Arthur C. Clarke was born in Somerset in 1917. He is a graduate of King's College, London (where he obtained a First Class Honours in Physics and Mathematics), a past Chairman of the British Interplanetary Society, and a member of the Academy of Astronautics, the Royal Astronomical Society, and many other scientific organizations. He served in the RAF during the Second World War and was in charge of the first radar talk-down equipment during its experimental trials. He wrote a monograph for *Wireless World* in 1945 predicting satellite communications, and did it so well that when the first commercial satellites were launched twenty years later they could not be patented.

He has written over sixty books, among them the science fiction classics *Childhood's End*, *The City and the Stars* and *Rendezvous with Rama* (which was unique in winning all three major science fiction trophies, the Hugo, Nebula and John W. Campbell Memorial Awards). In 1968 he shared an Oscar nomination with Stanley Kubrick for the screenplay of *2001 A Space Odyssey*. He became widely known for his non-fiction work with the television series *Arthur C. Clarke's Mysterious World*.

Arthur C. Clarke has for many years made his home in Sri Lanka. He is chancellor of a university there and founder of the Arthur C. Clarke Centre for Advanced Technology. He was awarded the CBE in 1989 and knighted in 1998.

2001 A Space Odyssey
2010 Odyssey Two
2061 Odyssey Three
Islands in the Sky
Prelude to Space
Against the Fall of Night
The Sands of Mars
Childhood's End
Expeditions to Earth
Earthlight
Reach for Tomorrow
The City and the Stars
Tales from the 'White Hart'
The Deep Range
The Other Side of the Sky
A Fall of Moondust
Tales of Ten Worlds
Dolphin Island
Glide Path
The Lion of Comarre
The Nine Billion Names of God
The Lost Worlds of 2001
The Wind From the Sun
Rendezvous with Rama
Imperial Earth
The Fountains of Paradise
1984: Spring
The Sentinel
Cradle (*with Gentry Lee*)
Rama II (*with Gentry Lee*)
Trigger (*with Michael Kube-McDowell*)
Greetings, Carbon-based Bipeds
The Light of Other Days (*with Stephen Baxter*)

Voyager

Arthur C. Clarke

3 0 0 1
THE FINAL ODYSSEY

THE SONGS OF DISTANT EARTH

Grafton

Voyager
An imprint of HarperCollins*Publishers*
77-85 Fulham Palace Road
Hammersmith, London w6 8jb

The *Voyager* website address is:
www.voyager-books.com

This omnibus edition published in 2004
by HarperCollins*Publishers*

ISBN 0 007 71208 1

Set in Palatino

Printed and bound in Great Britain by
Mackays of Chatham plc, Chatham, Kent

3001
THE FINAL ODYSSEY

CONTENTS

FOR CHERENE, TAMARA AND MELINDA –
may you be happy in
a far better century than mine

PROLOGUE

The Firstborn

Call them the Firstborn. Though they were not remotely human, they were flesh and blood, and when they looked out across the deeps of space, they felt awe, and wonder – and loneliness. As soon as they possessed the power, they began to seek for fellowship among the stars.

In their explorations, they encountered life in many forms, and watched the workings of evolution on a thousand worlds. They saw how often the first faint sparks of intelligence flickered and died in the cosmic night.

And because, in all the Galaxy, they had found nothing more precious than Mind, they encouraged its dawning everywhere. They became farmers in the fields of stars; they sowed, and sometimes they reaped.

1

And sometimes, dispassionately, they had to weed.

The great dinosaurs had long since passed away, their morning promise annihilated by a random hammerblow from space, when the survey ship entered the Solar System after a voyage that had already lasted a thousand years. It swept past the frozen outer planets, paused briefly above the deserts of dying Mars, and presently looked down on Earth.

Spread out beneath them, the explorers saw a world swarming with life. For years they studied, collected, catalogued. When they had learned all that they could, they began to modify. They tinkered with the destiny of many species, on land and in the seas. But which of their experiments would bear fruit, they could not know for at least a million years.

They were patient, but they were not yet immortal. There was so much to do in this universe of a hundred billion suns, and other worlds were calling. So they set out once more into the abyss, knowing that they would never come this way again. Nor was there any need: the servants they had left behind would do the rest.

On Earth, the glaciers came and went, while above them the changeless Moon still carried its secret from the stars. With a yet slower rhythm than the polar ice, the tides of civilization ebbed and flowed across the Galaxy. Strange and beautiful and terrible empires rose and fell, and passed on their knowledge to their successors.

And now, out among the stars, evolution was driving towards new goals. The first explorers of Earth had long since come to the limits of flesh and blood; as soon as their machines were better than their bodies, it was time

2

to move. First their brains, and then their thoughts alone, they transferred into shining new homes of metal and gemstone. In these, they roamed the Galaxy. They no longer built spaceships. They *were* spaceships.

But the age of the Machine-entities swiftly passed. In their ceaseless experimenting, they had learned to store knowledge in the structure of space itself, and to preserve their thoughts for eternity in frozen lattices of light.

Into pure energy, therefore, they presently transformed themselves; and on a thousand worlds, the empty shells they had discarded twitched for a while in a mindless dance of death, then crumbled into dust.

Now they were Lords of the Galaxy, and could rove at will among the stars, or sink like a subtle mist through the very interstices of space. Though they were freed at last from the tyranny of matter, they had not wholly forgotten their origin, in the warm slime of a vanished sea. And their marvellous instruments still continued to function, watching over the experiments started so many ages ago.

But no longer were they always obedient to the mandates of their creators; like all material things, they were not immune to the corruption of Time and its patient, unsleeping servant, Entropy.

And sometimes, they discovered and sought goals of their own.

I

STAR CITY

1

Comet Cowboy

Captain Dimitri Chandler [M2973.04.21/93.106//Mars// SpaceAcad3005] – or 'Dim' to his very best friends – was understandably annoyed. The message from Earth had taken six hours to reach the space-tug *Goliath*, here beyond the orbit of Neptune; if it had arrived ten minutes later he could have answered 'Sorry – can't leave now – we've just started to deploy the sun-screen.'

The excuse would have been perfectly valid: wrapping a comet's core in a sheet of reflective film only a few molecules thick, but kilometres on a side, was not the sort of job you could abandon while it was half-completed.

Still, it would be a good idea to obey this ridiculous request: he was already in disfavour sunwards, through

7

no fault of his own. Collecting ice from the rings of Saturn, and nudging it towards Venus and Mercury, where it was *really* needed, had started back in the 2700s – three centuries ago. Captain Chandler had never been able to see any real difference in the 'before and after' images the Solar Conservers were always producing, to support their accusations of celestial vandalism. But the general public, still sensitive to the ecological disasters of previous centuries, had thought otherwise, and the 'Hands off Saturn!' vote had passed by a substantial majority. As a result, Chandler was no longer a Ring Rustler, but a Comet Cowboy.

So here he was at an appreciable fraction of the distance to Alpha Centauri, rounding up stragglers from the Kuiper Belt. There was certainly enough ice out here to cover Mercury and Venus with oceans kilometres deep, but it might take centuries to extinguish their hell-fires and make them suitable for life. The Solar Conservers, of course, were still protesting against this, though no longer with so much enthusiasm. The millions dead from the tsunami caused by the Pacific asteroid in 2304 – how ironic that a land impact would have done much *less* damage! – had reminded all future generations that the human race had too many eggs in one fragile basket.

Well, Chandler told himself, it would be fifty years before this particular package reached its destination, so a delay of a week would hardly make much difference. But all the calculations about rotation, centre of mass, and thrust vectors would have to be redone, and radioed back to Mars for checking. It was a good idea to do your sums carefully, before nudging billions of tons of ice along an orbit that might take it within hailing distance of Earth.

As they had done so many times before, Captain Chandler's eyes strayed towards the ancient photograph above his desk. It showed a three-masted steamship, dwarfed by the iceberg that was looming above it – as, indeed, *Goliath* was dwarfed at this very moment.

How incredible, he had often thought, that only one long lifetime spanned the gulf between this primitive *Discovery* and the ship that had carried the same name to Jupiter! And what would those Antarctic explorers of a thousand years ago have made of the view from *his* bridge? They would certainly have been disoriented, for the wall of ice beside which *Goliath* was floating stretched both upwards and *downwards* as far as the eye could see. And it was strange-looking ice, wholly lacking the immaculate whites and blues of the frozen Polar seas. In fact, it looked *dirty* – as indeed it was. For only some ninety per cent was water-ice: the rest was a witch's brew of carbon and sulphur compounds, most of them stable only at temperatures not far above absolute zero. Thawing them out could produce unpleasant surprises: as one astrochemist had famously remarked, 'Comets have bad breath'.

'Skipper to all personnel,' Chandler announced. 'There's been a slight change of programme. We've been asked to delay operations, to investigate a target that Spaceguard radar has picked up.'

'Any details?' somebody asked, when the chorus of groans over the ship's intercom had died away.

'Not many, but I gather it's another Millennium Committee project they've forgotten to cancel.'

More groans: everyone had become heartily sick of all the events planned to celebrate the end of the 2000s. There had been a general sigh of relief when 1 January 3001 had passed uneventfully, and the human race could resume its normal activities.

'Anyway, it will probably be another false alarm, like the last one. We'll get back to work just as quickly as we can. Skipper out.'

This was the third wild-goose-chase, Chandler thought morosely, he'd been involved with during his career. Despite centuries of exploration, the Solar System could still produce surprises, and presumably Spaceguard had a good reason for its request. He only hoped that some imaginative idiot hadn't once again sighted the fabled Golden Asteroid. If it did exist – which Chandler did not for a moment believe – it would be no more than a mineralogical curiosity: it would be of far less *real* value than the ice he was nudging sunwards, to bring life to barren worlds.

There was one possibility, however, which he did take quite seriously. Already, the human race had scattered its robot probes through a volume of space a hundred light-years across – and the Tycho Monolith was sufficient reminder that much older civilizations had engaged in similar activities. There might well be other alien artefacts in the Solar System, or in transit through it. Captain Chandler suspected that Spaceguard had something like this in mind: otherwise it would hardly have diverted a Class I space-tug to go chasing after an unidentified radar blip.

Five hours later, the questing *Goliath* detected the echo at extreme range; even allowing for the distance, it seemed disappointingly small. However, as it grew clearer and stronger, it began to give the signature of a metallic object, perhaps a couple of metres long. It was travelling on an orbit heading out of the Solar System, so was almost certainly, Chandler decided, one of the myriad pieces of space-junk that Mankind had tossed towards the stars during the last millennium – and which might one day provide the only evidence that the human race had ever existed.

Then it came close enough for visual inspection, and Captain Chandler realized, with awed astonishment, that some patient historian was still checking the earliest records of the Space Age. What a pity that the computers had given him the answer, just a few years too late for the Millennium celebrations!

'*Goliath* here,' Chandler radioed Earthwards, his voice tinged with pride as well as solemnity. 'We're bringing aboard a thousand-year-old astronaut. And I can guess who it is.'

2
Awakening

Frank Poole awoke, but he did not remember. He was not even sure of his name.

Obviously, he was in a hospital room: even though his eyes were still closed, the most primitive, and evocative, of his senses told him that. Each breath brought the faint and not unpleasant tang of antiseptics in the air, and it triggered a memory of the time when – of course! – as a reckless teenager he had broken a rib in the Arizona Hang-gliding Championship.

Now it was all beginning to come back. I'm Deputy Commander Frank Poole, Executive Officer, USSS *Discovery*, on a Top Secret mission to Jupiter –

It seemed as if an icy hand had gripped his heart. He

remembered, in slow-motion playback, that runaway space-pod jetting towards him, metal claws outstretched. Then the silent impact – and the not-so-silent hiss of air rushing out of his suit. After that – one last memory, of spinning helplessly in space, trying in vain to reconnect his broken air-hose.

Well, whatever mysterious accident had happened to the space-pod controls, he was safe now. Presumably Dave had made a quick EVA and rescued him before lack of oxygen could do permanent brain damage.

Good old Dave! he told himself. I must thank – just a moment! – I'm obviously not aboard *Discovery* now – surely I haven't been unconscious long enough to be taken back to Earth!

His confused train of thought was abruptly broken by the arrival of a Matron and two nurses, wearing the immemorial uniform of their profession. They seemed a little surprised: Poole wondered if he had awakened ahead of schedule, and the idea gave him a childish feeling of satisfaction.

'Hello!' he said, after several attempts; his vocal cords appeared to be very rusty. 'How am I doing?'

Matron smiled back at him and gave an obvious 'Don't try to talk' command by putting a finger to her lips. Then the two nurses fussed swiftly over him with practised skill checking pulse, temperature, reflexes. When one of them lifted his right arm and let it drop again, Poole noticed something peculiar. It fell slowly, and did not seem to weigh as much as normal. Nor, for that matter, did his body, when he attempted to move.

So I must be on a planet, he thought. Or a space-station

with artificial gravity. Certainly not Earth – I don't weigh enough.

He was about to ask the obvious question when Matron pressed something against the side of his neck; he felt a slight tingling sensation, and sank back into a dreamless sleep. Just before he became unconscious, he had time for one more puzzled thought.

How odd – they never spoke a single word – all the time they were with me.

3
Rehabilitation

When he woke again, and found Matron and nurses standing round his bed, Poole felt strong enough to assert himself.

'Where *am* I? Surely you can tell me that!'

The three women exchanged glances, obviously uncertain what to do next. Then Matron answered, enunciating her words very slowly and carefully: 'Everything is fine, Mr Poole. Professor Anderson will be here in a minute . . . He will explain.'

Explain *what*? thought Poole with some exasperation. But at least she speaks English, even though I can't place her accent . . .

Anderson must have been already on his way, for the

15

door opened moments later – to give Poole a brief glimpse of a small crowd of inquisitive onlookers peering in at him. He began to feel like a new exhibit at a zoo.

Professor Anderson was a small, dapper man whose features seemed to have combined key aspects of several races – Chinese, Polynesian, Nordic – in a thoroughly confusing fashion. He greeted Poole by holding up his right palm, then did an obvious double-take and shook hands, with such a curious hesitation that he might have been rehearsing some quite unfamiliar gesture.

'Glad to see you're looking so well, Mr Poole . . . We'll have you up in no time.'

Again that odd accent and slow delivery – but the confident bedside manner was that of all doctors, in all places and all ages.

'I'm glad to hear it. Now perhaps you can answer a few questions . . .'

'Of course, of course. But just a minute.'

Anderson spoke so rapidly and quietly to the Matron that Poole could catch only a few words, several of which were wholly unfamiliar to him. Then the Matron nodded at one of the nurses, who opened a wall-cupboard and produced a slim metal band, which she proceeded to wrap around Poole's head.

'What's that for?' he asked – being one of those difficult patients, so annoying to doctors, who always want to know just what's happening to them. 'EEG readout?'

Professor, Matron and nurses looked equally baffled. Then a slow smile spread across Anderson's face.

'Oh – electro . . . enceph . . . alo . . . gram,' he said slowly, as if dredging the word up from the depth of memory.

16

'You're quite right. We just want to monitor your brain functions.'

My brain would function perfectly well if you'd let me use it, Poole grumbled silently. But at least we seem to be getting somewhere – finally.

'Mr Poole,' said Anderson, still speaking in that curious stilted voice, as if venturing in a foreign language, 'you know, of course, that you were – disabled – in a serious accident, while you were working outside *Discovery*.'

Poole nodded agreement.

'I'm beginning to suspect,' he said dryly, 'that "disabled" is a slight understatement.'

Anderson relaxed visibly, and a slow smile spread across his face.

'You're quite correct. Tell me what you *think* happened.'

'Well, the best case scenario is that, after I became unconscious, Dave Bowman rescued me and brought me back to the ship. How is Dave? No one will tell me anything!'

'All in due course ... and the *worst* case?'

It seemed to Frank Poole that a chill wind was blowing gently on the back of his neck. The suspicion that had been slowly forming in his mind began to solidify.

'That I died, but was brought back here – wherever "here" is – and you've been able to revive me. Thank you ...'

'Quite correct. And you're back on Earth. Well, very near it.'

What did he mean by 'very near it'? There was certainly a gravity field here – so he was probably inside the slowly turning wheel of an orbiting space-station. No matter: there was something much more important to think about.

Poole did some quick mental calculations. If Dave had put him in the hibernaculum, revived the rest of the crew, and completed the mission to Jupiter – why, he could have been 'dead' for as much as five years!

'Just what date is it?' he asked, as calmly as possible.

Professor and Matron exchanged glances. Again Poole felt that cold wind on his neck.

'I must tell you, Mr Poole, that Bowman did *not* rescue you. He believed – and we cannot blame him – that you were irrevocably dead. Also, he was facing a desperately serious crisis that threatened his own survival ...

'So you drifted on into space, passed through the Jupiter system, and headed out towards the stars. Fortunately, you were so far below freezing point that there was no metabolism – but it's a near-miracle that you were ever found at all. You are one of the luckiest men alive. No – ever to have lived!'

Am I? Poole asked himself bleakly. Five years, indeed! It could be a century – or even more.

'Let me have it,' he demanded.

Professor and Matron seemed to be consulting an invisible monitor: when they looked at each other and nodded agreement, Poole guessed that they were all plugged into the hospital information circuit, linked to the headband he was wearing.

'Frank,' said Professor Anderson, making a smooth switch to the role of long-time family physician, 'this will be a great shock to you, but you're capable of accepting it – and the sooner you know, the better.

'We're near the beginning of the Fourth Millennium. Believe me – you left Earth almost a thousand years ago.'

18

'I believe you,' Poole answered calmly. Then, to his great annoyance, the room started to spin around him, and he knew nothing more.

When he regained consciousness, he found that he was no longer in a bleak hospital room but in a luxurious suite with attractive – and steadily changing – images on the walls. Some of these were famous and familiar paintings, others showed land- and sea-scapes that might have been from his own time. There was nothing alien or upsetting: that, he guessed, would come later.

His present surroundings had obviously been carefully programmed: he wondered if there was the equivalent of a television screen somewhere (how many channels would the Fourth Millennium have?) but could see no sign of any controls near his bed. There was so much he would have to learn in this new world: he was a savage who had suddenly encountered civilization.

But first, he must regain his strength – and learn the language; not even the advent of sound recording, already more than a century old when Poole was born, had prevented major changes in grammar and pronunciation. And there were thousands of new words, mostly from science and technology, though often he was able to make a shrewd guess at their meaning.

More frustrating, however, were the myriad of famous and infamous personal names that had accumulated over the millennium, and which meant nothing to him. For weeks, until he had built up a data bank, most of his conversations had to be interrupted with potted biographies.

As Poole's strength increased, so did the number of his

visitors, though always under Professor Anderson's watchful eye. They included medical specialists, scholars of several disciplines, and – of the greatest interest to him – spacecraft commanders.

There was little that he could tell the doctors and historians that was not recorded somewhere in Mankind's gigantic data banks, but he was often able to give them research shortcuts and new insights about the events of his own time. Though they all treated him with the utmost respect and listened patiently as he tried to answer their questions, they seemed reluctant to answer his. Poole began to feel that he was being over-protected from culture shock, and half-seriously wondered how he could escape from his suite. On the few occasions he was alone, he was not surprised to discover that the door was locked.

Then the arrival of Doctor Indra Wallace changed everything. Despite her name, her chief racial component appeared to be Japanese, and there were times when with just a little imagination Poole could picture her as a rather mature Geisha Girl. It was hardly an appropriate image for a distinguished historian, holding a Virtual Chair at a university still boasting real ivy.

She was the first visitor with a fluent command of Poole's own English, so he was delighted to meet her.

'Mr Poole,' she began, in a very business-like voice, 'I've been appointed your official guide and – let's say – mentor. My qualifications – I've specialized in your period – my thesis was "The Collapse of the Nation-State, 2000–50". I believe we can help each other in many ways.'

'I'm sure we can. First I'd like you to get me out of here, so I can see a little of your world.'

'Exactly what we intend to do. But first we must give you an Ident. Until then you'll be – what was the term? – a non-person. It would be almost impossible for you to go anywhere, or get anything done. No input device would recognize your existence.'

'Just what I expected,' Poole answered, with a wry smile. 'It was starting to get that way in my own time – and many people hated the idea.'

'Some still do. They go off and live in the wilderness – there's a lot more on Earth than there was in your century! But they always take their compaks with them, so they can call for help as soon as they get into trouble. The median time is about five days.'

'Sorry to hear that. The human race has obviously deteriorated.'

He was cautiously testing her, trying to find the limits of her tolerance and to map out her personality. It was obvious that they were going to spend much time together, and that he would have to depend upon her in hundreds of ways. Yet he was still not sure if he would even like her: perhaps she regarded him merely as a fascinating museum exhibit.

Rather to Poole's surprise, she agreed with his criticism.

'That may be true – in some respects. Perhaps we're physically weaker, but we're healthier and better adjusted than most humans who have ever lived. The Noble Savage was always a myth.'

She walked over to a small rectangular plate, set at eye-level in the door. It was about the size of one of the countless magazines that had proliferated in the far-off Age of Print, and Poole had noticed that every room seemed to have at least one. Usually they were blank, but sometimes they contained lines of slowly scrolling text, completely meaningless to Poole even when most of the words were familiar. Once a plate in his suite had emitted urgent beepings, which he had ignored on the assumption that someone else would deal with the problem, whatever it was. Fortunately the noise stopped as abruptly as it had started.

Dr Wallace laid the palm of her hand upon the plate, then removed it after a few seconds. She glanced at Poole, and said smilingly: 'Come and look at this.'

The inscription that had suddenly appeared made a good deal of sense, when he read it slowly:-

WALLACE, INDRA [F2970.03.11:31.885//HIST.OXFORD]

'I suppose it means Female, date of birth 11 March 2970 – and that you're associated with the Department of History at Oxford. And I guess that 31.885 is a personal identification number. Correct?'

'Excellent, Mr Poole. I've seen some of your e-mail addresses and credit card numbers – hideous strings of alpha-numeric gibberish that no one could possibly remember! But we all know our date of birth, and not more than 99,999 other people will share it. So a five-figure number is all you'll ever need ... and even if you forget that, it doesn't really matter. As you see, it's a part of you.'

'Implant?'

'Yes – nanochip at birth, one in each palm for redundancy. You won't even feel yours when it goes in. But you've given us a small problem ...'

'What's that?'

'The readers you'll meet most of the time are too simple-

22

minded to believe your date of birth. So, with your permission, we've moved it up a thousand years.'

'Permission granted. And the rest of the Ident?'

'Optional. You can leave it empty, give your current interests and location – or use it for personal messages, global or targeted.'

Some things, Poole was quite sure, would not have changed over the centuries. A high proportion of those 'targeted' messages would be very personal indeed.

He wondered if there were still self- or state-appointed censors in this day and age – and if their efforts at improving other people's morals had been more successful than in his own time.

He would have to ask Dr Wallace about that, when he got to know her better.

4
A Room with a View

'Frank – Professor Anderson thinks you're strong enough to go for a little walk.'

'I'm very pleased to hear it. Do you know the expression "stir crazy"?'

'No – but I can guess what it means.'

Poole had so adapted to the low gravity that the long strides he was taking seemed perfectly normal. Half a gee, he had estimated – just right to give a sense of well-being. They met only a few people on their walk, all of them strangers, but every one gave a smile of recognition. By now, Poole told himself with a trace of smugness, I must be one of the best-known celebrities in this world. That should be a great help – when I decide what to do with

24

the rest of my life. At least another century, if I can believe Anderson . . .

The corridor along which they were walking was completely featureless apart from occasional numbered doors, each bearing one of the universal recog panels. Poole had followed Indra for perhaps two hundred metres when he came to a sudden halt, shocked because he had not realized something so blindingly obvious.

'This space-station must be *enormous*!' he exclaimed.

Indra smiled back at him.

'Didn't you have a saying – "You ain't seen anything yet"?'

' "Nothing",' he corrected, absent-mindedly. He was still trying to estimate the scale of this structure when he had another surprise. Who would have imagined a space-station large enough to boast a *subway* – admittedly a miniature one, with a single small coach capable of seating only a dozen passengers.

'Observation Lounge Three,' ordered Indra, and they drew silently and swiftly away from the terminal.

Poole checked the time on the elaborate wrist-band whose functions he was still exploring. One minor surprise had been that the whole world was now on Universal Time: the confusing patchwork of Time Zones had been swept away by the advent of global communications. There had been much talk of this, back in the twenty-first century, and it had even been suggested that Solar should be replaced by Sidereal Time. Then, during the course of the year, the Sun would move right round the clock: setting at the time it had risen six months earlier.

However, nothing had come of this 'Equal time in the

Sun' proposal – or of even more vociferous attempts to reform the calendar. *That* particular job, it had been cynically suggested, would have to wait for somewhat major advances in technology. Some day, surely, one of God's minor mistakes would be corrected, and the Earth's orbit would be adjusted, to give every year twelve months of thirty exactly equal days . . .

As far as Poole could judge by speed and elapsed time, they must have travelled at least three kilometres before the vehicle came to a silent stop, the doors opened, and a bland autovoice intoned, 'Have a good view. Thirty-five per cent cloud-cover today.'

At last, thought Poole, we're getting near the outer wall. But here was another mystery – despite the distance he had gone, neither the strength *nor the direction* of gravity had altered! He could not imagine a spinning space-station so huge that the gee-vector would not be changed by such a displacement . . . could he really be on some planet after all? But he would feel lighter – usually *much* lighter – on any other habitable world in the Solar System.

When the outer door of the terminal opened, and Poole found himself entering a small airlock, he realized that he must indeed be in space. But where were the spacesuits? He looked around anxiously: it was against all his instincts to be so close to vacuum, naked and unprotected. One experience of that was enough . . .

'We're nearly there,' said Indra reassuringly.

The last door opened, and he was looking out into the utter blackness of space, through a huge window that was curved both vertically and horizontally. He felt like a goldfish in its bowl, and hoped that the designers of this

26

audacious piece of engineering knew exactly what they were doing. They certainly possessed better structural materials than had existed in his time.

Though the stars must be shining out there, his light-adapted eyes could see nothing but black emptiness beyond the curve of the great window. As he started to walk towards it to get a wider view, Indra restrained him and pointed straight ahead.

'Look carefully,' she said. 'Don't you see it?'

Poole blinked, and stared into the night. Surely it must be an illusion – even, heaven forbid, a crack in the window!

He moved his head from side to side. No, it was real. But what could it be? He remembered Euclid's definition: 'A line has length, but no thickness'.

For spanning the whole height of the window, and obviously continuing out of sight above and below, was a thread of light quite easy to see when he looked for it, yet so one-dimensional that the word 'thin' could not even be applied. However, it was not completely featureless: there were barely visible spots of greater brilliance at irregular intervals along its length, like drops of water on a spider's web.

Poole continued walking towards the window, and the view expanded until at last he could see what lay below him. It was familiar enough: the whole continent of Europe and much of northern Africa, just as he had seen them many times from space. So he *was* in orbit after all – probably an equatorial one, at a height of at least a thousand kilometres.

Indra was looking at him with a quizzical smile.

'Go closer to the window,' she said, very softly. 'So that

you can look *straight* down. I hope you have a good head for heights.'

What a silly thing to say to an astronaut! Poole told himself as he moved forward. If I ever suffered from vertigo, I wouldn't be in this business . . .

The thought had barely passed through his mind when he cried 'My God!' and involuntarily stepped back from the window. Then, bracing himself, he dared to look again.

He was looking down on the distant Mediterranean from the face of a cylindrical tower, whose gently curving wall indicated a diameter of several kilometres. But that was nothing compared with its length, for it tapered away down, down, down – until it disappeared into the mist somewhere over Africa. He assumed that it continued all the way to the surface.

'How high are we?' he whispered.

'Two thousand kay. But now look *upwards*.'

This time, it was not such a shock: he had expected what he would see. The tower dwindled away until it became a glittering thread against the blackness of space, and he did not doubt that it continued all the way to the geostationary orbit, thirty-six thousand kilometres above the Equator. Such fantasies had been well known in Poole's day: he had never dreamed he would see the reality – and be living in it.

He pointed towards the distant thread reaching up from the eastern horizon.

'That must be another one.'

'Yes – the Asian Tower. We must look exactly the same to them.'

'How many are there?'

'Just four, equally spaced around the Equator. Africa, Asia, America, Pacifica. The last one's almost empty – only a few hundred levels completed. Nothing to see except water . . .'

Poole was still absorbing this stupendous concept when a disturbing thought occurred to him.

'There were already thousands of satellites, at all sorts of altitudes, in my time. How do you avoid collisions?'

Indra looked slightly embarrassed.

'You know – I never thought about that – it's not my field.' She paused for a moment, clearly searching her memory. Then her face brightened.

'I believe there was a big clean-up operation, centuries ago. There just aren't *any* satellites, below the stationary orbit.'

That made sense, Poole told himself. They wouldn't be needed – the four gigantic towers could provide all the facilities once provided by thousands of satellites and space-stations.

'And there have never been any accidents – any collisions with spaceships leaving earth, or re-entering the atmosphere?'

Indra looked at him with surprise.

'But they don't, any more.' She pointed to the ceiling. 'All the spaceports are where they should be – up there, on the outer ring. I believe it's four hundred years since the last rocket lifted off from the surface of the Earth.'

Poole was still digesting this when a trivial anomaly caught his attention. His training as an astronaut had made him alert to anything out of the ordinary: in space, that might be a matter of life or death.

29

The Sun was out of view, high overhead, but its rays streaming down through the great window painted a brilliant band of light on the floor underfoot. Cutting across that band at an angle was another, much fainter one, so that the frame of the window threw a double shadow.

Poole had to go almost down on his knees so that he could peer up at the sky. He had thought himself beyond surprise, but the spectacle of *two* suns left him momentarily speechless.

'What's *that*?' he gasped, when he had recovered his breath:

'Oh – haven't you been told? That's Lucifer.'

'Earth has another sun?'

'Well, it doesn't give us much heat, but it's put the Moon out of business ... Before the Second Mission went there to look for you, *that* was the planet Jupiter.'

I knew I would have much to learn in this new world, Poole told himself. But just *how* much, I never dreamed.

5
Education

Poole was both astonished and delighted when the television set was wheeled into the room and positioned at the end of his bed. Delighted because he was suffering from mild information starvation – and astonished because it was a model which had been obsolete even in his own time.

'We've had to promise the Museum we'll give it back,' Matron informed him. 'And I expect you know how to use *this.*'

As he fondled the remote-control, Poole felt a wave of acute nostalgia sweep over him. As few other artefacts could, it brought back memories of his childhood, and the days when most television sets were too stupid to understand spoken commands.

'Thank you, Matron. What's the best news channel?'

She seemed puzzled by his question, then brightened.

'Oh – I see what you mean. But Professor Anderson thinks you're not quite ready yet. So Archives has put together a collection that will make you feel at home.'

Poole wondered briefly what the storage medium was in this day and age. He could still remember compact disks, and his eccentric old Uncle George had been the proud possessor of a collection of vintage videotapes. But surely *that* technological contest must have finished centuries ago – in the usual Darwinian way, with the survival of the fittest.

He had to admit that the selection was well done, by someone (Indra?) familiar with the early twenty-first century. There was nothing disturbing – no wars or violence, and very little contemporary business or politics, all of which would now be utterly irrelevant. There were some light comedies, sporting events (how did they know that he had been a keen tennis fan?), classical and pop music, and wildlife documentaries.

And whoever had put this collection together had a sense of humour, or they would not have included episodes from each *Star Trek* series. As a very small boy, Poole had met both Patrick Stewart and Leonard Nimoy: he wondered what they would have thought if they could have known the destiny of the child who had shyly asked for their autographs.

A depressing thought occurred to him, soon after he had started exploring – much of the time in fast-forward – these relics of the past. He had read somewhere that by the turn of the century – *his* century! – there were approximately fifty thousand television stations broadcasting simultaneously. If that figure had been maintained – and it might well have increased – by now millions of *millions* of hours of TV programming must have gone on the air. So even the most hardened cynic would admit that there were probably at least a billion hours of worthwhile viewing . . . and millions that would pass the highest standards of excellence. How to find these few – well, few million – needles in so gigantic a haystack?

The thought was so overwhelming – indeed, so *demoralizing* – that after a week of increasingly aimless channel-surfing Poole asked for the set to be removed. Perhaps fortunately, he had less and less time to himself during his waking hours, which were steadily growing longer as his strength came back.

There was no risk of boredom, thanks to the continual parade not only of serious researchers but also inquisitive – and presumably influential – citizens who had managed to filter past the palace guard established by Matron and Professor Anderson. Nevertheless, he was glad when, one day, the television set reappeared; he was beginning to suffer from withdrawal symptoms – and this time, he resolved to be more selective in his viewing.

The venerable antique was accompanied by Indra Wallace, smiling broadly.

'We've found something you must see, Frank. We think it will help you to adjust – anyway, we're sure you'll enjoy it.'

Poole had always found that remark a recipe for guaranteed boredom, and prepared for the worst. But the opening had him instantly hooked, taking him back to his old life as few other things could have done. At once he recognized one of the most famous voices of his age, and remembered that he had seen this very programme before. Could it have been at its first transmission? No, he was only five then: must have been a repeat . . .

'Atlanta, 2000 December 31 . . .

'This is CNN International, five minutes from the dawn of the New Millennium, with all its unknown perils and promise . . .

'But before we try to explore the future, let's look *back* a thousand years, and ask ourselves: could any persons living in A.D. 1000 even *remotely* imagine our world, or understand it, if they were magically transported across the centuries?

'Almost the whole of the technology we take for granted was invented near the very end of our Millennium – the steam engine, electricity, telephones, radio, television, cinema, aviation, electronics. And, during a single lifetime, nuclear energy and space travel – what would the greatest minds of the past have made of these? How long could an Archimedes or a Leonardo have retained his sanity, if suddenly dumped into *our* world?

'It's tempting to think that we would do better, if we were transported a thousand years hence. Surely the fundamental scientific discoveries have already been made: though there will be major improvements in technology, will there be any devices, anything as magical and incomprehensible to us as a pocket calculator or a video camera would have been to Isaac Newton?

'Perhaps our age is indeed sundered from all those that have gone before. Telecommunications, the ability to record images and sounds once irrevocably lost, the conquest of the air and space – all these have created a civilization beyond the wildest fantasies of the past. And equally important, Copernicus, Newton, Darwin and Einstein have so changed our mode of thinking and our outlook on the universe that we might seem almost a new species to the most brilliant of our predecessors.

'And will our *successors*, a thousand years from now, look back on us with the same pity with which we regard our ignorant, superstitious, disease-ridden, short-lived ancestors? We believe that we know the answers to questions that they could not even ask: but what surprises does the Third Millennium hold for us?

'Well, here it comes –'

A great bell began to toll the strokes of midnight. The last vibration throbbed into silence . . .

'And that's the way it was – good-bye, wonderful and terrible twentieth century . . .'

Then the picture broke into a myriad fragments, and a new commentator took over, speaking with the accent which Poole could now easily understand, and which immediately brought him up to the present.

'Now, in the first minutes of the year *three* thousand and one, we can answer that question from the past . . .

'Certainly, the people of 2001 who you were just watching would not feel as utterly overwhelmed in our age as someone from 1001 would have felt in theirs. Many of our technological achievements they would have anticipated; indeed, they would have *expected* satellite cities, and colonies on the Moon and planets. They might even have been disappointed, because we are not yet immortal, and have sent probes only to the nearest stars . . .'

35

Abruptly, Indra switched off the recording.

'See the rest later, Frank: you're getting tired. But I hope it will help you to adjust.'

'Thank you, Indra. I'll have to sleep on it. But it's certainly proved one point.'

'What's that?'

'I should be grateful I'm not a thousand-and-oner, dropped into 2001. That would be too much of a quantum jump: I don't believe *anyone* could adjust to it. At least I know about electricity, and won't die of fright if a picture starts talking at me.'

I hope, Poole told himself, that confidence is justified. Someone once said that any sufficiently advanced technology is indistinguishable from magic. Will I meet magic in this new world – and be able to handle it?

6

Braincap

'I'm afraid you'll have to make an agonizing decision,' said Professor Anderson, with a smile that neutralized the exaggerated gravity of his words.

'I can take it, Doctor. Just give it to me straight.'

'Before you can be fitted with your Braincap, you have to be completely bald. So here's your choice. At the rate your hair grows, you'd have to be shaved at least once a month. Or you could have a permanent.'

'How's that done?'

'Laser scalp treatment. Kills the follicles at the root.'

'Hmm . . . is it reversible?'

'Yes, but that's messy and painful, and takes weeks.'

'Then I'll see how I like being hairless, before committing myself. I can't forget what happened to Samson.'

'Who?'

'Character in a famous old book. His girl-friend cut off his hair while he was sleeping. When he woke up, all his strength had gone.'

'Now I remember – pretty obvious medical symbolism!'

'Still, I wouldn't mind losing my beard – I'd be happy to stop shaving, once and for all.'

'I'll make the arrangements. And what kind of wig would you like?'

Poole laughed.

'I'm not particularly vain – think it would be a nuisance, and probably won't bother. Something else I can decide later.'

That everyone in this era was artificially bald was a surprising fact that Poole had been quite slow to discover; his first revelation had come when *both* his nurses removed their luxuriant tresses, without the slightest sign of embarrassment, just before several equally bald specialists arrived to give him a series of micro-biological checks. He had never been surrounded by so many hairless people, and his initial guess was that this was the latest step in the medical profession's endless war against germs.

Like many of his guesses, it was completely wrong, and when he discovered the true reason he amused himself by seeing how often he would have been sure, had he not known in advance, that his visitors' hair was not their own. The answer was: seldom with men, never with women; this was obviously the great age of the wig-maker.

Professor Anderson wasted no time: that afternoon the

nurses smeared some evil-smelling cream over Poole's head, and when he looked into the mirror an hour later he did not recognize himself. Well, he thought, perhaps a wig would be a good idea, after all . . .

The Braincap fitting took somewhat longer. First a mould had to be made, which required him to sit motionless for a few minutes until the plaster set. He fully expected to be told that his head was the wrong shape when his nurses – giggling most unprofessionally – had a hard time extricating him. 'Ouch – that hurt!' he complained.

Next came the skull-cap itself, a metal helmet that fitted snugly almost down to the ears, and triggered a nostalgic thought – wish my Jewish friends could see me now! After a few minutes, it was so comfortable that he was unaware of its presence.

Now he was ready for the installation – a process which, he realized with something akin to awe, had been the Rite of Passage for almost all the human race for more than half a millennium.

'There's no need to close your eyes,' said the technician, who had been introduced by the pretentious title of 'Brain Engineer' – almost always shortened to 'Brainman' in popular usage. 'When Setup begins, all your inputs will be taken over. Even if your eyes are open, you won't see anything.'

I wonder if everyone feels as nervous as this, Poole asked himself. Is this the last moment I'll be in control of my own mind? Still, I've learned to trust the technology of this age; up to now, it hasn't let me down. Of course, as the old saying goes, there's always a first time . . .

As he had been promised, he had felt nothing except a gentle tickling as the myriad of nano-wires wormed their way through his scalp. All his senses were still perfectly normal; when he scanned his familiar room, everything was exactly where it should be.

The Brainman – wearing his own skull-cap, wired, like Poole's, to a piece of equipment that could easily have been mistaken for a twentieth-century laptop computer – gave him a reassuring smile.

'Ready?' he asked.

There were times when the old clichés were the best ones.

'Ready as I'll ever be,' Poole answered.

Slowly, the light faded – or seemed to. A great silence descended, and even the gentle gravity of the Tower relinquished its hold upon him. He was an embryo, floating in a featureless void, though not in complete darkness. He had known such a barely visible, near ultra-violet tenebrosity, on the very edge of night, only once in his life – when he had descended further than was altogether wise down the face of a sheer cliff at the outer edge of the Great Barrier Reef. Looking down into hundreds of metres of crystalline emptiness, he had felt such a sense of disorientation that he experienced a brief moment of panic, and had almost triggered his buoyancy unit before regaining control. Needless to say, he had never mentioned the incident to the Space Agency physicians . . .

From a great distance a voice spoke out of the immense void that now seemed to surround him. But it did not reach him through his ears: it sounded softly in the echoing labyrinths of his brain.

'Calibration starting. From time to time you will be asked questions – you can answer mentally, but it may help to vocalize. Do you understand?'

'Yes,' Poole replied, wondering if his lips were indeed moving. There was no way that he could tell.

Something was appearing in the void – a grid of thin lines, like a huge sheet of graph paper. It extended up and down, right and left, to the limits of his vision. He tried to move his head, but the image refused to change.

Numbers started to flicker across the grid, too fast for him to read – but presumably some circuit was recording them. Poole could not help smiling (did his cheeks move?) at the familiarity of it all. This was just like the computer-driven eye examination that any oculist of his age would give a client.

The grid vanished, to be replaced by smooth sheets of colour filling his entire field of view. In a few seconds, they flashed from one end of the spectrum to the other. 'Could have told you *that*,' Poole muttered silently. 'My colour vision's perfect. Next for hearing, I suppose.'

He was quite correct. A faint, drumming sound accelerated until it became the lowest of audible Cs, then raced up the musical scale until it disappeared beyond the range of human hearing, into bat and dolphin territory.

That was the last of the simple, straightforward tests. He was briefly assailed by scents and flavours, most of them pleasant but some quite the reverse. Then he became, or so it seemed, a puppet on an invisible string.

He presumed that his neuromuscular control was being tested, and hoped that there were no external manifestations; if there were, he would probably look like someone

41

in the terminal stages of St Vitus's Dance. And for one moment he even had a violent erection, but was unable to give it a reality check before he fell into a dreamless sleep.

Or did he only dream that he slept? He had no idea how much time had elapsed before he awoke. The helmet had already gone, together with the Brainman and his equipment.

'Everything went fine,' beamed Matron. 'It will take a few hours to check that there are no anomalies. If your reading's KO – I mean OK – you'll have your Braincap tomorrow.'

Poole appreciated the efforts of his entourage to learn archaic English, but he could not help wishing that Matron had not made that unfortunate slip-of-the-tongue.

When the time came for the final fitting, Poole felt almost like a boy again, about to unwrap some wonderful new toy under the Christmas tree.

'You won't have to go through all that setting-up again,' the Brainman assured him. 'Download will start immediately. I'll give you a five-minute demo. Just relax and enjoy.'

Gentle, soothing music washed over him; though it was something very familiar, from his own time, he could not identify it. There was a mist before his eyes, which parted as he walked towards it . . .

Yes, he was *walking*! The illusion was utterly convincing; he could feel the impact of his feet on the ground, and now that the music had stopped he could hear a gentle wind blowing through the great trees that appeared to surround him. He recognized them as Californian redwoods, and hoped that they still existed in reality, somewhere on Earth.

He was moving at a brisk pace – too fast for comfort, as if time was slightly accelerated so he could cover as much ground as possible. Yet he was not conscious of any effort; he felt he was a guest in someone else's body. The sensation was enhanced by the fact that he had no control over his movements. When he attempted to stop, or to change direction, nothing happened. He was going along for the ride.

It did not matter; he was enjoying the novel experience – and could appreciate how addictive it could become. The 'dream machines' that many scientists of his own century had anticipated – often with alarm – were now part of everyday life. Poole wondered how Mankind had managed to survive: he had been told that much of it had not. Millions had been brain-burned, and had dropped out of life.

Of course, *he* would be immune to such temptations! He would use this marvellous tool to learn more about the world of the Fourth Millennium, and to acquire in minutes new skills that would otherwise take years to master. Well – he might, just occasionally, use the Braincap purely for fun . . .

He had come to the edge of the forest, and was looking out across a wide river. Without hesitation, he walked into it, and felt no alarm as the water rose over his head. It did seem a little strange that he could continue breathing naturally, but he thought it much more remarkable that he could see perfectly in a medium where the unaided human eye could not focus. He could count every scale on the magnificent trout that went swimming past, apparently oblivious to this strange intruder.

Then, a *mermaid*! Well, he had always wanted to meet one, but he had assumed that they were marine creatures.

Perhaps they occasionally came upstream – like salmon, to have their babies? She was gone before he could question her, to confirm or deny this revolutionary theory.

The river ended in a translucent wall; he stepped through it on to the face of a desert, beneath a blazing sun. Its heat burned him uncomfortably – yet he was able to look directly into its noonday fury. He could even see, with unnatural clarity, an archipelago of sunspots near one limb. And – this was surely impossible! – there was the tenuous glory of the corona, quite invisible except during total eclipse, reaching out like a swan's wings on either side of the Sun.

Everything faded to black: the haunting music returned, and with it the blissful coolness of his familiar room. He opened his eyes (had they ever been closed?) and found an expectant audience waiting for his reaction.

'Wonderful!' he breathed, almost reverently. 'Some of it seemed – well, realer than real!'

Then his engineer's curiosity, never far from the surface, started nagging him.

'Even that short demo must have contained an enormous amount of information. How's it stored?'

'In these tablets – the same your audio-visual system uses, but with much greater capacity.'

The Brainman handed Poole a small square, apparently made of glass, silvered on one surface; it was almost the same size as the computer diskettes of his youth, but twice the thickness. As Poole tilted it back and forth, trying to see into its transparent interior, there were occasional rainbow-hued flashes, but that was all.

He was holding, he realized, the end product of more

44

than a thousand years of electro-optical technology – as well as other technologies unborn in his era. And it was not surprising that, superficially, it resembled closely the devices he had known. There was a convenient shape and size for most of the common objects of everyday life – knives and forks, books, hand-tools, furniture ... and removable memories for computers.

'What's its capacity?' he asked. 'In my time, we were up to a terabyte in something this size. I'm sure you've done a lot better.'

'Not as much as you might imagine – there's a limit, of course, set by the structure of matter. By the way, what *was* a terabyte? Afraid I've forgotten.'

'Shame on you! Kilo, mega, giga, tera ... that's ten to the twelfth bytes. Then the petabyte – ten to the fifteenth – that's as far as I ever got.'

'That's about where we start. It's enough to record everything any person can experience during one lifetime.'

It was an astonishing thought, yet it should not have been so surprising. The kilogram of jelly inside the human skull was not much larger than the tablet Poole was holding in his hand, and it could not possibly be as efficient a storage device – it had so many other duties to deal with.

'And that's not all,' the Brainman continued. 'With some data compression, it could store not only the memories – but the actual person.

'And reproduce them again?'

'Of course; straightforward job of nanoassembly.'

So I'd heard, Poole told himself – but I never really believed it.

Back in his century, it seemed wonderful enough that

the entire lifework of a great artist could be stored on a single small disk.

And now, something no larger could hold – the artist as well.

7
Debriefing

'I'm delighted,' said Poole, 'to know that the Smithsonian still exists, after all these centuries.'

'You probably wouldn't recognize it,' said the visitor who had introduced himself as Dr Alistair Kim, Director of Astronautics. 'Especially as it's now scattered over the Solar System – the main off-Earth collections are on Mars and the Moon, and many of the exhibits that legally belong to us are still heading for the stars. Some day we'll catch up with them and bring them home. We're particularly anxious to get our hands on Pioneer 10 – the first man-made object to escape from the Solar System.'

'I believe *I* was on the verge of doing that, when they located me.'

'Lucky for you – and for us. You may be able to throw light on many things we don't know.'

'Frankly, I doubt it – but I'll do my best. I don't remember a thing after that runaway space-pod charged me. Though I still find it hard to believe, I've been told that Hal was responsible.'

'That's true, but it's a complicated story. Everything we've been able to learn is in this recording – about twenty hours, but you can probably Fast most of it.

'You know, of course, that Dave Bowman went out in the Number 2 Pod to rescue you – but was then locked outside the ship because Hal refused to open the pod-bay doors.'

'Why, for God's sake?'

Dr Kim winced slightly. It was not the first time Poole had noticed such a reaction.

(Must watch my language, he thought. 'God' seems to be a dirty word in this culture – must ask Indra about it.)

'There was a major programming error in Hal's instructions – he'd been given control of aspects of the mission you and Bowman didn't know about – it's all in the recording . . .

'Anyway, he also cut off the life-support systems to the three hybernauts – the Alpha Crew – and Bowman had to jettison their bodies as well.'

(So Dave and I were the Beta Crew – something else I didn't know . . .)

'What happened to them?' Poole asked. 'Couldn't they have been rescued, just as I was?'

'I'm afraid not: we've looked into it, of course. Bowman ejected them several hours after he'd taken back control from Hal, so their orbits were slightly different from yours. Just enough for them to burn up in Jupiter – while you skimmed by, and got a gravity boost that would have taken you to the Orion Nebula in a few thousand more years . . .

'Doing everything on manual override – really a fantastic performance! – Bowman managed to get *Discovery* into orbit round Jupiter. And there he encountered what the Second Expedition called Big Brother – an apparent twin of the Tycho Monolith, but hundreds of times larger.

'And that's where we lost him. He left *Discovery* in the remaining space-pod, and made a rendezvous with Big Brother. For almost a thousand years, we've been haunted by his last message: "By Deus – it's full of stars!"'

(Here we go again! Poole told himself. No way Dave could have said that . . . Must have been 'My God – it's full of stars!')

'Apparently the pod was drawn into the Monolith by some kind of inertial field, because it – and presumably Bowman – survived an acceleration which should have crushed them instantly. And that was the last information anyone had, for almost ten years, until the joint US–Russian *Leonov* mission.'

'Which made a rendezvous with the abandoned *Discovery* so that Dr Chandra could go aboard and reactivate Hal. Yes, I know that.'

Dr Kim looked slightly embarrassed

'Sorry – I wasn't sure how much you'd been told already. Anyway, that's when even stranger things started to happen.

'Apparently the arrival of *Leonov* triggered something inside Big Brother. If we did not have these recordings, no one would have believed what happened. Let me show you ... here's Dr Heywood Floyd keeping the midnight watch aboard *Discovery*, after power had been restored. Of course you'll recognize everything.'

(Indeed I do: and how strange to see the long-dead Heywood Floyd, sitting in my old seat with Hal's unblinking red eye surveying everything in sight. And even stranger to think that Hal and I have both shared the same experience of resurrection from the dead ...)

A message was coming up on one of the monitors, and Floyd answered lazily, 'OK, Hal. Who is calling?'

NO IDENTIFICATION.

Floyd looked slightly annoyed.

'Very well. Please give me the message.'

IT IS DANGEROUS TO REMAIN HERE. YOU MUST LEAVE WITHIN FIFTEEN DAYS.

'That is absolutely impossible. Our launch window does not open until twenty-six days from now. We do not have sufficient propellant for an earlier departure.'

I AM AWARE OF THESE FACTS. NEVERTHELESS YOU MUST LEAVE WITHIN FIFTEEN DAYS.

'I cannot take this warning seriously unless I know its origin ... who is speaking to me?'

I WAS DAVID BOWMAN. IT IS IMPORTANT THAT YOU BELIEVE ME. LOOK BEHIND YOU.

Heywood Floyd slowly turned in his swivel chair, away from the banked panels and switches of the computer display, towards the Velcro-covered catwalk behind.

('Watch this carefully,' said Dr Kim.

As if I needed telling, thought Poole ...)

The zero-gravity environment of *Discovery*'s observation

deck was much dustier than he remembered it: he guessed that the air-filtration plant had not yet been brought on line. The parallel rays of the distant yet still brilliant Sun, streaming through the great windows, lit up a myriad of dancing motes in a classic display of Brownian movement.

And now something strange was happening to these particles of dust; some force seemed to be marshalling them, herding them away from a central point yet bringing others towards it, until they all met on the surface of a hollow sphere. That sphere, about a metre across, hovered in the air for a moment like a giant soap bubble. Then it elongated into an ellipsoid, whose surface began to pucker, to form folds and indentations. Poole was not really surprised when it started to assume the shape of a man.

He had seen such figures, blown out of glass, in museums and science exhibitions. But this dusty phantom did not even approximate anatomical accuracy; it was like a crude clay figurine, or one of the primitive works of art found in the recesses of Stone Age caves. Only the head was fashioned with care; and the face, beyond all shadow of doubt, was that of Commander David Bowman.

HELLO, DR FLOYD. NOW DO YOU BELIEVE ME?

The lips of the figure never moved: Poole realized that the voice – yes, certainly Bowman's voice – was actually coming from the speaker grille.

THIS IS VERY DIFFICULT FOR ME, AND I HAVE LITTLE TIME. I HAVE BEEN ALLOWED TO GIVE THIS WARNING. YOU HAVE ONLY FIFTEEN DAYS.

'Why – and *what* are you?'

But the ghostly figure was already fading, its grainy

envelope beginning to dissolve back into the constituent particles of dust.

GOOD-BYE, DOCTOR FLOYD. WE CAN HAVE NO FURTHER CONTACT. BUT THERE MAY BE ONE MORE MESSAGE, IF ALL GOES WELL.

As the image dissolved, Poole could not help smiling at that old Space Age cliché. 'If all goes well' – how many times he had heard that phrase intoned before a mission!

The phantom vanished: only the motes of dancing dust were left, resuming their random patterns in the air. With an effort of will, Poole came back to the present.

'Well, Commander – what do you think of *that*?' asked Kim.

Poole was still shaken, and it was several seconds before he could reply.

'The face and the voice were Bowman's – I'd swear to that. But what *was* it?'

'That's what we're still arguing about. Call it a hologram, a projection – of course, there are plenty of ways it could be faked if anyone wanted to – but not in those circumstances! And then, of course, there's what happened next.'

'Lucifer?'

'Yes. Thanks to that warning, the *Leonov* had just sufficient time to get away before Jupiter detonated.'

'So whatever it was, the Bowman-thing was friendly and trying to help.'

'Presumably. And it may have been responsible for that "one more message" we did receive – it was sent only minutes before the detonation. Another warning.'

Dr Kim brought the screen to life once more. It showed plain text: ALL THESE WORLDS ARE YOURS – EXCEPT

EUROPA. ATTEMPT NO LANDINGS THERE. The same message was repeated about a hundred times, then the letters became garbled.

'And we never have tried to land there?' asked Poole.

'Only once, by accident, thirty-six years later – when the USSS *Galaxy* was hijacked and forced down there, and her sister ship *Universe* had to go to the rescue. It's all here – with what little our robot monitors have told us about the Europans.'

'I'm anxious to see them.'

'They're amphibious, and come in all shapes and sizes. As soon as Lucifer started melting the ice that covered their whole world, they began to emerge from the sea. Since then, they've developed at a speed that seems biologically impossible.'

'From what I remember about Europa, weren't there lots of cracks in the ice? Perhaps they'd already started crawling through and having a look round.'

'That's a widely accepted theory. But there's another, much more speculative, one. The Monolith may have been involved, in ways we don't yet understand. What triggered that line of thought was the discovery of TMA ZERO, right here on Earth, almost five hundred years after your time. I suppose you've been told about that?'

'Only vaguely – there's been so much to catch up with! I did think the name was ridiculous – since it wasn't a magnetic anomaly – and it was in Africa, not Tycho!'

'You're quite right, of course, but we're stuck with the name. And the more we learn about the Monoliths, the more the puzzle deepens. Especially as they're still the only real evidence for advanced technology beyond the Earth.'

53

'That's surprised me. I should have thought that by this time we'd have picked up radio signals from *somewhere*. The astronomers started searching when I was a boy!'

'Well, there is one hint – and it's so terrifying that we don't like to talk about it. Have you heard of Nova Scorpio?'

'I don't believe so.'

'Stars go nova all the time, of course – and this wasn't a particularly impressive one. But before it blew up, N Scorp was known to have several planets.'

'Inhabited?'

'Absolutely no way of telling; radio searches had picked up nothing. And here's the nightmare . . .

'Luckily, the automatic Nova Patrol caught the event at the very beginning. *And it didn't start at the star. One of the planets detonated first, and then triggered its sun.*'

'My Gah . . . sorry, go on.'

'You see the point. It's impossible for a *planet* to go nova – except in one way.'

'I once read a sick joke in a science-fiction novel – "super-novae are industrial accidents".'

'It wasn't a *super*nova – but that may be no joke. The most widely accepted theory is that someone else had been tapping vacuum energy – and had lost control.'

'Or it could have been a war.'

'Just as bad; we'll probably never know. But as our own civilization depends on the same energy source, you can understand why N Scorp sometimes gives us nightmares.'

'And *we* only had melting nuclear reactors to worry about!'

'Not any longer, thank Deus. But I really wanted to tell

you more about TMA ZERO's discovery, because it marked a turning point in human history.

'Finding TMA ONE on the Moon was a big enough shock, but five hundred years later there was a worse one. And it was much nearer home – in every sense of the word. Down there in Africa.'

8

Return to Olduvai

The Leakeys, Dr Stephen Del Marco often told himself, would never have recognized this place, even though it's barely a dozen kilometres from where Louis and Mary, five centuries ago, dug up the bones of our first ancestors. Global warming, and the Little Ice Age (truncated by miracles of heroic technology) had transformed the landscape, and completely altered its *biota*. Oaks and pine trees were still fighting it out, to see which would survive the changes in climatic fortune.

And it was hard to believe that, by this year 2513, there was anything left in Olduvai undug by enthusiastic anthropologists. However, recent flash-floods – which were not supposed to happen any more – had resculpted this area, and cut away several metres of topsoil. Del Marco had taken advantage of the opportunity: and there, at the limit of the deep-scan, was something he could not quite believe.

It had taken more than a year of slow and careful excavation to reach that ghostly image, and to learn that the reality was stranger than anything he had dared to imagine. Robot digging machines had swiftly removed the first few metres, then the traditional slave-crews of graduate students had taken over. They had been helped – or hindered – by a team of four kongs, who Del Marco considered more trouble than they were worth. However, the students adored the genetically-enhanced gorillas, whom they treated like retarded but much-loved children. It was rumoured that the relationships were not always completely Platonic.

For the last few metres, however, everything was the work of human hands, usually wielding toothbrushes – soft-bristled at that. And now it was finished: Howard Carter, seeing the first glint of gold in Tutankhamen's tomb, had never uncovered such a treasure as this. From this moment onwards, Del Marco knew, human beliefs and philosophies would be irrevocably changed.

The Monolith appeared to be the exact twin of that discovered on the Moon five centuries earlier: even the excavation surrounding it was almost identical in size. And like TMA ONE, it was totally non-reflective, absorbing with equal indifference the fierce glare of the African Sun and the pale gleam of Lucifer.

As he led his colleagues – the directors of the world's half-dozen most famous museums, three eminent anthropologists, the heads of two media empires – down into the pit, Del Marco wondered if such a distinguished group of men and women had ever been so silent, for so long. But that was the effect that this ebon rectangle had on all visitors, as they realized the implications of the thousands of artefacts that surrounded it.

For here was an archaeologist's treasure-trove – crudely-fashioned flint tools, countless bones – some animal, some human – *and almost all arranged in careful patterns*. For centuries – no, millennia – these pitiful gifts had been brought here, by creatures with only the first glimmer of intelligence, as tribute to a marvel beyond their understanding.

And beyond ours, Del Marco had often thought. Yet of two things he was certain, though he doubted if proof would ever be possible.

This was where – in time and space – the human species had really begun.

And this Monolith was the very first of all its multitudinous gods.

9

Skyland

'There were mice in my bedroom last night,' Poole complained, only half seriously. 'Is there any chance you could find me a cat?'

Dr Wallace looked puzzled, then started to laugh.

'You must have heard one of the cleaning microts – I'll get the programming checked so they don't disturb you. Try not to step on one if you catch it at work; if you do, it will call for help, and all its friends will come to pick up the pieces.'

So much to learn – so little time! No, that wasn't true, Poole reminded himself. He might well have a century ahead of him, thanks to the medical science of this age. The thought was already beginning to fill him with apprehension rather than pleasure.

At least he was now able to follow most conversations easily, and had learned to pronounce words so that Indra was not the only person who could understand him. He was very glad that Anglish was now the world language, though French, Russian and Mandarin still flourished.

'I've another problem, Indra – and I guess you're the only person who can help. When I say "God", why do people look embarrassed?'

Indra did not look at all embarrassed; in fact, she laughed.

'That's a very complicated story. I wish my old friend Dr Khan was here to explain it to you – but he's on Ganymede, curing any remaining True Believers he can find there. When all the old religions were discredited – let me tell you about Pope Pius XX sometime – one of the greatest men in history! – we still needed a word for the Prime Cause, or the Creator of the Universe – if there is one ...

'There were lots of suggestions – Deo – Theo – Jove – Brahma – they were all tried, and some of them are still around – especially Einstein's favourite, "The Old One". But Deus seems to be the fashion nowadays.'

'I'll try to remember; but it still seems silly to me.'

'You'll get used to it: I'll teach you some other reasonably polite expletives, to use when you want to express your feelings ...'

'You said that all the old religions have been discredited. So what *do* people believe nowadays?'

'As little as possible. We're all either Deists or Theists.'

'You've lost me. Definitions, please.'

'They were slightly different in your time, but here are

the latest versions. Theists believe there's not more than one God; Deists that there is not *less* than one God.'

'I'm afraid the distinction's too subtle for me.'

'Not for everyone; you'd be amazed at the bitter controversies it's aroused. Five centuries ago, someone used what's known as surreal mathematics to prove there's an infinite number of grades between Theists and Deists. Of course, like most dabblers with infinity, he went insane. By the way, the best-known Deists were Americans – Washington, Franklin, Jefferson.'

'A little before my time – though you'd be surprised how many people don't realize it.'

'Now I've some good news. Joe – Prof. Anderson – has finally given his – what was the phrase? – OK. You're fit enough to go for a little trip upstairs . . . to the Lunar Level.'

'Wonderful. How far is that?'

'Oh, about twelve thousand kilometres.'

'Twelve thousand! That will take hours!'

Indra looked surprised at his remark: then she smiled.

'Not as long as you think. No – we don't have a *Star Trek* Transporter yet – though I believe they're still working on it! But you'll need new clothes, and someone to show you how to wear them. And to help you with the hundreds of little everyday jobs that can waste so much time. So we've taken the liberty of arranging a *human* personal assistant for you. Come in, Danil . . .'

Danil was a small, light-brown man in his mid-thirties, who surprised Poole by not giving him the usual palm-to-palm salute, with its automatic exchange of information. Indeed, it soon appeared that Danil did not possess an

Ident: whenever it was needed, he produced a small rectangle of plastic that apparently served the same purpose as the twenty-first century's 'smart cards'.

'Danil will also be your guide and – what was that word? – I can never remember – rhymes with "ballet". He's been specially trained for the job. I'm sure you'll find him completely satisfactory.'

Though Poole appreciated this gesture, it made him feel a little uncomfortable. A valet, indeed! He could not recall ever meeting one; in his time, they were already a rare and endangered species. He began to feel like a character from an early-twentieth-century English novel.

'You have a choice,' said Indra, 'though I know which one you'll take. We can go up on an external elevator, and admire the view – or an interior one, and enjoy a meal and some light entertainment.'

'I can't imagine anyone wanting to stay *inside*.'

'You'd be surprised. It's too vertiginous for some people – especially visitors from down below. Even mountain climbers who say they've got a head for heights may start to turn green – when the heights are measured in thousands of kilometres, instead of metres.'

'I'll risk it,' Poole answered with a smile. 'I've been higher.'

When they had passed through a double set of airlocks in the exterior wall of the Tower (was it imagination, or *did* he feel a curious sense of disorientation then?) they entered what might have been the auditorium of a very small theatre. Rows of ten seats were banked up in five tiers: they all faced towards one of the huge picture windows which Poole still found disconcerting, as he could never quite forget the hundreds of tons of air pressure, striving to blast it out into space.

The dozen or so other passengers, who had probably never given the matter any thought, seemed perfectly at ease. They all smiled as they recognized him, nodded politely, then turned away to admire the view.

'Welcome to Skylounge,' said the inevitable autovoice. 'Ascent begins in five minutes. You will find refreshments and toilets on the lower floor.'

Just how long will this trip last? Poole wondered. We're going to travel over twenty thousand klicks, there and back: this will be like no elevator ride I've ever known on Earth . . .

While he was waiting for the ascent to begin, he enjoyed the stunning panorama laid out two thousand kilometres below. It was winter in the northern hemisphere, but the climate had indeed changed drastically, for there was little snow south of the Arctic Circle.

Europe was almost cloud-free, and there was so much detail that the eye was overwhelmed. One by one he identified the great cities whose names had echoed down the centuries; they had been shrinking even in his time, as the communications revolution changed the face of the world, and had now dwindled still further. There were also some bodies of water in improbable places – the northern Sahara's Lake Saladin was almost a small sea.

Poole was so engrossed by the view that he had forgotten the passage of time. Suddenly he realized that much more than five minutes had passed – yet the elevator was still stationary. Had something gone wrong – or were they waiting for late arrivals?

And then he noticed something so extraordinary that at first he refused to believe the evidence of his eyes. *The panorama had expanded, as if he had already risen hundreds of kilometres!* Even as he watched, he noticed new features of the planet below creeping into the frame of the window.

Then Poole laughed, as the obvious explanation occurred to him.

'You could have fooled me, Indra! I thought this was real – not a video projection!'

Indra looked back at him with a quizzical smile.

'Think again, Frank. We started to move about ten minutes ago. By now we must be climbing at, oh – at least a thousand kilometres an hour. Though I'm told these elevators can reach a hundred gee at maximum acceleration, we won't touch more than ten, on this short run.'

'That's impossible! Six is the maximum they ever gave me in the centrifuge, and I didn't enjoy weighing half a ton. I *know* we haven't moved since we stepped inside.'

Poole had raised his voice slightly, and suddenly became aware that the other passengers were pretending not to notice.

'I don't understand how it's done, Frank, but it's called an inertial field. Or sometimes a Sharp one – the "S" stands for a famous Russian scientist, Sakharov – I don't know who the others were.'

Slowly, understanding dawned in Poole's mind – and also a sense of awe-struck wonder. Here indeed was a 'technology indistinguishable from magic'.

'Some of my friends used to dream of "space drives" – energy fields that could replace rockets, and allow movement without any feeling of acceleration. Most of us thought they were crazy – but it seems they were right! I can still hardly believe it . . . and unless I'm mistaken, we're starting to lose weight.'

'Yes – it's adjusting to the lunar value. When we step out, you'll feel we're on the Moon. But for goodness' sake, Frank – forget you're an engineer, and simply enjoy the view.'

It was good advice, but even as he watched the whole of Africa, Europe and much of Asia flow into his field of vision, Poole could not tear his mind away from this astonishing revelation. Yet he should not have been wholly surprised: he knew that there had been major break-throughs in space propulsion systems since his time, but had not realized that they would have such dramatic applications to everyday life – if that term could be applied to existence in a thirty-six-thousand-kilometre-high sky-scraper.

And the age of the rocket must have been over, centuries ago. All his knowledge of propellant systems and combustion chambers, ion thrusters and fusion reactors, was totally obsolete. Of course, that no longer mattered – but he understood the sadness that the skipper of a wind-jammer must have felt, when sail gave way to steam.

His mood changed abruptly, and he could not help smiling, when the robovoice announced, 'Arriving in two minutes. Please make sure that you do not leave any of your personal belongings behind.'

How often he had heard that announcement, on some commercial flight! He looked at his watch, and was surprised to see that they had been ascending for less than half an hour. So that meant an average speed of at least twenty thousand kilometres an hour, yet they might never have moved. What was even stranger – for the last ten minutes or more they must actually have been *decelerating* so rapidly that by rights they should all have been standing on the roof, heads pointing towards Earth!

The doors opened silently, and as Poole stepped out he again felt the slight disorientation he had noticed on entering the elevator lounge. This time, however, he knew what it meant: he was moving through the transition zone where the inertial field overlapped with gravity – at this level, equal to the Moon's.

Indra and Danil followed him, walking carefully now at a third of their customary weight, as they went forward to meet the next of the day's wonders.

Though the view of the receding Earth had been awesome, even for an astronaut, there was nothing unexpected or surprising about it. But who would have imagined a gigantic chamber, apparently occupying the entire width of the Tower, so that the far wall was more than five kilometres away? Perhaps by this time there were larger enclosed volumes on the Moon and Mars, but this must surely be one of the largest in space itself.

They were standing on a viewing platform, fifty metres up on the outer wall, looking across an astonishingly varied panorama. Obviously, an attempt had been made to reproduce a whole range of terrestrial biomes. Immediately beneath them was a group of slender trees which Poole could not at first identify: then he realized that they were oaks, adapted to one-sixth of their normal gravity. What, he wondered, would palm trees look like here? Giant reeds, probably . . .

In the middle-distance there was a small lake, fed by a river that meandered across a grassy plain, then disappeared into something that looked like a single gigantic banyan tree. What was the source of the water? Poole had become aware of a faint drumming sound, and as he swept his gaze along the gently curving wall, he discovered a miniature Niagara, with a perfect rainbow hovering in the spray above it.

He could have stood here for hours, admiring the view and still not exhausting all the wonders of this complex and brilliantly contrived simulation of the planet below. As it spread out into new and hostile environments, perhaps the human race felt an ever-increasing need to remember its origins. Of course, even in his own time every city had its parks as – usually feeble – reminders of Nature. The same impulse must be acting here, on a much grander scale. Central Park, Africa Tower!

'Let's go down,' said Indra. 'There's so much to see, and I don't come here as often as I'd like.'

Followed by the silent but ever-present Danil, who always seemed to know when he was needed but otherwise kept out of the way, they began a leisurely exploration of this oasis in space. Though walking was almost effortless in this low gravity, from time to time they took advantage of a small monorail, and stopped once for refreshments at a café, cunningly concealed in the trunk of a redwood that must have been at least a quarter of a kilometre tall.

There were very few other people about – their fellow-passengers had long since disappeared into the landscape – so it was as if they had all this wonderland to themselves.

Everything was so beautifully maintained, presumably by armies of robots, that from time to time Poole was reminded of a visit he had made to Disney World as a small boy. But this was even better: there were no crowds, and indeed very little reminder of the human race and its artefacts.

They were admiring a superb collection of orchids, some of enormous size, when Poole had one of the biggest shocks of his life. As they walked past a typical small gardener's shed, the door opened – and the gardener emerged.

Frank Poole had always prided himself on his self-control, and never imagined that as a full-grown adult he would give a cry of pure fright. But like every boy of his generation, he had seen all the 'Jurassic' movies – and he knew a raptor when he met one eye to eye.

'I'm terribly sorry,' said Indra, with obvious concern. 'I never thought of warning you.'

Poole's jangling nerves returned to normal. Of course, there could be no danger, in this perhaps too-well-ordered world: but still . . . !

The dinosaur returned his stare with apparent total disinterest, then doubled back into the shed and emerged again with a rake and a pair of garden shears, which it dropped into a bag hanging over one shoulder. It walked away from them with a bird-like gait, never looking back as it disappeared behind some ten-metre-high sunflowers.

'I should explain,' said Indra contritely. 'We like to use bio-organisms when we can, rather than robots – I suppose it's carbon chauvinism! Now, there are only a few animals that have any manual dexterity, and we've used them all at one time or another.

'And here's a mystery that no one's been able to solve. You'd think that enhanced herbivores like orangutans and gorillas would be good at this sort of work. Well, they're not; they don't have the patience for it.

'Yet carnivores like our friend here are excellent, and easily trained. What's more – here's another paradox! – after they've been modified they're docile and good-natured. Of course, there's almost a thousand years of genetic engineering behind them, and look what primitive man did to the wolf, merely by trial and error!'

Indra laughed and continued: 'You may not believe this, Frank, but they also make good baby-sitters – children love them! There's a five-hundred-year-old joke: "Would you trust your kids to a dinosaur?" "What – and risk injuring it?"'

Poole joined in the laughter, partly in shame-faced reaction to his own fright. To change the subject, he asked Indra the question that was still worrying him.

'All *this*,' he said, 'it's wonderful – but why go to so much trouble, when anyone in the Tower can reach the real thing, just as quickly?'

Indra looked at him thoughtfully, weighing her words.

'That's not quite true. It's uncomfortable – even danger-ous – for anyone who lives above the half-gee level to go down to Earth, even in a hoverchair. So it has to be *this* – or, as you used to say, Virtual Reality.'

(Now I begin to understand, Poole told himself bleakly. That explains Anderson's evasiveness, and all the tests he's been doing to see if I've regained my strength. I've come all the way back from Jupiter, to within two thousand kilometres of Earth – but I may never again walk on the surface of my home planet. I'm not sure how I will be able to handle this . . .)

10

Homage to Icarus

His depression quickly passed: there was so much to do and see. A thousand lifetimes would not have been enough, and the problem was to choose which of the myriad distractions this age could offer. He tried, not always successfully, to avoid the trivia, and to concentrate on the things that mattered – notably his education.

The Braincap – and the book-sized player that went with it, inevitably called the Brainbox – was of enormous value here. He soon had a small library of 'instant knowledge' tablets, each containing all the material needed for a college degree. When he slipped one of these into the Brainbox, and gave it the speed and intensity adjustments that most suited him, there would be a flash of light, followed by a period of unconsciousness that might last as long as an hour. When he awoke, it seemed that new areas of his mind had been opened up, though he only knew they were there when he searched for them. It was almost as if he was the owner of a library who had suddenly discovered shelves of books he did not know he possessed.

To a large extent, he was the master of his own time. Out of a sense of duty – and gratitude – he acceded to as many requests as he could from scientists, historians, writers and artists working in media that were often incomprehensible to him. He also had countless invitations from other citizens of the four Towers, virtually all of which he was compelled to turn down.

Most tempting – and most hard to resist – were those that came from the beautiful planet spread out below. 'Of course,' Professor Anderson had told him, 'you'd *survive* if you went down for short time with the right life-support system, but you wouldn't enjoy it. And it might weaken your neuromuscular system even further. It's never really recovered from that thousand-year sleep.'

His other guardian, Indra Wallace, protected him from unnecessary intrusions, and advised him which requests he should accept – and which he should politely refuse. By himself, he would never understand the socio-political structure of this incredibly complex culture, but he soon gathered that, although in theory all class distinctions had vanished, there were a few thousand super-citizens. George Orwell had been right; some would always be more equal than others.

There had been times when, conditioned by his twenty-first-century experience, Poole had wondered who was paying for all this hospitality – would he one day be presented with the equivalent of an enormous hotel bill? But Indra had quickly reassured him: he was a unique and priceless museum exhibit, so would never have to worry about such mundane considerations. Anything he wanted – within reason – would be made available to him: Poole wondered what the limits were, never imagining that one day he would attempt to discover them.

All the most important things in life happen by accident, and he had set his wall display browser on random scan, silent, when a striking image caught his attention.

'Stop scan! Sound up!' he shouted, with quite unnecessary loudness.

He recognized the music, but it was a few minutes before he identified it; the fact that his wall was filled with winged humans circling gracefully round each other undoubtedly helped. But Tchaikovsky would have been utterly astonished to see this performance of *Swan Lake* – with the dancers *actually flying* . . .

Poole watched, entranced, for several minutes, until he was fairly confident that this was reality, and not a simulation: even in his own day, one could never be quite certain. Presumably the ballet was being performed in one of the many low-gravity environments – a very large one, judging by some of the images. It might even be here in Africa Tower.

I want to try that, Poole decided. He had never quite forgiven the Space Agency for banning one of his greatest pleasures – delayed parachute formation jumping – even though he could see the Agency's point in not wanting to risk a valuable investment. The doctors had been quite unhappy about his earlier hang-gliding accident; fortunately his teenage bones had healed completely.

'Well,' he thought, 'there's no one to stop me now . . . unless it's Prof. Anderson . . .'

To Poole's relief, the physician thought it an excellent idea, and he was also pleased to find that every one of the Towers had its own Aviary, up at the one-tenth-gee level.

Within a few days he was being measured for his wings, not in the least like the elegant versions worn by the performers of *Swan Lake*. Instead of feathers there was a flexible membrane, and when he grasped the handholds attached to the supporting ribs, Poole realized that he must look much more like a bat than a bird. However his 'Move over, Dracula!' was completely wasted on his instructor, who was apparently unacquainted with vampires.

For his first lessons he was restrained by a light harness, so that he did not move anywhere while he was taught the basic strokes – and, most important of all, learned control and stability. Like many acquired skills, it was not quite as easy as it looked.

He felt ridiculous in this safety-harness – how could anyone injure themselves at a tenth of a gravity! – and was glad that he needed only a few lessons; doubtless his astronaut training helped. He was, the Wingmaster told him, the best pupil he had ever taught: but perhaps he said that to all of them.

After a dozen free-flights in a chamber forty metres on a side, criss-crossed with various obstacles which he easily avoided, Poole was given the all-clear for his first solo – and felt nineteen years old again, about to take off in the Flagstaff Aero Club's antique Cesna.

The unexciting name 'The Aviary' had not prepared him for the venue of *this* maiden flight. Though it seemed even more enormous than the space holding the forests and gardens down at the lunar-gee level, it was almost the same size, since it too occupied an entire floor of the gently tapering Tower. A circular void, half a kilometre high and over four kilometres wide, it appeared truly enormous, as there were no features on which the eye could rest. Because the walls were a uniform pale blue, they contributed to the impression of infinite space.

Poole had not really believed the Wingmaster's boast, 'You can have any scenery you like', and intended to throw him what he was sure was an impossible challenge. But on this first flight, at the dizzy altitude of fifty metres, there were no visual distractions. Of course, a fall from the equivalent altitude of five metres in the ten-fold greater Earth gravity could break one's neck; however, even minor bruises were unlikely here, as the entire floor was covered with a network of flexible cables. The whole chamber was a giant trampoline; one could, thought Poole, have a lot of fun here – even without wings.

With firm, downward strokes, Poole lifted himself into the air. In almost no time, it seemed that he was a hundred metres in the air, and still rising.

'Slow down!' said the Wingmaster, 'I can't keep up with you!'

Poole straightened out, then attempted a slow roll. He felt light-headed as well as light-bodied (less than ten kilograms!) and wondered if the concentration of oxygen had been increased.

This was wonderful – quite different from zero gravity, as it posed more of a physical challenge. The nearest thing to it was scuba diving: he wished there were birds here, to emulate the equally colourful coral fish who had so often accompanied him over tropical reefs.

One by one, the Wingmaster put him through a series of manoeuvres – rolls, loops, upside-down flying, hovering ... Finally he said: 'Nothing more I can teach you. Now let's enjoy the view.'

Just for a moment, Poole almost lost control – as he was probably expected to do. For, without the slightest warning, he was surrounded by snow-capped mountains, and was flying down a narrow pass, only metres from some unpleasantly jagged rocks.

Of course, this could not be real: those mountains were as insubstantial as clouds, and he could fly right through them if he wished. Nevertheless, he veered away from the cliff-face (there was an eagle's nest on one of its ledges, holding two eggs which he felt he could touch if he came closer) and headed for more open space.

The mountains vanished; suddenly, it was night. And then the stars came out – not the miserable few thousand in the impoverished skies of Earth, but legions beyond counting. And not only stars, but the spiral whirlpools of distant galaxies, the teeming, close-packed sun-swarms of globular clusters.

There was no possible way *this* could be real, even if he had been magically transported to some world where such skies existed. For those galaxies were receding even as he watched; stars were fading, exploding, being born in stellar nurseries of glowing fire-mist. Every second, a million years must be passing . . .

The overwhelming spectacle disappeared as quickly as it had come: he was back in the empty sky, alone except for his instructor, in the featureless blue cylinder of the Aviary.

'I think that's enough for one day,' said the Wingmaster, hovering a few metres above Poole. 'What scenery would you like, the next time you come here?'

Poole did not hesitate. With a smile, he answered the question.

11

Here be Dragons

He would never have believed it possible, even with the technology of this day and age. How many terabytes – petabytes – was there a large enough word? – of information must have been accumulated over the centuries, and in what sort of storage medium? Better not think about it, and follow Indra's advice: 'Forget you're an engineer – and enjoy yourself.'

He was certainly enjoying himself now, though his pleasure was mixed with an almost overwhelming sense of nostalgia. For he was flying, or so it seemed, at an altitude of about two kilometres, above the spectacular and unforgotten landscape of his youth. Of course, the perspective was false, since the Aviary was only half a kilometre high, but the illusion was perfect.

He circled Meteor Crater, remembering how he had scrambled up its sides during his earlier astronaut training. How incredible that anyone could ever have doubted its origin, and the accuracy of its name! Yet well into the twentieth century, distinguished geologists had argued that it was volcanic: not until the coming of the Space Age was it – reluctantly – accepted that all planets were still under continual bombardment.

Poole was quite sure that his comfortable cruising speed was nearer twenty than two hundred kilometres an hour, yet he had been allowed to reach Flagstaff in less than fifteen minutes. And there were the whitely-gleaming domes of the Lowell Observatory, which he had visited so often as a boy, and whose friendly staff had undoubtedly been responsible for his choice of career. He had sometimes wondered what his profession might have been, had he not been born in Arizona, near the very spot where the most long-enduring and influential of Martian fantasies had been created. Perhaps it was imagination, but Poole thought he could just see Lowell's unique tomb, close to the great telescope, which had fuelled his dreams.

From what year, and what season, had this image been captured? He guessed it had come from the spy satellites which had watched over the world of the early twenty-first century. It could not be much later than his own time, for the layout of the city was just as he remembered. Perhaps if he went low enough he would even see himself . . .

But he knew that was absurd; he had already discovered that this was the nearest he could get. If he flew any closer, the image would start to break up, revealing its basic pixels. It was better to keep his distance, and not destroy the beautiful illusion.

And there – it was incredible! – was the little park where he had played with his junior- and high-school friends. The City Fathers were always arguing about its maintenance, as the water supply became more and more critical. Well, at least it had survived to this time – whenever *that* might be.

And then another memory brought tears to his eyes. Along those narrow paths, whenever he could get home from Houston or the Moon, he had walked with his beloved Rhodesian Ridgeback, throwing sticks for him to retrieve, as man and dog had done from time immemorial.

Poole had hoped, with all his heart, that Rikki would still be there to greet him when he returned from Jupiter, and had left him in the care of his younger brother Martin. He almost lost control, and sank several metres before regaining stability, as he once more faced the bitter truth that both Rikki and Martin had been dust for centuries.

When he could see properly again, he noticed that the dark band of the Grand Canyon was just visible on the far horizon. He was debating whether to head for it – he was growing a little tired – when he became aware that he was not alone in the sky. Something else was approaching, and it was certainly not a human flyer. Although it was difficult to judge distances here, it seemed much too large for that.

Well, he thought, I'm not particularly surprised to meet a pterodactyl here – indeed, it's just the sort of thing I'd expect. I hope it's friendly – or that I can outfly it if it isn't. Oh, no!

A pterodactyl was not a bad guess: maybe eight points out of ten. What was approaching him now, with slow flaps of its great leathery wings, was a dragon straight out of Fairyland. And, to complete the picture, there was a beautiful lady riding on its back. At least, Poole assumed she was beautiful. The traditional image was rather spoiled by one trifling detail: much of her face was concealed by a large pair of aviator's goggles that might have come straight from the open cockpit of a World War I biplane.

Poole hovered in mid-air, like a swimmer treading water, until the oncoming monster came close enough for him to hear the flapping of its great wings. Even when it was less than twenty metres away, he could not decide whether it was a machine or a bio-construct: probably both.

And then he forgot about the dragon, for the rider removed her goggles.

The trouble with clichés, some philosopher remarked, probably with a yawn, is that they are so boringly true.

But 'love at first sight' is never boring.

Danil could provide no information, but then Poole had not expected any from him. His ubiquitous escort – he certainly would not pass muster as a classic valet – seemed so limited in his functions that Poole sometimes wondered if he was mentally handicapped, unlikely though that seemed. He understood the functioning of all the household appliances, carried out simple orders with speed and efficiency, and knew his way about the Tower. But that was all; it was impossible to have an intelligent conversation with him, and any polite queries about his family were met with a look of blank incomprehension. Poole had even wondered if he too was a bio-robot.

Indra, however, gave him the answer he needed right away.

'Oh, you've met the Dragon Lady!'

'Is that what you call her? What's her real name – and can you get me her Ident? We were hardly in a position to touch palms.'

'Of course – no problemo.'

'Where did you pick up *that*?'

Indra looked uncharacteristically confused.

'I've no idea – some old book or movie. Is it a good figure of speech?'

'Not if you're over fifteen.'

'I'll try to remember. Now tell me what happened – unless you want to make me jealous.'

They were now such good friends that they could discuss any subject with perfect frankness. Indeed, they had laughingly lamented their total lack of romantic interest in each other – though Indra had once commented, 'I guess that if we were both marooned on a desert asteroid, with no hope of rescue, we could come to some arrangement.'

'First, you tell me who she is.'

'Her name's Aurora McAuley; among many other things, she's President of the Society for Creative Anachronisms. And if you thought Draco was impressive, wait until you see some of their other – ah – creations. Like Moby Dick – and a whole zooful of dinosaurs Mother Nature never thought of.'

This is too good to be true, thought Poole.

I am the biggest anachronism on Planet Earth.

12

Frustration

Until now, he had almost forgotten that conversation with the Space Agency psychologist.

'You may be gone from Earth for at least three years. If you like, I can give you a harmless anaphrodisiac implant that will last out the mission. I promise we'll more than make it up, when you get home.'

'No thanks,' Poole had answered, trying to keep his face straight when he continued, 'I think I can handle it.'

Nevertheless, he had become suspicious after the third or fourth week – and so had Dave Bowman.

'I've noticed it too,' Dave said. 'I bet those damn doctors put something in our diet.'

Whatever that something was – if indeed it had ever

existed – it was certainly long past its shelf-life. Until now, Poole had been too busy to get involved in any emotional entanglements, and had politely turned down generous offers from several young (and not so young) ladies. He was not sure whether it was his physique or his fame that appealed to them: perhaps it was nothing more than simple curiosity about a man who, for all they knew, might be an ancestor from twenty or thirty generations in the past.

To Poole's delight, Mistress McAuley's Ident conveyed the information that she was currently between lovers, and he wasted no further time in contacting her. Within twenty-four hours he was pillion-riding, with his arms enjoyably around her waist. He had also learned why aviator's goggles were a good idea, for Draco was entirely robotic, and could easily cruise at a hundred klicks. Poole doubted if any real dragons had ever attained such speeds.

He was not surprised that the ever-changing landscapes below them were straight out of legend. Ali Baba had waved angrily at them, as they overtook his flying carpet, shouting 'Can't you see where you're going!' Yet he must be a long way from Baghdad, because the dreaming spires over which they now circled could only be Oxford.

Aurora confirmed his guess as she pointed down: 'That's the pub – the inn – where Lewis and Tolkien used to meet their friends, the Inklings. And look at the river – that boat just coming out from the bridge – do you see the two little girls and the clergyman in it?'

'Yes,' he shouted back against the gentle sussuration of Draco's slipstream. 'And I suppose one of them is Alice.'

Aurora turned and smiled at him over her shoulder: she seemed genuinely delighted.

'Quite correct: she's an accurate replica, based on the Reverend's photos. I was afraid you wouldn't know. So many people stopped reading soon after your time.'

Poole felt a glow of satisfaction.

I believe I've passed another test, he told himself smugly. Riding on Draco must have been the first. How many more, I wonder? Fighting with broadswords?

But there were no more, and the answer to the immemorial 'Your place or mine?' was – Poole's.

The next morning, shaken and mortified, he contacted Professor Anderson.

'Everything was going splendidly,' he lamented, 'when she suddenly became hysterical and pushed me away. I was afraid I'd hurt her somehow –

'Then she called the roomlight – we'd been in darkness – and jumped out of bed. I guess I was just staring like a fool . . .' He laughed ruefully. 'She was certainly worth staring at.'

'I'm sure of it. Go on.'

'After a few minutes she relaxed and said something I'll never be able to forget.'

Anderson waited patiently for Poole to compose himself.

'She said: "I'm really sorry, Frank. We could have had a good time. But I didn't know that you'd been – *mutilated*."'

The professor looked baffled, but only for a moment.

'Oh – I understand. I'm sorry too, Frank – perhaps I should have warned you. In my thirty years of practice, I've only seen half a dozen cases – all for valid medical reasons, which certainly didn't apply to you . . .

'Circumcision made a lot of sense in primitive times –

and even in your century – as a defence against some unpleasant – even fatal – diseases in backward countries with poor hygiene. But otherwise there was absolutely no excuse for it – and several arguments against, as you've just discovered!

'I checked the records after I'd examined you the first time, and found that by mid-twenty-first century there had been so many malpractice suits that the American Medical Association had been forced to ban it. The arguments among the contemporary doctors are very entertaining.'

'I'm sure they are,' said Poole morosely.

'In some countries it continued for another century: then some unknown genius coined a slogan – please excuse the vulgarity – "God designed us: circumcision is blasphemy". That more or less ended the practice. But if you want, it would be easy to arrange a transplant – you wouldn't be making medical history, by any means.'

'I don't think it would work. Afraid I'd start laughing every time.'

'That's the spirit – you're already getting over it.'

Somewhat to his surprise, Poole realized that Anderson's prognosis was correct. He even found himself *already* laughing.

'Now what, Frank?'

'Aurora's "Society for Creative Anachronisms". I'd hoped it would improve my chances. Just my luck to have found one anachronism she doesn't appreciate.'

13

Stranger in a Strange Time

Indra was not quite as sympathetic as he had hoped: perhaps, after all, there was some sexual jealousy in their relationship. And – much more serious – what they wryly labelled the Dragon Debacle led to their first real argument.

It began innocently enough, when Indra complained:

'People are always asking me why I've devoted my life to such a horrible period of history, and it's not much of an answer to say that there were even worse ones.'

'Then why *are* you interested in my century?'

'Because it marks the transition between barbarism and civilization.'

'Thank you. Just call me Conan.'

'Conan? The only one I know is the man who invented Sherlock Holmes.'

'Never mind – sorry I interrupted. Of course, we in the so-called developed countries thought we were civilized. At least war wasn't respectable any more, and the United Nations was always doing its best to stop the wars that did break out.'

'Not very successfully: I'd give it about three out of ten. But what we find incredible is the way that people – right up to the early 2000s! – calmly accepted behaviour we would consider atrocious. And believed in the most mind-boggled –'

'Boggling.'

'– nonsense, which surely any rational person would dismiss out of hand.'

'Examples, please.'

'Well, your really trivial loss started me doing some research, and I was appalled by what I found. Did you know that every year in some countries thousands of little girls were hideously mutilated to preserve their virginity? Many of them died – but the authorities turned a blind eye.'

'I agree that was terrible – but what could *my* government do about it?'

'A great deal – if it wished. But that would have offended the people who supplied it with oil – and bought its weapons, like the landmines that killed and maimed civilians by the thousand.'

'You don't understand, Indra. Often we had no choice: we couldn't reform the whole world. And didn't somebody once say "Politics is the art of the possible"?'

'Quite true – which is why only second-rate minds go into it. Genius likes to challenge the impossible.'

'Well, I'm glad you have a good supply of genius, so you can put things right.'

'Do I detect a hint of sarcasm? Thanks to our computers, we can run political experiments in cyberspace before trying them out in practice. Lenin was unlucky; he was born a hundred years too soon. Russian communism might have worked – at least for a while – if it had had microchips. And had managed to avoid Stalin.'

Poole was constantly amazed by Indra's knowledge of his age – as well as by her ignorance of so much that he took for granted. In a way, he had the reverse problem. Even if he lived the hundred years that had been confidently promised him, he could never learn enough to feel at home. In any conversation, there would always be references he did not understand, and jokes that would go over his head. Worse still, he would always feel on the verge of some *faux pas* – about to create some social disaster that would embarrass even the best of his new friends . . .

. . . Such as the occasion when he was lunching, fortunately in his own quarters, with Indra and Professor Anderson. The meals that emerged from the autochef were always perfectly acceptable, having been designed to match his physiological requirements. But they were certainly nothing to get excited about, and would have been the despair of a twenty-first-century gourmet.

Then, one day, an unusually tasty dish appeared, which brought back vivid memories of the deer-hunts and barbecues of his youth. However, there was something unfamiliar about both flavour and texture, so Poole asked the obvious question.

Anderson merely smiled, but for a few seconds Indra looked as if she was about to be sick. Then she recovered and said: '*You* tell him – *after* we've finished eating.'

Now what have I done wrong? Poole asked himself. Half an hour later, with Indra rather pointedly absorbed in a video display at the other end of the room, his knowledge of the Third Millennium made another major advance.

'Corpse-food was on the way out even in your time,' Anderson explained. 'Raising animals to – ugh – *eat* them became economically impossible. I don't know how many acres of land it took to feed one cow, but at least ten humans could survive on the plants it produced. And probably a hundred, with hydroponic techniques.

'But what finished the whole horrible business was not economics – but disease. It started first with cattle, then spread to other food animals – a kind of virus, I believe, that affected the brain, and caused a particularly nasty death. Although a cure was eventually found, it was too late to turn back the clock – and anyway, synthetic foods were now far cheaper, and you could get them in any flavour you liked.'

Remembering weeks of satisfying but unexciting meals, Poole had strong reservations about this. For why, he wondered, did he still have wistful dreams of spare-ribs and *cordon bleu* steaks?

Other dreams were far more disturbing, and he was afraid that before long he would have to ask Anderson for medical assistance. Despite everything that was being done to make him feel at home, the strangeness and sheer complexity of this new world were beginning to over-whelm him. During sleep, as if in an unconscious effort to escape, he often reverted to his earlier life: but when he awoke, that only made matters worse.

He had travelled across to America Tower and looked down, in reality and not in simulation, on the landscape of his youth – and it had not been a good idea. With optical aid, when the atmosphere was clear, he'd got so close that he could see individual human beings as they went about their affairs, sometimes along streets that he remembered . . .

And always, at the back of his mind, was the knowledge that down there had once lived everyone he had ever loved. Mother, Father (before he had gone off with that Other Woman), dear Uncle George and Aunt Lil, brother Martin – and, not least, a succession of dogs, beginning with the warm puppies of his earliest childhood and culminating in Rikki.

Above all, there was the memory – and mystery – of Helena . . .

It had begun as a casual affair, in the early days of his astrotraining, but had become more and more serious as the years went by. Just before he had left for Jupiter, they had planned to make it permanent – when he returned.

And if he did not, Helena wished to have his child. He still recalled the blend of solemnity and hilarity with which they had made the necessary arrangements . . .

Now, a thousand years later, despite all his efforts, he had been unable to find if Helena had kept her promise. Just as there were now gaps in his own memory, so there were also in the collective records of Mankind. The worst was that created by the devastating electromagnetic pulse from the 2304 asteroid impact, which had wiped out several per cent of the world's information banks, despite all backups and safety systems. Poole could not help wondering if, among all the exabytes that were irretrievably lost, were the records of his own children: even now, his descendants of the thirtieth generation might be walking the Earth; but he would never know.

It helped a little to have discovered that – unlike Aurora – some ladies of this era did not consider him to be damaged goods. On the contrary: they often found his alteration quite exciting, but this slightly bizarre reaction made it impossible for Poole to establish any close relationship. Nor was he anxious to do so; all that he really needed was the occasional healthy, mindless exercise.

Mindless – that was the trouble. He no longer had any purpose in life. And the weight of too many memories was upon him; echoing the title of a famous book he had read in his youth, he often said to himself, 'I am a Stranger in a Strange Time.'

There were even occasions when he looked down at the beautiful planet on which – if he obeyed doctor's orders – he could never walk again, and wondered what it would be like to make a second acquaintance with the vacuum of space. Though it was not easy to get through the airlocks without triggering some alarm, it had been done: every few years, some determined suicide made a brief meteoric display in the Earth's atmosphere.

Perhaps it was just as well that deliverance was on its way, from a completely unexpected direction.

* * *

'Nice to meet you, Commander Poole – for the second time.'

'I'm sorry – don't recall – but then I see so many people.'

'No need to apologize. First time was out round Neptune.'

'Captain Chandler – delighted to see you! Can I get something from the autochef?'

'Anything with over twenty per cent alcohol will be fine.'

'And what are you doing back on Earth? They told me you never come inside Mars orbit.'

'Almost true – though I was born here, I think it's a dirty, smelly place – too many people – creeping up to a *billion* again!'

'More than ten billion in my time. By the way, did you get my "Thank you" message?'

'Yes – and I know I should have contacted you. But I waited until I headed sunwards again. So here I am. Your good health!'

As the Captain disposed of his drink with impressive speed, Poole tried to analyse his visitor. Beards – even small goatees like Chandler's – were very rare in this society, and he had never known an astronaut who wore one: they did not co-exist comfortably with space-helmets. Of course, a Captain might go for years between EVs, and in any case most outside jobs were done by robots; but there was always the risk of the unexpected, when one might have to get suited in a hurry. It was obvious that Chandler was something of an eccentric, and Poole's heart warmed to him.

'You've not answered my question. If you don't like Earth, what are you doing here?'

'Oh, mostly contacting old friends – it's wonderful to forget hour-long delays, and to have real-time conversations! But of course *that's* not the reason. My old rust-bucket is having a refit, up at the Rim shipyard. And the armour has to be replaced; when it gets down to a few centimetres thick, I don't sleep too well.'

'Armour?'

'Dust shield. Not such a problem in your time, was it? But it's a dirty environment out round Jupiter, and our normal cruise speed is several thousand klicks – a *second*! So there's a continuous gentle pattering, like raindrops on the roof.'

'You're joking!'

'Course I am. If we really could hear anything, we'd be dead. Luckily, this sort of unpleasantness is very rare – last serious accident was twenty years ago. We know all the main comet streams, where most of the junk is, and are careful to avoid them – except when we're matching velocity to round up ice.

'But why don't you come aboard and have a look around, before we take off for Jupiter?'

'I'd be delighted . . . did you say Jupiter?'

'Well, Ganymede, of course – Anubis City. We've a lot of business there, and several of us have families we haven't seen for months.'

Poole scarcely heard him.

Suddenly – unexpectedly – and perhaps none too soon, he had found a reason for living.

Commander Frank Poole was the sort of man who hated

to leave a job undone -- and a few specks of cosmic dust, even moving at a thousand kilometres a second, were not likely to discourage him.

He had unfinished business at the world once known as Jupiter.

II

GOLIATH

14

A Farewell to Earth

'Anything you want – within reason,' he had been told. Frank Poole was not sure if his hosts would consider that returning to Jupiter was a reasonable request; indeed, he was not quite sure himself, and was beginning to have second thoughts.

He had already committed himself to scores of engagements, weeks in advance. Most of them he would be happy to miss, but there were some he would be sorry to forgo. In particular, he hated to disappoint the senior class from his old high school – how astonishing that it still existed! – when they planned to visit him next month.

However, he was relieved – and a little surprised – when both Indra and Professor Anderson agreed that it was an excellent idea. For the first time, he realized that they had been concerned with his mental health; perhaps a holiday from Earth would be the best possible cure.

And, most important of all, Captain Chandler was delighted. 'You can have my cabin,' he promised. 'I'll kick the First Mate out of hers.' There were times when Poole wondered if Chandler, with his beard and swagger, was not another anachronism. He could easily picture him on the bridge of a battered three-master, with Skull and Cross-bones flying overhead.

Once his decision had been made, events moved with surprising speed. He had accumulated very few possessions, and fewer still that he needed to take with him. The most important was Miss Pringle, his electronic *alter ego* and secretary, now the storehouse of both his lives, and the small stack of terabyte memories that went with her.

Miss Pringle was not much larger than the hand-held personal assistants of his own age, and usually lived, like the Old West's Colt 45, in a quick-draw holster at his waist. She could communicate with him by audio or Braincap, and her prime duty was to act as an information filter and a buffer to the outside world. Like any good secretary, she knew when to reply, in the appropriate format: 'I'll put you through now' or – much more frequently: 'I'm sorry – Mr Poole is engaged. Please record your message and he will get back to you as soon as possible.' Usually, this was never.

There were very few farewells to be made: though real-time conversations would be impossible owing to the sluggish velocity of radio waves, he would be in constant touch with Indra and Joseph – the only genuine friends he had made.

Somewhat to his surprise, Poole realized that he would miss his enigmatic but useful 'valet', because he would now have to handle all the small chores of everyday life by himself. Danil bowed slightly when they parted, but otherwise showed no sign of emotion, as they took the long ride up to the outer curve of the world-circling wheel, thirty-six thousand kilometres above central Africa.

'I'm not sure, Dim, that you'll appreciate the comparison. But do you know what *Goliath* reminds me of?'

They were now such good friends that Poole could use the Captain's nickname – but only when no one else was around.

'Something unflattering, I assume.'

'Not really. But when I was a boy, I came across a whole pile of old science-fiction magazines that my Uncle George had abandoned – "pulps", they were called, after the cheap paper they were printed on . . . most of them were already falling to bits. They had wonderful garish covers, showing strange planets and monsters – and, of course, spaceships!

'As I grew older, I realized how ridiculous those spaceships were. They were usually rocket-driven – but there was never any sign of propellant tanks! Some of them had rows of windows from stem to stern, just like ocean liners. There was one favourite of mine with a huge glass dome – a space-going conservatory . . .

'Well, those old artists had the last laugh: too bad they could never know. *Goliath* looks more like their dreams than the flying fuel-tanks we used to launch from the Cape.

Your Inertial Drive still seems too good to be true – no visible means of support, unlimited range and speed ... sometimes I think *I'm* the one who's dreaming!'

Chandler laughed and pointed to the view outside.

'Does that look like a dream?'

It was the first time that Poole had seen a genuine horizon since he had come to Star City, and it was not quite as far away as he had expected. After all, he was on the outer rim of a wheel seven times the diameter of Earth, so surely the view across the roof of this artificial world should extend for several hundred kilometres ...

He used to be good at mental arithmetic – a rare achievement even in his time, and probably much rarer now. The formula to give the horizon distance was a simple one: the square root of twice your height times the radius – the sort of thing you never forgot, even if you wanted to ...

Let's see – we're about 8 metres up – so root 16 – this is easy! – say big R is 40,000 – knock off those three zeros to make it all klicks – 4 times root 40 – hmm – just over 25 ...

Well, twenty-five kilometres was a fair distance, and certainly no spaceport on Earth had ever seemed this huge. Even knowing perfectly well what to expect, it was uncanny to watch vessels many times the size of his long-lost *Discovery* lifting off, not only with no sound, but with no apparent means of propulsion. Though Poole missed the flame and fury of the old-time countdowns, he had to admit that this was cleaner, more efficient – and far safer.

Strangest of all, though, was to sit up here on the Rim, in the Geostationary Orbit itself – and to feel weight! Just metres away, outside the window of the tiny observation lounge, servicing robots and a few spacesuited humans were gliding gently about their business; yet here inside *Goliath* the inertial field was maintaining standard Mars-gee.

'Sure you don't want to change your mind, Frank?' Captain Chandler had asked jokingly, as he left for the bridge. 'Still ten minutes before lift-off.'

'Wouldn't be very popular if I did, would I? No – as they used to say back in the old days – we have commit. Ready or not, here I come.'

Poole felt the need to be alone when the drive went on, and the tiny crew – only four men and three women – respected his wish. Perhaps they guessed how he must be feeling, to leave Earth for the second time in a thousand years – and, once again, to face an unknown destiny.

Jupiter-Lucifer was on the other side of the Sun, and the almost straight line of *Goliath*'s orbit would take them close to Venus. Poole looked forward to seeing, with his own unaided eyes, if Earth's sister planet was now beginning to live up to that description, after centuries of terraforming.

From a thousand kilometres up, Star City looked like a gigantic metal band around Earth's Equator, dotted with gantries, pressure domes, scaffolding holding half-completed ships, antennas, and other more enigmatic structures. It was diminishing swiftly as *Goliath* headed upwards, and presently Poole could see how incomplete it was: there were huge gaps spanned only by a spider's web of scaffolding, which would probably never be completely enclosed.

And now they were falling below the plane of the ring; it was midwinter in the northern hemisphere, so the slim halo of Star City was inclined at over twenty degrees to the Sun. Already Poole could see the American and Asian towers, as shining threads stretching outwards and away, beyond the blue haze of the atmosphere.

He was barely conscious of time as *Goliath* gained speed, moving more swiftly than any comet that had ever fallen sunwards from interstellar space. The Earth, almost full, still spanned his field of view, and he could now see the full length of the Africa Tower which had been his home in the life he was now leaving – perhaps, he could not help thinking, leaving for ever.

When they were fifty thousand kilometres out, he was able to view the whole of Star City, as a narrow ellipse enclosing the Earth. Though the far side was barely visible, as a hair-line of light against the stars, it was awe-inspiring to think that the human race had now set this sign upon the heavens.

Then Poole remembered the rings of Saturn, infinitely more glorious. The astronautical engineers still had a long, long way to go, before they could match the achievements of Nature.

Or, if that was the right word, Deus.

15

Transit of Venus

When he woke the next morning, they were already at Venus. But the huge, dazzling crescent of the still cloud-wrapped planet was not the most striking object in the sky: *Goliath* was floating above an endless expanse of crinkled silver foil, flashing in the sunlight with ever-changing patterns as the ship drifted across it.

Poole remembered that in his own age there had been an artist who had wrapped whole buildings in plastic sheets: how he would have loved this opportunity to package billions of tons of ice in a glittering envelope! Only in this way could the core of a comet be protected from evaporation on its decades-long journey sunwards.

'You're in luck, Frank,' Chandler had told him. 'This is

something I've never seen myself. It should be spectacular. Impact due in just over an hour. We've given it a little nudge, to make sure it comes down in the right place. Don't want anyone to get hurt.'

Poole looked at him in astonishment.

'You mean – there are already people on Venus?'

'About fifty mad scientists, near the South Pole. Of course, they're well dug in, but we should shake them up a bit – even though Ground Zero is on the other side of the planet. Or I should say "Atmosphere Zero" – it will be days before anything except the shockwave gets down to the surface.'

As the cosmic iceberg, sparkling and flashing in its protective envelope, dwindled away towards Venus, Poole was struck with a sudden, poignant memory. The Christmas trees of his childhood had been adorned with just such ornaments, delicate bubbles of coloured glass. And the comparison was not completely ludicrous: for many families on Earth, this was still the right season for gifts, and Goliath was bringing a present beyond price to another world.

The radar image of the tortured Venusian landscape – its weird volcanoes, pancake domes, and narrow, sinuous canyons – dominated the main screen of Goliath's control centre, but Poole preferred the evidence of his own eyes. Although the unbroken sea of clouds that covered the planet revealed nothing of the inferno beneath, he wanted to see what would happen when the stolen comet struck. In a matter of seconds, the myriad of tons of frozen hydrates that had been gathering speed for decades on the downhill run from Neptune would deliver all their energy . . .

The initial flash was even brighter than he had expected. How strange that a missile made of ice could generate temperatures that must be in the tens of thousands of degrees! Though the filters of the view-port would have absorbed all the dangerous shorter wave-lengths, the fierce blue of the fireball proclaimed that it was hotter than the Sun.

It was cooling rapidly as it expanded – through yellow, orange, red ... The shockwave would now be spreading outwards at the velocity of sound – and what a sound *that* must be! – so in a few minutes there should be some visible indication of its passage across the face of Venus.

And there it was! Only a tiny black ring – like an insignificant puff of smoke, giving no hint of the cyclonic fury that must be blasting its way outwards from the point of impact. As Poole watched, it slowly expanded, though owing to its scale there was no sense of visible movement: he had to wait for a full minute before he could be quite sure that it had grown larger.

After a quarter of an hour, however, it was the most prominent marking on the planet. Though much fainter – a dirty grey, rather than black – the shockwave was now a ragged circle more than a thousand kilometres across. Poole guessed that it had lost its original symmetry while sweeping over the great mountain ranges that lay beneath it.

Captain Chandler's voice sounded briskly over the ship's address system.

'Putting you through to Aphrodite Base. Glad to say they're not shouting for help –'

'– shook us up a bit, but just what we expected. Monitors

indicate some rain already over the Nokomis Mountains – it will soon evaporate, but that's a beginning. And there seems to have been a flash-flood in Hecate Chasm – too good to be true, but we're checking. There *was* a temporary lake of boiling water there after the last delivery –'

I don't envy them, Poole told himself – but I certainly admire them. They prove that the spirit of adventure still exists in this perhaps too-comfortable and too-well-adjusted society.

' – and thanks again for bringing this little load down in the right place. With any luck – and if we can get that sun-screen up into sync orbit – we'll have some permanent seas before long. And *then* we can plant coral reefs, to make lime and pull the excess CO_2 out of the atmosphere ... hope I live to see it!'

I hope you do, thought Poole in silent admiration. He had often dived in the tropical seas of Earth, admiring weird and colourful creatures so bizarre that it was hard to believe anything stranger would be found, even on the planets of other suns.

'Package delivered on time, and receipt acknowledged,' said Captain Chandler with obvious satisfaction. 'Good-bye Venus – Ganymede, here we come.'

MISS PRINGLE

FILE – WALLACE

Hello, Indra. Yes, you were quite right. I do miss our little arguments. Chandler and I get along fine, and at first the crew treated me – this will amuse you – rather like a holy relic. But they're beginning to accept me, and have even started to pull my leg (do you know that idiom?).

It's annoying not to be able to have a real conversation – we've crossed the orbit of Mars, so radio round-trip is already over an hour. But there's one advantage – you won't be able to interrupt me . . .

Even though it will take us only a week to reach Jupiter, I thought I'd have time to relax. Not a bit of it: my fingers started to itch, and I couldn't resist going back to school. So I've begun basic training, all over again, in one of *Goliath*'s minishuttles. Maybe Dim will actually let me solo . . .

It's not much bigger than *Discovery*'s pods – but what a difference! First of all, of course, it doesn't use rockets: I can't get used to the luxury of the inertial drive, and unlimited range. Could fly back to Earth if I had to – though I'd probably get – remember the phrase I used once, and you guessed its meaning? – 'stir crazy'.

The biggest difference, though, is the control system. It's been a big challenge for me to get used to hands-off operation.

– and the computer has had to learn to recognize my voice commands. At first it was asking every five minutes 'Do you *really* mean that?' I know it would be better to use the Braincap – but I'm still not completely confident with that gadget. Not sure if I'll *ever* get used to something reading my mind . . .

By the way, the shuttle's called *Falcon*. It's a nice name – and I was disappointed to find that no one aboard knew that it goes all the way back to the Apollo missions, when we first landed on the Moon . . .

Uh-huh – there was a lot more I wanted to say, but

the skipper is calling. Back to the classroom – love and out.

STORE

TRANSMIT

Hello Frank – Indra calling – if that's right word! – on my new Thoughtwriter – old one had nervous breakdown ha ha – so be lots of mistakes – no time to edit before I send. Hope you can make sense.

COMSET! Channel one oh three – record from twelve thirty – correction – thirteen thirty. Sorry . . .

Hope I can get old unit fixed – knew all my short-cuts and abbrieves – maybe should get psychoanalysed like in your time – never understood how that Fraudian – mean Freudian ha ha – nonsense lasted as long as it did –

Reminds me – came across late Twentieth defin other day – may amuse you – something like this – quote – Psychoanalysis – contagious disease originating Vienna circa 1900 – now extinct in Europe but occasional outbreaks among rich Americans. Unquote. Funny?

Sorry again – trouble with Thoughtwriters – hard to stick to point –

xz 12£ w 888 8****** js9812yebdc DAMN . . . STOP . . . BACKUP

Did I do something wrong then? Will try again.

You mentioned Danil . . . sorry we always evaded your questions about him – knew you were curious, but we had very good reason – remember you once called him a non-person? . . . not bad guess . . . !

Once you asked me about crime nowadays – I said any such interest pathological – maybe prompted by the endless sickening television programmes of your time – never able to watch more than few minutes myself . . . disgusting!

DOOR – ACKNOWLEDGE! – OH, HELLO MELINDA – EXCUSE – SIT DOWN – NEARLY FINISHED . . .

Yes – crime. Always some . . . Society's irreducible noise level. What to do?

Your solution – prisons. State-sponsored perversion factories – costing ten times average family income to hold one inmate! Utterly crazy . . . Obviously something very wrong with people who shouted loudest for more prisons – *they* should be psychoanalysed! But let's be fair – really no alternative before electronic monitoring and control perfected – you should see the joyful crowds smashing the prison walls then – nothing like it since Berlin fifty years earlier!

Yes – Danil. I don't know what his crime was – wouldn't tell you if I did – but presume his psych profile suggested he'd make a good – what was the word? – ballet – no, valet. Very hard to get people for some jobs – don't know how we'd manage if crime level zero! Anyway hope he's soon decontrolled and back in normal society.

SORRY MELINDA – NEARLY FINISHED.

That's it, Frank – regards to Dimitri – you must be half-way to Ganymede now – wonder if they'll ever repeal Einstein so we can *talk* across space in real-time!

Hope this machine soon gets used to me. Otherwise be looking round for genuine antique twentieth century word processor . . . Would you believe – once even mastered that QWERTYUIOP nonsense, which you took a couple of hundred years to get rid of?

Love and good-bye.

* * *

Hello Frank – here I am again. Still waiting acknowledgement of my last . . .

Strange you should be heading towards Ganymede, and my old friend Ted Khan. But perhaps it's not such a coincidence: he was drawn by the same enigma that you were . . .

First I must tell you something about him. His parents played a dirty trick, giving him the name Theodore. That shortens – don't ever call him that! – to Theo. See what I mean?

Can't help wondering if that's what drives him. Don't know anyone else who's developed such an interest in religion – no, *obsession*. Better warn you; he can be quite a bore.

By the way, how am I doing? I miss my old Thinkwriter, but seem to be getting this machine under control. Haven't made any bad – what did you call them? – bloopers – glitches – fluffs – so far at least –

Not sure I should tell you this, in case you accidentally blurt it out, but my private nickname for Ted is 'The Last Jesuit'. You must know something about them – the Order was still very active in your time.

Amazing people – often great scientists – superb scholars – did a tremendous amount of good as well as much harm. One of history's supreme ironies – sincere and brilliant seekers of knowledge and truth, yet their whole philosophy hopelessly distorted by superstition . . .

Xuedn2k3jn deer 21eidj dwpp

Damn. Got emotional and lost control. One, two, three, four . . . now is the time for all good men to come to the aid of the party . . . *that's* better.

Anyway, Ted has that same brand of high-minded

determination; don't get into any arguments with him – he'll go over you like a steam-roller.

By the way what *were* steam-rollers? Used for pressing clothes? Can see how that could be very uncomfortable . . .

Trouble with Thinkwriters . . . too easy to go off in all directions, no matter how hard you try to discipline yourself . . . something to be said for keyboards after all . . . sure I've said that before . . .

Ted Khan . . . Ted Khan . . . Ted Khan

He's still famous back on Earth for at least two of his sayings: 'Civilization and Religion are incompatible' and 'Faith is believing what you know isn't true'. Actually, I don't think the last one is original; if it is, that's the nearest he ever got to a joke. He never cracked a smile when I tried one of my favourites on him – hope you haven't heard it before. It obviously dates from your time . . .

The Dean's complaining to his Faculty. 'Why do you scientists need such expensive equipment? Why can't you be like the Maths Department, which only needs a blackboard and a waste-paper basket? Better still, like the Department of Philosophy. *That* doesn't even need a waste-paper basket . . .' Well, perhaps Ted had heard it before . . . I expect most philosophers have . . .

Anyway, give him my regards – and don't, repeat don't, get into any arguments with him!

Love and best wishes from Afran Tower

TRANSCRIBE. STORE.

TRANSMIT – POOLE

16
The Captain's Table

The arrival of such a distinguished passenger had caused a certain disruption in the tight little world of *Goliath*, but the crew had adapted to it with good humour. Every day, at 18.00 hours, all personnel gathered for dinner in the wardroom, which in zero-gee could hold at least thirty people in comfort, if spread uniformly around the walls. However, most of the time the ship's working areas were held at lunar gravity, so there was an undeniable floor – and more than eight bodies made a crowd.

The semi-circular table that unfolded around the auto-chef at mealtimes could just seat the entire seven-person crew, with the Captain at the place of honour. One extra created such insuperable problems that somebody now had to eat alone for every meal. After much good-natured debate, it was decided to make the choice in alphabetical order – not of proper names, which were hardly ever used, but of nicknames. It had taken Poole some time to get used to them: 'Bolts' (structural engineering); 'Chips' (computers and communications); 'First' (First Mate); 'Life' (medical and life-support systems); 'Props' (propulsion and power); and 'Stars' (orbits and navigation).

During the ten-day voyage, as he listened to the stories, jokes and complaints of his temporary shipmates, Poole learned more about the solar system than during his months on Earth. All aboard were obviously delighted to have a new and perhaps naïve listener as an attentive one-man audience, but Poole was seldom taken in by their more imaginative stories.

Yet sometimes it was hard to know where to draw the line. No one *really* believed in the Golden Asteroid, which was usually regarded as a twenty-fourth-century hoax. But what about the Mercurian plasmoids, which had been reported by at least a dozen reliable witnesses during the last five hundred years?

The simplest explanation was that they were related to ball-lightning, responsible for so many 'Unidentified Flying Object' reports on Earth and Mars. But some observers swore that they had shown purposefulness – even inquisitiveness – when they were encountered at close quarters. Nonsense, answered the sceptics – merely electrostatic attraction!

Inevitably, this led to discussions about life in the Universe, and Poole found himself – not for the first time – defending his own era against its extremes of credulity and scepticism. Although the 'Aliens are among us' mania had already subsided when he was a boy, even as late as the 2020s the Space Agency was still plagued by lunatics who claimed to have been contacted – or abducted – by visitors from other worlds. Their delusions had been reinforced by sensational media exploitation, and the whole syndrome was later enshrined in the medical literature as 'Adamski's Disease'.

The discovery of TMA ONE had, paradoxically, put an end to this sorry nonsense, by demonstrating that though there was indeed intelligence elsewhere, it had apparently not concerned itself with Mankind for several million years. TMA ONE had also convincingly refuted the handful of scientists who argued that life above the bacterial level was such an improbable phenomenon that the human race was alone in this Galaxy – if not the Cosmos.

Goliath's crew was more interested in the technology than the politics and economics of Poole's era, and were particularly fascinated by the revolution that had taken place in his own lifetime – the end of the fossil-fuel age, triggered by the harnessing of vacuum energy. They found it hard to imagine the smog-choked cities of the twentieth century, and the waste, greed and appalling environmental disasters of the Oil Age.

'Don't blame *me*,' said Poole, fighting back gamely after one round of criticism. 'Anyway, see what a mess the twenty-*first* century made.'

There was a chorus of 'What do you mean?'s around the table.

'Well, as soon as the so-called Age of Infinite Power got under way, and everyone had thousands of kilowatts of cheap, clean energy to play with – you know what happened!'

'Oh, you mean the Thermal Crisis. But that was fixed.'

'Eventually – after you'd covered half the Earth with reflectors to bounce the Sun's heat back into space. Otherwise it would have been as parboiled as Venus by now.'

The crew's knowledge of Third Millennium history was so surprisingly limited that Poole – thanks to the intensive education he had received in Star City – could often amaze them with details of events centuries after his own time. However, he was flattered to discover how well-acquainted they were with *Discovery*'s log; it had become one of the classic records of the Space Age. They looked on it as he might have regarded a Viking saga; often he had to remind himself that he was midway in time between *Goliath* and the first ships to cross the western ocean.

'On your Day 86,' Stars reminded him, at dinner on the fifth evening, 'you passed within two thousand kay of asteroid 7794 – and shot a probe into it. Do you remember?'

'Of course I do,' Poole answered rather brusquely. 'To me, it happened less than a year ago.'

'Um, sorry. Well, tomorrow we'll be even closer to 13,445. Like to have a look? With autoguidance and freeze-frame, we should have a window all of ten milliseconds wide.'

A hundredth of a second! That few minutes in *Discovery* had seemed hectic enough, but now everything would happen fifty times faster . . .

'How large is it?' Poole asked.

'Thirty by twenty by fifteen metres,' Stars replied. 'Looks like a battered brick.'

'Sorry we don't have a slug to fire at it,' said Props. 'Did you ever wonder if 7794 would hit back?'

'Never occurred to us. But it did give the astronomers a lot of useful information, so it was worth the risk ... Anyway, a hundredth of a second hardly seems worth the bother. Thanks all the same.'

'I understand. When you've seen one asteroid, you've seen them –'

'Not true, Chips. When I was on Eros –'

'As you've told us at least a dozen times –'

Poole's mind tuned out the discussion, so that it was a background of meaningless noise. He was a thousand years in the past, recalling the only excitement of *Discovery*'s mission before the final disaster. Though he and Bowman were perfectly aware that 7794 was merely a lifeless, airless chunk of rock, that knowledge scarcely affected their feelings. It was the only solid matter they would meet this side of Jupiter, and they had stared at it with the emotions of sailors on a long sea voyage, skirting a coast on which they could not land.

It was turning slowly end over end, and there were mottled patches of light and shade distributed at random over its surface. Sometimes it sparkled like a distant window, as planes or outcroppings of crystalline material flashed in the Sun ...

He remembered, also, the mounting tension as they waited to see if their aim had been accurate. It was not easy to hit such a small target, two thousand kilometres away, moving at a relative velocity of twenty kilometres a second.

Then, against the darkened portion of the asteroid, there

had been a sudden, dazzling explosion of light. The tiny slug – pure Uranium 238 – had impacted at meteoric speed: in a fraction of a second, all its kinetic energy had been transformed into heat. A puff of incandescent gas had erupted briefly into space, and *Discovery*'s cameras were recording the rapidly fading spectral lines, looking for the tell-tale signatures of glowing atoms. A few hours later, back on Earth, the astronomers learned for the first time the composition of an asteroid's crust. There were no major surprises, but several bottles of champagne changed hands.

Captain Chandler himself took little part in the very democratic discussions around his semi-circular table: he seemed content to let his crew relax and express their feelings in this informal atmosphere. There was only one unspoken rule: no serious business at mealtimes. If there were any technical or operational problems, they had to be dealt with elsewhere.

Poole had been surprised – and a little shocked – to discover that the crew's knowledge of *Goliath*'s systems was very superficial. Often he had asked questions which should have been easily answered, only to be referred to the ship's own memory banks. After a while, however, he realized that the sort of in-depth training he had received in his days was no longer possible: far too many complex systems were involved for any man or woman's mind to master. The various specialists merely had to know *what* their equipment did, not how. Reliability depended on redundancy and automatic checking, and human intervention was much more likely to do harm than good.

Fortunately none was required on this voyage: it had been as uneventful as any skipper could have hoped, when the new sun of Lucifer dominated the sky ahead.

III

THE WORLDS OF GALILEO

(Extract, text only, *Tourist's Guide to Outer Solar System*, v 219.3)

Even today, the giant satellites of what was once Jupiter present us with major mysteries. Why are four worlds, orbiting the same primary and very similar in size, so different in most other respects?

Only in the case of Io, the innermost satellite, is there a convincing explanation. It is so close to Jupiter that the gravitational tides constantly kneading its interior generate colossal quantities of heat – so much, indeed, that Io's surface is semi-molten. It is the most volcanically active world in the Solar System; maps of Io have a half-life of only a few decades.

123

Though no permanent human bases have ever been established in such an unstable environment, there have been numerous landings and there is continuous robot monitoring. (For the tragic fate of the 2571 Expedition, see Beagle 5.)

Europa, second in distance from Jupiter, was originally entirely covered in ice, and showed few surface features except a complicated network of cracks. The tidal forces which dominate Io were much less powerful here, but produced enough heat to give Europa a global ocean of liquid water, in which many strange life-forms have evolved.

In 2010 the Chinese ship *Tsien* touched down on Europa on one of the few outcrops of solid rock protruding through the crust of ice. In doing so it disturbed a creature of the Europan abyss and was destroyed (see Spacecraft *Tsien*, *Galaxy*, *Universe*).

Since the conversion of Jupiter into the mini-sun Lucifer in 2061, virtually all of Europa's ice-cover has melted, and extensive vulcanism has created several small islands.

As is well-known, there have been no landings on Europa for almost a thousand years, but the satellite is under continuous surveillance.

Ganymede, largest moon in the Solar System (diameter 5260 kilometres), has also been affected by the creation of a new sun, and its equatorial regions are warm enough to sustain terrestrial life-forms, though it does not yet have a breathable atmosphere. Most of its population is actively engaged in terraforming and scientific research; the main settlement is Anubis (pop 41,000), near the South Pole.

Callisto is again wholly different. Its entire surface is covered by impact craters of all sizes, so numerous that they overlap. The bombardment must have continued for millions of years, for the newer craters have completely obliterated the earlier ones. There is no permanent base on Callisto, but several automatic stations have been established there.

17

Ganymede

It was unusual for Frank Poole to oversleep, but he had been kept awake by strange dreams. Past and present were inextricably mixed; sometimes he was on *Discovery*, sometimes in the Africa Tower – and sometimes he was a boy again, among friends he had thought long-forgotten.

Where am I? he asked himself as he struggled up to consciousness, like a swimmer trying to get back to the surface. There was a small window just above his bed, covered by a curtain not thick enough to completely block the light from outside. There had been a time, around the mid-twentieth century, when aircraft had been slow enough to feature First Class sleeping accommodation: Poole had never sampled this nostalgic luxury, which some tourist organizations had still advertised in his own day, but he could easily imagine that he was doing so now.

He drew the curtain and looked out. No, he had not awakened in the skies of Earth, though the landscape unrolling below was not unlike the Antarctic. But the South Pole had never boasted two suns, both rising at once as *Goliath* swept towards them.

The ship was orbiting less than a hundred kilometres above what appeared to be an immense ploughed field, lightly dusted with snow. But the ploughman must have been drunk – or the guidance system must have gone crazy – for the furrows meandered in every direction, sometimes cutting across each other or turning back on themselves. Here and there the terrain was dotted with faint circles – ghost craters from meteor impacts aeons ago.

So this is Ganymede, Poole wondered drowsily. Mankind's furthest outpost from home! Why should any sensible person want to live here? Well, I've often thought that when I've flown over Greenland or Iceland in wintertime . . .

There was a knock on the door, a 'Mind if I come in?', and Captain Chandler did so without waiting for a reply.

'Thought we'd let you sleep until we landed – that end-of-trip party did last longer than I'd intended, but I couldn't risk a mutiny by cutting it short.'

Poole laughed.

'Has there *ever* been a mutiny in space?'

'Oh, quite a few – but not in my time. Now we've mentioned the subject, you might say that Hal started the tradition . . . sorry – perhaps I shouldn't – look – there's Ganymede City!'

Coming up over the horizon was what appeared to be a criss-cross pattern of streets and avenues, intersecting almost at right-angles but with the slight irregularity typical of any settlement that had grown by accretion, without central planning. It was bisected by a broad river – Poole recalled that the equatorial regions of Ganymede were now warm enough for liquid water to exist – and it reminded him of an old wood-cut he had seen of medieval London.

Then he noticed that Chandler was looking at him with an expression of amusement ... and the illusion vanished as he realized the scale of the 'city'.

'The Ganymedeans,' he said dryly, 'must have been rather large, to have made roads five or ten kilometres wide.'

'Twenty in some places. Impressive, isn't it? And all the result of ice stretching and contracting. Mother Nature *is* ingenious ... I could show you some patterns that look even more artificial, though they're not as large as this one.'

'When I was a boy, there was a big fuss about a face on Mars. Of course, it turned out to be a hill that had been carved by sand-storms ... lots of similar ones in Earth's deserts.'

'Didn't someone say that history always repeats itself? Same sort of nonsense happened with Ganymede City – some nuts claimed it had been built by aliens. But I'm afraid it won't be around much longer.'

'Why?' asked Poole in surprise.

'It's already started to collapse, as Lucifer melts the permafrost. You won't recognize Ganymede in another hundred years . . . there's the edge of Lake Gilgamesh – if you look carefully – over on the right –'

'I see what you mean. What's happening – surely the water's not *boiling*, even at this low pressure?'

'Electrolysis plant. Don't know how many skillions of kilograms of oxygen a day. Of course, the hydrogen goes up and gets lost – we hope.'

Chandler's voice trailed off into silence. Then he resumed, in an unusually diffident tone: 'All that beautiful water down there – Ganymede doesn't need half of it! Don't tell anyone, but I've been working out ways of getting some to Venus.'

'Easier than nudging comets?'

'As far as energy is concerned, yes – Ganymede's escape velocity is only three klicks per second. And much, *much* quicker – years instead of decades. But there are a few practical difficulties . . .'

'I can appreciate that. Would you shoot it off by a mass-launcher?'

'Oh no – I'd use towers reaching up through the atmosphere, like the ones on Earth, but much smaller. We'd pump the water up to the top, freeze it down to near absolute zero, and let Ganymede sling it off in the right direction as it rotated. There would be some evaporation loss in transit, but most of it would arrive – what's so funny?'

'Sorry – I'm not laughing at the idea – it makes good sense. But you've brought back such a vivid memory. We used to have a garden sprinkler – driven round and round by its water jets. What you're planning is the same thing – on a slightly bigger scale . . . using a whole world . . .'

Suddenly, another image from his past obliterated all else. Poole remembered how, in those hot Arizona days, he and Rikki had loved to chase each other through the clouds of moving mist, from the slowly revolving spray of the garden sprinkler.

Captain Chandler was a much more sensitive man than he pretended to be: he knew when it was time to leave.

'Gotta get back to the bridge,' he said gruffly. 'See you when we land at Anubis.'

Grand Hotel

The Grand Ganymede Hotel – inevitably known throughout the Solar System as 'Hotel Grannymede' was certainly not grand, and would be lucky to get a rating of one-and-a-half stars on Earth. As the nearest competition was several hundred million kilometres away, the management felt little need to exert itself unduly.

Yet Poole had no complaints, though he often wished that Danil was still around, to help him with the mechanics of life and to communicate more efficiently with the semi-intelligent devices with which he was surrounded. He had known a brief moment of panic when the door had closed behind the (human) bellboy, who had apparently been too awed by his guest to explain how any of the room's services functioned. After five minutes of fruitless talking to the unresponsive walls, Poole had finally made contact with a system that understood his accent and his commands. What an 'All Worlds' news item it would have made – 'Historic astronaut starves to death, trapped in Ganymede hotel room'!

And there would have been a double irony. Perhaps the naming of the Grannymede's only luxury suite was inevitable, but it had been a real shock to meet an ancient life-size holo of his old shipmate, in full-dress uniform, as he was led into – the Bowman Suite. Poole even recognized the image: his own official portrait had been made at the same time, a few days before the mission began.

He soon discovered that most of his *Goliath* crewmates had domestic arrangements in Anubis, and were anxious for him to meet their Significant Others during the ship's planned twenty-day stop. Almost immediately he was caught up in the social and professional life of this frontier settlement, and it was Africa Tower that now seemed a distant dream.

Like many Americans, in their secret hearts, Poole had a nostalgic affection for small communities where everyone knew everyone else – in the real world, and not the virtual one of cyberspace. Anubis, with a resident population less than that of his remembered Flagstaff, was not a bad approximation to this ideal.

The three main pressure domes, each two kilometres in diameter, stood on a plateau overlooking an ice-field which stretched unbroken to the horizon. Ganymede's second sun – once known as Jupiter – would never give sufficient heat to melt the polar caps. This was the principal reason for establishing Anubis in such an inhospitable spot: the city's foundations were not likely to collapse for at least several centuries.

And inside the domes, it was easy to be completely indifferent to the outside world. Poole, when he had mastered the mechanisms of the Bowman Suite, discovered that he had a limited but impressive choice of environments. He could sit beneath palm trees on a Pacific beach, listening to the gentle murmur of the waves – or, if he preferred, the roar of a tropical hurricane. He could fly slowly along the peaks of the Himalayas, or down the immense canyons of Mariner Valley. He could walk through the gardens of Versailles or down the streets of half a dozen great cities, at several widely spaced times in their history. Even if the Hotel Grannymede was not one of the Solar System's most highly acclaimed resorts, it boasted facilities which would have astounded all its more famous predecessors on Earth.

But it was ridiculous to indulge in terrestrial nostalgia, when he had come half-way across the Solar System to visit a strange new world. After some experimenting, Poole arranged a compromise, for enjoyment – and inspiration – during his steadily fewer moments of leisure.

To his great regret, he had never been to Egypt, so it was delightful to relax beneath the gaze of the Sphinx – as it was before its controversial 'restoration' – and to watch tourists scrambling up the massive blocks of the Great Pyramid. The illusion was perfect, apart from the no-man's-land where the desert clashed with the (slightly worn) carpet of the Bowman Suite.

The sky, however, was one that no human eyes had seen until five thousand years after the last stone was laid at

Giza. But it was not an illusion; it was the complex and ever-changing reality of Ganymede.

Because this world – like its companions – had been robbed of its spin aeons ago by the tidal drag of Jupiter, the new sun born from the giant planet hung motionless in its sky. One side of Ganymede was in perpetual Lucifer-light – and although the other hemisphere was often referred to as the 'Night Land', that designation was as misleading as the much earlier phrase 'The dark side of the Moon'. Like the lunar Farside, Ganymede's 'Night Land' had the brilliant light of old Sol for half of its long day.

By a coincidence more confusing than useful, Ganymede took almost exactly one week – seven days, three hours – to orbit its primary. Attempts to create a 'One Mede day = one Earth week' calendar had generated so much chaos that they had been abandoned centuries ago. Like all the other residents of the Solar System, the locals employed Universal Time, identifying their twenty-four-hour standard days by numbers rather than names.

Since Ganymede's newborn atmosphere was still extremely thin and almost cloudless, the parade of heavenly bodies provided a never-ending spectacle. At their closest, Io and Callisto each appeared about half the size of the Moon as seen from Earth – but that was the only thing they had in common. Io was so close to Lucifer that it took less than two days to race around its orbit, and showed visible movement even in a matter of minutes. Callisto, at over four times Io's distance, required two Mede days – or sixteen Earth ones – to complete its leisurely circuit.

The physical contrast between the two worlds was even more remarkable. Deep-frozen Callisto had been almost unchanged by Jupiter's conversion into a mini-sun: it was still a wasteland of shallow ice craters, so closely packed that there was not a single spot on the entire satellite that had escaped from multiple impacts, in the days when Jupiter's enormous gravity field was competing with Saturn's to gather up the debris of the outer Solar System. Since then, apart from a few stray shots, nothing had happened for several billion years.

On Io, something was happening every week. As a local wit had remarked, before the creation of Lucifer it had been Hell – now it was Hell warmed up.

Often, Poole would zoom into that burning landscape and look into the sulphurous throats of volcanoes that were continually reshaping an area larger than Africa. Sometimes incandescent fountains would soar briefly hundreds of kilometres into space, like gigantic trees of fire growing on a lifeless world.

As the floods of molten sulphur spread out from volcanoes and vents, the versatile element changed through a narrow spectrum of reds and oranges and yellows when, chameleon-like, it was transformed into its vari-coloured allotropes. Before the dawn of the Space Age, no one had ever imagined that such a world existed. Fascinating though it was to observe it from his comfortable vantage point, Poole found it hard to believe that men had ever risked landing there, where even robots feared to tread . . .

His main interest, however, was Europa, which at its closest appeared almost exactly the same size as Earth's solitary Moon, but raced through its phases in only four days. Though Poole had been quite unconscious of the symbolism when he chose his private landscape, it now seemed wholly appropriate that Europa should hang in the sky above another great enigma – the Sphinx.

Even with no magnification, when he requested the naked-eye view, Poole could see how greatly Europa had changed in the thousand years since *Discovery* had set out for Jupiter. The spider's web of narrow bands and lines that had once completely enveloped the smallest of the four Galilean satellites had vanished, except around the poles. Here the global crust of kilometre-thick ice remained unmelted by the warmth of Europa's new sun: elsewhere, virgin oceans seethed and boiled in the thin atmosphere, at what would have been comfortable room temperature on Earth.

It was also a comfortable temperature to the creatures who had emerged, after the melting of the unbroken ice shield that had both trapped and protected them. Orbiting spysats, showing details only centimetres across, had watched one Europan species starting to evolve into an amphibious stage: though they still spent much of their time underwater, the 'Europs' had even begun the construction of simple buildings.

That this could happen in a mere thousand years was astonishing, but no one doubted that the explanation lay in the last and greatest of the Monoliths – the many-kilometre-long 'Great Wall' standing on the shore of the Sea of Galilee.

And no one doubted that, in its own mysterious way, it was watching over the experiment it had started on *this* world – as it had done on Earth four million years before.

19

The Madness of Mankind

MISS PRINGLE

FILE – INDRA

My dear Indra – sorry I've not even voice-mailed you before – usual excuse, of course, so I won't bother to give it.

To answer your question – yes, I'm now feeling quite at home at the Grannymede, but am spending less and less time there, though I've been enjoying the sky display I've had piped into my suite. Last night the Io flux tube put on a fine performance – that's a kind of lightning discharge between Io and Jupiter – I mean Lucifer. Rather like Earth's aurora, but much more spectacular. Discovered by the radio astronomers even before I was born.

And talking about ancient times – did you know that

Anubis has a *Sheriff*? I think that's overdoing the frontier spirit. Reminds me of the stories my grandfather used to tell me about Arizona ... Must try some of them on the Medes ...

This may sound silly – I'm still not used to being in the *Bowman* Suite. I keep looking over my shoulder ...

How do I spend my time? Much the same as in Africa Tower. I'm meeting the local intelligentsia, though as you might expect they're rather thin on the ground (hope no one is bugging this). And I've interacted – real and virtual – with the educational system – very good, it seems, though more technically oriented than you'd approve. That's inevitable, of course, in this hostile environment ...

But it's helped me to understand why people live here. There's a challenge – a sense of purpose, if you like – that I seldom found on Earth.

It's true that most of the Medes were born here, so don't know any other home. Though they're – usually – too polite to say so, they think that the Home Planet is becoming decadent. Are you? And if so, what are you Terries – as the locals call you – going to do about it? One of the teenage classes I've met hopes to wake you up. They're drawing up elaborate Top Secret plans for the Invasion of Earth. Don't say I didn't warn you ...

I've made one trip outside Anubis, into the so-called Night Land, where they never see Lucifer. Ten of us – Chandler, two of *Goliath*'s crew, six Medes – went into Farside, and chased the Sun down to the horizon so it really *was* night. Awesome – much like polar winters on Earth, but with the sky completely black ... almost felt I was in space.

We could see all the Galileans beautifully, and watched Europa eclipse – sorry, occult – Io. Of course, the trip had been timed so we could observe this . . .

Several of the smaller satellites were just also visible, but the double star Earth-Moon was much more conspicuous. Did I feel homesick? Frankly, no – though I miss my new friends back there . . .

And I'm sorry – I still haven't met Dr Khan, though he's left several messages for me. I promise to do it in the next few days – Earth days, not Mede ones!

Best wishes to Joe – regards to Danil, if you know what's happened to him – is he a real person again? – and my love to yourself . . .

STORE – TRANSMIT

Back in Poole's century, a person's name often gave a clue to his/her appearance, but that was no longer true thirty generations later. Dr Theodore Khan turned out to be a Nordic blond who might have looked more at home in a Viking longboat than ravaging the steppes of Central Asia: however, he would not have been too impressive in either role, being less than a hundred and fifty centimetres tall. Poole could not resist a little amateur psychoanalysis: small people were often aggressive over-achievers – which, from Indra Wallace's hints, appeared to be a good description of Ganymeda's sole resident philosopher. Khan probably needed these qualifications, to survive in such a practically-minded society.

Anubis City was far too small to boast a university campus – a luxury which still existed on the other worlds, though many believed that the telecommunications revolution had made it obsolete. Instead, it had something much more appropriate, as well as centuries older – an Academy, complete with a grove of olive trees that would have fooled Plato himself, until he had attempted to walk through it. Indra's joke about departments of philosophy requiring no more equipment than blackboards clearly did not apply in this sophisticated environment.

'It's built to hold seven people,' said Dr Khan proudly, when they had settled down on chairs obviously designed to be not-too-comfortable, 'because that's the maximum one can efficiently interact with. And, if you count the ghost of Socrates, it was the number present when Phaedo delivered his famous address . . .'

'The one on the immortality of the soul?'

Khan was so obviously surprised that Poole could not help laughing.

'I took a crash course in philosophy just before I graduated – when the syllabus was planned, someone decided that we hairy-knuckled engineers should be exposed to a little culture.'

'I'm delighted to hear it. That makes things so much easier. You know – I still can't credit my luck. Your arrival here almost tempts me to believe in miracles! I'd even thought of going to Earth to meet you – has dear Indra told you about my – ah – obsession?'

'No,' Poole answered, not altogether truthfully.

Dr Khan looked very pleased; he was clearly delighted to find a new audience.

'You may have heard me called an atheist, but that's not quite true. Atheism is unprovable, so uninteresting. Equally, however unlikely it is, we can never be certain that God once existed – and has now shot off to infinity, where no one can ever find him . . . Like Gautama Buddha, I take no position on this subject. My field of interest is the psychopathology known as Religion.'

'Psychopathology? That's a harsh judgement.'

'Amply justified by history. Imagine that you're an intelligent extraterrestrial, concerned only with verifiable truths. You discover a species which has divided itself into thousands – no by now *millions* – of tribal groups holding an incredible variety of beliefs about the origin of the universe and the way to behave in it. Although many of them have ideas in common, even when there's a ninety-nine per cent overlap, the remaining one per cent is enough to set them killing and torturing each other, over trivial points of doctrine, utterly meaningless to outsiders.

'How to account for such irrational behaviour? Lucretius hit it on the nail when he said that religion was the by-product of fear – a reaction to a mysterious and often hostile universe. For much of human prehistory, it may have been a necessary evil – but why was it so much more evil than necessary – and *why* did it survive when it was no longer necessary?

'I said evil – and I mean it, because fear leads to cruelty. The slightest knowledge of the Inquisition makes one ashamed to belong to the human species . . . One of the most revolting books ever published was the *Hammer of Witches*, written by a couple of sadistic perverts and describing the tortures the Church authorized – encouraged! – to extract "confessions" from thousands of harmless old women, before it burned them alive . . . The Pope himself wrote an approving foreword!

141

'But most of the other religions, with a few honourable exceptions, were just as bad as Christianity ... Even in your century, little boys were kept chained and whipped until they'd memorized whole volumes of pious gibberish, and robbed of their childhood *and* manhood to become monks ...

'Perhaps the most baffling aspect of the whole affair is how obvious madmen, century after century, would proclaim that they – and they alone! – had received messages from God. If *all* the messages had agreed, that would have settled the matter. But of course they were wildly discordant – which never prevented self-styled messiahs from gathering hundreds – sometimes millions – of adherents, who would fight to the death against equally deluded believers of a microscopically differing faith.'

Poole thought it was about time he got a word in edgeways.

'You've reminded me of something that happened in my home-town when I was a kid. A holy man – quote, unquote – set up shop, claimed he could work miracles – and collected a crowd of devotees in next to no time. And they weren't ignorant or illiterate; often they came from the best families. Every Sunday I used to see expensive cars parked round his – ah – temple.'

'The "Rasputin Syndrome", it's been called: there are *millions* of such cases, all through history, in every country. And about one time in a thousand the cult survives for a couple of generations. What happened in this case?'

'Well, the competition was very unhappy, and did its best to discredit him. Wish I could remember his name –

he used a long Indian one – Swami something-or-other – but it turned out he came from Alabama. One of his tricks was to produce holy objects out of thin air, and hand them to his worshippers. As it happened, our local rabbi was an amateur conjuror, and gave public demonstrations showing exactly how it was done. Didn't make the slightest difference – the faithful said that their man's magic was *real*, and the rabbi was just jealous.

'At one time, I'm sorry to say, Mother took the rascal seriously – it was soon after Dad had run off, which may have had something to do with it – and dragged me to one of his sessions. I was only about ten, but I thought I'd never seen anyone so unpleasant-looking. He had a beard that could have held several birds' nests, and probably did.'

'He sounds like the standard model. How long did he flourish?'

'Three or four years. And then he had to leave town in a hurry: he was caught running teenage orgies. Of course, he claimed he was using mystical soul-saving techniques. And you won't believe this –'

'Try me.'

'Even then, lots of his dupes still had faith in him. *Their* god could do no wrong, so he must have been framed.'

'Framed?'

'Sorry – convicted by faked evidence – sometimes used by the police to catch criminals, when all else fails.'

'Hmm. Well, your swami was perfectly typical: I'm rather disappointed. But he does help to prove my case – that most of humanity has always been insane, at least some of the time.'

'Rather an unrepresentative sample – one small Flagstaff suburb.'

'True, but I could multiply it by *thousands* – not only in your century, but all down the ages. There's never been anything, however absurd, that countless people weren't prepared to believe, often so passionately that they'd fight to the death rather than abandon their illusions. To me, that's a good operational definition of insanity.'

'Would you argue that *anyone* with strong religious beliefs was insane?'

'In a strictly technical sense, yes – if they really were sincere, and not hypocrites. As I suspect ninety per cent were.'

'I'm certain that Rabbi Berenstein was sincere – and he was one of the sanest men I ever knew, as well as one of the finest. And how do you account for this? The only real genius I ever met was Dr Chandra, who led the HAL project. I once had to go into his office – there was no reply when I knocked, and I thought it was unoccupied.

'He was praying to a group of fantastic little bronze statues, draped with flowers. One of them looked like an elephant . . . another had more than the regular number of arms . . . I was quite embarrassed, but luckily he didn't hear me and I tiptoed out. Would you say *he* was insane?'

'You've chosen a bad example: genius often is! So let's say: not insane, but mentally impaired, owing to childhood conditioning. The Jesuits claimed: "Give me a boy for six years, and he is mine for life." If they'd got hold of little Chandra in time, he'd have been a devout Catholic – not a Hindu.'

'Possibly. But I'm puzzled – why were you so anxious

to meet me? I'm afraid I've never been a devout anything. What have I got to do with all this?'

Slowly, and with the obvious enjoyment of a man unburdening himself of a heavy, long-hoarded secret, Dr Khan told him.

20

Apostate

RECORD – POOLE

Hello, Frank ... So you've finally met Ted. Yes, you could call him a crank – if you define that as an enthusiast with no sense of humour. But cranks often get that way because they know a Big Truth – can you hear my capitals? – and no one will listen ... I'm glad *you* did – and I suggest you take him quite seriously.

You said you were surprised to see a Pope's portrait prominently displayed in Ted's apartment. That would have been his hero, Pius XX – I'm sure I mentioned him to you. Look him up – he's usually called the *Impius*! It's a fascinating story, and exactly parallels something that happened just before you were born. You must know how

Mikhail Gorbachev, the President of the Soviet Empire, brought about its dissolution at the end of the twentieth century, by exposing its crimes and excesses.

He didn't *intend* to go that far – he'd hoped to reform it, but that was no longer possible. We'll never know if Pius XX had the same idea, because he was assassinated by a demented cardinal soon after he'd horrified the world by releasing the secret files of the Inquisition . . .

The religious were still shaken by the discovery of TMA ZERO only a few decades earlier – that had a great impact on Pius XX, and certainly influenced his actions . . .

But you still haven't told me how Ted, that old crypto-Deist, thinks you can help him in *his* search for God. I believe he's still mad at him for hiding so successfully. Better not say I told you that.

On second thoughts, why not?

Love – Indra.

STORE

TRANSMIT

MISS PRINGLE

RECORD

Hello – Indra – I've had another session with Dr Ted, though I've still not told him just why you think he's angry with God!

But I've had some very interesting arguments – no, dialogues – with him, though he does most of the talking. Never thought I'd get into philosophy again after all these years of engineering. Perhaps I had to go through them first, to appreciate it. Wonder how he'd grade me as a student?

Yesterday I tried this line of approach, to see his reaction. Perhaps it's original, though I doubt it. Thought you'd like to hear it – will be interested in your comments. Here's our discussion –

MISS PRINGLE – COPY AUDIO 94.

'Surely, Ted, you can't deny that most of the greatest works of human art have been inspired by religious devotion. Doesn't that prove *something*?'

'Yes – but not in a way that will give much comfort to any believers! From time to time, people amuse themselves making lists of the Biggests and Greatests and Bests – I'm sure that was a popular entertainment in your day.'

'It certainly was.'

'Well, there have been some famous attempts to do this with the arts. Of course such lists can't establish absolute – eternal – values, but they're interesting and show how tastes change from age to age . . .

'The last list I saw – it was on the Earth Artnet only a few years ago – was divided into Architecture, Music, Visual Arts . . . I remember a few of the examples . . . the Parthenon, the Taj Mahal . . . Bach's *Toccata and Fugue* was first in music, followed by Verdi's *Requiem Mass*. In art – the Mona Lisa, of course. Then – not sure of the order – a group of Buddha statues somewhere in Ceylon, and the golden death-mask of young King Tut.

'Even if I could remember all the others – which of course I can't – it doesn't matter: the important thing is their cultural and religious backgrounds. Overall, *no* single religion dominated – except in music. And that could be due to a purely technological accident: the organ and the other pre-electronic musical instruments were perfected in the Christianized West. It could have worked out quite differently ... if, for example, the Greeks or the Chinese had regarded machines as something more than toys.

'But what really settles the argument, as far as I'm concerned, is the general consensus about the single greatest work of human art. Over and over again, in almost every listing – it's Angkor Wat. Yet the religion that inspired *that* has been extinct for centuries – no one even knows precisely what it was, except that it involved *hundreds* of gods, not merely one!'

'Wish I could have thrown that at dear old Rabbi Berenstein – I'm sure he'd have had a good answer.'

'I don't doubt it. I wish I could have met him myself. And I'm glad he never lived to see what happened to Israel.'

END AUDIO.

There you have it, Indra. Wish the Grannymede had Angkor Wat on its menu – I've never seen it – but you can't have everything ...

Now, the question you really wanted answered ... why is Dr Ted so delighted that I'm here?

As you know, he's convinced that the key to many mysteries lies on Europa – where no one has been allowed to land for a thousand years.

He thinks I may be an exception. He believes I have a friend there. Yes – Dave Bowman, or whatever he's now become ...

We know that he survived being drawn into the Big Brother Monolith – and somehow revisited Earth afterwards. But there's more, that I didn't know. Very few people do, because the Medes are embarrassed to talk about it . . .

Ted Khan has spent years collecting the evidence, and is now quite certain of the facts – even though he can't explain them. On at least six occasions, about a century apart, reliable observers here in Anubis have reported seeing an – apparition – just like the one that Heywood Floyd met aboard *Discovery*. Though not one of them knew about that incident, they were all able to identify Dave when they were shown his hologram. And there was another sighting aboard a survey ship that made a close approach to Europa, six hundred years ago . . .

Individually, no one would take these cases seriously – but altogether they make a pattern. Ted's quite sure that Dave Bowman survives in some form, presumably associated with the Monolith we call the Great Wall. And he still has some interest in our affairs.

Though he's made no attempt at communication, Ted hopes we can make contact. He believes that I'm the only human who can do it . . .

I'm still trying to make up my mind. Tomorrow, I'll talk it over with Captain Chandler. Will let you know what we decide. Love, Frank.

STORE

TRANSMIT – INDRA

21

Quarantine

'Do you believe in ghosts, Dim?'

'Certainly not: but like every sensible man, I'm afraid of them. Why do you ask?'

'If it wasn't a ghost, it was the most vivid dream I've ever had. Last night I had a conversation with Dave Bowman.'

Poole knew that Captain Chandler would take him seriously, when the occasion required; nor was he disappointed.

'Interesting – but there's an obvious explanation. You've been *living* here in the Bowman Suite, for Deus's sake! You told me yourself it feels haunted.'

'I'm sure – well, ninety-nine per cent sure – that you're right, and the whole thing was prompted by the discussions I've been having with Prof. Ted. Have you heard the reports that Dave Bowman occasionally appears in Anubis? About once every hundred years? Just as he did to Dr Floyd aboard *Discovery*, after she'd been reactivated.'

'What happened there? I've heard vague stories, but never taken them seriously.'

'Dr Khan does – and so do I – I've seen the original recordings. Floyd's sitting in my old chair when a kind of dust-cloud forms behind him, and shapes itself into Dave – though only the head has detail. Then it gives that famous message, warning him to leave.'

'Who wouldn't have? But that was a thousand years ago. Plenty of time to fake it.'

'What would be the point? Khan and I were looking at it yesterday. I'd bet my life it's authentic.'

'As a matter of fact, I agree with you. And I *have* heard those reports . . .'

Chandler's voice trailed away, and he looked slightly embarrassed.

'Long time ago, I had a girl-friend here in Anubis. She told me that her grandfather had seen Bowman. I laughed.'

'I wonder if Ted has that sighting on his list. Could you put him in touch with your friend?'

'Er – rather not. We haven't spoken for years. For all I know, she may be on the Moon, or Mars . . . Anyway, why is Professor Ted interested?'

'That's what I really wanted to discuss with you.'

'Sounds ominous. Go ahead.'

'Ted thinks that Dave Bowman – or whatever he's become – may still exist – up there on Europa.'

'After a thousand years?'

'Well – look at me.'

'One sample ·is poor statistics, my maths prof. used to say. But go on.'

'It's a complicated story – or maybe a jigsaw, with most of the pieces missing. But it's generally agreed that something crucial happened to our ancestors when that Monolith appeared in Africa, four million years ago. It marks a turning point in prehistory – the first appearance of tools – and weapons – *and* religion . . . That can't be pure coincidence. The Monolith must have done *something* to us – surely it couldn't have just stood there, passively accepting worship . . .

'Ted's fond of quoting a famous palaeontologist who said "TMA ZERO gave us an evolutionary kick in the pants". He argues that the kick wasn't in a wholly desirable direction. Did we *have* to become so mean and nasty to survive? Maybe we did . . . As I understand him, Ted believes that there's something fundamentally wrong with the wiring of our brains, which makes us incapable of consistent logical thinking. To make matters worse, though all creatures need a certain amount of aggressiveness to survive, we seem to have far more than is absolutely necessary. And *no* other animal tortures its fellows as we do. Is this an evolutionary accident – a piece of genetic bad luck?

'It's also widely agreed that TMA ONE was planted on the Moon to keep track of the project – experiment – whatever it was – and to report to Jupiter – the obvious place for Solar System Mission Control. That's why another Monolith – Big Brother – was waiting there. Had been waiting four million years, when *Discovery* arrived. Agreed so far?'

'Yes; I've always thought that was the most plausible theory.'

'Now for the more speculative stuff. Bowman was apparently swallowed up by Big Brother, yet something of his personality seems to have survived. Twenty years after that encounter with Heywood Floyd in the *second* Jupiter expedition, they had another contact aboard *Universe*, when Floyd joined it for the 2061 rendezvous with Halley's Comet. At least, so he tells us in his memoirs – though he was well over a hundred when he dictated them.'

'Could have been senile.'

'Not according to all the contemporary accounts! Also – perhaps even more significant – his grandson Chris had some equally weird experiences when *Galaxy* made its forced landing on Europa. And, of course, that's where the Monolith – or *a* Monolith – is, right now! Surrounded by Europans . . .'

'I'm beginning to see what Dr Ted's driving at. This is where we came in – the whole cycle's starting over again. The Europs are being groomed for stardom.'

'Exactly – everything fits. Jupiter ignited to give them a sun, to thaw out their frozen world. The warning to us to keep our distance – presumably so that we wouldn't interfere with their development . . .'

'Where have I heard *that* idea before? Of course, Frank – it goes back a thousand years – to your own time! "The Prime Directive"! We still get lots of laughs from those old *Star Trek* programmes.'

'Did I ever tell you I once met some of the actors? They would have been surprised to see me now . . . And I've always had two thoughts about that non-interference policy. The Monolith certainly violated it with us, back there in Africa. One might argue that *did* have disastrous results . . .'

'So better luck next time – on Europa!'

Poole laughed, without much humour.

'Khan used those exact words.'

'And what does he think we should do about it? Above all – where do *you* come into the picture?'

'First of all, we must find what's *really* happening on Europa – and why. Merely observing it from space is not enough.'

'What else can we do? All the probes the Medes have sent there were blown up, just before landing.'

'And ever since the mission to rescue *Galaxy*, crew-carrying ships have been diverted by some field of force, which no one can figure out. Very interesting: it proves that whatever is down there is protective, but not malevolent. And – this is the important point – it must have some way of scanning what's on the way. It can distinguish between robots and humans.'

'More than I can do, sometimes. Go on.'

'Well, Ted thinks there's one human being who might make it down to the surface of Europa – because his old friend is there, and may have some influence with the powers-that-be.'

Captain Dimitri Chandler gave a long, low whistle.

'And you're willing to risk it?'

'Yes: what have I got to lose?'

'One valuable shuttle craft, if I know what you have in mind. Is that why you've been learning to fly *Falcon*?'

'Well, now that you mention it . . . the idea had occurred to me.'

'I'll have to think it over – I'll admit I'm intrigued, but there are lots of problems.'

'Knowing you, I'm sure they won't stand in the way – once you've decided to help me.'

22

Venture

MISS PRINGLE – LIST PRIORITY MESSAGES FROM EARTH
  RECORD

Dear Indra – I'm not trying to be dramatic, but this may be my last message from Ganymede. By the time you receive it, I will be on my way to Europa.

Though it's a sudden decision – and no one is more surprised than I am – I've thought it over very carefully. As you'll have guessed, Ted Khan is largely responsible ... let him do the explaining, if I don't come back.

Please don't misunderstand me – in no way do I regard this as a suicide mission! But I'm ninety per cent convinced by Ted's arguments, and he's aroused my curiosity so much that I'd never forgive myself if I turned down this once-in-a-lifetime opportunity. Maybe I should say once in two lifetimes . . .

I'm flying *Goliath*'s little one-person shuttle *Falcon* – how I'd have loved to demonstrate her to my old colleagues back at the Space Administration! Judging by past records, the most likely outcome is that I'll be diverted away from Europa before I can land. Even this will teach me something . . .

And if it – presumably the local Monolith, the Great Wall – decides to treat me like the robot probes it's zapped in the past, I'll never know. That's a risk I'm prepared to take.

Thank you for everything, and my very best to Joe. Love from Ganymede – and soon, I hope, from Europa.
STORE
TRANSMIT

IV

THE KINGDOM OF SULPHUR

23

Falcon

'Europa's about four hundred thousand kay from Ganymede at the moment,' Captain Chandler informed Poole. 'If you stepped on the gas – thanks for teaching me that phrase! – *Falcon* could get you there in an hour. But I wouldn't recommend it: our mysterious friend might be alarmed by anyone coming in that fast.'

'Agreed – and I want time to think. I'm going to take several hours, at least. And I'm still hoping ...' Poole's voice trailed off into silence.

'Hoping what?'

'That I can make some sort of contact with Dave, or whatever it is, before I attempt to land.'

'Yes, it's always rude to drop in uninvited – even with

people you know, let alone perfect strangers like the Europs. Perhaps you should take some gifts – what did the old-time explorers use? I believe mirrors and beads were once popular.'

Chandler's facetious tone did not disguise his real concern, both for Poole and for the valuable piece of equipment he proposed to borrow – and for which the skipper of *Goliath* was ultimately responsible.

'I'm still trying to decide how we work this. If you come back a hero, I want to bask in your reflected glory. But if you lose *Falcon* as well as yourself, what shall I say? That you stole the shuttle while we weren't looking? I'm afraid no one would buy that story. Ganymede Traffic Control's very efficient – has to be! If you left without advance notice, they'd be on to you in a microsec – well, a millisecond. *No* way you could leave unless I file your flight-plan ahead of time.

'So this is what I propose to do, unless I think of something better.

'You're taking *Falcon* out for a final qualification test – everyone knows you've already soloed. You'll go into a two-thousand-kilometre-high orbit above Europa – nothing unusual about that – people do it all the time, and the local authorities don't seem to object.

'Estimated total flight time five hours plus or minus ten minutes. If you suddenly change your mind about coming home, no one can do anything about it – at least, no one on Ganymede. Of course, I'll make some indignant noises, and say how astonished I am by such gross navigational errors, etc., etc. Whatever will look best in the subsequent Court of Enquiry.'

'Would it come to that? I don't want to do anything that will get you into trouble.'

'Don't worry – it's time there was a little excitement round here. But only you and I know about this plot; try not to mention it to the crew – I want them to have – what was that other useful expression you taught me? – "plausible deniability".'

'Thanks, Dim – I really appreciate what you're doing. And I hope you'll never have to regret hauling me aboard *Goliath*, out round Neptune.'

Poole found it hard to avoid arousing suspicion, by the way he behaved towards his new crew-mates as they prepared *Falcon* for what was supposed to be a short, routine flight. Only he and Chandler knew that it might be nothing of the kind.

Yet he was not heading into the totally unknown, as he and Dave Bowman had done a thousand years ago. Stored in the shuttle's memory were high-resolution maps of Europa showing details down to a few metres across. He knew exactly where he wished to go; it only remained to see if he would be allowed to break the centuries-long quarantine.

24

Escape

'Manual control, please.'

'Are you sure, Frank?'

'Quite sure, *Falcon* . . . Thank you.'

Illogical though it seemed, most of the human race had found it impossible *not* to be polite to its artificial children, however simple-minded they might be. Whole volumes of psychology, as well as popular guides (*How Not to Hurt Your Computer's Feelings; Artificial Intelligence – Real Irritation* were two of the best-known titles) had been written on the subject of Man–Machine etiquette. Long ago it had been decided that, however inconsequential rudeness to robots might appear to be, it should be discouraged. All too easily, it could spread to human relationships as well.

Falcon was now in orbit, just as her flight-plan had promised, at a safe two thousand kilometres above Europa. The giant moon's crescent dominated the sky ahead, and even the area not illuminated by Lucifer was so brilliantly lit by the much more distant Sun that every detail was clearly visible. Poole needed no optical aid to see his planned destination, on the still-icy shore of the Sea of Galilee, not far from the skeleton of the first spacecraft to land on this world. Though the Europans had long ago removed all its metal components, the ill-fated Chinese ship still served as a memorial to its crew; and it was appropriate that the only 'town' – even if an alien one – on this whole world should have been named 'Tsienville'.

Poole had decided to come down over the Sea, and then fly very slowly towards Tsienville – hoping that this approach would appear friendly, or at least non-aggressive. Though he admitted to himself that this was very naïve, he could think of no better alternative.

Then, suddenly, just as he was dropping below the thousand-kilometre level, there was an interruption – not of the kind he had hoped for, but one which he had been expecting.

'This is Ganymede Control calling *Falcon*. You have departed from your flight-plan. Please advise immediately what is happening.'

It was hard to ignore such an urgent request, but in the circumstances it seemed the best thing to do.

Exactly thirty seconds later, and a hundred kilometres closer to Europa, Ganymede repeated its message. Once again Poole ignored it – but *Falcon* did not.

'Are you quite sure you want to do this, Frank?' asked

the shuttle. Though Poole knew perfectly well that he was imagining it, he would have sworn there was a note of anxiety in its voice.

'Quite sure, *Falcon*. I know exactly what I'm doing.'

That was certainly untrue, and any moment now further lying might be necessary, to a more sophisticated audience.

Seldom-activated indicator lights started to flash near the edge of the control board. Poole smiled with satisfaction: everything was going according to plan.

'This is Ganymede Control! Do you receive me, *Falcon*? You are operating on manual override, so I am unable to assist you. What is happening? You are still descending towards Europa. Please acknowledge immediately.'

Poole began to experience mild twinges of conscience. He thought he recognized the Controller's voice, and was almost certain that it was a charming lady he had met at a reception given by the Mayor, soon after his arrival at Anubis. She sounded genuinely alarmed.

Suddenly, he knew how to relieve her anxiety – as well as to attempt something which he had previously dismissed as altogether too absurd. Perhaps, after all, it was worth a try: it certainly wouldn't do any harm – and it might even work.

'This is Frank Poole, calling from *Falcon*. I am perfectly OK – but something seems to have taken over the controls, and is bringing the shuttle down towards Europa. I hope you are receiving this – I will continue to report as long as possible.'

Well, he hadn't actually lied to the worried Controller, and one day he hoped he would be able to face her with a clear conscience.

He continued to talk, trying to sound as if he was completely sincere, instead of skirting the edge of truth.

'This is Frank Poole aboard the shuttle *Falcon*, descending towards Europa. I assume that some outside force has taken charge of my spacecraft, and will be landing it safely.

'Dave – this is your old shipmate Frank. Are you the entity that is controlling me? I have reason to think that you are on Europa.

'If so – I look forward to meeting you – wherever or whatever you are.'

Not for a moment did he imagine there would be any reply: even Ganymede Control appeared to be shocked into silence.

And yet, in a way, he had an answer. *Falcon* was still being permitted to descend towards the Sea of Galilee.

Europa was only fifty kilometres below; with his naked eyes Poole could now see the narrow black bar where the greatest of the Monoliths stood guard – if indeed it was doing that – on the outskirts of Tsienville.

No human being had been allowed to come so close for a thousand years.

25

Fire in the Deep

For millions of years it had been an ocean world, its hidden waters protected from the vacuum of space by a crust of ice. In most places the ice was kilometres thick, but there were lines of weakness where it had cracked open and torn apart. Then there had been a brief battle between two implacably hostile elements that came into direct contact on no other world in the Solar System. The war between Sea and Space always ended in the same stalemate; the exposed water simultaneously boiled and froze, repairing the armour of ice.

The seas of Europa would have frozen completely solid long ago without the influence of nearby Jupiter. Its gravity continually kneaded the core of the little world; the forces that convulsed Io were also working there, though with much less ferocity. Everywhere in the deep was evidence of that tug-of-war between planet and satellite, in the continual roar and thunder of submarine earthquakes, the shriek of gases escaping from the interior, the infrasonic pressure waves of avalanches sweeping over the abyssal plains. By comparison with the tumultuous ocean that covered Europa, even the noisy seas of Earth were muted.

Here and there, scattered over the deserts of the deep, were oases that would have amazed and delighted any terrestrial biologist. They extended for several kilometres around tangled masses of pipes and chimneys deposited by mineral brines gushing from the interior. Often they created natural parodies of Gothic castles, from which black, scalding liquids pulsed in a slow rhythm, as if driven by the beating of some mighty heart. And like blood, they were the authentic sign of life itself.

The boiling fluids drove back the deadly cold leaking down from above, and formed islands of warmth on the sea-bed. Equally important, they brought from Europa's interior all the chemicals of life. Such fertile oases, offering food and energy in abundance, had been discovered by the twentieth-century explorers of Earth's oceans. Here they were present on an immensely larger scale, and in far greater variety.

Delicate, spidery structures that seemed to be the analogue of plants flourished in the 'tropical' zones closest to the sources of heat. Crawling among these were bizarre slugs and worms, some feeding on the plants, others obtaining their food directly from the mineral-laden waters around them. At greater distances from the submarine

169

fires around which all these creatures warmed themselves lived sturdier, more robust organisms, not unlike crabs or spiders.

Armies of biologists could have spent lifetimes studying one small oasis. Unlike the Palaeozoic terrestrial seas, the Europan abyss was not a stable environment, so evolution had progressed with astonishing speed, producing multitudes of fantastic forms. And all were under the same indefinite stay of execution; sooner or later, each fountain of life would weaken and die, as the forces that powered it moved their focus elsewhere. All across the Europan sea-bed was evidence of such tragedies; countless circular areas were littered with the skeletons and mineral-encrusted remains of dead creatures, where entire chapters of evolution had been deleted from the book of life. Some had left as their only memorial huge, empty shells like convoluted trumpets, larger than a man. And there were clams of many shapes – bivalves, and even trivalves, as well as spiral stone patterns, many metres across – exactly like the beautiful ammonites that disappeared so mysteriously from Earth's oceans at the end of the Cretaceous Period.

Among the greatest wonders of the Europan abyss were rivers of incandescent lava, pouring from the calderas of submarine volcanoes. The pressure at these depths was so great that the water in contact with the red-hot magma could not flash into steam, so the two liquids co-existed in an uneasy truce.

There, on another world and with alien actors, something like the story of Egypt had been played out long before the coming of Man. As the Nile had brought life to a narrow ribbon of desert, so this river of warmth had vivified the Europan deep. Along its banks, in a band never more than a few kilometres wide, species after species had evolved and flourished and passed away. And some had left permanent monuments.

Often, they were not easy to distinguish from the natural formations around the thermal vents, and even when they were clearly not due to pure chemistry, one would be hard put to decide whether they were the product of instinct or intelligence. On Earth, the termites reared condominiums almost as impressive as any found in the single vast ocean that enveloped this frozen world.

Along the narrow band of fertility in the deserts of the deep, whole cultures and even civilizations might have risen and fallen, armies might have marched – or swum – under the command of Europan Tamberlanes or Napoleons. And the rest of their world would never have known, for all their oases were as isolated from one another as the planets themselves. The creatures who basked in the glow of the lava rivers, and fed around the hot vents, could not cross the hostile wilderness between their lonely islands. If they had ever produced historians and philosophers, each culture would have been convinced that it was alone in the Universe.

Yet even the space between the oases was not altogether empty of life; there were hardier creatures who had dared its rigours. Some were the Europan analogues of fish – streamlined torpedoes, propelled by vertical tails, steered by fins along their bodies. The resemblance to the most successful dwellers in Earth's oceans was inevitable; given the same engineering problems, evolution must produce very similar answers. Witness the dolphin and the shark – superficially almost identical, yet from far distant branches of the tree of life.

There was, however, one very obvious difference between the fish of the Europan seas and those in terrestrial oceans; they had no gills, for there was hardly a trace of oxygen to be extracted from the waters in which they swam. Like the creatures around Earth's own geothermal vents, their metabolism was based on sulphur compounds, present in abundance in this volcanic environment.

And very few had eyes. Apart from the flickering glow of lava outpourings, and occasional bursts of bioluminescence from creatures seeking mates, or hunters questing prey, it was a lightless world.

It was also a doomed one. Not only were its energy sources sporadic and constantly shifting, but the tidal forces that drove them were steadily weakening. Even if they developed true intelligence, the Europans were trapped between fire and ice.

Barring a miracle, they would perish with the final freezing of their little world.

Lucifer had wrought that miracle.

26

Tsienville

In the final moments, as he came in over the coast at a sedate hundred kilometres an hour, Poole wondered if there might be some last-minute intervention. But nothing untoward happened, even when he moved slowly along the black, forbidding face of the Great Wall.

It was the inevitable name for the Europa Monolith as, unlike its little brothers on Earth and Moon, it was lying horizontally, and was more than twenty kilometres long. Although it was literally billions of times greater in volume than TMA ZERO and TMA ONE, its proportions were exactly the same – that intriguing ratio 1:4:9, inspirer of so much numerological nonsense over the centuries.

As the vertical face was almost ten kilometres high, one

plausible theory maintained that among its other functions the Great Wall served as a wind-break, protecting Tsienville from the ferocious gales that occasionally roared in from the Sea of Galilee. They were much less frequent now that the climate had stabilized, but a thousand years earlier they would have been a severe discouragement to any life-forms emerging from the ocean.

Though he had fully intended to do so, Poole had never found time to visit the Tycho Monolith – still Top Secret when he had left for Jupiter – and Earth's gravity made its twin at Olduvai inaccessible to him. But he had seen their images so often that they were much more familiar than the proverbial back of the hand (and how many people, he had often wondered, *would* recognize the backs of their hands?). Apart from the enormous difference in scale, there was absolutely no way of distinguishing the Great Wall from TMA ONE and TMA ZERO – or, for that matter, the 'Big Brother' Monolith that *Discovery* and the *Leonov* had encountered orbiting Jupiter.

According to some theories, perhaps crazy enough to be true, there was only one archetypal Monolith, and all the others – whatever their size – were merely projections or images of it. Poole recalled these ideas when he noticed the spotless, unsullied smoothness of the Great Wall's towering ebon face. Surely, after so many centuries in such a hostile environment, it should have collected a few patches of grime! Yet it looked as immaculate as if an army of window-cleaners had just polished every square centimetre.

Then he recalled that although everyone who had ever come to view TMA ONE and TMA ZERO felt an irresistible urge to touch their apparently pristine surfaces, no one had ever succeeded. Fingers – diamond drills – laser knives – all skittered across the Monoliths as if they were coated by an impenetrable film. Or as if – and this was another popular theory – they were not quite in this universe, but somehow separated from it by an utterly impassable fraction of a millimetre.

He made one complete, leisurely circuit of the Great Wall, which remained totally indifferent to his progress. Then he brought the shuttle – still on manual, in case Ganymede Control made any further attempts to 'rescue' him – to the outer limits of Tsienville, and hovered there looking for the best place to land.

The scene through *Falcon*'s small panoramic window was wholly familiar to him; he had examined it so often in Ganymede recordings, never imagining that one day he would be observing it in reality. The Europs, it seemed, had no idea of town planning; hundreds of hemispherical structures were scattered apparently at random over an area about a kilometre across. Some were so small that even human children would feel cramped in them; though others were big enough to hold a large family, none was more than five metres high.

And they were all made from the same material, which gleamed a ghostly white in the double daylight. On Earth, the Esquimaux had found the identical answer to the challenge of their own frigid, materials-poor environment; Tsienville's igloos were also made of ice.

In lieu of streets, there were canals – as best suited creatures who were still amphibious, and apparently returned to the water to sleep. Also, it was believed, to feed and to mate, though neither hypothesis had been proved.

Tsienville had been called 'Venice, made of ice', and Poole had to agree that it was an apt description. However, there were no Venetians in sight; the place looked as if it had been deserted for years.

And here was another mystery; despite the fact that Lucifer was fifty times brighter than the distant Sun, and was a permanent fixture in the sky, the Europs still seemed locked to an ancient rhythm of night and day. They returned to the ocean at sunset, and emerged with the rising of the Sun – despite the fact that the level of illumination had changed by only a few per cent. Perhaps there was a parallel on Earth, where the life cycles of many creatures were controlled as much by the feeble Moon as the far more brilliant Sun.

It would be sunrise in another hour, and then the inhabitants of Tsienville would return to land and go about their leisurely affairs – as by human standards, they certainly were. The sulphur-based biochemistry that powered the Europs was not as efficient as the oxygen-driven one that energized the vast majority of terrestrial animals. Even a sloth could outrun a Europ, so it was difficult to regard them as potentially dangerous. That was the Good News; the Bad News was that even with the best intentions on both sides, attempts at communication would be extremely slow – perhaps intolerably tedious.

It was about time, Poole decided, that he reported back to Ganymede Control. They must be getting very anxious, and he wondered how his co-conspirator, Captain Chandler, was dealing with the situation.

'*Falcon* calling Ganymede. As you can doubtless see, I have – er – been brought to rest just above Tsienville. There is no sign of hostility, and as it's still solar night here all the Europs are underwater. Will call you again as soon as I'm on the ground.'

Dim would have been proud of him, Poole thought, as he brought *Falcon* down gently as a snowflake on a smooth patch of ice. He was taking no chances with its stability, and set the inertial drive to cancel all but a fraction of the shuttle's weight – just enough, he hoped, to prevent it being blown away by any wind.

He was on Europa – the first human in a thousand years. Had Armstrong and Aldrin felt this sense of elation, when *Eagle* touched down on the Moon? Probably they were too busy checking their Lunar Module's primitive and totally unintelligent systems. *Falcon*, of course, was doing all this automatically. The little cabin was now very quiet, apart from the inevitable – and reassuring – murmur of well-tempered electronics. It gave Poole a considerable shock when Chandler's voice, obviously pre-recorded, interrupted his thoughts.

'So you made it! Congratulations! As you know, we're scheduled to return to the Belt week after next, but that should give you plenty of time.

'After five days, *Falcon* knows what to do. She'll find her way home, with or without you. So good luck!'

MISS PRINGLE
    ACTIVATE CRYPTO PROGRAM
    STORE
    Hello, Dim – thanks for that cheerful message! I feel rather silly using this program – as if I'm a secret agent in one of the spy melodramas that used to be so popular

before I was born. Still, it will allow some privacy, which may be useful. Hope Miss Pringle has downloaded it properly ... of course, Miss P, I'm only joking!

By the way, I'm getting a barrage of requests from all the news media in the Solar System. Please try to hold them off – or divert them to Dr Ted. He'll enjoy handling them ...

Since Ganymede has me on camera all the time, I won't waste breath telling you what I'm seeing. If all goes well, we should have some action in a few minutes – and we'll know if it really was a good idea to let the Europs find me already sitting here peacefully, waiting to greet them when they come to the surface ...

Whatever happens, it won't be as big a surprise to me as it was to Dr Chang and his colleagues, when they landed here a thousand years ago! I played his famous last message again, just before leaving Ganymede. I must confess it gave me an eerie feeling – couldn't help wondering if something like that could possibly happen again ... wouldn't like to immortalize myself the way poor Chang did ...

Of course, I can always lift off if something starts going wrong ... and here's an interesting thought that's just occurred to me ... I wonder if the Europs have any history – any kind of records ... any memory of what happened just a few kilometres from here, a thousand years ago?

27

Ice and Vacuum

... This is Dr Chang, calling from Europa. I hope you can hear me, especially Dr Floyd – I know you're aboard *Leonov* ... I may not have much time ... aiming my suit antenna where I think you are ... please relay this information to Earth.

Tsien was destroyed three hours ago. I'm the only survivor. Using my suit radio – no idea if it has enough range, but it's the only chance. Please listen carefully ...

THERE IS LIFE ON EUROPA. I repeat: THERE IS LIFE ON EUROPA ...

We landed safely, checked all the systems, and ran out the hoses so we could start pumping water into our propellant tanks immediately ... just in case we had to leave in a hurry.

Everything was going according to plan ... it seemed almost too good to be true. The tanks were half full when Dr Lee and I went out to check the pipe insulation. *Tsien* stands – stood – about thirty metres from the edge of the Grand Canal. Pipes went directly from it and down through the ice. Very thin – not safe to walk on.

Jupiter was quarter full, and we had five kilowatts of lighting strung up on the ship. She looked like a Christmas tree – beautiful, reflected on the ice ...

Lee saw it first – a huge dark mass rising up from the depths. At first we thought it was a school of fish – too large for a single organism – then it started to break through the ice, and began moving towards us.

It looked rather like huge strands of wet seaweed, crawling along the ground. Lee ran back to the ship to get a camera – I stayed to watch, reporting over the radio. The thing moved so slowly I could easily outrun it. I was much more excited than alarmed. Thought I knew what kind of creature it was – I've seen pictures of the kelp forests off California – but I was quite wrong.

... I could tell it was in trouble. It couldn't possibly survive at a temperature a hundred and fifty below its normal environment. It was freezing solid as it moved forward – bits were breaking off like glass – but it was still advancing towards the ship, a black tidal wave, slowing down all the time.

I was still so surprised that I couldn't think straight and I couldn't imagine what it was trying to do. Even though it was heading towards *Tsien* it still seemed completely harmless, like – well, a small forest on the move. I remember smiling – it reminded me of *Macbeth*'s Birnam Wood ...

Then I suddenly realized the danger. Even if it was completely inoffensive – it was *heavy* – with all the ice it was carrying, it must have weighed several tons, even in this low gravity.

And it was slowly, painfully climbing up our landing gear ... the legs were beginning to buckle, all in slow motion, like something in a dream – or a nightmare ...

Not until the ship started to topple did I realize what the thing was trying to do – and then it was far too late. We could have saved ourselves – if we'd only switched off our lights!

Perhaps it's a phototrope, its biological cycle triggered by the sunlight that filters down through the ice. Or it could have been attracted like a moth to a candle. Our floodlights must have been more brilliant than anything that Europa has ever known, even the Sun itself ...

Then the ship crashed. I saw the hull split, a cloud of snowflakes form as moisture condensed. All the lights went out, except for one, swinging back and forth on a cable a couple of metres above the ground.

I don't know what happened immediately after that. The next thing I remember, I was standing under the light, beside the wreck of the ship, with a fine powdering of fresh snow all around me. I could see my footsteps in it very clearly. I must have run there; perhaps only a minute or two had elapsed ...

The plant – I still thought of it as a plant – was motionless. I wondered if it had been damaged by the impact; large sections – as thick as a man's arms – had splintered off, like broken twigs.

Then the main trunk started to move again. It pulled

away from the hull, and began to crawl towards me. That was when I knew for certain that the thing was light-sensitive: I was standing immediately under the thousand-watt lamp, which had stopped swinging now.

Imagine an oak tree – better still, a banyan with its multiple trunks and roots – flattened out by gravity and trying to creep along the ground. It got to within five metres of the light, then started to spread out until it had made a perfect circle around me. Presumably that was the limit of its tolerance – the point at which photo-attraction turned to repulsion.

After that, nothing happened for several minutes, I wondered if it was dead – frozen solid at last.

Then I saw that large buds were forming on many of the branches. It was like watching a time-lapse film of flowers opening. In fact I thought they *were* flowers – each about as big as a man's head.

Delicate, beautifully coloured membranes started to unfold. Even then, it occurred to me that no one – no *thing* – could ever have seen these colours properly, until we brought our lights – our fatal lights – to this world.

Tendrils, stamens, waving feebly ... I walked over to the living wall that surrounded me, so that I could see exactly what was happening. Neither then, or at any other time, had I felt the slightest fear of the creature. I was certain that it was not malevolent – if indeed it was conscious at all.

There were scores of the big flowers, in various stages of unfolding. Now they reminded me of butterflies, just emerging from the chrysalis – wings crumpled, still feeble – I was getting closer and closer to the truth.

But they were freezing – dying as quickly as they formed. Then, one after another, they dropped off from the parent buds. For a few moments they flopped around like fish stranded on dry land – and at last I realized exactly what they were. Those membranes weren't petals – they were fins, or their equivalent. This was the free-swimming larval stage of the creature. Probably it spends much of its life rooted on the sea-bed, then sends these mobile offspring in search of new territory. Just like the corals of Earth's oceans.

I knelt down to get a closer look at one of the little creatures. The beautiful colours were fading now, to a drab brown. Some of the petal-fins had snapped off, becoming brittle shards as they froze. But it was still moving feebly, and as I approached it tried to avoid me. I wondered how it sensed my presence.

Then I noticed that the stamens – as I'd called them – all carried bright blue dots at their tips. They looked like tiny star sapphires – or the blue eyes along the mantle of a scallop – aware of light, but unable to form true images. As I watched, the vivid blue faded, the gems became dull, ordinary stones . . .

Dr Floyd – or anyone else who is listening – I haven't much more time; my life-support system alarm has just sounded. But I've almost finished.

I know then what I had to do. The cable to that thousand-watt lamp was hanging almost to the ground. I gave it a few tugs, and the light went out in a shower of sparks.

I wondered whether it was too late. For a few minutes nothing happened. So I walked over to the wall of tangled branches around me – and kicked it.

Slowly, the creature started to unweave itself, and to retreat back to the Canal. I followed it all the way back to the water, encouraging it with more kicks when it slowed down, feeling the fragments of ice crunching all the time beneath my boots ... As it neared the Canal, it seemed to gain strength and energy, as if it knew it was approaching its natural home. I wondered if it would survive, to bud again.

It disappeared through the surface, leaving a few last dead larvae on the alien land. The exposed free water bubbled for a few minutes until a scab of protective ice sealed it from the vacuum above. Then I walked back to the ship to see if there was anything to salvage – I don't want to talk about that.

I've only two requests to make, Doctor. When the taxonomists classify this creature , I hope they'll name it after me.

And – when the next ship comes home – ask them to take our bones back to China.

I'll lose power in a few minutes – wish I knew whether anyone was receiving me. Anyway, I'll repeat this message as long as I can ...

This is Professor Chang on Europa, reporting the destruction of the spaceship *Tsien*. We landed beside the Grand Canal and set up our pumps at the edge of the ice –

28

The Little Dawn

MISS PRINGLE
  RECORD

Here comes the Sun! Strange – how quickly it seems to rise, on this slowly turning world! Of course, of course – the disc's so small that the whole of it pops above the horizon in no time ... Not that it makes much difference to the light – if you weren't looking in that direction, you'd never notice that there was another sun in the sky.

But I hope the Europs have noticed. Usually it takes them less than five minutes to start coming ashore after the Little Dawn. Wonder if they already know I'm here, and are scared ...

No – could be the other way round. Perhaps they're

inquisitive – even anxious to see what strange visitor has come to Tsienville ... I rather hope so ...

Here they come! Hope your spysats are watching – *Falcon*'s cameras recording ...

How slowly they move! I'm afraid it's going to be very boring trying to communicate with them ... even if they want to talk to me ...

Rather like the thing that overturned *Tsien*, but much smaller ... They remind me of little trees, walking on half a dozen slender trunks. And with hundreds of branches, dividing into twigs, which divide again ... and again. Just like many of our general-purpose robots ... what a long time it took us to realize that imitation humanoids were ridiculously clumsy, and the proper way to go was with myriad of small manipulators! Whenever we invent something clever, we find that Mother Nature's already thought of it ...

Aren't the little ones cute – like tiny bushes on the move. Wonder how they reproduce – budding? I hadn't realized how beautiful they are. Almost as colourful as coral reef fish – maybe for the same reasons ... to attract mates, or fool predators by pretending to be something else ...

Did I say they looked like bushes? Make that *rose*-bushes – they've actually got thorns! Must have a good reason for them ...

I'm disappointed. They don't seem to have noticed me. They're all heading into town, as if a visiting spacecraft was an everyday occurrence ... only a few left ... maybe this will work ...

I suppose they can detect sound vibrations – most marine creatures can – though this atmosphere may be too thin to carry my voice very far ...

FALCON – EXTERNAL SPEAKER . . .

HELLO, CAN YOU HEAR ME? MY NAME IS FRANK POOLE . . . AHEM . . . I COME IN PEACE FOR ALL MANKIND . . .

Makes me feel rather stupid, but can you suggest anything better? And it will be good for the record . . .

Nobody's taking the slightest notice. Big ones and little ones, they're all creeping towards their igloos. Wonder what they actually *do* when they get there – perhaps I should follow. I'm sure it would be perfectly safe – I can move so much faster –

I've just had an amusing flashback. All these creatures going in the same direction – they look like the commuters who used to surge back and forth twice a day between home and office, before electronics made it unnecessary.

Let's try again, before they all disappear . . .

HELLO THERE – THIS IS FRANK POOLE, A VISITOR FROM PLANET EARTH. CAN YOU HEAR ME?

I HEAR YOU, FRANK. THIS IS DAVE.

29

The Ghosts in the Machine

Frank Poole's immediate reaction was one of utter astonishment, followed by overwhelming joy. He had never
really believed that he would make any kind of contact,
either with the Europs or the Monolith. Indeed, he had
even had fantasies of kicking in frustration against that
towering ebon wall and shouting angrily, 'Is there anybody
home?'

Yet he should not have been so amazed: some intelligence must have monitored his approach from Ganymede,
and permitted him to land. He should have taken Ted
Khan more seriously.

'Dave,' he said slowly, 'is that *really* you?'

Who else could it be? a part of his mind asked. Yet it

was not a foolish question. There was something curiously mechanical – impersonal – about the voice that came from the small speaker on *Falcon*'s control board.

YES, FRANK. I AM DAVE.

There was a very brief pause: then the same voice continued, without any change of intonation:

HELLO FRANK. THIS IS HAL.

MISS PRINGLE
RECORD

Well – Indra, Dim – I'm glad I recorded all that, otherwise you'd never believe me . . .

I guess I'm still in a state of shock. First of all, how should I feel about someone who tried to – who *did* – kill me – even if it was a thousand years ago! But I understand now that Hal wasn't to blame; nobody was. There's a very good piece of advice I've often found useful: 'Never attribute to malevolence what is merely due to incompetence'. I can't feel any anger towards a bunch of programmers I never knew, who've been dead for centuries.

I'm glad this is encrypted, as I don't know how it should be handled, and a lot that I tell you may turn out to be complete nonsense. I'm already suffering from information overload, and had to ask Dave to leave me for a while – after all the trouble I've gone through to meet him! But I don't think I hurt his feelings; I'm not sure yet if he *has* any feelings . . .

What *is* he – good question! Well, he really is Dave Bowman, but with most of the humanity stripped away – like – ah – like the synopsis of a book or a technical paper. You know how an abstract can give all the basic information –

but no hint of the author's personality? Yet there were moments when I felt that something of the old Dave was still there. I wouldn't go so far as to say he's *pleased* to meet me again – moderately satisfied might be more like it ... For myself, I'm still very confused. Like meeting an old friend after a long separation, and finding that they're now a different person. Well, it *has* been a thousand years – and I can't imagine what experiences he's known, though as I'll show you presently, he's tried to share some of them with me.

And Hal – he's here too, without question. Most of the time, there's no way I can tell which of them is speaking to me. Aren't there examples of multiple personalities in the medical records? Maybe it's something like that.

I asked him how this had happened to them both, and he – they – dammit, *Halman*! – tried to explain. Let me repeat – I may have got it partly wrong, but it's the only working hypothesis I have.

Of course, the Monolith – in its various manifestations – is the key – no, that's the wrong word – didn't someone once say it was a kind of cosmic Swiss Army knife? You still have them, I've noticed, though both Switzerland and its army disappeared centuries ago. It's a general-purpose device that can do anything it wants to. Or was programmed to do ...

Back in Africa, four million years ago, it gave us that evolutionary kick in the pants, for better or for worse. Then its sibling on the Moon waited for us to climb out of the cradle. That we've already guessed, and Dave's confirmed it.

I said that he doesn't have many human feelings, but

he still has curiosity – he wants to learn. And what an opportunity he's had!

When the Jupiter Monolith absorbed him – can't think of a better word – it got more than it bargained for. Though it used him – apparently as a captured specimen, and a probe to investigate Earth – he's also been using *it*. With Hal's assistance – and who should understand a super-computer better than another one? – he's been exploring its memory, and trying to find its purpose.

Now, this is something that's very hard to believe. The Monolith is a fantastically powerful machine – look what it did to Jupiter! – but it's no more than that. It's running on automatic – *it has no consciousness*. I remember once thinking that I might have to kick the Great Wall and shout 'Is there anyone there?' And the correct answer would have to be – no one, except Dave and Hal . . .

Worse still, some of its systems may have started to fail; Dave even suggests that, in a fundamental way, it's become *stupid*! Perhaps it's been left on its own for too long – it's time for a service check.

And he believes the Monolith has made at least one misjudgement. Perhaps that's not the right word – it may have been deliberate, carefully considered . . .

In any event, it's – well, truly awesome, and terrifying in its implications. Luckily, I can show it to you, so you can decide for yourselves. Yes, even though it happened a thousand years ago, when *Leonov* flew the second mission to Jupiter! And all this time, no one has ever guessed . . .

I'm certainly glad you got me fitted with the Braincap. Of course it's been invaluable – I can't imagine life without

191

it – but now it's doing a job it was never designed for. And doing it remarkably well.

It took Halman about ten minutes to find how it worked, and to set up an interface. Now we have mind-to-mind contact – which is quite a strain on me, I can tell you. I have to keep asking them to slow down, and use baby-talk. Or should I say baby-think . . .

I'm not sure how well this will come through. It's a thousand-year-old recording of Dave's own experience, somehow stored in the Monolith's enormous memory, then retrieved by Dave and injected into my Braincap – don't ask me exactly how – and finally transferred and beamed to you by Ganymede Central. Phew. Hope you don't get a headache downloading it.

Over to Dave Bowman at Jupiter, early twenty-first century . . .

30

Foamscape

The million-kilometre-long tendrils of magnetic force, the sudden explosion of radio waves, the geysers of electrified plasma wider than the planet Earth – they were as real and clearly visible to him as the clouds banding the planet in multi-hued glory. He could understand the complex pattern of their interactions, and realized that Jupiter was much more wonderful than anyone had ever guessed.

Even as he fell through the roaring heart of the Great Red Spot, with the lightning of its continent-wide thunderstorms detonating under him, he knew why it had persisted for centuries though it was made of gases far less substantial than those that formed the hurricanes of Earth. The thin scream of hydrogen wind faded as he sank into the calmer depths, and a sheet of waxen snowflakes – some already coalescing into barely palpable mountains of hydrocarbon foam – descended from the heights above. It was already warm enough for liquid water to exist, but there were no oceans there; this purely gaseous environment was too tenuous to support them.

He descended through layer after layer of cloud, until he entered a region of such clarity that even human vision could have scanned an area more than a thousand kilometres across. It was only a minor eddy in the vaster gyre of the Great Red Spot; and it held a secret that men had long guessed, but never proved. Skirting the foothills of the drifting foam mountains were myriad of small, sharply defined clouds, all about the same size and patterned with similar red and brown mottling. They were small only as compared with the inhuman scale of their surroundings; the very least would have covered a fair-sized city.

They were clearly alive, for they were moving with slow deliberation along the flanks of the aerial mountains, browsing off their slopes like colossal sheep. And they were calling to each other in the metre band, their radio voices faint but clear against the cracklings and concussions of Jupiter itself.

Nothing less than living gasbags, they floated in the narrow zone between freezing heights and scorching depths. Narrow, yes – but a domain far larger than all the biosphere of Earth.

They were not alone. Moving swiftly among them were other creatures so small that they could easily have been overlooked. Some of them bore an almost uncanny resemblance to terrestrial aircraft, and were of about the same size. But they too were alive – perhaps predators, perhaps parasites, perhaps even herdsmen.

A whole new chapter of evolution, as alien as that which he had glimpsed on Europa, was opening before him. There were jet-propelled torpedoes like the squids of the terrestrial oceans, hunting and devouring the huge gas-bags. But the balloons were not defenceless; some of them fought back with electric thunderbolts and with clawed tentacles like kilometre-long chainsaws.

There were even stranger shapes, exploiting almost every possibility of geometry – bizarre, translucent kites, tetrahedra, spheres, polyhedra, tangles of twisted ribbons ... The gigantic plankton of the Jovian atmosphere, they were designed to float like gossamer in the uprising currents, until they had lived long enough to reproduce; then they would be swept down into the depths to be carbonized and recycled in a new generation.

He was searching a world more than a hundred times the area of Earth, and though he saw many wonders, nothing there hinted of intelligence. The radio voices of the great balloons carried only simple messages of warning or of fear. Even the hunters, who might have been expected to develop higher degrees of organization, were like the sharks in Earth's oceans – mindless automata.

And for all its breathtaking size and novelty, the biosphere of Jupiter was a fragile world, a place of mists and foam, of delicate silken threads and paper-thin tissues spun from the continual snowfall of petrochemicals formed by lightning in the upper atmosphere. Few of its constructs were more substantial than soap bubbles; its most awesome predators could be torn to shreds by even the feeblest of terrestrial carnivores.

Like Europa, but on a vastly grander scale, Jupiter was an evolutionary *cul-de-sac*. Intelligence would never emerge here; even if it did, it would be doomed to a stunted existence. A purely aerial culture might develop, but in an environment where fire was impossible, and solids scarcely existed, it could never even reach the Stone Age.

31

Nursery

MISS PRINGLE
  RECORD

Well, Indra – Dim – I hope that came through in good shape – I still find it hard to believe. All those fantastic creatures – surely we should have detected their radio voices, even if we couldn't understand them! – wiped out in a moment, so that Jupiter could be made into a sun.

And now we can understand why. It was to give the Europs their chance. What pitiless logic: is intelligence the only thing that matters? I can see some long arguments with Ted Khan over this –

The next question is: will the Europs make the grade – or will they remain forever stuck in the kindergarten – not even that – the nursery? Though a thousand years is a very short time, one would have expected some progress, but according to Dave they're exactly the same now as when they left the sea. Perhaps that's the trouble; they still have one foot – or one twig! – in the water.

And here's another thing we got completely wrong. We thought they went back into the water to sleep. It's just the other way round – they go back to eat, and sleep when they come on land! As we might have guessed from their structure – that network of branches – they're plankton feeders . . .

I asked Dave about the igloos they've built. Aren't they a technological advance? And he said: not really – they're only adaptations of structures they make on the sea-bed, to protect themselves from various predators – especially something like a flying carpet, as big as a football field . . .

There's one area, though, where they have shown initiative – even creativity. They're fascinated by metals, presumably because they don't exist in pure form in the ocean. That's why *Tsien* was stripped – the same thing's happened to the occasional probes that have come down in their territory. What do they do with the copper and beryllium and titanium they collect? Nothing useful, I'm afraid. They pile it all together in one place, in a fantastic heap that they keep reassembling. They could be developing an aesthetic sense – I've seen worse in the Museum of Modern Art . . . But I've got another theory – did you ever hear of cargo cults? During the twentieth century, some of the few primitive tribes that still existed made imitation aeroplanes out of bamboo, in the hope of attracting the big birds in the sky that occasionally brought them wonderful gifts. Perhaps the Europs have the same idea.

Now that question you keep asking me . . . What *is* Dave? And how did he – and Hal – become whatever it is they are now?

The quick answer, of course, is that they're both emulations – simulations – in the Monolith's gigantic memory. Most of the time they're inactivated; when I asked Dave about this, he said he'd been 'awake' – his actual word – for only fifty years altogether, in the thousand since his er – metamorphosis.

When I asked if he resented this takeover of his life, he said, 'Why should I resent it? I am performing my functions perfectly.' Yes, that sounds exactly like Hal! But I believe it *was* Dave – if there's any distinction now.

Remember that Swiss Army knife analogy? Halman is one of this cosmic knife's myriad of components.

But he's not a completely passive tool – when he's awake, he has some autonomy, some independence – presumably within limits set by the Monolith's overriding control. During the centuries, he's been used as a kind of intelligent probe to examine Jupiter – as you've just seen – as well as Ganymede and the Earth. That confirms those mysterious events in Florida, reported by Dave's old girl-friend, and the nurse who was looking after his mother, just moments before her death . . . as well as the encounters in Anubis City.

And it also explains another mystery. I asked Dave directly: why was I allowed to land on Europa, when everyone else has been turned away for centuries? *I* fully expected to be!

The answer's ridiculously simple. The Monolith uses Dave – Halman – from time to time, to keep an eye on us.

Dave knew all about my rescue – even saw some of the media interviews I made, on Earth *and* on Ganymede. I must say I'm still a little hurt he made no attempt to contact me! But at least he put out the Welcome mat when I did arrive . . .

Dim – I still have forty-eight hours before *Falcon* leaves – with or without me! I don't think I'll need them, now I've made contact with Halman; we can keep in touch just as easily from Anubis . . . if he wants to do so.

And I'm anxious to get back to the Grannymede as quickly as possible. *Falcon*'s a fine little spacecraft, but her plumbing could be improved – it's beginning to smell in here, and I'm itching for a shower.

Look forward to seeing you – and especially Ted Khan. We have much to talk about, before I return to Earth.
TRANSMIT
STORE

V

TERMINATION

The toil of all that be
Heals not the primal fault;
It rains into the sea,
And still the sea is salt.

A. E. Housman, *More Poems*

32

A Gentleman of Leisure

On the whole, it had been an interesting but uneventful three decades, punctuated by the joys and sorrows which Time and Fate bring to all mankind. The greatest of those joys had been wholly unexpected; in fact, before he left Earth for Ganymede, Poole would have dismissed the very idea as preposterous.

There is much truth in the saying that absence makes the heart grow fonder. When he and Indra Wallace met again, they discovered that, despite their bantering and occasional disagreements, they were closer than they had imagined. One thing led to another – including, to their mutual joy, Dawn Wallace and Martin Poole.

It was rather late in life to start a family – quite apart

from that little matter of a thousand years – and Professor Anderson had warned them that it might be impossible. Or even worse . . .

'You were lucky in more ways than you realize,' he told Poole. 'Radiation damage was surprisingly low, and we were able to make all essential repairs from your intact DNA. But until we do some more tests, I can't promise genetic integrity. So enjoy yourselves – but don't start a family until I give the OK.'

The tests had been time-consuming, and as Anderson had feared, further repairs were necessary. There was one major set-back – something that could never have lived, even if it had been allowed to go beyond the first few weeks after conception – but Martin and Dawn were perfect, with just the right number of heads, arms and legs. They were also handsome and intelligent, and barely managed to escape being spoiled by their doting parents – who continued to be the best of friends when, after fifteen years, each opted for independence again. Because of their Social Achievement Rating, they would have been permitted – indeed, encouraged – to have another child, but they decided not to put any more of a burden on their astonishingly good luck.

One tragedy had shadowed Poole's personal life during this period – and indeed had shocked the whole Solar community. Captain Chandler and his entire crew had been lost when the nucleus of a comet they were reconnoitring exploded suddenly, destroying *Goliath* so completely that only a few fragments were ever located. Such explosions – caused by reactions among unstable molecules which existed at very low temperatures – were a well-known danger to comet-collectors, and Chandler had encountered several during his career. No one would ever know the exact circumstances which caused so experienced a spaceman to be taken by surprise.

Poole missed Chandler very badly: he had played a unique role in his life, and there was no one to replace him – no one, except Dave Bowman, with whom he had shared so momentous an adventure. He and Chandler had often made plans to go into space together again, perhaps all the way out to the Oort Cloud with its unknown mysteries and its remote but inexhaustible wealth of ice. Yet some conflict of schedules had always upset their plans, so this was a wished-for future that would never exist.

Another long-desired goal Poole had managed to achieve – despite doctor's orders. He had been down to Earth: and once was quite enough.

The vehicle in which he had travelled looked almost identical to the wheelchairs used by the luckier paraplegics of his own time. It was motorized, and had balloon tyres which allowed it to roll over reasonably smooth surfaces. However, it could also fly – at an altitude of about twenty centimetres – on an aircushion produced by a set of small but very powerful fans. Poole was surprised that so primitive a technology was still in use, but inertia-control devices were too bulky for such small-scale applications.

Seated comfortably in his hoverchair, he was scarcely conscious of his increasing weight as he descended into the heart of Africa; though he did notice some difficulty in breathing, he had experienced far worse during his astronaut training. What he was not prepared for was the blast of furnace-heat that smote him as he rolled out of the gigantic, sky-piercing cylinder that formed the base of the Tower. Yet it was still morning: what would it be like at noon?

He had barely accustomed himself to the heat when his sense of smell was assailed. A myriad odours – none unpleasant, but all unfamiliar – clamoured for his attention. He closed his eyes for a few minutes, in an attempt to avoid overloading his input circuits.

Before he had decided to open them again, he felt some large, moist object palpating the back of his neck.

'Say hello to Elizabeth,' said his guide, a burly young man dressed in traditional Great White Hunter garb, much too smart to have seen any real use: 'she's our official greeter.'

Poole twisted round in his chair, and found himself looking into the soulful eyes of a baby elephant.

'Hello, Elizabeth,' he answered, rather feebly. Elizabeth lifted her trunk in salute, and emitted a sound not usually heard in polite society, though Poole felt sure it was well-intentioned.

Altogether, he spent less than an hour on Planet Earth, skirting the edge of a jungle whose stunted trees compared unfavourably with Skyland's, and encountering much of the local fauna. His guides apologized for the friendliness of the lions, who had been spoilt by tourists – but the malevolent expressions of the crocodiles more than compensated; here was Nature raw and unchanged.

Before he returned to the Tower, Poole risked taking a few steps away from his hoverchair. He realized that this would be the equivalent of carrying his own weight on his back, but that did not seem an impossible feat, and he would never forgive himself unless he attempted it.

It was not a good idea; perhaps he should have tried it in a cooler climate. After no more than a dozen steps, he was glad to sink back into the luxurious clutches of the chair.

'That's enough,' he said wearily. 'Let's go back to the Tower.'

As he rolled into the elevator lobby, he noticed a sign which he had somehow overlooked during the excitement of his arrival. It read:

WELCOME TO AFRICA!
'In wildness is the preservation of the world.'
HENRY DAVID THOREAU
(1817–1862)

Observing Poole's interest, the guide asked 'Did you know him?'

It was the sort of question Poole heard all too often, and at the moment he did not feel equipped to deal with it.

'I don't think so,' he answered wearily, as the great doors closed behind them, shutting out the sights, scents and sounds of Mankind's earliest home.

His vertical safari had satisfied his need to visit Earth, and he did his best to ignore the various aches and pains acquired there when he returned to his apartment at Level 10,000 – a prestigious location, even in this democratic society. Indra, however, was mildly shocked by his appearance, and ordered him straight to bed.

'Just like Antaeus – but in reverse!' she muttered darkly.

'Who?' asked Poole: there were times when his wife's erudition was a little overwhelming, but he had determined never to let it give him an inferiority complex.

'Son of the Earth Goddess, Gaea. Hercules wrestled with him – but every time he was thrown to the ground, Antaeus renewed his strength.'

'Who won?'

'Hercules, of course – by holding Antaeus in the air, so Ma couldn't recharge his batteries.'

'Well, I'm sure it won't take me long to recharge mine. And I've learned one lesson. If I don't get more exercise, I may have to move up to Lunar Gravity level.'

Poole's good resolution lasted a full month: every morning he went for a brisk five-kilometre walk, choosing a different level of the Africa Tower each day. Some floors were still vast, echoing deserts of metal which would probably never be occupied, but others had been landscaped and developed over the centuries in a bewildering variety of architectural styles. Many were borrowings from past ages and cultures; others hinted at futures which Poole would not care to visit. At least there was no danger of boredom, and on many of his walks he was accompanied, at a respectful distance, by small groups of friendly children. They were seldom able to keep up with him for long.

One day, as Poole was striding down a convincing – though sparsely populated – imitation of the Champs Élysées, he suddenly spotted a familiar face.

'Danil!' he called.

The other man took not the slightest notice, even when Poole called again, more loudly.

'Don't you remember me?'

Danil – and now that he had caught up with him, Poole

did not have the slightest doubt of his identity – looked genuinely baffled.

'I'm sorry,' he said. 'You're Commander Poole, of course. But I'm sure we've never met before.'

Now it was Poole's turn to be embarrassed.

'Stupid of me,' he apologized. 'Must have mistaken you for someone else. Have a good day.'

He was glad of the encounter, and was pleased to know that Danil was back in normal society. Whether his original crime had been axe-murders or overdue library books should no longer be the concern of his one-time employer; the account had been settled, the books closed. Although Poole sometimes missed the cops-and-robbers dramas he had often enjoyed in his youth, he had grown to accept the current wisdom: excessive interest in pathological behaviour was itself pathological.

With the help of Miss Pringle, Mk III, Poole had been able to schedule his life so that there were even occasional blank moments when he could relax and set his Braincap on Random Search, scanning his areas of interest. Outside his immediate family, his chief concerns were still among the moons of Jupiter/Lucifer, not least because he was recognized as the leading expert on the subject, and a permanent member of the Europa Committee.

This had been set up almost a thousand years ago, to consider what, if anything, could and should be done about the mysterious satellite. Over the centuries, it had accumulated a vast amount of information, going all the way back to the Voyager flybys of 1979 and the first detailed surveys from the orbiting Galileo spacecraft of 1996.

Like most long-lived organizations, the Europa Committee had become slowly fossilized, and now met only when there was some new development. It had woken up with a start after Halman's reappearance, and appointed an energetic new chairperson whose first act had been to co-opt Poole.

Though there was little that he could contribute that was not already recorded, Poole was very happy to be on the Committee. It was obviously his duty to make himself available, and it also gave him an official position he would otherwise have lacked. Previously his status was what had once been called a 'national treasure', which he found faintly embarrassing. Although he was glad to be supported in luxury by a world wealthier than all the dreams of war-ravaged earlier ages could have imagined, he felt the need to justify his existence.

He also felt another need, which he seldom articulated even to himself. Halman had spoken to him, if only briefly, at their strange encounter two decades ago. Poole was certain that, if he wished, Halman could easily do so again. Were all human contacts no longer of interest to him? He hoped that was not the case; yet that might be one explanation of his silence.

He was frequently in touch with Theodore Khan – as active and acerbic as ever, and now the Europa Committee's representative on Ganymede. Ever since Poole had returned to Earth, Ted had been trying in vain to open a channel of communication with Bowman. He could not understand why long lists of important questions on subjects of vital philosophical and historic interest received not even brief acknowledgements.

'Does the Monolith keep your friend Halman so busy

that he can't talk to me?' he complained to Poole. 'What does he do with his time, anyway?'

It was a very reasonable question; and the answer came, like a thunderbolt out of a cloudless sky, from Bowman himself – as a perfectly commonplace vidphone call.

33
Contact

'Hello, Frank. This is Dave. I have a very important message for you. I assume that you are now in your suite in Africa Tower. If you are there, please identify yourself by giving the name of our instructor in orbital mechanics. I will wait for sixty seconds, and if there is no reply will try again in exactly one hour.'

That minute was hardly long enough for Poole to recover from the shock. He felt a brief surge of delight, as well as astonishment, before another emotion took over. Glad though he was to hear from Bowman again, that phrase 'a very important message' sounded distinctly ominous.

At least it was fortunate, Poole told himself, that he's asked for one of the few names I can remember. Yet who *could* forget a Scot with a Glasgow accent so thick it had taken them a week to master it? But he had been a brilliant lecturer – once you understood what he was saying.

'Dr Gregory McVitty.'

'Accepted. Now please switch on your Braincap receiver. It will take three minutes to download this message. Do not attempt to monitor: I am using ten-to-one compression. I will wait two minutes before starting.'

How is he managing to do this? Poole wondered. Jupiter/Lucifer was now over fifty light-minutes away, so this message must have left almost an hour ago. It must have been sent with an intelligent agent in a properly addressed package on the Ganymede–Earth beam – but that would have been a trivial feat to Halman, with the resources he had apparently been able to tap inside the Monolith.

The indicator light on the Brainbox was flickering. The message was coming through.

At the compression Halman was using, it would take half an hour for Poole to absorb the message in real-time. But he needed only ten minutes to know that his peaceful life-style had come to an abrupt end.

213

34

Judgement

In a world of universal and instantaneous communication, it was very difficult to keep secrets. This was a matter, Poole decided immediately, for face-to-face discussion.

The Europa Committee had grumbled, but all its members had assembled in his apartment. There were seven of them – the lucky number, doubtless suggested by the phases of the Moon, that had always fascinated Mankind. It was the first time Poole had met three of the Committee's members, though by now he knew them all more thoroughly than he could possibly have done in a pre-Braincapped lifetime.

'Chairperson Oconnor, members of the Committee – I'd like to say a few words – only a few, I promise! – before you download the message I've received from Europa. And this is something I prefer to do verbally; that's more natural for me – I'm afraid I'll never be quite at ease with direct mental transfer.

'As you all know, Dave Bowman and Hal have been stored as emulations in the Monolith on Europa. Apparently it never discards a tool it once found useful, and from time to time it activates Halman, to monitor our affairs – when they begin to concern it. As I suspect my arrival may have done – though perhaps I flatter myself.

'But Halman isn't just a passive tool. The Dave component still retains something of its human origins – even emotions. And because we were trained together – shared almost everything for years – he apparently finds it much easier to communicate with me than with anyone else. I would like to think he enjoys doing it, but perhaps that's too strong a word . . .

'He's also curious – inquisitive – and perhaps a little resentful of the way he's been collected, like a specimen of wildlife. Though that's probably what we are, from the viewpoint of the intelligence that created the Monolith.

'And where *is* that intelligence now? Halman apparently knows the answer, and it's a chilling one.

'As we always suspected, the Monolith is part of a galactic network of some kind. And the nearest node – the Monolith's controller, or immediate superior – is 450 light-years away.

'Much too close for comfort! This means that the report on us and our affairs that was transmitted early in the twenty-first century was received half a millennium ago. If the Monolith's – let's say Supervisor – replied at once, any further instructions should be arriving just about now.

'And that's exactly what seems to be happening. During the last few days, the Monolith has been receiving a continuous string of messages, and has been setting up new programs, presumably in accordance with these.

'Unfortunately, Halman can only make guesses about the nature of those instructions. As you'll gather when you've downloaded this tablet, he has some limited access to many of the Monolith's circuits and memory banks, and can even carry on a kind of dialogue with it. If that's the right word – since you need two people for that! I still can't really grasp the idea that the Monolith, for all its powers, doesn't possess consciousness – doesn't even know that it exists!

'Halman's been brooding over the problem for a thousand years – on and off – and has come to the same answer that most of us have done. But his conclusion must surely carry far more weight, because of his inside knowledge.

'Sorry! I wasn't intending to make a joke – but what else could you call it?

'Whatever went to the trouble of creating us – or at least tinkering with our ancestors' minds and genes – is deciding what to do next. And Halman is pessimistic. No – that's an exaggeration. Let's say he doesn't think much of our chances, but is now too detached an observer to be unduly worried. The future – the *survival*! – of the human race isn't much more than an interesting problem to him, but he's willing to help.'

Poole suddenly stopped talking, to the surprise of his intent audience.

'That's strange. I've just had an amazing flashback . . .

I'm sure it explains what's happening. Please bear with me.

'Dave and I were walking together one day, along the beach at the Cape, a few weeks before launch, when we noticed a large beetle lying on the sand. As often happens, it had fallen on its back and was waving its legs in the air, struggling to get right-way-up.

'I ignored it – we were engaged in some complicated technical discussion – but not Dave. He stepped aside, and carefully flipped it over with his shoe. As it flew away I commented, "Are you sure that was a good idea? Now it will go off and chomp somebody's prize chrysanthemums." And he answered, "Maybe you're right. But I'd like to give it the benefit of the doubt."

'My apologies – I'd promised to say only a few words! But I'm very glad I remembered that incident: I really believe it puts Halman's message in the right perspective. He's giving the human race the benefit of the doubt . . .

'Now please check your Braincaps. This is a high-density recording – top of the u.v. band, Channel 110. Make yourselves comfortable, but be sure you're in line of sight. Here we go . . .'

35

Council of War

No one asked for a replay. Once was sufficient.

There was a brief silence when the playback finished; then Chairperson Dr Oconnor removed her Braincap, massaged her shining scalp, and said slowly:

'You taught me a phrase from your period that seems very appropriate now. This *is* a can of worms.'

'But only Bowman – Halman – has opened it,' said one of the Committee members. 'Does he really understand the operation of something as complex as the Monolith? Or is this whole scenario a figment of his imagination?'

'I don't think he has much imagination,' Dr Oconnor answered. 'And everything checks perfectly. Especially the reference to Nova Scorpio. We assumed that was an accident; apparently it was a – *judgement.*'

'First Jupiter – now Scorpio,' said Dr Kraussman, the distinguished physicist who was popularly regarded as a reincarnation of the legendary Einstein. A little plastic surgery, it was rumoured, had also helped. 'Who will be next in line?'

'We always guessed,' said the Chair, 'that the TMAs were monitoring us.' She paused for a moment, then added ruefully: 'What bad – what incredibly bad! – luck that the final report went off, just after the very worst period in human history!'

There was another silence. Everyone knew that the twentieth century had often been branded 'The Century of Torture'.

Poole listened without interrupting, while he waited for some consensus to emerge. Not for the first time, he was impressed by the quality of the Committee. No one was trying to prove a pet theory, score debating points, or inflate an ego: he could not help drawing a contrast with the often bad-tempered arguments he had heard in his own time, between Space Agency engineers and administrators, Congressional staffs, and industrial executives.

Yes, the human race *had* undoubtedly improved. The Braincap had not only helped to weed out misfits, but had enormously increased the efficiency of education. Yet there had also been a loss; there were very few memorable characters in this society. Offhand he could think of only four – Indra, Captain Chandler, Dr Khan and the Dragon Lady of wistful memory.

The Chairperson let the discussion flow smoothly back

and forth until everyone had had a say, then began her summing up.

'The obvious first question – how seriously should we take this threat – isn't worth wasting time on. Even if it's a false alarm, or a misunderstanding, it's potentially so grave that we must assume it's real, until we have absolute proof to the contrary. Agreed?

'Good. And we don't know how much time we have. So we must assume that the danger is immediate. Perhaps Halman may be able to give us some further warning, but by then it may be too late.

'So the only thing we have to decide is: how can we protect ourselves, against something as powerful as the Monolith? Look what happened to Jupiter! And, apparently, Nova Scorpio . . .

'I'm sure that brute force would be useless, though perhaps we should explore that option. Dr Kraussman – how long would it take to build a super-bomb?'

'Assuming that the designs still exist, so that no research is necessary – oh, perhaps two weeks. Thermonuclear weapons are rather simple, and use common materials – after all, they made them back in the Second Millennium! But if you wanted something sophisticated – say an anti-matter bomb, or a mini-black-hole – well, that might take a few months.'

'Thank you: could you start looking into it? But as I've said, I don't believe it would work; surely something that can *handle* such powers must also be able to protect itself against them. So – any other suggestions?'

'Can we negotiate?' one councillor asked, not very hopefully.

'With what ... or whom?' Kraussman answered. 'As we've discovered, the Monolith is essentially a pure mechanism, doing just what it's been programmed to do. Perhaps that program is flexible enough to allow of changes, but there's no way we can tell. And we certainly can't appeal to Head Office – that's half a thousand light-years away!'

Poole listened without interrupting; there was nothing he could contribute to the discussion, and indeed much of it was completely over his head. He began to feel an insidious sense of depression; would it have been better, he wondered, not to pass on this information? Then, if it was a false alarm, no one would be any the worse. And if it was not – well, humanity would still have peace of mind, before whatever inescapable doom awaited it.

He was still mulling over these gloomy thoughts when he was suddenly alerted by a familiar phrase.

A quiet little member of the Committee, with a name so long and difficult that Poole had never been able to remember, still less pronounce it, had abruptly dropped just two words into the discussion.

'Trojan Horse!'

There was one of those silences generally described as 'pregnant', then a chorus of 'Why didn't I think of that!' 'Of course!' 'Very good idea!' until the Chairperson, for the first time in the session, had to call for order.

'Thank you, Professor Thirugnanasampanthamoorthy,' said Dr Oconnor, without missing a beat. 'Would you like to be more specific?'

'Certainly. If the Monolith is indeed, as everyone seems to think, essentially a machine without consciousness – and hence with only limited self-monitoring ability – we may already have the weapons that can defeat it. Locked up in the Vault.'

'And a delivery system – Halman!'

'Precisely.'

'Just a minute, Dr T. We know nothing – absolutely nothing – about the Monolith's architecture. How can we be sure that anything our primitive species ever designed would be effective against it?'

'We can't – but remember this. However sophisticated it is, the Monolith has to obey exactly the same universal laws of logic that Aristotle and Boole formulated, centuries ago. That's why it may – no, *should*! – be vulnerable to the things locked up in the Vault. We have to assemble them in such a way that at least one of them will work. It's our only hope – unless anybody can suggest a better alternative.'

'Excuse me,' said Poole, finally losing patience. 'Will someone kindly tell me – what and where is this famous Vault you're talking about?'

36

Chamber of Horrors

History is full of nightmares, some natural, some man-made.

By the end of the twenty-first century, most of the natural ones – smallpox, the Black Death, AIDS, the hideous viruses lurking in the African jungle – had been eliminated, or at least brought under control, by the advance of medicine. However, it was never wise to underestimate the ingenuity of Mother Nature, and no one doubted that the future would still have unpleasant biological surprises in store for Mankind.

It seemed a sensible precaution, therefore, to keep a few specimens of all these horrors for scientific study – carefully guarded, of course, so that there was no possibility of them escaping and again wreaking havoc on the human race. But how could one be *absolutely* sure that there was no danger of this happening?

There had been – understandably – quite an outcry in the late twentieth century when it was proposed to keep the last known smallpox viruses at Disease Control Centres in the United States and Russia. However unlikely it might be, there was a finite possibility that they might be released by such accidents as earthquakes, equipment failures – or even deliberate sabotage by terrorist groups.

A solution that satisfied everyone (except a few 'Preserve the lunar wilderness!' extremists) was to ship them to the Moon, and to keep them in a laboratory at the end of a kilometre-long shaft drilled into the isolated mountain Pico, one of the most prominent features of the Mare Imbrium. And here, over the years, they were joined by some of the most outstanding examples of misplaced human ingenuity – indeed, insanity.

There were gases and mists that, even in microscopic doses, caused slow or instant death. Some had been created by religious cultists who, though mentally deranged, had managed to acquire considerable scientific knowledge. Many of them believed that the end of the world was at hand (when, of course, only their followers would be saved). In case God was absent-minded enough not to perform as scheduled, they wanted to make sure that they could rectify His unfortunate oversight.

The first assaults of these lethal cultists were made on such vulnerable targets as crowded subways, World Fairs, sports stadiums, pop concerts . . . tens of thousands were killed, and many more injured, before the madness was brought under control in the early twenty-first century. As often happens, some good came out of evil, because it forced the world's law-enforcement agencies to co-operate as never before; even rogue states which had promoted political terrorism were unable to tolerate this random and wholly unpredictable variety.

The chemical and biological agents used in these attacks – as well as in earlier forms of warfare – joined the deadly collection in Pico. Their antidotes, when they existed, were also stored with them. It was hoped that none of this material would ever concern humanity again – but it was still available, under heavy guard, if it was needed in some desperate emergency.

The third category of items stored in the Pico vault, although they could be classified as plagues, had never killed or injured anyone – directly. They had not even existed before the late twentieth century, but in a few decades they had done billions of dollars' worth of damage, and often wrecked lives as effectively as any bodily illness could have done. They were the diseases which attacked Mankind's newest and most versatile servant, the computer.

Taking names from the medical dictionaries – viruses, prions, tapeworms – they were programs that often mimicked, with uncanny accuracy, the behaviour of their organic relatives. Some were harmless – little more than playful jokes, contrived to surprise or amuse computer operators by unexpected messages and images on their visual displays. Others were far more malicious – deliberately designed agents of catastrophe.

In most cases their purpose was entirely mercenary; they

were the weapons that sophisticated criminals used to blackmail the banks and commercial organizations that now depended utterly upon the efficient operation of their computer systems. On being warned that their data banks would be erased automatically at a certain time, unless they transferred a few megadollars to some anonymous offshore number, most victims decided not to risk possibly irreparable disaster. They paid up quietly, often – to avoid public or even private embarrassment – without notifying the police.

This understandable desire for privacy made it easy for the network highwaymen to conduct their electronic hold-ups: even when they were caught, they were treated gently by legal systems which did not know how to handle such novel crimes – and, after all, they had not really *hurt* any-one, had they? Indeed, after they had served their brief sentences, many of the perpetrators were quietly hired by their victims, on the old principle that poachers make the best game-keepers.

These computer criminals were driven purely by greed, and certainly did not wish to destroy the organizations they preyed upon: no sensible parasite kills its host. But there were other, and much more dangerous, enemies of society at work . . .

Usually, they were maladjusted individuals – typically adolescent males – working entirely alone, and of course in complete secrecy. Their aim was to create programs which would simply create havoc and confusion, when they had been spread over the planet by the world-wide cable and radio networks, or on physical carriers such as diskettes and CD ROMS. Then they would enjoy the resulting chaos, basking in the sense of power it gave their pitiful psyches.

Sometimes, these perverted geniuses were discovered and adopted by national intelligence agencies for their own secretive purposes – usually, to break into the data banks of their rivals. This was a fairly harmless line of employment, as the organizations concerned did at least have some sense of civic responsibility.

Not so the apocalyptic sects, who were delighted to discover this new armoury, holding weapons far more effective, and more easily disseminated, than gas or germs. And much more difficult to counter, since they could be broadcast instantaneously to millions of offices and homes.

The collapse of the New York-Havana Bank in 2005, the launching of Indian nuclear missiles in 2007 (luckily with their warheads unactivated), the shutdown of Pan-European Air Traffic Control in 2008, the paralysis of the North American telephone network in that same year – all these were cult-inspired rehearsals for Doomsday. Thanks to brilliant feats of counterintelligence by normally uncooperative, and even warring, national agencies, this menace was slowly brought under control.

At least, so it was generally believed: there had been no serious attacks at the very foundations of society for several hundred years. One of the chief weapons of victory had been the Braincap – though there were some who believed that this achievement had been bought at too great a cost.

Though arguments over the freedom of the Individual versus the duties of the State were old when Plato and Aristotle attempted to codify them, and would probably continue until the end of time, some consensus had been reached in the Third Millennium. It was generally agreed that Communism was the most perfect form of government; unfortunately it had been demonstrated – at the cost of some hundreds of millions of lives – that it was only applicable to social insects, Robots Class II, and similar restricted categories. For imperfect human beings, the least-worst answer was Demosocracy, frequently defined as 'individual greed, moderated by an efficient but not *too* zealous government'.

Soon after the Braincap came into general use, some highly intelligent – and maximally zealous – bureaucrats realized that it had a unique potential as an early-warning system. During the setting-up process, when the new wearer was being mentally 'calibrated' it was possible to detect many forms of psychosis before they had a chance of becoming dangerous. Often this suggested the best therapy, but when no cure appeared possible the subject could be electronically tagged – or, in extreme cases, segregated from society. Of course, this mental monitoring could test only those who were fitted with a Braincap – but by the end of the Third Millennium this was as essential for everyday life as the personal telephone had been at its beginning. In fact, anyone who did *not* join the vast majority was automatically suspect, and checked as a potential deviant.

Needless to say, when 'mind-probing', as its critics called it, started coming into general use, there were cries of outrage from civil-rights organizations; one of their most effective slogans was 'Braincap or Braincop?' Slowly – even reluctantly – it was accepted that this form of monitoring was a necessary precaution against far worse evils; and it was no coincidence that with the general improvement in mental health, religious fanaticism also started its rapid decline.

When the long-drawn-out war against the cybernet criminals ended, the victors found themselves owning an embarrassing collection of spoils, all of them utterly incomprehensible to any past conqueror. There were, of course, hundreds of computer viruses, most of them very difficult to detect and kill. And there were some entities – for want of a better name – that were much more terrifying. They were brilliantly invented diseases for which there was no cure – in some cases, not even the *possibility* of a cure . . .

Many of them had been linked to great mathematicians who would have been horrified by this corruption of their discoveries. As it is a human characteristic to belittle a real danger by giving it an absurd name, the designations were often facetious: the Gödel Gremlin, the Mandelbrot Maze, the Combinatorial Catastrophe, the Transfinite Trap, the Conway Conundrum, the Turing Torpedo, the Lorentz Labyrinth, the Boolean Bomb, the Shannon Snare, the Cantor Cataclysm . . .

If any generalization was possible, all these mathematical horrors operated on the same principle. They did not depend for their effectiveness on anything as naïve as memory-erasure or code corruption – on the contrary. Their approach was more subtle; they persuaded their host machine to initiate a program which could not be completed before the end of the universe, or which – the Mandelbrot Maze was the deadliest example – involved a literally infinite series of steps.

A trivial example would be the calculation of Pi, or any

other irrational number. However, even the most stupid electro-optic computer would not fall into such a simple trap: the day had long since passed when mechanical morons would wear out their gears, grinding them to powder as they tried to divide by zero . . .

The challenge to the demon programmers was to convince their targets that the task set them had a definite conclusion that could be reached in a finite time. In the battle of wits between man (seldom woman, despite such role-models as Lady Ada Lovelace, Admiral Grace Hopper and Dr Susan Calvin) and machine, the machine almost invariably lost.

It would have been possible – though in some cases difficult and even risky – to destroy the captured obscenities by ERASE/OVERWRITE commands, but they represented an enormous investment in time and ingenuity which, however misguided, seemed a pity to waste. And, more important, perhaps they should be kept for study, in some secure location, as a safeguard against the time when some evil genius might reinvent and deploy them.

The solution was obvious. The digital demons should be sealed with their chemical and biological counterparts, it was hoped for ever, in the Pico Vault.

37

Operation Damocles

Poole never had much contact with the team who
assembled the weapon everyone hoped would never have
to be used. The operation – ominously, but aptly, named
Damocles – was so highly specialized that he could contribute nothing directly, and he saw enough of the task force
to realize that some of them might almost belong to an
alien species. Indeed, one key member was apparently in
a lunatic asylum – Poole had been surprised to find that
such places still existed – and Chairperson Oconnor sometimes suggested that at least two others should join him.

'Have you ever heard of the Enigma Project?' she
remarked to Poole, after a particularly frustrating session.

When he shook his head, she continued: 'I'm surprised

– it was only a few decades before you were born: I came across it while when I was researching material for Damocles. Very similar problem – in one of your wars, a group of brilliant mathematicians was gathered together, in great secrecy, to break an enemy code . . . incidentally, they built one of the very first real computers, to make the job possible.

'And there's a lovely story – I hope it's true – that reminds me of our own little team. One day the Prime Minister came on a visit of inspection, and afterwards he said to Enigma's Director: "When I told you to leave no stone unturned to get the men you needed, I didn't expect you to take me so literally".'

Presumably all the right stones had been turned for Project Damocles. However, as no one knew whether they were working against a deadline of days, weeks or years, at first it was hard to generate any sense of urgency. The need for secrecy also created problems; since there was no point in spreading alarm throughout the Solar System, not more than fifty people knew of the project. But they were the people who mattered – who could marshal all the forces necessary, and who alone could authorize the opening of the Pico Vault, for the first time in five hundred years.

When Halman reported that the Monolith was receiving messages with increasing frequency, there seemed little doubt that *something* was going to happen. Poole was not the only one who found it hard to sleep in those days, even with the help of the Braincap's anti-insomnia programs. Before he finally did get to sleep, he often wondered if he would wake up again. But at last all the components of the weapon were assembled – a weapon invisible, untouchable – and unimaginable to almost all the warriors who had ever lived.

Nothing could have looked more harmless and innocent than the perfectly standard terabyte memory tablet, used with millions of Braincaps every day. But the fact that it was encased in a massive block of crystalline material, criss-crossed with metal bands, indicated that it was something quite out of the ordinary. Poole received it with reluctance; he wondered if the courier who had been given the awesome task of carrying the Hiroshima atom bomb's core to the Pacific airbase from which it was launched had felt the same way. And yet, if all their fears were justified, his responsibility might be even greater.

And he could not be certain that even the first part of his mission would be successful. Because no circuit could be absolutely secure, Halman had not yet been informed about Project Damocles; Poole would do that when he returned to Ganymede.

Then he could only hope that Halman would be willing to play the role of Trojan Horse – and, perhaps, be destroyed in the process.

38

Pre-emptive Strike

It was strange to be back in the Hotel Grannymede after all these years – strangest of all, because it seemed completely unchanged, despite everything that had happened. Poole was still greeted by the familiar image of Bowman as he walked into the suite named after him: and, as he expected, Bowman/Halman was waiting, looking slightly less substantial than the ancient hologram.

Before they could even exchange greetings, there was an interruption that Poole would have welcomed – at any other time than this. The room vidphone gave its urgent trio of rising notes – also unchanged since his last visit – and an old friend appeared on the screen.

'Frank!' cried Theodore Khan, 'why didn't you tell me

you were coming! When can we meet? Why no video –
someone with you? And who were all those official-looking
types who landed at the same time –'

'*Please* Ted! Yes, I'm sorry – but believe me, I've got very
good reasons – I'll explain later. And I *do* have someone
with me – call you back just as soon as I can. Good-bye!'

As he belatedly gave the 'Do Not Disturb' order, Poole
said apologetically: 'Sorry about that – you know who it
was, of course.'

'Yes – Dr Khan. He often tried to get in touch with me.'

'But you never answered. May I ask why?' Though there
were far more important matters to worry about, Poole
could not resist putting the question.

'Ours was the only channel I wished to keep open. Also,
I was often away. Sometimes for years.'

That was surprising – yet it should not have been. Poole
knew well enough that Halman had been reported in many
places, in many times. Yet – 'away for years'? He might
have visited quite a few star systems – perhaps that was
how he knew about Nova Scorpio, only forty light-years
distant. But he could never have gone all the way to the
Node; there and back would have been a nine-hundred-
year journey.

'How lucky that you were here when we needed you!'

It was very unusual for Halman to hesitate before reply-
ing. There was much longer than the unavoidable three-
second time-lag before he said slowly: 'Are you sure that
it was luck?'

'What do you mean?'

'I do not wish to talk about it, but twice I have – glimpsed
– powers – entities – far superior to the Monoliths, and

perhaps even their makers. We may both have less freedom than we imagine.'

That was indeed a chilling thought; Poole needed a deliberate effort of will to put it aside and concentrate on the immediate problem.

'Let us hope we have enough free-will to do what is necessary. Perhaps this is a foolish question. Does the Monolith know that we are meeting? Could it be – suspicious?'

'It is not capable of such an emotion. It has numerous fault-protection devices, some of which I understand. But that is all.'

'Could it be overhearing us now?'

'I do not believe so.'

I wish that I could be sure it was such a naïve and simple-minded super-genius, thought Poole as he unlocked his briefcase and took out the sealed box containing the tablet. In this low gravity its weight was almost negligible; it was impossible to believe that it might hold the destiny of Mankind.

'There was no way we could be certain of getting a secure circuit to you, so we couldn't go into details. This tablet contains programs which we hope will prevent the Monolith from carrying out any orders which threaten Mankind. There are twenty of the most devastating viruses ever designed on this, most of which have no known antidote; in some cases, it is believed that none is possible. There are five copies of each. We would like you to release them when – and if – you think it is necessary. Dave – Hal – no one has ever been given such a responsibility. But we have no other choice.'

Once again, the reply seemed to take longer than the three-second round trip from Europa.

'If we do this, all the Monolith's functions may cease. We are uncertain what will happen to us then.'

'We have considered that, of course. But by this time, you must surely have many facilities at your command – some of them probably beyond our understanding. I am also sending you a petabyte memory tablet. Ten to the fifteenth bytes is more than sufficient to hold all the memories and experiences of many lifetimes. This will give you one escape route: I suspect you have others.'

'Correct. We will decide which to use at the appropriate time.'

Poole relaxed – as far as was possible in this extraordinary situation. Halman was willing to co-operate: he still had sufficient links with his origins.

'Now, we have to get this tablet to you – physically. Its contents are too dangerous to risk sending over *any* radio or optical channel. I know you possess long-range control of matter: did you not once detonate an orbiting bomb? Could you transport it to Europa? Alternatively, we could send it in an auto-courier, to any point you specify.'

'That would be best: I will collect it in Tsienville. Here are the co-ordinates . . .'

Poole was still slumped in his chair when the Bowman Suite monitor admitted the head of the delegation that had accompanied him from Earth. Whether Colonel Jones was a genuine Colonel – or even if his name was Jones – were minor mysteries which Poole was not really interested in solving; it was sufficient that he was a superb organizer and had handled the mechanics of Operation Damocles with quiet efficiency.

'Well, Frank – it's on its way. Will be landing in one hour, ten minutes. I assume that Halman can take it from there, but I don't understand how he can actually handle – is that the right word? – these tablets.'

'I wondered about that, until someone on the Europa Committee explained it. There's a well-known – though not to me! – theorem stating that any computer can emulate any other computer. So I'm sure that Halman knows exactly what he's doing. He would never have agreed otherwise.'

'I hope you're right,' replied the Colonel. 'If not – well, I don't know what alternative we have.'

There was a gloomy pause, until Poole did his best to relieve the tension.

'By the way, have you heard the local rumour about our visit?'

'Which particular one?'

'That we're a special commission sent here to investigate crime and corruption in this raw frontier township. The Mayor and the Sheriff are supposed to be running scared.'

'How I envy them,' said 'Colonel Jones'. 'Sometimes it's quite a relief to have something trivial to worry about.'

39
Deicide

Like all the inhabitants of Anubis City (population now 56,521), Dr Theodore Khan woke soon after local midnight to the sound of the General Alarm. His first reaction was 'Not another Icequake, for Deus's sake!'

He rushed to the window, shouting 'Open' so loudly that the room did not understand, and he had to repeat the order in a normal voice. The light of Lucifer should have come streaming in, painting the patterns on the floor that so fascinated visitors from Earth, because they never moved even a fraction of a millimetre, no matter how long they waited . . .

That unvarying beam of light was no longer there. As Khan stared in utter disbelief through the huge, transparent

239

bubble of the Anubis Dome, he saw a sky that Ganymede had not known for a thousand years. It was once more ablaze with stars; Lucifer had gone.

And then, as he explored the forgotten constellations, Kahn noticed something even more terrifying. Where Lucifer *should* have been was a tiny disc of absolute blackness, eclipsing the unfamiliar stars.

There was only one possible explanation, Khan told himself numbly. Lucifer has been swallowed by a Black Hole. And it may be our turn next.

On the balcony of the Grannymede Hotel, Poole was watching the same spectacle, but with more complex emotions. Even before the general alarm, his comsec had woken him with a message from Halman.

'It is beginning. We have infected the Monolith. But one – perhaps several – of the viruses have entered our own circuits. We do not know if we will be able to use the memory tablet you have given us. If we succeed, we will meet you in Tsienville.'

Then came the surprising and strangely moving words whose exact emotional content would be debated for generations:

'If we are unable to download, remember us.'

From the room behind him, Poole heard the voice of the Mayor, doing his best to reassure the now sleepless citizens of Anubis. Though he opened with that most terrifying of official statements – 'No cause for alarm' – the Mayor did indeed have words of comfort.

'We don't know what's happening – but Lucifer's still shining normally! I repeat – Lucifer is still shining! We've just received news from the interorbit shuttle *Alcyone*, which left for Callisto half an hour ago. Here's their view –'

Poole left the balcony and rushed into his room just in time to see Lucifer blaze reassuringly on the vidscreen.

'What's happened,' the Mayor continued breathlessly, 'is that something has caused a temporary eclipse – we'll zoom in to look at it . . . Callisto Observatory, come in please . . .'

How does he know it's 'temporary'? thought Poole, as he waited for the next image to come up on the screen.

Lucifer vanished, to be replaced by a field of stars. At the same time, the Mayor faded out and another voice took over:

'– two-metre telescope, but almost any instrument will do. It's a disc of perfectly black material, just over ten thousand kilometres across, so thin it shows no visible thickness. And it's placed exactly – obviously *deliberately* – to block Ganymede from receiving any light.

'We'll zoom in to see if it shows any details, though I rather doubt it . . .'

From the viewpoint of Callisto, the occulting disc was foreshortened into an oval, twice as long as it was wide. It expanded until it completely filled the screen; thereafter, it was impossible to tell whether the image was being zoomed, as it showed no structure whatsoever.

'As I thought – there's nothing to see. Let's pan over to the edge of the thing . . .'

Again there was no sense of motion, until a field of stars suddenly appeared, sharply defined by the curving edge of the world-sized disc. It was exactly as if they were look-ing past the horizon of an airless, perfectly smooth planet.

No, it was not perfectly smooth . . .

'That's interesting,' commented the astronomer, who until now had sounded remarkably matter-of-fact, as if this sort of thing was an everyday occurrence. 'The edge looks jagged – but in a very regular fashion – like a saw-blade . . .'

A circular saw Poole muttered under his breath. Is it going to carve us up? Don't be ridiculous . . .

'This is as close as we can get before diffraction spoils the image – we'll process it later and get much better detail.'

The magnification was now so great that all trace of the disc's circularity had vanished. Across the vidscreen was a black band, serrated along its edge with triangles so identical that Poole found it hard to avoid the ominous analogy of a saw-blade. Yet something else was nagging at the back of his mind . . .

Like everyone else on Ganymede, he watched the infinitely more distant stars drifting in and out of those geometrically perfect valleys. Very probably, many others jumped to the same conclusion even before he did.

If you attempt to make a disc out of rectangular blocks – whether their proportions are 1:4:9 or any other – it cannot possibly have a smooth edge. Of course, you can make it as near a perfect circle as you like, by using smaller and smaller blocks. Yet why go to that trouble, if you merely wanted to build a screen large enough to eclipse a sun?

The Mayor was right; the eclipse was indeed temporary. But its ending was the precise opposite of a solar one.

First light broke through at the exact *centre*, not in the usual necklace of Bailey's Beads along the very edge. Jagged lines radiated from a dazzling pinhole – and now, under the highest magnification, the structure of the disc was being revealed. It was composed of millions of

identical rectangles, perhaps the same size as the Great
Wall of Europa. And now they were splitting apart: it was
as if a gigantic jigsaw puzzle was being dismantled.

Its perpetual, but now briefly interrupted, daylight was
slowly returning to Ganymede, as the disc fragmented and
the rays of Lucifer poured through the widening gaps.
Now the components themselves were evaporating, almost
as if they needed the reinforcement of each other's contact
to maintain reality.

Although it seemed like hours to the anxious watchers
in Anubis City, the whole event lasted for less than fifteen
minutes. Not until it was all over did anyone pay attention
to Europa itself.

The Great Wall was gone: and it was almost an hour
before the news came from Earth, Mars and Moon that the
Sun itself had appeared to flicker for a few seconds, before
resuming business as usual.

It had been a highly selective set of eclipses, obviously
targeted at humankind. Nowhere else in the Solar System
would anything have been noticed.

In the general excitement, it was a little longer before
the world realized that TMA ZERO and TMA ONE had
both vanished, leaving only their four-million-year-old
imprints on Tycho and Africa.

It was the first time the Europs could ever have met
humans, but they seemed neither alarmed nor surprised by
the huge creatures moving among them at such lightning
speed. Of course, it was not too easy to interpret the
emotional state of something that looked like a small,
leafless bush, with no obvious sense organs or means of

communication. But if they were frightened by the arrival of *Alcyone*, and the emergence of its passengers, they would surely have remained hiding in their igloos.

As Frank Poole, slightly encumbered by his protective suit and the gift of shining copper wire he was carrying, walked into the untidy suburbs of Tsienville, he wondered what the Europs thought of recent events. For them, there had been no eclipse of Lucifer, but the disappearance of the Great Wall must surely have been a shock. It had stood there for a thousand years, as a shield and doubtless much more; then, abruptly, it was gone, as if it had never been . . .

The petabyte tablet was waiting for him, with a group of Europs standing around it, demonstrating the first sign of curiosity that Poole had ever observed in them. He wondered if Halman had somehow told them to watch over this gift from space, until he came to collect it.

And to take it back, since it now contained not only a sleeping friend but terrors which some future age might exorcise, to the only place where it could be safely stored.

Midnight: Pico

It would be hard, Poole thought, to imagine a more peaceful scene – especially after the trauma of the last weeks. The slanting rays of a nearly full Earth revealed all the subtle details of the waterless Sea of Rains – not obliterating them, as the incandescent fury of the Sun would do.

The small convoy of mooncars was arranged in a semicircle a hundred metres from the inconspicuous opening at the base of Pico that was the entrance to the Vault. From this viewpoint, Poole could see that the mountain did not live up to the name that the early astronomers, misled by its pointed shadow, had given to it. It was more like a rounded hill than a sharp peak, and he could well believe that one of the local pastimes was bicycle-riding to the summit. Until now, none of those sportsmen and -women could have guessed at the secret hidden beneath their wheels: he hoped that the sinister knowledge would not discourage their healthy exercise.

An hour ago, with a sense of mingled sadness and triumph, he had handed over the tablet he had brought – never letting it out of his sight – from Ganymede directly to the Moon.

'Good-bye, old friends,' he had murmured. 'You've done well. Perhaps some future generation will reawaken you. But on the whole – I rather hope not.'

He could imagine, all too clearly, one desperate reason why Halman's knowledge might be needed again. By now, surely, some message was on its way to that unknown control centre, bearing the news that its servant on Europa no longer existed. With reasonable luck, it would take 950 years, give or take a few, before any response could be expected.

Poole had often cursed Einstein in the past; now he blessed him. Even the powers behind the Monoliths, it now appeared certain, could not spread their influence faster than the speed of light. So the human race should have almost a millennium to prepare for the next encounter – if there was to be one. Perhaps by that time, it would be better prepared.

Something was emerging from the tunnel – the track-mounted, semi-humanoid robot that had carried the tablet into the Vault. It was almost comic to see a machine enclosed in the kind of isolation suit used as protection against deadly germs – and here on the airless Moon! But no one was taking any chances, however unlikely they might seem. After all, the robot had moved among those carefully sequestered nightmares, and although according to its video cameras everything appeared in order, there was always a chance that some vial had leaked, or some canister's seal had broken. The Moon was a very stable environment, but during the centuries it had known many quakes and meteor impacts.

The robot came to a halt fifty metres outside the tunnel. Slowly, the massive plug that sealed the Vault swung back into place, and began to rotate in its threads, like a giant bolt being screwed into the mountain.

'All not wearing dark glasses, please close your eyes or look away from the robot!' said an urgent voice over the mooncar radio. Poole twisted round in his seat, just in time to see an explosion of light on the roof of the vehicle. When he turned back to look at Pico, all that was left of the robot was a heap of glowing slag; even to someone who had spent much of his life surrounded by vacuum, it seemed altogether wrong that tendrils of smoke were not slowly spiralling up from it.

'Sterilization completed,' said the voice of the Mission Controller. 'Thank you, everybody. Now returning to Plato City.'

How ironic – that the human race had been saved by the skilful deployment of its own insanities! What moral, Poole wondered, could one possibly draw from that?

He looked back at the beautiful blue Earth, huddling beneath its tattered blanket of clouds for protection against the cold of space. Up there, a few weeks from now, he hoped to cradle his first grandson in his arms.

Whatever godlike powers and principalities lurked

beyond the stars, Poole reminded himself, for ordinary humans only two things were important – Love and Death.

His body had not yet aged a hundred years: he still had plenty of time for both.

EPILOGUE

'Their little universe is very young, and its god is still a child. But it is too soon to judge them; when We return in the Last Days, We will consider what should be saved.'

SOURCES AND
ACKNOWLEDGEMENTS

SOURCES

Chapter 1: The Kuiper Belt
For a description of Captain Chandler's hunting ground, discovered as recently as 1992, see 'The Kuiper Belt' by Jane X. Luu and David C. Jewitt (*Scientific American*, May 1996)

Chapter 3: Rehabilitation
I believed that I had invented the palm-to-palm transfer of information, so it was mortifying to discover that Nicholas (*Being Digital*) Negroponte (Hodder and Stoughton, 1995) and his MIT Media Lab have been working on the idea for years . . .

Chapter 4: Star City
The concept of a 'ring around the world' in the geostationary orbit (GEO), linked to the Earth by towers at the Equator, may seem utterly fantastic but in fact has a firm scientific basis. It is an obvious extension of the 'space elevator' invented by the St Petersburg engineer Yuri Artsutanov, whom I had the pleasure of meeting in 1982, when his city had a different name.

Yuri pointed out that it was theoretically possible to lay a cable between the Earth and a satellite hovering over the same spot on the Equator – which it does when placed in the GEO, home of most of today's communications satellites. From this beginning, a space elevator (or in Yuri's picturesque phrase, 'cosmic funicular') could be established, and payloads could be carried up to the GEO purely by electrical energy. Rocket propulsion would be needed only for the remainder of the journey.

In addition to avoiding the danger, noise and environmental hazards of rocketry, the space elevator would make possible quite astonishing reductions in the cost of all space missions. Electricity is cheap, and it would require only about a hundred dollars' worth to take one person to orbit. And the round trip would cost about *ten* dollars, as most of the energy would be recovered on the downward journey! (Of course, catering and inflight movies would put up the price of the ticket. Would you believe a thousand dollars to GEO and back?)

The theory is impeccable: but does any material exist with sufficient tensile strength to hang all the way down to the Equator from an altitude of 36,000 kilometres, with enough margin left over to raise useful payloads? When Yuri wrote his paper, only one substance met these rather stringent specifications – crystalline carbon, better known as diamond. Unfortunately, the necessary megaton quantities are not readily available on the open market, though in *2061: Odyssey Three* I gave reasons for thinking that they might exist at the core of Jupiter. In *The Fountains of Paradise* I suggested a more accessible source – orbiting factories where diamonds might be grown under zero-gravity conditions.

The first 'small step' towards the space elevator was attempted in August 1992 on the Shuttle *Atlantis*, when one experiment involved the release – and retrieval – of a payload on a 21-kilometre-long tether. Unfortunately the playing-out mechanism jammed after only a few hundred metres.

I was very flattered when the *Atlantis* crew produced *The Fountains of Paradise* during their orbital press conference, and Mission Specialist Jeffrey Hoffman sent me the autographed copy on their return to Earth.

The second tether experiment, in February 1996, was slightly more successful: the payload was indeed deployed to its full distance, but during retrieval the cable was severed, owing to an electrical discharge caused by faulty insulation. This may have been a lucky accident – perhaps the equivalent of a blown fuse: I cannot help recalling that some of Ben Franklin's contemporaries were killed when they attempted to repeat his famous – and risky – experiment of flying a kite during a thunderstorm.

Apart from possible dangers, playing-out tethered payloads

from the Shuttle appears rather like fly-fishing: is not as easy as it looks. But eventually the final 'giant leap' will be made – all the way down to the Equator.

Meanwhile, the discovery of the *third* form of carbon, buckminsterfullerene (C60) has made the concept of the space elevator much more plausible. In 1990 a group of chemists at Rice University, Houston, produced a tubular form of C60 – which has far greater tensile strength than diamond. The group's leader, Dr Smalley, even went so far as to claim it was the strongest material *that could ever exist* – and added that it would make possible the construction of the space elevator.

(Stop Press News: I am delighted to know that Dr Smalley has shared the 1996 Nobel Prize in Chemistry for this work.)

And now for a truly amazing coincidence – one so eerie that it makes me wonder Who Is In Charge.

Buckminster Fuller died in 1983, so never lived to see the discovery of the 'buckyballs' and 'buckytubes' which have given him much greater posthumous fame. During one of the last of his many world trips, I had the pleasure of flying him and his wife Anne around Sri Lanka, and showed them some of the locations featured in *The Fountains of Paradise*. Shortly afterwards, I made a recording from the novel on a 12" (remember them?) LP record (Caedmon TC 1606) and Bucky was kind enough to write the sleeve notes. They ended with a surprising revelation, which may well have triggered my own thinking about 'Star City':

'In 1951 I designed a free-floating tensegrity ring-bridge to be installed way out from and around the Earth's equator. Within this "halo" bridge, the Earth would continue its spinning while the circular bridge would revolve at its own rate. I foresaw Earthian traffic vertically ascending to the bridge, revolving and descending at preferred Earth loci.'

I have no doubt that, if the human race decides to make such an investment (a trivial one, according to some estimates of economic growth), 'Star City' could be constructed. In addition to providing new styles of living, and giving visitors from low-gravity worlds like Mars and the Moon better access to the Home Planet, it would eliminate all rocketry from the Earth's surface and relegate it to deep space, where it belongs. (Though I hope there would be occasional anniversary re-enactments at Cape Kennedy, to bring back the excitement of the pioneering days.)

Almost certainly most of the City would be empty scaffolding, and only a very small fraction would be occupied or used for scientific or technological purposes. After all, each of the Towers would be the equivalent of a *ten-million-floor* skyscraper – and the circumference of the ring around the geostationary orbit would be more than half the distance to the Moon! Many times the entire population of the human race could be housed in such a volume of space, if it was all enclosed. (This would pose some interesting logistics problems, which I am content to leave as 'an exercise for the student'.)

Chapter 5: Education

I was astonished to read in a newspaper on 19 July 1996 that Dr Chris Winter, head of British Telecom's Artificial Life Team, believes that the information and storage device I described in this chapter could be developed within *30 years*! (In my 1956 novel *The City and the Stars* I put it more than a billion years in the future . . . obviously a serious failure of imagination.) Dr Winter states that it would allow us to 'recreate a person physically, emotionally and spiritually', and estimates that the memory requirements would be about 10 terabytes (10e13 bytes), two orders of magnitude less than the petabyte (10e15 bytes) I suggest.

And I wish I'd thought of Dr Winter's name for this device, which will certainly start some fierce debates in ecclesiastical circles: the 'Soul Catcher' . . . For its application to interstellar travel, see following note on Chapter 9.

For an excellent history of the 'Beanstalk' concept (as well as many other even farther-out ideas such as anti-gravity and space-warps) see Robert L. Forward's *Indistinguishable From Magic* (Baen 1995).

Chapter 7: Infinite Energy

If the inconceivable energy of the Zero Point Field (sometimes referred to as 'quantum fluctuations' or 'vacuum energy') can ever

be tapped, the impact upon our civilization will be incalculable.
All present sources of power – oil, coal, nuclear, hydro, solar –
would become obsolete, and so would many of our fears about
environmental pollution. They would all be wrapped up in one
big worry – heat pollution. All energy eventually degrades to
heat, and if everyone had a few million kilowatts to play with,
this planet would soon be heading the way of Venus – several
hundred degrees in the shade.

However, there is a bright side to the picture: there may be no
other way of averting the next Ice Age, which otherwise is inevitable. ('Civilization is an interval between Ice Ages' – Will Durant:
The Story of Civilization, Fine Communications, US, 1993)

Even as I write this, many competent engineers, in laboratories
all over the world, claim to be tapping this new energy source.
Some idea of its magnitude is contained in a famous remark by
the physicist Richard Feynman, to the effect that the energy in a
coffee-mug's volume (any such volume, anywhere!) is *enough to
boil all the oceans of the world*. This, surely, is a thought to give one
pause. By comparison, nuclear energy looks as feeble as a damp
match.

And how many supernovae, I wonder, really are industrial
accidents?

Chapter 9: Skyland

One of the main problems of getting around in Star City would
be caused by the sheer distances involved: if you wanted to visit
a friend in the next Tower (and communications will never completely replace contact, despite all advances in Virtual Reality) it
could be the equivalent of a trip to the Moon. Even with the
fastest elevators this would involve days rather than hours, or
else accelerations quite unacceptable to people who had adapted
to low-gravity life.

The concept of an 'inertialess drive' – i.e. a propulsion system that
acts on every atom of a body so that no strains are produced when
it accelerates – was probably invented by the master of the 'Space
Opera', E.E. Smith, in the 1930s. It is not as improbable as it sounds
– because a gravitational field acts in precisely this manner.

If you fall freely near the Earth (neglecting the effects of air resistance) you will increase speed by just under ten metres per second, every second. Yet you will feel weightless – there will be no sense of acceleration, even though your velocity is increasing by one kilometre a second, every minute and a half!

And this would still be true if you were falling in Jupiter's gravity (just over two-and-a-half times Earth's) or even the enormously more powerful field of a white dwarf or neutron star (millions or *billions* of times greater). You would feel nothing, even if you had approached the velocity of light from a standing start in a matter of minutes. However, if you were foolish enough to get within a few radii of the attracting object, its field would no longer be uniform over the whole length of your body, and tidal forces would soon tear you to pieces. For further details, see my deplorable but accurately-titled short story 'Neutron Tide' (in *The Wind from the Sun*).

An 'inertialess drive', which would act exactly like a controllable gravity field, had never been discussed seriously outside the pages of science fiction until very recently. But in 1994 three American physicists did exactly this, developing some ideas of the great Russian physicist Andrei Sakharov.

'Inertia as a Zero-Point Field Lorentz Force' by B. Haisch, A. Rueda & H. E. Puthoff (*Physics Review A*, February 1994) may one day be regarded as a landmark paper, and for the purposes of fiction I have made it so. It addresses a problem so fundamental that it is normally taken for granted, with a that's-just-the-way-the-universe-is-made shrug of the shoulders.

The question HR&P asked is: 'What gives an object mass (or inertia) so that it requires an effort to start it moving, and exactly the same effort to restore it to its original state?'

Their provisional answer depends on the astonishing – and outside the physicists' ivory towers – little-known fact that so-called 'empty' space is actually a cauldron of seething energies – the Zero-Point Field (see note above). HR&P suggest that both inertia *and gravitation* are electromagnetic phenomena, resulting from interaction with this field.

There have been countless attempts, going all the way back to Faraday, to link gravity and magnetism, and although many experimenters have claimed success, none of their results has ever been verified. However, if HR&P's theory can be proved, it opens up the prospect – however remote – of anti-gravity, 'space drives' and the even more fantastic possibility of controlling inertia. This could lead to some interesting situations: if you gave someone the gentlest touch, they would promptly disappear at thousands of kilometres an hour, until they bounced off the other side of the room a fraction of a millisecond later. The good news is that traffic accidents would be virtually impossible; automobiles – and passengers – could collide harmlessly at any speed.

(And you think that today's life-styles are already too hectic?)

The 'weightlessness' which we now take for granted in space missions – and which millions of tourists will be enjoying in the next century – would have seemed like magic to our grandparents. But the abolition – or merely the reduction – of inertia is quite another matter, and may be completely impossible.* But it's a nice thought, for it could provide the equivalent of 'teleportation': you could travel anywhere (at least on Earth) almost instantaneously. Frankly, I don't know how 'Star City' could manage without it . . .

One of the assumptions I have made in this novel is that Einstein is correct, and that no signal – or object – can exceed the speed of light. A number of highly mathematical papers have recently appeared suggesting that, as countless science-fiction writers have taken for granted, galactic hitch-hikers may not have to suffer this annoying disability.

On the whole, I hope they are right – but there seems one fundamental objection. If FTL is possible, where *are* all those hitch-hikers – or at least the well-heeled tourists?

One answer is that no sensible ETs will ever build interstellar vehicles, for precisely the same reason that we have never

---

* As every Trekker knows, the Starship *Enterprise* uses 'inertial dampers' to solve this particular problem. When asked how these work, the series' technical advisor gave the only possible answer: 'Very well, thank you.' (See *The Physics of Star Trek* by Lawrence Krauss: HarperCollins, 1996.)

developed coal-fuelled airships: there are much better ways of doing the job.

The surprisingly small number of 'bits' required to define a human being, or to store all the information one could possibly acquire in a lifetime, is discussed in 'Machine Intelligence, the Cost of Interstellar Travel and Fermi's Paradox' by Louis K. Scheffer (*Quarterly Journal of the Royal Astronomical Society*, Vol. 35, No. 2, June 1994: pp. 157–75). This paper (surely the most mind-stretching that the staid *QJRAS* has published in its entire career!) estimates that the total mental state of a 100-year-old human with a perfect memory could be represented by 10 to the 15th bits (one petabit). Even today's optical fibres could transmit this amount of information in a matter of minutes.

My suggestion that a *Star Trek* transporter would still be unavailable in 3001 may therefore appear ludicrously short-sighted a mere century from now* and the present lack of inter-stellar tourists is simply due to the fact that no receiving equipment has yet been set up on Earth. Perhaps it's already on its way by slow-boat . . .

Chapter 15: Falcon

It gives me particular pleasure to pay this tribute to the crew of Apollo 15. On their return from the Moon they sent me the beauti-ful relief map of *Falcon*'s landing site, which now has pride of place in my office. It shows the routes taken by the Lunar Rover during its three excursions, one of which skirted Earthlight Crater. The map bears the inscription: 'To Arthur Clarke from the crew of Apollo 15 with many thanks for your visions of space. Dave Scott, Al Worden, Jim Irwin.' In return, I have now dedicated *Earthlight* (which, written in 1953, was set in the territory the Rover was to drive over in 1971): 'To Dave Scott and Jim Irwin,

---

* However, for a diametrically opposing view, see the above-mentioned *Physics of Star Trek*.

the first men to enter this land, and to Al Worden, who watched over them from orbit.'

After covering the Apollo 15 landing in the CBS studio with Walter Cronkite and Wally Schirra, I flew to Mission Control to watch the re-entry and splashdown. I was sitting beside Al Worden's little daughter when she was the first to notice that one of the capsule's three parachutes had failed to deploy. It was a tense moment, but luckily the remaining two were quite adequate for the job.

Chapter 16: Asteroid 7794

See Chapter 18 of *2001: A Space Odyssey* for the description of the probe's impact. Precisely such an experiment is now being planned for the forthcoming Clementine 2 mission.

I am a little embarrassed to see that in my first *Space Odyssey* the discovery of Asteroid 7794 was attributed to the Lunar Observatory – in 1997! Well, I'll move it to 2017 – in time for my 100th birthday.

Just a few hours after writing the above, I was delighted to learn that Asteroid 4923 (1981 EO27), discovered by S. J. Bus at Siding Spring, Australia, on 2 March 1981, has been named Clarke, partly in recognition of Project Spaceguard (see *Rendezvous with Rama* and *The Hammer of God*). I was informed, with profound apologies, that owing to an unfortunate oversight Number 2001 was no longer available, having been allocated to somebody named A. Einstein. Excuses, excuses . . .

But I was very pleased to learn that Asteroid 5020, discovered on the same day as 4923, has been named Asimov – though saddened by the fact that my old friend could never know.

Chapter 17: Ganymede

As explained in the Valediction, and in the Author's Notes to *2010 Odyssey Two* and *2061 Odyssey Three*, I had hoped that the ambitious Galileo Mission to Jupiter and its moons would by now have given us much more detailed knowledge – as well as stunning close-ups – of these strange worlds.

Well, after many delays, Galileo reached its first objective –

Jupiter itself – and is performing admirably. But, alas, there is a problem – for some reason, the main antenna never unfolded. This means that images have to be sent back via a low-gain antenna, at an agonizingly slow rate. Although miracles of onboard computer reprogramming have been done to compensate for this, it will still require hours to receive information that should have been sent in minutes.

So we must be patient – and I was in the tantalizing position of exploring Ganymede in fiction just before Galileo started to do so in reality, on 27 June 1996.

On 11 July 1996, just two days before finishing this book, I downloaded the first images from JPL; luckily nothing – so far! – contradicts my descriptions. But if the current vistas of cratered ice-fields suddenly give way to palm trees and tropical beaches – or, worse still, YANKEE GO HOME signs, I'll be in real trouble . . .

I am particularly looking forward to close-ups of 'Ganymede City' (Chapter 17). This striking formation is exactly as I described it – though I hesitated to do so for fear that my 'discovery' might be front-paged by the *National Prevaricator*. To my eyes it appears considerably more artificial than the notorious 'Mars Face' and its surroundings. And if its streets and avenues are ten kilometres wide – so what? Perhaps the Medes were BIG . . .

The city will be found on the NASA *Voyager* images 20637.02 and 20637.29, or more conveniently in Figure 23.8 of John H. Rogers's monumental *The Giant Planet Jupiter* (Cambridge University Press, 1995).

Chapter 19: The Madness of Mankind
For visual evidence supporting Khan's startling assertion that most of mankind has been at least partially insane, see Episode 22, 'Meeting Mary', in my television series *Arthur C. Clarke's Mysterious Universe*. And bear in mind that Christians represent only a very small subset of our species: far greater numbers of devotees than have ever worshipped the Virgin Mary have given equal reverence to such totally incompatible divinities as Rama, Kali, Siva, Thor, Wotan, Jupiter, Osiris, etc. etc. . . .

The most striking – and pitiful – example of a brilliant man whose beliefs turned him into a raving lunatic is that of Conan Doyle. Despite endless exposures of his favourite psychics as frauds, his faith in them remained unshaken. And the creator of Sherlock Holmes even tried to convince the great magician Harry Houdini that he 'dematerialized' himself to perform his feats of escapology – often based on tricks which, as Dr Watson was fond of saying, were 'absurdly simple'. (See the essay 'The Irrelevance of Conan Doyle' in Martin Gardner's *The Night is Large*, St Martin's Press, US, 1996.)

For details of the Inquisition, whose pious atrocities make Pol Pot look positively benign, see Carl Sagan's devastating attack on New Age Nitwittery, *The Demon-Haunted World: Science as a Candle in the Dark* (Headline, 1995). I wish it – and Martin's book – could be made required reading in every high school and college.

At least the US Department of Immigration has taken action against one religion-inspired barbarity. *Time Magazine* ('Milestones', 24 June 1996) reports that asylum *must* now be granted to girls threatened with genital mutilation in their countries of origin.

I had already written this chapter when I came across Anthony Storr's *Feet of Clay: A Study of Gurus* (HarperCollins, 1996), which is a virtual textbook on this depressing subject. It is hard to believe that one holy fraud, by the time the US Marshals belatedly arrested him, had accumulated ninety-three Rolls-Royces! Even worse – eighty-three per cent of his thousands of American dupes had been to college, and thus qualify for my favourite definition of an intellectual: 'Someone who has been educated beyond his/her intelligence.'

Chapter 26: Tsienville

In the 1982 preface to *2010: Odyssey Two*, I explained why I named the Chinese spaceship which landed on Europa after Dr Tsien Hsue-shen, one of the founders of the United States and Chinese rocket programmers. As Iris Chang states in her biography *Thread of the Silkworm* (Basic Books, 1995) 'his life is one of the supreme ironies of the Cold War'.

Born in 1911, Tsien won a scholarship which brought him from

China to the United States in 1935, where he became student and later colleague of the brilliant Hungarian aerodynamicist Theodore von Karman. Later, as first Goddard Professor at the California Institute of Technology, he helped establish the Guggenheim Aeronautical Laboratory – the direct ancestor of Pasadena's famed Jet Propulsion Laboratory.

With top secret clearance, he contributed greatly to American rocket research in the 1950s, but during the hysteria of the McCarthy era was arrested on trumped-up security charges when he attempted to pay a visit to his native China. After many hearings and a prolonged period of arrest, he was finally deported to his homeland – with all his unrivalled knowledge and expertise. As many of his distinguished colleagues affirmed, it was one of the most stupid (as well as most disgraceful) things the United States ever did.

After his expulsion, according to Zhuang Fenggan, Deputy Director, China National Space Administration, Tsien 'started the rocket business from nothing .. Without him, China would have suffered a twenty-year lag in technology.' And a corresponding delay, perhaps, in the deployment of the deadly 'Silkworm' anti-ship missile and the 'Long March' satellite launcher . . .

Shortly after I had completed this novel, the International Academy of Astronautics honoured me with its highest distinction, the von Karman Award – to be given in Beijing! This was an offer I couldn't refuse, especially when I learned that Dr Tsien is now a resident of that city. Unfortunately, when I arrived there I discovered that he was in hospital for observation, and his doctors would not permit visitors.

I am therefore extremely grateful to his personal assistant, Major-General Wang Shouyun, for carrying suitably inscribed copies of 2010 and 2061 to Dr Tsien. In return the General presented me with the massive volume he has edited, Collected Works of H. S. Tsien: 1938–1956 (1991, Science Press, 16, Donghuangcheggen North Street, Beijing 100707). It is a fascinating collection, beginning with numerous collaborations with von Karman on problems in aerodynamics, and ending with solo papers on rockets and satellites. The very last entry, 'Thermonuclear Power Plants' (Jet Propulsion, July 1956) was written while Dr Tsien was still a virtual prisoner of the FBI, and deals with a subject that is even more topical today – though very little progress has been made towards 'a power station utilizing the deuterium fusion reaction'.

Just before I left Beijing on 13 October 1996 I was happy to learn that, despite his current age (85) and disability, Dr Tsien is still pursuing his scientific studies. I sincerely hope that he enjoyed *2010* and *2061*, and look forward to sending him this Final Odyssey as an additional tribute.

Chapter 36: Chamber of Horrors

As the result of a series of Senate Hearings on Computer Security in June 1996, on 15 July 1996 President Clinton signed Executive Order 13010 to deal with 'computer-based attacks on the information or communications components that control critical infrastructures ("cyber threats").' This will set up a task force to counter cyberterrorism, and will have representatives from the CIA, NSA, defense agencies, etc.

Pico, here we come . . .

Since writing the above paragraph, I have been intrigued to learn that the *finale* of the movie *Independence Day*, which I have not yet seen, also involves the use of computer viruses as Trojan horses! I am also informed that its opening is identical to that of *Childhood's End* (1953), and that it contains every known science-fiction cliché since Méliès's *Trip to the Moon* (1903).

I cannot decide whether to congratulate the script-writers on their one stroke of originality – or to accuse them of the transtemporal crime of pre-cognitive plagiarism. In any event, I fear there's nothing I can do to stop John Q. Popcorn thinking that *I* have ripped off the ending of *ID4*.

The following material has been taken – usually with major editing – from the earlier books in the series:

From *2001 A Space Odyssey*: Chapter 18 Through the Asteroids and Chapter 37 Experiment.

From *2010: Odyssey Two*: Chapter 11 Ice and Vacuum; Chapter 36 Fire in the Deep: Chapter 38 Foamscape.

ACKNOWLEDGEMENTS

My thanks to IBM for presenting me with the beautiful little Thinkpad 755CD on which this book was composed. For many years I have been embarrassed by the – totally unfounded – rumour that the name HAL was derived by one-letter displacement from IBM. In an attempt to exorcise this computer-age myth, I even went to the trouble of getting Dr Chandra, HAL's inventor, to deny it in *2010 Odyssey Two*. However, I was recently assured that, far from being annoyed by the association, Big Blue is now quite proud of it. So I will abandon any future attempts to put the record straight – and send my congratulations to all those participating in HAL's 'birthday party' at (of course) the University of Illinois, Urbana, on 12 March 1997.

Rueful gratitude to my Del Rey Books editor, Shelly Shapiro, for ten pages of niggles which, when dealt with, made a vast improvement to the final product. (Yes, I've been an editor myself, and do not suffer from the usual author's conviction that the members of this trade are frustrated butchers.)

Finally, and most important of all: my deepest thanks to my old friend Cyril Gardiner, Chairman of the Galle Face Hotel, for the hospitality of his magnificent (and enormous) personal suite while I was writing this book: he gave me a Tranquillity Base in a time of troubles. I hasten to add that, even though it may not provide such extensive imaginary landscapes, the facilities of the Galle Face are far superior to those offered by the 'Grannymede', and never in my life have I worked in more comfortable surroundings.

Or, for that matter, in more inspirational ones, for a large plaque at the entrance lists more than a hundred of the Heads of State and other distinguished visitors who have been entertained here. They include Yuri Gagarin, the crew of Apollo 12 – the second mission to the Moon's surface – and a fine collection of stage and movie stars: Gregory Peck, Alec Guinness, Noël Coward, Carrie Fisher of *Star Wars* fame . . . As well as Vivien Leigh and Laurence Olivier – both of whom make brief appearances in *2061 Odyssey Three* (Chapter 37). I am honoured to see my name listed among them.

It seems appropriate that a project begun in one famous hotel – New York's Chelsea, that hotbed of genuine and imitation genius – should be concluded in another, half a world away. But it's strange to hear the monsoon-lashed Indian Ocean roaring just a few yards outside my window, instead of the traffic along far-off and fondly remembered 23rd Street.

IN MEMORIAM: 18 SEPTEMBER 1996

It was with the deepest regret that I heard – literally while editing this acknowledgements – that Cyril Gardiner died a few hours ago.

It is some consolation to know that he had already seen the above tribute, and was delighted with it.

VALEDICTION

'Never explain, never apologize' may be excellent advice for politicians, Hollywood moguls and business tycoons, but an author should treat his readers with more consideration. So, though I have no intention of apologizing for anything, perhaps the complicated genesis of the Odyssey Quartet requires a little explaining.

It all began at Christmas 1948 – yes, 1948! – with a 4,000-word short story which I wrote for a contest sponsored by the British Broadcasting Corporation. 'The Sentinel' described the discovery of a small pyramid on the Moon, set there by some alien civilization to await the emergence of mankind as a planet-faring species. Until then, it was implied, we would be too primitive to be of any interest.* The BBC rejected my modest effort, and it was not published until almost three years later in the one-and-only (Spring 1951) issue of *10 Story Fantasy* – a magazine which, as the invaluable *Encyclopaedia of Science Fiction* wryly comments, is 'primarily remembered for its poor arithmetic (there were 13 stories)'.

'The Sentinel' remained in limbo for more than a decade, until Stanley Kubrick contacted me in the spring of 1964 and asked if I had any ideas for the 'proverbial' (i.e. still non-existent) 'good science-fiction movie'. During the course of our many brainstorming sessions, as recounted in *The Lost Worlds of 2001* (Sidgwick and Jackson, 1972) we decided that the patient watcher on

---

* The search for alien artefacts in the Solar System should be a perfectly legitimate branch of science ('exo-archaeology'?). Unfortunately, it has been largely discredited by claims that such evidence has already been found – and has been deliberately suppressed by NASA! It is incredible that anyone would believe such nonsense: far more likely that the space agency would deliberately fake ET artefacts – to solve its budget problems! (Over to you, NASA Administrators . . .)

the Moon might provide a good starting point for our story. Eventually it did much more than that, as somewhere during production the pyramid evolved into the now famous black monolith.

To put the Odyssey series in perspective, it must be remembered that when Stanley and I started planning what we privately called 'How the Solar System was Won' the Space Age was barely seven years old, and no human had travelled more than a hundred kilometres from the home planet. Although President Kennedy had announced that the United States intended to go to the Moon 'in this decade', to most people that must still have seemed like a far-off dream. When filming started just west of London* on a freezing 29 December 1965, we did not even know what the lunar surface looked like at close quarters. There were still fears that the first word uttered by an emerging astronaut would be 'Help!' as he disappeared into a talcum-power-like layer of moondust. On the whole, we guessed fairly well: only the fact that our lunar landscapes are more jagged than the real ones – smoothed by aeons of sand-blasting by meteoric dust – reveals that *2001* was made in the pre-Apollo era.

Today, of course, it seems ludicrous that we could have imagined giant space-stations, orbiting Hilton Hotels, and expeditions to Jupiter as early as 2001. It is now difficult to realize that back in the 1960s there were serious plans for permanent Moon bases and Mars landings – by 1990! Indeed, in the CBS studio, immediately after the Apollo 11 launch, I heard the Vice-President of the United States proclaim exuberantly: 'Now we must go to Mars!'

As it turned out, *he* was lucky not to go to prison. That scandal, plus Vietnam and Watergate, is one of the reasons why these optimistic scenarios never materialized.

When the movie and book of *2001 A Space Odyssey* made their appearance in 1968, the possibility of a sequel had never crossed my mind. But in 1979 a mission to Jupiter really did take place,

* At Shepperton, destroyed by the Martians in one of the most dramatic scenes in Wells's masterpiece, *The War of the Worlds.*

and we obtained our first close-ups of the giant planet and its astonishing family of moons.

The Voyager space-probes* were, of course, unmanned, but the images they sent back made real – and totally unexpected – worlds from what had hitherto been merely points of light in the most powerful telescopes. The continually erupting sulphur volcanoes of Io, the multiply-impacted face of Callisto, the weirdly contoured landscape of Ganymede – it was almost as if we had discovered a whole new Solar System. The temptation to explore it was irresistible; hence *2010 Odyssey Two*, which also gave me the opportunity to find out what happened to David Bowman, after he had awakened in that enigmatic hotel room.

In 1981, when I started writing the new book, the Cold War was still in progress, and I felt I was going out on a limb – as well as risking criticism – by showing a joint US–Russian mission. I also underlined my hope of future co-operation by dedicating the novel to Nobelist Andrei Sakharov (then still in exile) and Cosmonaut Alexei Leonov – who, when I told him in 'Star Village' that the ship would be named after him, exclaimed with typical ebullience, 'Then it will be a good ship!'

It still seems incredible to me that, when Peter Hyams made his excellent film version in 1983, he was able to use the actual close-ups of the Jovian moons obtained in the Voyager missions (some of them after helpful computer processing by the Jet Propulsion Laboratory, source of the originals). However, far better images were expected from the ambitious *Galileo* mission, due to carry out a detailed survey of the major satellites over a period of many months. Our knowledge of this new territory, previously obtained only from a brief flyby, would be enormously expanded – and I would have no excuse for not writing *Odyssey Three*.

Alas – something tragic on the way to Jupiter. It had been planned to launch *Galileo* from the Space Shuttle in 1986 – but the *Challenger* disaster ruled out that option, and it soon became clear

---

* Which employed a 'slingshot' or 'gravity-assist' manoeuvre by flying close to Jupiter – precisely as was done by *Discovery* in the book version of *2001*.

that we would get no new information from Io and Europa, Ganymede and Callisto, for at least another decade.

I decided not to wait, and the (1985) return of Halley's Comet to the inner Solar System gave me an irresistible theme. Its next appearance in 2061 would be good timing for a third Odyssey, though as I was not certain when I could deliver it I asked my publisher for a rather modest advance. It is with much sadness that I quote the dedication of *2061 Odyssey Three*:

TO THE MEMORY OF
JUDY-LYNN DEL REY,
EDITOR EXTRAORDINARY,

who bought this book for one dollar
– but never knew if she got her money's worth.

Obviously there is no way in which a series of four science-fiction novels, written over a period of more than thirty years of the most breathtaking developments in technology (especially in space exploration) and politics, could be mutually consistent. As I wrote in the introduction to *2061*: 'Just as *2010* was not a direct sequel to *2001*, so this book is a not a linear sequel to *2010*. They must all be considered as variations on the same theme, involving many of the same characters and situations, but not necessarily happening in the same universe.' If you want a good analogy from another medium, listen to what Rachmaninoff and Andrew Lloyd Webber did to the same handful of notes by Paganini.

So this Final Odyssey has discarded many of the elements of its precursors, but developed others – and I hope more important ones – in much greater detail. And if any readers of the earlier books feel disorientated by such transmutations, I hope I can dissuade them from sending me angry letters of denunciation by adapting one of the more endearing remarks of a certain US President: 'It's fiction, stupid!'

And it's all my *own* fiction, in case you hadn't noticed. Though I have much enjoyed my collaborations with Gentry Lee,* Michael

---

* By an unlikely coincidence, Gentry was Chief Engineer on the Galileo and Viking projects. (See Introduction to *Rama II*). It wasn't his fault that the Galileo antenna didn't unfurl ...

Kube-McDowell and the late Mike McQuay – and won't hesitate again to call on the best hired guns in the business if I have future projects that are too big to handle myself – this particular Odyssey had to be a solo job.

So every word is mine: well, almost every word. I must confess that I found Professor Thirugnanasampanthamoorthy (Chapter 35) in the Colombo Telephone Directory; I hope the present owner of that name will not object to the loan. There are also a few borrowings from the great Oxford English Dictionary. And what do you know – to my delighted surprise, I find it uses no fewer than 66 quotations from my own books to illustrate the meaning and use of words!

Dear OED, if you find any useful examples in these pages, please be my guest – again.

I apologize for the number of modest coughs (about ten, at last count) in this Afterword; but the matters to which they drew attention seemed too relevant to be omitted.

Finally, I would like to assure my many Buddhist, Christian, Hindu, Jewish and Muslim friends that I am sincerely happy that the religion which Chance has given you has contributed to your peace of mind (and often, as Western medical science now reluctantly admits, to your physical well-being).

Perhaps it is better to be un-sane and happy, than sane and un-happy. But it is best of all to be sane *and* happy.

Whether our descendants can achieve that goal will be the greatest challenge of the future. Indeed, it may well decide whether we *have* any future.

Arthur C. Clarke
Colombo, Sri Lanka
19 September 1996

The Songs of
Distant Earth

For Tamara and Cherene,
Valerie and Hector
– for love and loyalty

Contents

IV KRAKAN

V THE BOUNTY SYNDROME

VI THE FORESTS OF THE SEA

VII   AS THE SPARKS FLY UPWARD

VIII   THE SONGS OF DISTANT EARTH

IX   SAGAN 2

Nowhere in all space or on a thousand worlds will there be men to share our loneliness. There may be wisdom; there may be power; somewhere across space great instruments ... may stare vainly at our floating cloud wrack, their owners yearning as we yearn. Nevertheless, in the nature of life and in the principles of evolution we have had our answer. Of men elsewhere, and beyond, there will be none forever ...

Loren Eiseley, *The Immense Journey* (1957)

I have written a wicked book, and feel spotless as the lamb.

Melville to Hawthorne (1851)

Author's Note

This novel is based on an idea developed almost thirty years ago in a short story of the same name (now in my collection *The Other Side of the Sky*). However, this version was directly – and *negatively* – inspired by the recent rash of space-operas on TV and movie screen. (Query: what is the opposite of inspiration – expiration?)

Please do not misunderstand me: I have enormously enjoyed the best of *Star Trek* and the Lucas/Spielberg epics, to mention only the most famous examples of the *genre*. But these works are fantasy, not science fiction in the strict meaning of the term. It now seems almost certain that in the real universe we may never exceed the velocity of light. Even the very closest star systems will always be decades or centuries apart; no Warp Six will ever get you from one episode to another in time for next week's instalment. The great Producer in the Sky did not arrange his programme planning that way.

In the last decade, there has also been a significant, and rather surprising, change in the attitude of scientists towards the problem of Extraterrestrial Intelligence. The whole subject did not become respectable (except among dubious characters like the writers of science fiction) until the 1960s: Shklovskii and Sagan's *Intelligent Life in the Universe* (1966) is the landmark here.

But now there has been a backlash. The total failure to find any trace of life in this solar system, or to pick up any of the interstellar radio signals that our great antennae should be easily able to detect, has prompted some scientists to argue 'Perhaps we *are* alone in the Universe ...' Dr Frank Tipler, the best-known exponent of this view, has (doubtless deliberately) outraged the Saganites by giving one of his papers the provocative title 'There Are No Intelligent Extra-Terrestrials'. Carl Sagan *et al* argue (and I agree with them) that it is much too early to jump to such far-reaching conclusions.

Meanwhile, the controversy rages; as has been well said, *either* answer will be awe-inspiring. The question can only be settled by evidence, not by any amount of logic, however plausible. I would like to see the whole debate given a decade or two of benign neglect, while the radioastronomers, like gold-miners panning for dust, quietly sieve through the torrents of noise pouring down from the sky.

This novel is, among other things, my attempt to create a wholly *realistic* piece of fiction on the interstellar theme – just as, in *Prelude to Space* (1951), I used known or foreseeable technology to depict mankind's first voyage beyond the Earth. There is nothing in this book which defies or denies known principles; the only really wild extrapolation is the 'quantum drive', and even this has a highly respectable paternity. (See Acknowledgements.) Should it turn out to be a pipe-dream, there are several possible alternatives; and if we twentieth-century primitives can imagine them, future science will undoubtedly discover something much better.

Arthur C. Clarke
COLOMBO, SRI LANKA
JULY 1985

I
Thalassa

1

The Beach at Tarna

Even before the boat came through the reef, Mirissa could tell that Brant was angry. The tense attitude of his body as he stood at the wheel – the very fact that he had not left the final passage in Kumar's capable hands – showed that something had upset him.

She left the shade of the palm trees and walked slowly down the beach, the wet sand tugging at her feet. When she reached the water's edge, Kumar was already furling the sail. Her 'baby' brother – now almost as tall as she was, and solid muscle – waved to her cheerfully. How often she had wished that Brant shared Kumar's easygoing good nature, which no crisis ever seemed capable of disturbing ...

Brant did not wait for the boat to hit the sand, but jumped into the water while it was still waist-deep and came splashing angrily towards her. He was carrying a twisted mass of metal festooned with broken wires and held it up for her inspection.

'Look!' he cried. 'They've done it again!'

With his free hand, he waved towards the northern horizon.

'This time – I'm not going to let them get away with it! And the mayor can say what she damn well pleases!'

Mirissa stood aside while the little catamaran, like some primeval sea-beast making its first assault on the dry land, heaved itself slowly up the beach on its spinning outboard rollers. As soon as it was above the high-water line, Kumar stopped the engine, and jumped out to join his still-fuming skipper.

'I keep telling Brant,' he said, 'that it must be an accident –

maybe a dragging anchor. After all, why should the Northers do something like this *deliberately?*'

'I'll tell you,' Brant retorted. 'Because they're too lazy to work out the technology themselves. Because they're afraid we'll catch too many fish. Because – '

He caught sight of the other's grin and sent the cat's cradle of broken wires spinning in his direction. Kumar caught it effortlessly.

'Anyway – even if it *is* an accident, they shouldn't be anchoring here. That area's clearly marked on the chart: KEEP OUT – RESEARCH PROJECT. So I'm still going to lodge a protest.'

Brant had already recovered his good humour; even his most furious rages seldom lasted more than a few minutes. To keep him in the right mood, Mirissa started to run her fingers down his back and spoke to him in her most soothing voice.

'Did you catch any good fish?'

'Of course not,' Kumar answered. 'He's only interested in catching statistics – kilograms per kilowatt – that sort of nonsense. Lucky I took my rod. We'll have tuna for dinner.'

He reached into the boat and pulled out almost a metre of streamlined power and beauty, its colours fading rapidly, its sightless eyes already glazed in death.

'Don't often get one of these,' he said proudly. They were still admiring his prize when History returned to Thalassa, and the simple, carefree world they had known all their young lives came abruptly to its end.

The sign of its passing was written there upon the sky, as if a giant hand had drawn a piece of chalk across the blue dome of heaven. Even as they watched, the gleaming vapour trail began to fray at the edges, breaking up into wisps of cloud, until it seemed that a bridge of snow had been thrown from horizon to horizon.

And now a distant thunder was rolling down from the edge of space. It was a sound that Thalassa had not heard for seven hundred years but which any child would recognize at once.

Despite the warmth of the evening, Mirissa shivered and her

hand found Brant's. Though his fingers closed about hers, he scarcely seemed to notice; he was still staring at the riven sky.

Even Kumar was subdued, yet he was the first to speak.

'One of the colonies must have found us.'

Brant shook his head slowly but without much conviction.

'Why should they bother? They must have the old maps – they'll know that Thalassa is almost all ocean. It wouldn't make any sense to come here.'

'Scientific curiosity?' Mirissa suggested. 'To see what's happened to us? I always said we should repair the communications link …'

This was an old dispute, which was revived every few decades. One day, most people agreed, Thalassa really should rebuild the big dish on East Island, destroyed when Krakan erupted four hundred years ago. But meanwhile there was so much that was more important – or simply more amusing.

'Building a starship's an *enormous* project,' Brant said thoughtfully. 'I don't believe that any colony would do it – unless it had to. Like Earth …'

His voice trailed off into silence. After all these centuries, that was still a hard name to say.

As one person, they turned towards the east, where the swift equatorial night was advancing across the sea.

A few of the brighter stars had already emerged, and just climbing above the palm trees was the unmistakable, compact little group of the Triangle. Its three stars were of almost equal magnitude – but a far more brilliant intruder had once shone, for a few weeks, near the southern tip of the constellation.

Its now-shrunken husk was still visible, in a telescope of moderate power. But no instrument could show the orbiting cinder that had been the planet Earth.

2

The Little Neutral One

More than a thousand years later, a great historian had called the period 1901–2000 'the Century when everything happened'. He added that the people of the time would have agreed with him – but for entirely the wrong reasons.

They would have pointed, often with justified pride, to the era's scientific achievements – the conquest of the air, the release of atomic energy, the discovery of the basic principles of life, the electronics and communications revolution, the beginnings of artificial intelligence – and most spectacular of all, the exploration of the solar system and the first landing on the Moon. But as the historian pointed out, with the 20/20 accuracy of hindsight, not one in a thousand would even have heard of the discovery that transcended all these events by threatening to make them utterly irrelevant.

It seemed as harmless, and as far from human affairs, as the fogged photographic plate in Becquerel's laboratory that led, in only fifty years, to the fireball above Hiroshima. Indeed, it was a by-product of that same research, and began in equal innocence.

Nature is a very strict accountant, and always balances her books. So physicists were extremely puzzled when they discovered certain nuclear reactions in which, after all the fragments were added up, something seemed to be missing on one side of the equation.

Like a bookkeeper hastily replenishing the petty cash to keep one jump ahead of the auditors, the physicists were forced to invent a new particle. And, to account for the discrepancy, it had to be a most peculiar one – with neither mass nor charge, and so fantastically penetrating that it could pass, without noticeable inconvenience, through a wall of lead *billions* of kilometres thick.

This phantom was given the nickname 'neutrino' – neutron plus bambino. There seemed no hope of ever detecting so elusive an entity; but in 1956, by heroic feats of instrumentation, the physicists had caught the first few specimens. It was also a triumph for the theoreticians, who now found their unlikely equations verified.

The world as a whole neither knew nor cared; but the countdown to doomsday had begun.

3

Village Council

Tarna's local network was never more than ninety-five per cent operational – but on the other hand never *less* than eighty-five per cent of it was working at any one time. Like most of the equipment on Thalassa, it had been designed by long-dead geniuses so that catastrophic breakdowns were virtually impossible. Even if many components failed, the system would still continue to function reasonably well until someone was sufficiently exasperated to make repairs.

The engineers called this 'graceful degradation' – a phrase that, some cynics had declared, rather accurately described the Lassan way of life.

According to the central computer, the network was now hovering around its normal ninety-five per cent serviceability, and Mayor Waldron would gladly have settled for less. Most of the village had called her during the past half-hour, and at least fifty adults and children were milling round in the council chamber – which was more than it could comfortably hold, let alone seat. The quorum for an ordinary meeting was twelve, and it sometimes took draconian measures to collect even that number of warm bodies in one place. The rest of Tarna's five hundred and sixty inhabitants preferred to watch – and vote, if they felt sufficiently interested – in the comfort of their own homes.

There had also been two calls from the provincial governor, one from the president's office, and one from one North Island news service, all making the same completely unnecessary request. Each had received the same short answer: Of course we'll tell you if anything happens ... and thanks for your interest.

Mayor Waldron did not like excitement, and her moderately successful career as a local administrator had been based on avoiding it. Sometimes, of course, that was impossible; her veto would hardly have deflected the hurricane of '09, which – until today – had been the century's most notable event.

'Quiet, everybody!' she cried. 'Reena – leave those shells alone – someone went to a lot of trouble arranging them! Time you were in bed, anyway! Billy – off the table! *Now!*'

The surprising speed with which order was restored showed that, for once, the villagers were anxious to hear what their mayor had to say. She switched off the insistent beeping of her wristphone and routed the call to the message centre.

'Frankly, I don't know much more than you do – and it's not likely we'll get any more information for several hours. But it certainly *was* some kind of spacecraft, and it had already reentered – I suppose I should say entered – when it passed over us. Since there's nowhere else for it to go on Thalassa, presumably it will come back to the Three Islands sooner or later. That might take hours if it's going right round the planet.'

'Any attempt at radio contact?' somebody asked.

'Yes, but no luck so far.'

'Should we even try?' an anxious voice said.

A brief hush fell upon the whole assembly; then Councillor Simmons, Mayor Waldron's chief gadfly, gave a snort of disgust.

'That's ridiculous. Whatever we do, they can find us in about ten minutes. Anyway, they probably know exactly where we are.'

'I agree completely with the councillor,' Mayor Waldron said, relishing this unusual opportunity. 'Any colony ship will certainly have maps of Thalassa. They may be a thousand years old – but they'll show First Landing.'

'But suppose – just suppose – that they *are* aliens?'

The mayor sighed; she thought that thesis had died through sheer exhaustion, centuries ago.

'There are no aliens,' she said firmly. 'At least, none intelligent enough to go starfaring. Of course, we can never be one hundred per cent certain – but Earth searched for a thousand years with every conceivable instrument.'

'There's another possibility,' said Mirissa, who was standing with Brant and Kumar near the back of the chamber. Every head turned towards her, but Brant looked slightly annoyed. Despite his love for Mirissa, there were times when he wished that she was not quite so well-informed, and that her family had not been in charge of the Archives for the last five generations.

'What's that, my dear?'

Now it was Mirissa's turn to be annoyed, though she concealed her irritation. She did not enjoy being condescended to by someone who was not really very intelligent, though undoubtedly shrewd – or perhaps cunning was the better word. The fact that Mayor Waldron was always making eyes at Brant did not bother Mirissa in the least; it merely amused her, and she could even feel a certain sympathy for the older woman.

'It could be another robot seedship, like the one that brought our ancestor's gene patterns to Thalassa.'

'But *now* – so late?'

'Why not? The first seeders could only reach a few per cent of light velocity. Earth kept improving them – right up to the time it was destroyed. As the later models were almost ten times faster, the earlier ones were overtaken in a century or so; many of them must still be on the way. Don't you agree, Brant?'

Mirissa was always careful to bring him into any discussion and, if possible, to make him think he had originated it. She was well aware of his feelings of inferiority and did not wish to add to them.

Sometimes it was rather lonely being the brightest person in Tarna; although she networked with half a dozen of her mental peers on the Three Islands, she seldom met them in the face-to-face encounters that, even after all these millennia, no communications technology could really match.

'It's an interesting idea,' Brant said. 'You could be right.'

Although history was not his strong point, Brant Falconer had a technician's knowledge of the complex series of events that had led to the colonization of Thalassa. 'And what shall we do,' he asked, 'if it's another seedship, and tries to colonize us all over again? Say "Thanks very much, but not today"?'

There were a few nervous little laughs; then Councillor Simmons remarked thoughtfully, 'I'm sure we could handle a seedship if we had to. And wouldn't its robots be intelligent enough to cancel their program when they saw that the job had already been done?'

'Perhaps. But they might think they could do a better one. Anyway, whether it's a relic from Earth or a later model from one of the colonies, it's bound to be a robot of some kind.'

There was no need to elaborate; everyone knew the fantastic difficulty and expense of *manned* interstellar flight. Even though technically possible, it was completely pointless. Robots could do the job a thousand times more cheaply.

'Robot or relic – what are we going to do about it?' one of the villagers demanded.

'It may not be our problem,' the mayor said. 'Everyone seems to have assumed that it will head for First Landing, but why should it? After all, North Island is much more likely – '

The mayor had often been proved wrong, but never so swiftly. This time the sound that grew in the sky above Tarna was no distant thunder from the ionosphere but the piercing whistle of a low, fast-flying jet. Everyone rushed out of the council chamber in unseemly haste; only the first few were in time to see the blunt-nosed delta-wing eclipsing the stars as it headed purposefully towards the spot still sacred as the last link with Earth.

Mayor Waldron paused briefly to report to central, then joined the others milling around outside.

'Brant – you can get there first. Take the kite.'

Tarna's chief mechanical engineer blinked; it was the first time he had ever received so direct an order from the mayor. Then he looked a little abashed.

'A coconut went through the wing a couple of days ago. I've not had time to repair it because of that problem with the fishtraps. Anyway, it's not equipped for night flying.'

The mayor gave him a long, hard look.

'I hope my car's working,' she said sarcastically.

'Of course,' Brant answered, in a hurt voice. 'All fuelled up, and ready to go.'

It was quite unusual for the mayor's car to go anywhere; one could walk the length of Tarna in twenty minutes, and all local transport of food and equipment was handled by small sandrollers. In seventy years of official service the car had clocked up less than a hundred thousand kilometres, and, barring accidents, should still be going strong for at least a century to come.

The Lassans had experimented cheerfully with most vices; but planned obsolescence and conspicuous consumption were not among them. No one could have guessed that the vehicle was older than any of its passengers as it started on the most historic journey it would ever make.

4

Tocsin

No one heard the first tolling of Earth's funeral bell – not even the scientists who made the fatal discovery, far underground, in an abandoned Colorado gold mine.

It was a daring experiment, quite inconceivable before the mid-twentieth century. Once the neutrino had been detected, it was quickly realized that mankind had a new window on the universe. Something so penetrating that it passed through a planet as easily as light through a sheet of glass could be used to look into the hearts of suns.

Especially *the* Sun. Astronomers were confident that they understood the reactions powering the solar furnace, upon which all life on Earth ultimately depended. At the enormous pressures and temperatures at the Sun's core, hydrogen was fused to helium, in a series of reactions that liberated vast amounts of energy. And, as an incidental by-product, neutrinos.

Finding the trillions of tons of matter in their way no more obstacle than a wisp of smoke, those solar neutrinos raced up from their birthplace at the velocity of light. Just two seconds later they emerged into space, and spread outward across the universe. However many stars and planets they encountered, most of them would still have evaded capture by the insubstantial ghost of 'solid' matter when Time itself came to an end.

Eight minutes after they had left the Sun, a tiny fraction of the solar torrent swept through the Earth – and an even smaller fraction was intercepted by the scientists in Colorado. They had buried their equipment more than a kilometre underground so that all the less penetrating radiations would be filtered out and they could trap the rare, genuine messengers from the heart of the Sun. By counting the captured neutrinos, they hoped to study in detail conditions at a spot that, as any philosopher could easily prove, was forever barred from human knowledge or observation.

The experiment worked; solar neutrinos were detected. But – *there were far too few of them.* There should have been three or four times as many as the massive instrumentation had succeeded in capturing.

Clearly, something was wrong, and during the 1970s the Case of the Missing Neutrinos escalated to a major scientific scandal. Equipment was checked and rechecked, theories were over-hauled, and the experiment rerun scores of times – always with the same baffling result.

By the end of the twentieth century, the astrophysicists had been forced to accept a disturbing conclusion – though as yet, no one realized its full implications.

There was nothing wrong with the theory, or with the equipment. The trouble lay inside the Sun.

The first secret meeting in the history of the International Astronomical Union took place in 2008 at Aspen, Colorado – not far from the scene of the original experiment, which had now been repeated in a dozen countries. A week later IAU Special Bulletin No. 55/08, bearing the deliberately low-key title 'Some Notes on Solar Reactions', was in the hands of every government on Earth.

One might have thought that as the news slowly leaked out, the announcement of the End of the World would have produced a certain amount of panic. In fact, the general reaction was a stunned silence – then a shrug of the shoulders and the resumption of normal, everyday business.

Few governments had ever looked more than an election ahead, few individuals beyond the lifetimes of their grandchildren. And anyway, the astronomers might be wrong ...

Even if humanity was under sentence of death, the date of

execution was still indefinite. The Sun would not blow up for at least a thousand years; and who could weep for the fortieth generation?

5

Night Ride

Neither of the two moons had risen when the car set off along Tarna's most famous road, carrying Brant, Mayor Waldron, Councillor Simmons, and two senior villagers. Though he was driving with his usual effortless skill, Brant was still smouldering slightly from the mayor's reprimand. The fact that her plump arm was accidentally draped over his bare shoulders did little to improve matters.

But the peaceful beauty of the night and the hypnotic rhythm of the palm trees as they swept steadily through the car's moving fan of light quickly restored his normal good humour. And how could such petty personal feelings be allowed to intrude, at such an historic moment as this?

In ten minutes, they would be at First Landing and the beginning of their history. What was waiting for them there? Only one thing was certain; the visitor had homed on the still-operating beacon of the ancient seedship. It knew where to look, so it must be from some other human colony in this sector of space.

On the other hand – Brant was suddenly struck by a disturbing thought. Anyone – any*thing* – could have detected that beacon, signalling to all the universe that Intelligence had once passed this way. He recalled that, a few years ago, there had been a move to switch off the transmission on the grounds that it served no useful purpose and might conceivably do harm. The motion had been rejected by a narrow margin, for reasons that were sentimental and emotional rather than logical. Thalassa might soon regret that decision, but it was certainly much too late to do anything about it.

Councillor Simmons, leaning across from the back seat, was talking quietly to the mayor.

'Helga,' he said – and it was the first time Brant had ever heard him use the mayor's first name – 'do you think we'll still be able to communicate? Robot languages evolve very rapidly, you know.'

Mayor Waldron didn't know, but she was very good at concealing ignorance.

'That's the least of our problems; let's wait until it arises. Brant – could you drive a little more slowly? I'd like to get there alive.'

Their present speed was perfectly safe on this familiar road, but Brant dutifully slowed to forty klicks. He wondered if the mayor was trying to postpone the confrontation; it was an awesome responsibility, facing only the second outworld spacecraft in the history of the planet. The whole of Thalassa would be watching.

'Krakan!' swore one of the passengers in the back seat. 'Did anybody bring a camera?'

'Too late to go back,' Councillor Simmons answered. 'Anyway, there will be plenty of time for photographs. I don't suppose they'll take off again right after saying "hello!"'

There was a certain mild hysteria in his voice, and Brant could hardly blame him. Who could tell *what* was waiting for them just over the brow of the next hill?

'I'll report just as soon as there's anything to tell you, Mr President,' said Mayor Waldron to the car radio. Brant had never even noticed the call; he had been too lost in a reverie of his own. For the first time in his life, he wished he had learned a little more history.

Of course, he was familiar enough with the basic facts; every child on Thalassa grew up with them. He knew how, as the centuries ticked remorselessly by, the astronomers' diagnosis became ever more confident, the date of their prediction steadily more precise. In the year 3600, plus or minus 75, the Sun would become a nova. Not a very spectacular one – but big enough...

An old philosopher had once remarked that it settles a man's mind wonderfully to know that he will be hanged in the morning. Something of the same kind occurred with the entire human race, during the closing years of the Fourth Millennium. If there was a single moment when humanity at last faced the truth with both resignation and determination, it was at the December midnight when the year 2999 changed to 3000. No one who saw that first 3 appear could forget that there would never be a 4.

Yet more than half a millennium remained; much could be done by the thirty generations that would still live and die on Earth as had their ancestors before them. At the very least, they could preserve the knowledge of the race, and the greatest creations of human art.

Even at the dawn of the space age, the first robot probes to leave the solar system had carried recordings of music, messages, and pictures in case they were ever encountered by other explorers of the cosmos. And though no sign of alien civilizations had ever been detected in the home galaxy, even the most pessimistic believed that intelligence must occur *somewhere* in the billions of other island universes that stretched as far as the most powerful telescope could see.

For centuries, terabyte upon terabyte of human knowledge and culture were beamed towards the Andromeda Nebula and its more distant neighbours. No one, of course, would ever know if the signals were received – or, if received, could be interpreted. But the motivation was one that most men could share; it was the impulse to leave some last message – some signal saying, 'Look – I, too, was once alive!'

By the year 3000, astronomers believed that their giant orbiting telescopes had detected all planetary systems within five hundred light-years of the Sun. Dozens of approximately Earth-size worlds had been discovered, and some of the closer ones had been crudely mapped. Several had atmospheres bearing that unmistakable signature of life, an abnormally high percentage of oxygen. There was a reasonable chance that men could survive there – if they could reach them.

Men could not, but Man could.

The first seedships were primitive, yet even so they stretched technology to the limit. With the propulsion systems available by 2500, they could reach the nearest planetary system in two hundred years, carrying their precious burden of frozen embryos.

But that was the least of their tasks. They also had to carry the automatic equipment that would revive and rear these potential humans, and teach them how to survive in an unknown but probably hostile environment. It would be useless – indeed, cruel – to decant naked, ignorant children on to worlds as unfriendly as the Sahara or the Antarctic. They had to be educated, given tools, shown how to locate and use local resources. After it had landed and the seedship became a Mother Ship, it might have to cherish its brood for generations.

Not only humans had to be carried, but a complete *biota*. Plants (even though no one knew if there would be soil for them), farm animals, and a surprising variety of essential insects and microorganisms also had to be included in case normal food–production systems broke down and it was necessary to revert to basic agricultural techniques.

There was one advantage in such a new beginning. All the diseases and parasites that had plagued humanity since the beginning of time would be left behind, to perish in the sterilizing fire of Nova Solis.

Data banks, 'expert systems' able to handle any conceivable situation, robots, repair and backup mechanisms – all these had to be designed and built. And they had to function over a timespan at least as long as that between the Declaration of Independence and the first landing on the Moon.

Though the task seemed barely possible, it was so inspiring that almost the whole of mankind united to achieve it. Here was a long-term goal – the *last* long-term goal – that could now give some meaning to life, even after Earth had been destroyed.

The first seedship left the solar system in 2553, heading towards the Sun's near twin, Alpha Centauri A. Although the climate of the Earth-sized planet Pasadena was subject to violent extremes, owing to nearby Centauri B, the next likely target was more than twice as far away. The voyage time to Sirius X would be over four hundred years; when the seeder arrived, Earth might no longer exist.

But if Pasadena could be successfully colonized, there would be ample time to send back the good news. Two hundred years for the voyage, fifty years to secure a foothold and build a small transmitter, and a mere four years for the signal to get back to Earth – why, with luck, there would be shouting in the streets, around the year 2800 ...

In fact, it was 2786; Pasadena had done better than predicted. The news was electrifying, and gave renewed encouragement to the seeding programme. By this time, a score of ships had been launched, each with more advanced technology than its precursor. The latest models could reach a twentieth of the velocity of light, and more than fifty targets lay within their range.

Even when the Pasadena beacon became silent after beaming no more than the news of the initial landing, discouragement was only momentary. What had been done once could be done again – and yet again – with greater certainty of success.

By 2700 the crude technique of frozen embryos was abandoned. The genetic message that Nature encoded in the spiral structure of the DNA molecule could now be stored more easily, more safely, and even more compactly, in the memories of the ultimate computers, so that a million genotypes could be carried in a seedship no larger than an ordinary thousand-passenger aircraft. An entire unborn nation, with all the replicating equipment needed to set up a new civilization, could be contained in a few hundred cubic metres, and carried to the stars.

This, Brant knew, was what had happened on Thalassa seven

hundred years ago. Already, as the road climbed up into the hills, they had passed some of the scars left by the first robot excavators as they sought the raw materials from which his own ancestors had been created. In a moment, they would see the long-abandoned processing plants and –

'What's *that*?' Councillor Simmons whispered urgently.

'Stop!' the mayor ordered. 'Cut the engine, Brant.' She reached for the car microphone.

'Mayor Waldron. We're at the seven-kilometre mark. There's a light ahead of us – we can see it through the trees – as far as I can tell it's exactly at First Landing. We can't hear anything. Now we're starting up again.'

Brant did not wait for the order, but eased the speed control gently forward. This was the second most exciting thing that had happened to him in his entire life, next to being caught in the hurricane of '09.

That had been more than exciting; he had been lucky to escape alive. Perhaps there was also danger here, but he did not really believe so. Could robots be hostile? Surely there was nothing that any outworlders could possibly want from Thalassa, except knowledge and friendship ...

'You know,' Councillor Simmons said, 'I had a good view of the thing before it went over the trees, and I'm certain it was some kind of aircraft. Seedships never had wings and streamlining, of course. And it was very small.'

'Whatever it is,' Brant said, 'we'll know in five minutes. Look at that light – it's come down in Earth Park – the obvious place. Should we stop the car and walk the rest of the way?'

Earth Park was the carefully tended oval of grass on the eastern side of First Landing, and it was now hidden from their direct view by the black, looming column of the Mother Ship, the oldest and most revered monument on the planet. Spilling round the edges of the still-untarnished cylinder was a flood of light, apparently from a single brilliant source.

'Stop the car just before we reach the ship,' the mayor ordered.

'Then we'll get out and peek around it. Switch off your lights so they won't see us until we want them to.'

'Them – or It?' asked one of the passengers, just a little hysterically. Everyone ignored him.

The car came to a halt in the ship's immense shadow, and Brant swung it round through a hundred and eighty degrees.

'Just so we can make a quick getaway,' he explained, half seriously, half out of mischief; he still could not believe that they were in any real danger. Indeed, there were moments when he wondered if this was really happening. Perhaps he was still asleep, and this was merely a vivid dream.

They got quietly out of the car and walked up to the ship, then circled it until they came to the sharply defined wall of light. Brant shielded his eyes and peered around the edge, squinting against the glare.

Councillor Simmons had been perfectly correct. It *was* some kind of aircraft – or aerospacecraft – and a very small one at that. Could the Northers? – No, that was absurd. There was no conceivable use for such a vehicle in the limited area of the Three Islands, and its development could not possibly have been concealed.

It was shaped like a blunt arrowhead and must have landed vertically, for there were no marks on the surrounding grass. The light came from a single source in a streamlined dorsal housing, and a small red beacon was flashing on and off just above that. Altogether, it was a reassuringly – indeed, disappointingly – ordinary machine. One that could not conceivably have travelled the dozen light-years to the nearest known colony.

Suddenly, the main light went out, leaving the little group of observers momentarily blind. When he recovered his night vision, Brant could see that there were windows in the forepart of the machine, glowing faintly with internal illumination. Why – it looked almost like a *manned* vehicle, not the robot craft they had taken for granted!

Mayor Waldron had come to exactly the same astonishing conclusion.

'It's not a robot – there are people in it! Let's not waste any more time. Shine your flashlight on me, Brant, so they can see us.'

'Helga!' Councillor Simmons protested.

'Don't be an ass, Charlie. Let's go, Brant.'

What was it that the first man on the Moon had said, almost two millennia ago? 'One small step ...' They had taken about twenty when a door opened in the side of the vehicle, a double-jointed ramp flipped rapidly downward, and two humanoids walked out to meet them.

That was Brant's first reaction. Then he realized that he had been misled by the colour of their skin – or what he could see of it, through the flexible, transparent film that covered them from head to foot.

They were not humanoids – they were *human*. If he never went out into the sun again, he might become almost as bleached as they were.

The Mayor was holding out her hands in the traditional 'See – no weapons!' gesture as old as history.

'I don't suppose you'll understand me,' she said, 'but welcome to Thalassa.'

The visitors smiled, and the older of the two – a handsome, grey-haired man in his late sixties – held up his hands in response.

'On the contrary,' he answered, in one of the deepest and most beautifully modulated voices that Brant had ever heard, 'we understand you perfectly. We're delighted to meet you.'

For a moment, the welcoming party stood in stunned silence. But it was silly, thought Brant, to have been surprised. After all, they did not have the slightest difficulty understanding the speech of men who had lived two thousand years ago. When sound recording was invented, it froze the basic phoneme patterns of all languages. Vocabularies would expand, syntax and grammar might be modified – but pronunciation would remain stable for millennia.

Mayor Waldron was the first to recover.

'Well, that certainly saves a lot of trouble,' she said rather lamely. 'But where have you come from? I'm afraid we've lost touch with – our neighbours – since our deep-space antenna was destroyed.'

The older man glanced at his much taller companion, and some silent message flashed between them. Then he again turned towards the waiting mayor.

There was no mistaking the sadness in that beautiful voice, as he made his preposterous claim.

'It may be difficult for you to believe this,' he said. 'But we're not from any of the colonies. We've come straight from Earth.'

II
Magellan

6

Planetfall

Even before he opened his eyes, Loren knew exactly where he was, and he found this quite surprising. After sleeping for two hundred years, some confusion would have been understandable, but it seemed only yesterday that he had made his last entry in the ship's log. And as far as he could remember, he had not had a single dream. He was thankful for that.

Still keeping his eyes closed, he concentrated one at a time on all his other sense channels. He could hear a soft murmur of voices, quietly reassuring. There was the familiar sighing of the air exchangers, and he could feel a barely perceptible current, wafting pleasant antiseptic smells across his face.

The one sensation he did not feel was that of weight. He lifted his right arm effortlessly: it remained floating in midair, awaiting his next order.

'Hello, Mister Lorenson,' a cheerfully bullying voice said. 'So you've condescended to join us again. How do you feel?'

Loren finally opened his eyes and tried to focus them on the blurred figure floating beside his bed.

'Hello ... doctor. I'm fine. And hungry.'

'That's always a good sign. You can get dressed – don't move too quickly for a while. And you can decide later if you want to keep that beard.'

Loren directed his still-floating hand towards his chin; he was surprised at the amount of stubble he found there. Like the majority of men, he had never taken the option of permanent eradication – whole volumes of psychology had been written on *that* subject. Perhaps it was time to think about doing so; amusing how such trivia cluttered up the mind, even at a moment like this.

'We've arrived safely?'

'Of course – otherwise you'd still be asleep. Everything's gone according to plan. The ship started to wake us a month ago – now we're in orbit above Thalassa. The maintenance crews have checked all the systems; now it's your turn to do some work. And we have a little surprise for you.'

'A pleasant one, I hope.'

'So do we. Captain Bey has a briefing two hours from now, in Main Assembly. If you don't want to move yet, you can watch from here.'

'I'll come to assembly – I'd like to meet everyone. But can I have breakfast first? It's been a long time ...'

Captain Sirdar Bey looked tired but happy as he welcomed the fifteen men and women who had just been revived, and introduced them to the thirty who formed the current A and B crews. According to ship's regulations, C crew was supposed to be sleeping – but several figures were lurking at the back of the Assembly room, pretending not to be there.

'I'm happy you've joined us,' he told the newcomers. 'It's good to see some fresh faces around here. And it's better still to see a planet and to know that our ship's carried out the first two hundred years of the mission plan without any serious anomalies. Here's Thalassa, right on schedule.'

Everyone turned towards the visual display covering most of one wall. Much of it was devoted to data and state-of-ship information, but the largest section might have been a window looking out into space. It was completely filled by a stunningly beautiful image of a blue-white globe, almost fully illuminated. Probably everyone in the room had noticed the heart-breaking similarity to the Earth as seen from high above the Pacific – almost all water, with only a few isolated landmasses.

And there was land here – a compact grouping of three islands, partly hidden by a veil of cloud. Loren thought of Hawaii, which he had never seen and which no longer existed. But there was one fundamental difference between the two planets. The other hemisphere of Earth was mostly land; the other hemisphere of Thalassa was *entirely* ocean.

'There it is,' the captain said proudly. 'Just as the mission planners predicted. But there's one detail they didn't expect, which will certainly affect our operations.

'You'll recall that Thalassa was seeded by a Mark 3A fifty-thousand unit module which left Earth in 2751 and arrived in 3109. Everything went well, and the first transmissions were received a hundred and sixty years later. They continued intermittently for almost two centuries, then suddenly stopped, after a brief message reporting a major volcanic eruption. Nothing more was ever heard, and it was assumed that our colony on Thalassa had been destroyed – or at any rate reduced to barbarism as seems to have happened in several other cases.

'For the benefit of the newcomers, let me repeat what we've found. Naturally, we listened out on all frequencies when we entered the system. Nothing – not even power-system leakage radiation.

'When we got closer, we realized that didn't prove a thing. Thalassa has a very dense ionosphere. There might be a lot of medium- and short-wave chatter going on beneath it, and nobody outside would ever know. Microwaves would go through, of course, but maybe they don't need them, or we haven't been lucky enough to intercept a beam.

'Anyway, there's a well-developed civilization down there. We saw the lights of their cities – towns, at least – as soon as we had a good view of the nightside. There are plenty of small industries, a little coastal traffic – no large ships – and we've even spotted a couple of aircraft moving at all of five hundred klicks, which will get them anywhere in fifteen minutes.

'Obviously, they don't need much air transport in such a compact community, and they have a good system of roads. But we've still not been able to detect any communications. And no satellites, either – not even meteorological ones, which you'd think they'd need ... though perhaps not, as their ships probably never get out of sight of land. There's simply no other land to go to, of course.

'So there we are. It's an interesting situation – and a very pleasant surprise. At least, I *hope* it will be. Now, any questions? Yes, Mister Lorenson?'

'Have we tried to contact them, sir?'

'Not yet; we thought it inadvisable until we know the exact level of their culture. Whatever we do, it may be a considerable shock.'

'Do they know we're here?'

'Probably not.'

'But surely – our drive – they must have seen *that!*'

It was a reasonable question, since a quantum ramjet at full power was one of the most dramatic spectacles ever contrived by man. It was as brilliant as an atomic bomb, and it lasted much longer – months instead of milliseconds.

'Possibly, but I doubt it. We were on the other side of the sun when we did most of our braking. They wouldn't have seen us in its glare.'

Then someone asked the question that everybody had been thinking.

'Captain, how will this affect our mission?'

Sirdar Bey looked thoughtfully at the speaker.

'At this stage, it's still quite impossible to say. A few hundred thousand other humans – or whatever the population is – could make things a lot easier for us. Or at least much more pleasant. On the other hand, if they don't like us –'

He gave an expressive shrug.

'I've just remembered a piece of advice that an old explorer gave to one of his colleagues. If you assume that the natives are friendly, they usually are. And *vice versa*.

'So until they prove otherwise, we'll assume that they're friendly. And if they're not ...'

The Captain's expression hardened, and his voice became that of a commander who had just brought a great ship across fifty light-years of space.

'I've never claimed that might is right, but it's always very comforting to have it.'

7

Lords of the Last Days

It was hard to believe that he was really and truly awake, and that life could begin again.

Lieutenant Commander Loren Lorenson knew that he could never wholly escape from the tragedy that had shadowed more than forty generations and had reached its climax in his own lifetime. During the course of his first new day, he had one continuing fear. Not even the promise, and mystery, of the beautiful ocean-world hanging there below *Magellan* could keep at bay the thought: what dreams will come when I close my eyes tonight in *natural* sleep for the first time in two hundred years?

He had witnessed scenes that no one could ever forget and which would haunt Mankind until the end of time. Through the ship's telescopes, he had watched the death of the solar system. With his own eyes, he had seen the volcanoes of Mars erupt for the first time in a billion years; Venus briefly naked as her atmosphere was blasted into space before she herself was consumed; the gas giants exploding into incandescent fireballs. But these were empty, meaningless spectacles compared with the tragedy of Earth.

That, too, he had watched through the lenses of cameras that had survived a few minutes longer than the devoted men who had sacrificed the last moments of their lives to set them up. He had seen ...

... the Great Pyramid, glowing dully red before it slumped into a puddle of molten stone ...

... the floor of the Atlantic, baked rock-hard in seconds, before it was submerged again, by the lava gushing from the volcanoes of the Mid-ocean Rift ...

... the Moon rising above the flaming forests of Brazil and now itself shining almost as brilliantly as had the Sun, on its last setting, only minutes before ...

... the continent of Antarctica emerging briefly after its long burial, as the kilometres of ancient ice were burned away ...

... the mighty central span of the Gibraltar Bridge, melting even as it slumped downward through the burning air ...

In that last century the Earth was haunted with ghosts – not of the dead, but of those who now could never be born. For five hundred years the birthrate had been held at a level that would reduce the human population to a few millions when the end finally came. Whole cities – even countries – had been deserted as mankind huddled together for History's closing act.

It was a time of strange paradoxes, of wild oscillations between despair and feverish exhilaration. Many, of course, sought oblivion through the traditional routes of drugs, sex, and dangerous sports – including what were virtually miniature wars, carefully monitored and fought with agreed weapons. Equally popular was the whole spectrum of electronic catharsis, from endless video games, interactive dramas, and direct stimulation of the brain's centres.

Because there was no longer any reason to take heed for the future on *this* planet, Earth's resources and the accumulated wealth of all the ages could be squandered with a clear conscience. In terms of material goods, all men were millionaires, rich beyond the wildest dreams of their ancestors, the fruits of whose toil they had inherited. They called themselves wryly, yet not without a certain pride, the Lords of the Last Days.

Yet though myriads sought forgetfulness, even more found satisfaction, as some men had always done, in working for goals beyond their own lifetimes. Much scientific research continued, using the immense resources that had now been freed. If a physicist needed a hundred tons of gold for an experiment, that was merely a minor problem in logistics, not budgeting.

Three themes dominated. First was the continual monitoring of the Sun – not because there was any remaining doubt but to predict the moment of detonation to the year, the day, the hour ...

Second was the search for extraterrestrial intelligence, neglected after centuries of failure, now resumed with desperate urgency – and, even to the end, with no greater success than before. To all Man's questioning, the Universe still gave a dusty answer.

And the third, of course, was the seeding of the nearby stars in the hope that the human race would not perish with the dying of its Sun.

By the dawn of the final century, seedships of ever-increasing speed and sophistication had been sent to more than fifty targets. Most, as expected, had been failures, but ten had radioed back news of at least partial success. Even greater hopes were placed on the later and more advanced models, though they would not reach their distant goals until long after Earth had ceased to exist. The very last to be launched could cruise at a twentieth of the speed of light and would make planetfall in nine hundred and fifty years – if all went well.

Loren could still remember the launching of *Excalibur* from its construction cradle at the Lagrangian point between Earth and Moon. Though he was only five, even then he knew that this seedship would be the very last of its kind. But *why* the centuries-long programme had been cancelled just when it had reached technological maturity, he was still too young to understand. Nor could he have guessed how his own life would be changed, by the stunning discovery that had transformed the entire situation and given mankind a new hope, in the very last decades of terrestrial history.

Though countless theoretical studies had been made, no one had ever been able to make a plausible case for *manned* space-flight even to the nearest star. That such a journey might take a century was not the decisive factor; hibernation could solve that problem. A rhesus monkey had been sleeping in the Louis Pasteur satellite hospital for almost a thousand years and still showed perfectly normal brain activity. There was no reason to suppose that human beings could not do the same – though the record, held by a patient suffering from a peculiarly baffling form of cancer, was less than two centuries.

The biological problem had been solved; it was the engineering one that appeared insuperable. A vessel that could carry thousands of sleeping passengers, and all they needed for a new life on another world, would have to be as large as one of the great ocean liners that had once ruled the seas of Earth.

It would be easy enough to build such a ship beyond the orbit of Mars and using the abundant resources of the asteroid belt. However, it was impossible to devise engines that could get it to the stars in any reasonable length of time.

Even at a tenth of the speed of light, all the most promising targets were more than five hundred years away. Such a velocity had been attained by robot probes – flashing through nearby star systems and radioing back their observations during a few hectic hours of transit. But there was no way in which they could slow down for rendezvous or landing; barring accidents, they would continue speeding through the galaxy forever.

This was the fundamental problem with rockets – and no one had ever discovered any alternative for deep-space propulsion. It was just as difficult to lose speed as to acquire it, and carrying the necessary propellant for deceleration did not merely *double* the difficulty of a mission; it *squared* it.

A full-scale hibership could indeed be built to reach a tenth of the speed of light. It would require about a million tons of somewhat exotic elements as propellant; difficult, but not impossible.

But in order to cancel that velocity at the end of the voyage, the ship must start not with a million – but a preposterous million, *million* tons of propellant. This, of course, was so completely out of the question that no one had given the matter any serious thought for centuries.

And then, by one of history's greatest ironies, Mankind was given the keys to the Universe – and barely a century in which to use them.

8

Remembrance of Love Lost

How glad I am, thought Moses Kaldor, that I never succumbed to that temptation – the seductive lure that art and technology had first given to mankind more than a thousand years ago. Had I wished, I could have brought Evelyn's electronic ghost with me into exile, trapped in a few gigabytes of programming. She could have appeared before me, in any one of the backgrounds we both loved, and carried on a conversation so utterly convincing that a stranger could never have guessed that no one – *nothing* – was really there.

But I would have known, after five or ten minutes unless I deluded myself by a deliberate act of will. And that I could never do. Though I am still not sure why my instincts revolt against it, I always refused to accept the false solace of a dialogue with the dead. I do not even possess, now, a simple recording of her voice.

It is far better this way, to watch her moving in silence, in the little garden of our last home, knowing that this is no illusion of the image-makers but that it really *did* happen, two hundred years ago on Earth.

And the only voice will be mine, here and now, speaking to the memory that still exists in my own human, living brain.

Private recording One. Alpha scrambler. Autoerase program.

You were right, Evelyn, and I was wrong. Even though I am the oldest man on the ship, it seems that I can still be useful.

When I awoke, Captain Bey was standing beside me. I felt flattered – as soon as I was able to feel anything.

'Well, Captain,' I said, 'this is quite a surprise. I half expected you to dump me in space as unnecessary mass.'

He laughed and answered. 'It could still happen, Moses; the voyage isn't over yet. But we certainly need you now. The Mission planners were wiser than you gave them credit.'

'They listed me on the ship's manifest as quote Ambassador-Counsellor unquote. In which capacity am I required?'

'Probably both. And perhaps in your even better-known role as –'

'Don't hesitate if you wanted to say crusader, even though I never liked the word and never regarded myself as a leader of any movement. I only tried to make people think for themselves – I never wanted anyone to follow me blindly. History has seen too many leaders.'

'Yes, but not all have been bad ones. Consider your namesake.'

'Much overrated, though I can understand if you admire him. After all, you, too, have the task of leading homeless tribes into a promised land. I assume that some slight problem has arisen.'

The captain smiled and answered. 'I'm happy to see that you're fully alert. At this stage, there's not even a problem, and there's no reason why there should be. But a situation has arisen that no one expected, and you're our official diplomat. You have the one skill we never thought we'd need.'

I can tell you, Evelyn, *that* gave me a shock. Captain Bey must have read my mind very accurately when he saw my jaw drop.

'Oh,' he said quickly, 'we haven't run into aliens! But it turns

out that the human colony on Thalassa wasn't destroyed as we'd
imagined. In fact, it's doing very well.'

That, of course, was another surprise, though quite a pleasant
one. Thalassa – the Sea, the Sea! – was a world I had never
expected to set eyes upon. When *I* awoke, it should have been
light-years behind and centuries ago.

'What are the people like? Have you made contact with them?'

'Not yet; that's your job. You know better than anyone else the
mistakes that were made in the past. We don't want to repeat
them here. Now, if you're ready to come up to the bridge, I'll give
you a bird's-eye view of our long-lost cousins.'

That was a week ago, Evelyn; how pleasant it is to have no time
pressures after decades of unbreakable – and all too literal –
deadlines! Now we know as much about the Thalassans as we can
hope to do without actually meeting them face-to-face. And this
we shall do tonight.

We have chosen common ground to show that we recognize
our kinship. The site of the first landing is clearly visible and has
been well kept, like a park – possibly a shrine. That's a very good
sign: I only hope that *our* landing there won't be taken as sacrilege.
Perhaps it will confirm that we are gods, which should make it
easier for us. If the Thalassans have invented gods – that's one
thing I want to find out.

I am beginning to live again, my darling. Yes, yes – you were
wiser than I, the so-called philosopher! No man has a right to die
while he can still help his fellows. It was selfish of me to have
wished otherwise ... to have hoped to lie forever beside you, in the
spot we had chosen, so long ago, so far away ... Now I can even
accept the fact that you are scattered across the solar system, with
all else that I ever loved on Earth.

But now there is work to be done; and while I talk to your
memory, you are still alive.

The Quest for Superspace

Of all the psychological hammer blows that the scientists of the twentieth century had to endure, perhaps the most devastating – and unexpected – was the discovery that nothing was more crowded than 'empty' space.

The old Aristotelian doctrine that Nature abhorred a vacuum was perfectly true. Even when every atom of seemingly solid matter was removed from a given volume, what remained was a seething inferno of energies of an intensity and scale unimaginable to the human mind. By comparison, even the most condensed form of matter – the hundred-million-tons-to-the-cubic-centimetre of a neutron star – was an impalpable ghost, a barely perceptible perturbation in the inconceivably dense, yet foamlike structure of 'superspace.'

That there was much more to space than naive intuition suggested was first revealed by the classic work of Lamb and Rutherford in 1947. Studying the simplest of elements – the hydrogen atom – they discovered that something very odd happened when the solitary electron orbited the nucleus. Far from travelling in a smooth curve, it behaved as if being continually buffeted by incessant waves on a sub-submicroscopic scale. Hard though it was to grasp the concept, there were fluctuations *in the vacuum itself.*

Since the time of the Greeks, philosophers had been divided into two schools – those who believed that the operations of Nature flowed smoothly and those who argued that this was an illusion; everything really happened in discrete jumps or jerks too small to be perceptible in everyday life. The establishment of the atomic theory was a triumph for the second school of thought; and when Planck's Quantum Theory demonstrated that even light and energy came in little packets, not continuous streams, the argument finally ended.

In the ultimate analysis, the world of Nature was granular – discontinuous. Even if, to the naked human eye, a waterfall and a shower of bricks appeared very different, they were really much the same. The tiny 'bricks' of H_2O were too small to be visible to the unaided senses, but they could be easily discerned by the instruments of the physicists.

And now the analysis was taken one step further. What made the granularity of space so hard to envisage was not only its sub-submicroscopic scale – but its sheer *violence*.

No one could really imagine a *million*th of a centimetre, but at least the number itself – a thousand thousands – was familiar in such human affairs as budgets and population statistics. To say that it would require a million viruses to span the distance of a centimetre did convey something to the mind.

But a million-*millionth* of a centimetre? That was comparable to the size of the electron, and already it was far beyond visualization. It could perhaps be grasped intellectually, but not emotionally.

And yet the scale of events in the structure of space was unbelievably smaller than this – so much so that, in comparison, an ant and an elephant were of virtually the same size. If one imagined it as a bubbling, foamlike mass (almost hopelessly misleading, yet a first approximation to the truth) then those bubbles were ...

a thousandth of a millionth of a millionth of a millionth of a millionth of a millionth ...

... of a centimetre across.

And now imagine them continually exploding with energies comparable to those of nuclear bombs – and then reabsorbing that energy, and spitting it out again, and so on forever and forever.

This, in a grossly simplified form, was the picture that some late twentieth-century physicists had developed of the fundamental structure of space. That its intrinsic energies might ever be tapped must, at the time, have seemed completely ridiculous.

So, a lifetime earlier, had been the idea of releasing the new-found forces of the atomic nucleus; yet that had happened in less than half a century. To harness the 'quantum fluctuations' that embodied the energies of space itself was a task orders of magnitude more difficult – and the prize correspondingly greater.

Among other things, it would give mankind the freedom of the universe. A spaceship could accelerate literally forever, since it would no longer need any fuel. The only practical limit to speed would, paradoxically, be that which the early aircraft had to contend with – the friction of the surrounding medium. The space between the stars contained appreciable quantities of hydrogen and other atoms, which could cause trouble long before one reached the ultimate limit set by the velocity of light.

The quantum drive might have been developed at any time after the year 2500, and the history of the human race would then have been very different. Unfortunately – as had happened many times before in the zig-zag progress of science – faulty observations and erroneous theories delayed the final breakthrough for almost a thousand years.

The feverish centuries of the Last Days produced much brilliant – though often decadent – art but little new fundamental knowledge. Moreover, by that time the long record of failure had convinced almost everyone that tapping the energies of space was like perpetual motion, impossible even in theory, let alone in practice. However – unlike perpetual motion – it had not yet been *proved* to be impossible, and until this was demonstrated beyond all doubt, some hope still remained.

Only a hundred and fifty years before the end, a group of physicists in the Lagrange 1 zero-gravity research satellite announced that they had at last found such a proof; there were fundamental reasons why the immense energies of superspace, though they were real enough, could never be tapped. No one was in the least interested in this tidying-up of an obscure corner of science.

A year later, there was an embarrassed cough from Lagrange 1. A slight mistake had been found in the proof. It was the sort of thing that had happened often enough in the past though never with such momentous consequences.

A minus sign had been accidentally converted into a plus.

Instantly, the whole world was changed. The road to the stars had been opened up – five minutes before midnight.

III

South Island

10

First Contact

Perhaps I should have broken it more gently, Moses Kaldor told himself; they all seem in a state of shock. But that in itself is very instructive; even if these people are technologically backward (just look at that car!) they must realize that only a miracle of engineering could have brought us from Earth to Thalassa. First they will wonder how we did it, and then they will start to wonder *why*.

That, in fact, was the very first question that had occurred to Mayor Waldron. These two men in one small vehicle were obviously only the vanguard. Up there in orbit might be thousands – even millions. And the population of Thalassa, thanks to strict regulation, was already within ninety per cent of ecological optimum ...

'My name is Moses Kaldor,' the older of the two visitors said. 'And this is Lieutenant Commander Loren Lorenson, Assistant Chief Engineer, Starship *Magellan*. We apologize for these bubble suits – you'll realize that they are for our mutual protection. Though *we* come in friendship, our bacteria may have different ideas.'

What a beautiful voice, Mayor Waldron told herself – as well she might. Once it had been the best-known in the world, consoling – and sometimes provoking – millions in the decades before the End.

The mayor's notoriously roving eye did not, however remain long on Moses Kaldor; he was obviously well into his sixties, and a little too old for her. The younger man was much more to her liking, though she wondered if she could ever really grow accustomed to that ugly white pallor. Loren Lorenson (what a charming name!) was nearly two metres in height, and his hair was so blond as to be almost silver. He was not as husky as – well, Brant – but he was certainly more handsome.

Mayor Waldron was a good judge both of men and of women, and she classified Lorenson very quickly. Here were intelligence, determination, perhaps even ruthlessness – she would not like to have him as an enemy, but she was certainly interested in having him as a friend. Or better …

At the same time, she did not doubt that Kaldor was a much *nicer* person. In his face and voice she could already discern wisdom, compassion, and also a profound sadness. Little wonder, considering the shadow under which he must have spent the whole of his life.

All the other members of the reception committee had now approached and were introduced one by one. Brant, after the briefest of courtesies, headed straight for the aircraft and began to examine it from end to end.

Loren followed him; he recognized a fellow engineer when he saw one and would be able to learn a good deal from the Thalassan's reactions. He guessed, correctly, what Brant's first question would be about. Even so, he was taken off balance.

'What's the propulsion system? Those jet orifices are ridiculously small – *if* that's what they are.'

It was a very shrewd observation; these people were not the technological savages they had seemed at first sight. But it would never do to show that he was impressed. Better to counterattack and let him have it right between the eyes.

'It's a derated quantum ramjet, adapted for atmospheric flight by using air as a working fluid. Taps the Planck fluctuations – you know, ten to the minus thirty-three centimetres. So of course it has infinite range, in air or in space.' Loren felt rather pleased with that 'of course'.

Once again he had to give Brant credit; the Lassan barely

blinked and even managed to say, 'Very interesting,' as if he really meant it.

'Can I go inside?'

Loren hesitated. It might seem discourteous to refuse, and after all, they were anxious to make friends as quickly as possible. Perhaps more important, this would show who *really* had the mastery here.

'Of course,' he answered. 'But be careful not to touch anything.' Brant was much too interested to notice the absence of 'please'.

Loren led the way into the spaceplane's tiny airlock. There was just enough room for the two of them, and it required complicated gymnastics to seal Brant into the spare bubble suit.

'I hope these won't be necessary for long,' Loren explained, 'but we have to wear them until the microbiology checks are complete. Close your eyes until we've been through the sterilization cycle.'

Brant was aware of a faint violet glow, and there was a brief hissing of gas. Then the inner door opened, and they walked into the control cabin.

As they sat down side by side, the tough, yet scarcely visible films around them barely hindered their movements. Yet it separated them as effectively as if they were on different worlds – which, in many senses, they still were.

Brant was a quick learner, Loren had to admit. Give him a few hours and he could handle this machine – even though he would never be able to grasp the underlying theory. For that matter, legend had it that only a handful of men had ever *really* comprehended the geodynamics of superspace – and they were now centuries dead.

They quickly became so engrossed in technical discussions that they almost forgot the outside world. Suddenly, a slightly worried voice remarked from the general direction of the control panel, 'Loren? Ship calling. What's happening? We've not heard from you for half an hour.'

Loren reached lazily for a switch.

'Since you're monitoring us on six video and five audio channels, that's a slight exaggeration.' He hoped that Brant had got the message: We're in full charge of the situation, and we're not taking anything for granted. 'Over to Moses – he's doing all the talking as usual.'

Through the curved windows, they could see that Kaldor and the mayor were still in earnest discussion, with Councillor Simmons joining in from time to time. Loren threw a switch, and their amplified voices suddenly filled the cabin, more loudly than if they had been standing beside them.

' – our hospitality. But you realize, of course, that this is an extraordinarily small world, as far as land surface is concerned. How many people did you say were aboard your ship?'

'I don't think I mentioned a figure, Madame Mayor. In any event, only a very few of us will ever come down to Thalassa, beautiful though it is. I fully understand your – ah – concern, but there's no need to feel the slightest apprehension. In a year or two, if all goes well, we'll be on our way again.

'At the same time, this isn't a social call – after all, we never expected to meet anyone here! But a starship doesn't delta-vee through half the velocity of light except for *very* good reasons. You have something that we need, and we have something to give you.'

'What, may I ask?'

'From us, if you will accept it, the final centuries of human art and science. But I should warn you – consider what such a gift may do to your own culture. It might not be wise to accept everything we can offer.'

'I appreciate your honesty – and your understanding. You must have treasures beyond price. What can we possibly offer in exchange?'

Kaldor gave his resonant laugh.

'Luckily, *that's* no problem. You wouldn't even notice, if we took it without asking.

'All we want from Thalassa is a hundred thousand tons of water. Or, to be more specific, *ice*.'

11

Delegation

The President of Thalassa had been in office for only two months and was still unreconciled to his misfortune. But there was nothing he could do about it, except to make the best of a bad job for the three years it would last. Certainly it was no use demanding a recount; the selection program, which involved the generation and interleaving of thousand–digit random numbers, was the nearest thing to pure chance that human ingenuity could devise.

There were exactly five ways to avoid the danger of being dragged into the Presidential Palace (twenty rooms, one large enough to hold almost a hundred guests). You could be under thirty or over seventy; you could be incurably ill; you could be mentally defective; or you could have committed a grave crime. The only option really open to President Edgar Farradine was the last, and he had given it serious thought.

Yet he had to admit that, despite the personal inconvenience it had caused him, this was probably the best form of government that mankind had ever devised. The mother planet had taken some ten thousand years to perfect it, by trial and often hideous error.

As soon as the entire adult population had been educated to the limits of its intellectual ability (and sometimes, alas, beyond) genuine democracy became possible. The final step required the development of instantaneous personal communications, linked with central computers. According to the historians, the first true democracy on Earth was established in the (Terran) year 2011, in a country called New Zealand.

Thereafter, selecting a head of state was relatively unimportant. Once it was universally accepted that anyone who *deliberately* aimed at the job should automatically be disqualified, almost any system would serve equally well, and a lottery was the simplest procedure.

'Mr President,' the secretary to the cabinet said, 'the visitors are waiting in the library.'

'Thank you, Lisa. And without their bubble suits?'

'Yes – all the medical people agree that it's perfectly safe. But I'd better warn you, sir. They – ah – *smell* a little odd.'

'Krakan! In what way?'

The secretary smiled.

'Oh, it's not unpleasant – at least, *I* don't think so. It must be something to do with their food; after a thousand years, our biochemistries may have diverged. "Aromatic" is probably the best word to describe it.'

The president was not quite sure what that meant and was debating whether to ask when a disturbing thought occurred to him.

'And how,' he said, 'do you suppose we smell to *them*?'

To his relief, his five guests showed no obvious signs of olfactory distress when they were introduced, one at a time. But Secretary Elisabeth Ishihara was certainly wise to have warned him; now he knew exactly what the word 'aromatic' implied. She was also correct in saying that it was not unpleasant; indeed, he was reminded of the spices his wife used when it was her turn to do the cooking in the palace.

As he sat down at the curve of the horseshoe-shaped conference table, the President of Thalassa found himself musing wryly about Chance and Fate – subjects that had never much concerned him in the past. But Chance, in its purest form, had put him in his present position. Now it – or its sibling, Fate – had struck again. How odd that *he*, an unambitious manufacturer of sporting equipment, had been chosen to preside at this historic meeting! Still, somebody had to do it; and he had to admit that he was beginning to enjoy himself. At the very least, no one could stop him from making his speech of welcome ...

... It was, in fact, quite a good speech, though perhaps a little longer than necessary even for such an occasion as this. Towards the end he became aware that his listeners' politely attentive expressions were becoming a trifle glazed, so he cut out some of the productivity statistics and the whole section about the new power grid on South Island. When he sat down, he felt confident that he had painted a picture of a vigorous, progressive society with a high level of technical skills. Any superficial impressions to the contrary notwithstanding, Thalassa was neither backward nor decadent, and still sustained the finest traditions of its great ancestors. Et cetera.

'Thank you very much, Mr President,' Captain Bey said in the appreciative pause that followed. 'It was indeed a welcome surprise when we discovered that Thalassa was not only inhabited but flourishing. It will make our stay here all the more pleasant, and we hope to leave again with nothing but goodwill on both sides.'

'Pardon me for being so blunt – it may even seem rude to raise the question just as soon as guests arrive – but how long *do* you expect to be here? We'd like to know as soon as possible, so that we can make any necessary arrangements.'

'I quite understand, Mr President. We can't be specific at this stage, because it depends partly on the amount of assistance you can give us. My guess is at least one of your years – more probably two.'

Edgar Farradine, like most Lassans, was not good at concealing his emotions, and Captain Bey was alarmed by the sudden gleeful – one might even say crafty – expression that spread across the chief executive's countenance.

'I hope, Your Excellency, that won't create any problems?' he asked anxiously.

'On the contrary,' the president said, practically rubbing his hands. 'You may not have heard, but our 200th Olympic Games are due in two years.' He coughed modestly. 'I got a bronze in the 1000 metres when I was a young man, so they've put me in charge of the arrangements. We could do with some competition from outside.'

'Mr President,' the secretary to the cabinet said, 'I'm not sure that the rules – '

'Which *I* make,' continued the president firmly. 'Captain, please consider this an invitation. Or a challenge, if you prefer.'

The commander of the starship *Magellan* was a man accustomed to making swift decisions, but for once he was taken completely aback. Before he could think of a suitable reply, his chief medical officer stepped into the breach.

'That's extremely kind of you, Mr President,' Surgeon-Commander Mary Newton said. 'But as a medperson, may I point out that all of us are over thirty, we're completely out of training – and Thalassa's gravity is six per cent stronger than Earth's, which would put us at a severe disadvantage. So unless your Olympics includes chess or card games ...'

The president looked disappointed, but quickly recovered.

'Oh, well – at least, Captain Bey, I'd like you to present some of the prizes.'

'I'd be delighted,' the slightly dazed commander said. He felt that the meeting was getting out of hand and determined to return to the agenda.

'May I explain what we hope to do here, Mr President?'

'Of course,' was the somewhat uninterested reply. His Excellency's thoughts still seemed elsewhere. Perhaps he was still reliving the triumphs of his youth. Then, with an obvious effort, he focused his attention upon the present. 'We were flattered, but rather puzzled, by your visit. There seems very little that our world can offer you. I'm told there was some talk of *ice*; surely that was a joke.'

'No, Mr President – we're absolutely serious. That's all we need of Thalassa, though now we've sampled some of your food products – I'm thinking especially of the cheese and wine we had at lunch – we may increase our demands considerably. But *ice* is the essential; let me explain. First image, please.'

The starship *Magellan*, two metres long, floated in front of the president. It looked so real that he wanted to reach out and touch it, and would certainly have done so had there been no spectators to observe such naive behaviour.

'You'll see that the ship is roughly cylindrical – length four kilometres, diameter one. Because our propulsion system taps the energies of space itself, there's no theoretical limit to speed, up to the velocity of light. But in practice, we run into trouble at about a fifth of that speed, owing to interstellar dust and gas. Tenuous though that is, an object moving through it at sixty thousand kilometres a second or more hits a surprising amount of material – and at that velocity even a single hydrogen atom can do appreciable damage.

'So *Magellan*, just like the first primitive spaceships, carries an ablation shield ahead of it. Almost any material would do, as long as we use enough of it. And at the near-zero temperature between the stars, it's hard to find anything better than ice. Cheap, easily worked, and surprisingly strong! This blunt cone is what our little iceberg looked like when we left the solar system, two hundred years ago. And this is what it's like now.'

The image flickered, then reappeared. The ship was unchanged, but the cone floating ahead of it had shrunk to a thin disc.

'That's the result of drilling a hole fifty light-years long, through this rather dusty sector of the galaxy. I'm pleased to say the rate of ablation is within five per cent of estimate, so we were never in any danger – though of course there was always the remote possibility that we might hit something *really* big. No shield could protect us against that – whether it was made of ice, or the best armour-plate steel.

'We're still good for another ten light-years, but that's not enough. Our final destination is the planet Sagan 2 – seventy-five lights to go.

'So now you understand, Mr President, why we stopped at Thalassa. We would like to borrow – well, beg, since we can hardly promise to return it – a hundred or so thousand tons of water from you. We must build another iceberg, up there in orbit, to sweep the path ahead of us when we go on to the stars.'

'How can we possibly help you to do that? Technically, you must be centuries ahead of us.'

'I doubt it – except for the quantum drive. Perhaps Deputy Captain Malina can outline our plans – subject to your approval, of course.'

'Please go ahead.'

'First we have to locate a site for the freezing plant. There are many possibilities – it could be on any isolated stretch of coastline. It will cause absolutely no ecological disturbance, but if you wish, we'll put it on East Island – and hope that Krakan won't blow before we've finished!

'The plant design is virtually complete, needing only minor modifications to match whatever site we finally choose. Most of the main components can go into production right away. They're all very straightforward – pumps, refrigerating systems, heat exchangers, cranes – good old-fashioned Second Millennium technology!

'If everything goes smoothly, we should have our first ice in ninety days. We plan to make standard-sized blocks, each weighing six hundred tons – flat, hexagonal plates – someone's christened them snowflakes, and the name seems to have stuck.

'When production's started, we'll lift one snowflake every day. They'll be assembled in orbit and keyed together to build up the shield. From first lift to final structural test should take two hundred and fifty days. Then we'll be ready to leave.'

When the deputy captain had finished, President Farradine sat in silence for a moment, a faraway look in his eye. Then he said, almost reverently. 'Ice – I've never seen any, except at the bottom of a drink ...'

*   *   *

As he shook hands with the departing visitors, President Farradine became aware of something strange. Their aromatic odour was now barely perceptible.

Had he grown accustomed to it already – or was he losing his sense of smell?

Although both answers were correct, around midnight he would have accepted only the second. He woke up with his eyes watering, and his nose so clogged that it was difficult to breathe.

'What's the matter, dear?' Mrs President said anxiously.

'Call the – *atischoo*! – doctor,' the chief executive answered. 'Ours – *and* the one up in the ship. I don't believe there's a damn thing they can do, but I want to give them – *atischoo* – a piece of my mind. And I hope *you* haven't caught it as well.'

The president's lady started to reassure him, but was interrupted by a sneeze.

They both sat up in bed and looked at each other unhappily.

'I believe it took seven days to get over it,' sniffed the president. 'But perhaps medical science has advanced in the last few centuries.'

His hope was fulfilled, though barely. By heroic efforts, and with no loss of life, the epidemic was stamped out – in six miserable days.

It was not an auspicious beginning for the first contact between star-sundered cousins in almost a thousand years.

12

Heritage

We've been here two weeks, Evelyn – though it doesn't seem like it as that's only eleven of Thalassa's days. Sooner or later we'll have to abandon the old calendar, but my heart will always beat to the ancient rhythms of Earth.

It's been a busy time, and on the whole a pleasant one. The only real problem was medical; despite all precautions, we broke quarantine too soon, and about twenty per cent of the Lassans caught some kind of virus. To make us feel even guiltier, none of *us* developed any symptoms whatsoever. Luckily no one died, though I'm afraid we can't give the local doctors too much credit for that. Medical science is definitely backward here; they've grown to rely on automated systems so much that they can't handle anything out of the ordinary.

But we've been forgiven; the Lassans are very good-natured, easygoing people. They have been incredibly lucky – perhaps too lucky! – with their planet; it makes the contrast with Sagan 2 even bleaker.

Their only real handicap is lack of land, and they've been wise enough to hold the population well below the sustainable maximum. If they're ever tempted to exceed it, they have the records of Earth's city-slums as a terrible warning.

Because they're such beautiful and charming people, it's a great temptation to help them instead of letting them develop their own culture in their own way. In a sense, they're our children – and all parents find it hard to accept that, sooner or later, they must cease to interfere.

To some extent, of course, we can't help interfering; our very presence does that. We're unexpected – though luckily not unwelcome – guests on their planet. And they can never forget that *Magellan* is orbiting just above the atmosphere, the last emissary from the world of their own ancestors.

I've revisited First Landing – *their* birthplace – and gone on the tour that every Lassan makes at least once in his life. It's a combination of museum and shrine, the only place on the whole planet to which the word 'sacred' is remotely applicable. Nothing has changed in seven hundred years. The seedship, though it is now an empty husk, looks as if it has only just landed. All around it are the silent machines – the excavators and constructors and chemical processing plants with their robot attendants. And, of course, the nurseries and schools of Generation One.

There are almost no records of those first decades – perhaps deliberately. Despite all the skills and precautions of the planners, there must have been biological accidents, ruthlessly eliminated by the overriding program. And the time when those who had no organic parents gave way to those who did, must have been full of psychological traumas.

But the tragedy and sadness of the Genesis Decades is now centuries in the past. Like the graves of all pioneers, it has been forgotten by the builders of the new society.

I would be happy to spend the rest of my life here; there's material on Thalassa for a whole army of anthropologists and psychologists and social scientists. Above all, how I wish I could meet some of my long-dead colleagues and let them know how many of our endless arguments have been finally resolved!

It is possible to build a rational and humane culture completely free from the threat of supernatural restraints. Though in principle I don't approve of censorship, it seems that those who prepared the archives for the Thalassan colony succeeded in an almost-impossible task. They purged the history and literature of ten thousand years, and the result has justified their efforts. We must be very cautious before replacing anything that was lost – however beautiful, however moving a work of art.

The Thalassans were never poisoned by the decay products of dead religions, and in seven hundred years no prophet has arisen here to preach a new faith. The very word 'God' has almost vanished from their language, and they're quite surprised – or amused – when we happen to use it.

My scientist friends are fond of saying that one sample makes very poor statistics, so I wonder if the total lack of religion in this society really proves anything. We know that the Thalassans were also very carefully selected genetically to eliminate as many undesirable social traits as possible. Yes, yes – I know that only about fifteen per cent of human behaviour is determined by the genes – but that fraction is *very* important! The Lassans certainly seem remarkably free from such unpleasant traits as envy, intolerance, jealousy, anger. Is this entirely the result of cultural conditioning?

How I would love to know what happened to the seedships that were sent out by those religious groups in the twenty-sixth century! The Mormons' *Ark of the Covenant*, the *Sword of the Prophet* – there were half a dozen of them. I wonder if any of them succeeded, and if so what part religion played in their success or their failure. Perhaps one day, when the local communications grid is established, we'll find what happened to those early pioneers.

One result of Thalassa's total atheism is a serious shortage of expletives. When a Lassan drops something on his toe, he's at a loss for words. Even the usual references to bodily functions aren't much help because they're all taken for granted. About the only general-purpose exclamation is 'Krakan!' and that's badly overworked. But it does show what an impression Mount Krakan made when it erupted four hundred years ago; I hope I'll have a chance of visiting it before we leave.

That's still many months ahead, yet already I fear it. Not for the possible danger – if anything happens to the ship, I'll never know. But because it will mean that another link with Earth has been broken – and, my dearest, with you.

13

Task Force

'The president's not going to like this,' Mayor Waldron said with relish. 'He's set his heart on getting you to North Island.'

'I know,' Deputy Captain Malina answered. 'And we'll be sorry to disappoint him – he's been very helpful. But North Island's far too rocky; the only suitable coastal areas are already developed. Yet there's a completely deserted bay, with a gently sloping beach, only nine kilometres from Tarna – it will be perfect.'

'Sounds too good to be true. *Why* is it deserted, Brant?'

'That was the Mangrove Project. All the trees died – we still don't know why – and no one's had the heart to tidy up the mess. It looks terrible, and smells worse.'

'So it's already an ecological disaster area – you're welcome, Captain! You can only improve matters.'

'I can assure you that our plant will be very handsome and won't damage the environment in the slightest. And of course it will all be dismantled when we leave. Unless you want to keep it.'

'Thank you – but I doubt if we'd have much use for several hundred tons of ice a day. Meanwhile, what facilities can Tarna offer – accommodation, catering, transport? – we'll be happy to oblige. I assume that quite a number of you will be coming down to work here.'

'Probably about a hundred, and we appreciate your offer of hospitality. But I'm afraid we'd be terrible guests: we'll be having conferences with the ship at all hours of the day and night. So we have to stick together – and as soon as we've assembled our little prefabricated village, we'll move into it with all our equipment. I'm sorry if this seems ungracious – but any other arrangement simply wouldn't be practical.'

'I suppose you're right,' the mayor sighed. She had been wondering how she could bend protocol and offer what passed for the hospitality suite to the spectacular Lieutenant Commander Lorenson instead of to Deputy Captain Malina. The problem had appeared insoluble; now, alas, it would not even arise.

She felt so discouraged that she was almost tempted to call North Island and invite her last official consort back for a vacation. But the wretch would probably turn her down again, and she simply couldn't face that.

14

Mirissa

Even when she was a very old woman, Mirissa Leonidas could still remember the exact moment when she first set eyes on Loren. There was no one else – not even Brant – of which this was true.

Novelty had nothing to do with it; she had already met several of the Earthmen before encountering Loren, and they had made no unusual impression on her. Most of them could have passed as Lassans if they had been left out in the sun for a few days.

But not Loren; his skin never tanned, and his startling hair became, if anything, even more silvery. That was certainly what had first drawn her notice as he was emerging from Mayor Waldron's office with two of his colleagues – all of them bearing that slightly frustrated look which was the usual outcome of a session with Tarna's lethargic and well-entrenched bureaucracy.

Their eyes had met, but for a moment only. Mirissa took a few more paces; then, without any conscious volition, she came to a dead halt and looked back over her shoulder – to see that the visitor was staring at her. Already, they both knew that their lives had been irrevocably changed.

Later that night, after they had made love, she asked Brant, 'Have they said how long they're staying?'

'You do choose the worst times,' he grumbled sleepily. 'At least a year. Maybe two. Goodnight – *again*.'

She knew better than to ask any more questions even though she still felt wide awake. For a long time she lay open-eyed, watching the swift shadows of the inner moon sweep across the floor while the cherished body beside her sank gently into sleep.

She had known not a few men before Brant, but since they had been together she had been utterly indifferent to anyone else. Then why this sudden interest – she still pretended it was no stronger than that – in a man she had glimpsed only for a few seconds and whose very name she did not even know? (Though that would certainly be one of tomorrow's first priorities.)

Mirissa prided herself on being honest and clear-sighted; she looked down on women – or men – who let themselves be ruled by their emotions. Part of the attraction, she was quite sure, was the element of novelty, the glamour of vast new horizons. To be able to speak to someone who had actually walked through the cities of Earth – had witnessed the last hours of the solar system – and was now on the way to new suns was a wonder beyond her wildest dreams. It made her once more aware of that underlying dissatisfaction with the placid tempo of Thalassan life despite her happiness with Brant.

Or was it merely contentment and not true happiness? What did she *really* want? Whether she could find it with these strangers from the stars she did not know, but before they left Thalassa forever, she meant to try.

That same morning, Brant had also visited Mayor Waldron, who greeted him with slightly less than her usual warmth when he dumped the fragments of his fish-trap on her desk.

'I know you've been busy with more important matters,' he said, 'but what are we going to do about *this*?'

The mayor looked without enthusiasm at the tangled mess of cables. It was hard to focus on the day-to-day routine after the heady excitements of interstellar politics.

'What do *you* think happened?' she asked.

'It's obviously deliberate – see how this wire was twisted until it broke. Not only was the grid damaged, but sections have been taken away. I'm sure no one on South Island would do such a thing. What motive would they have? And I'd be bound to find out, sooner or later ...'

Brant's pregnant pause left no doubt as to what would happen then.

'Who do you suspect?'

'Ever since I started experimenting with electric trapping, I've been fighting not only the Conservers but those crazy people who believe that *all* food should be synthetic because it's wicked to eat living creatures, like animals – or even plants.'

'The Conservers, at least, may have a point. If your trap is as efficient as you claim, it could upset the ecological balance they're always talking about.'

'The regular reef census would tell us if *that* was happening, and we'd just switch off for a while. Anyway, it's the pelagics I'm really after; my field seems to attract them from up to three or four kilometres away. And even if everyone on the Three Islands ate nothing but fish, we couldn't make a dent in the oceanic population.'

'I'm sure you're right – as far as the indigenous pseudofish are concerned. And much good that does, since most of them are too poisonous to be worth processing. Are you *sure* that the Terran stock has established itself securely? You might be the last straw, as the old saying goes.'

Brant looked at the mayor with respect; she was continually surprising him with shrewd questions like this. It never occurred to him that she would not have held her position for so long if there was not a great deal more in her than met the eye.

'I'm afraid the tuna aren't going to survive; it will be a few billion years before the oceans are salty enough for them. But the trout and salmon are doing very well.'

'And they're certainly delicious; they might even overcome the moral scruples of the Synthesists. Not that I really accept your interesting theory. Those people may talk, but they don't *do* anything.'

'They released a whole herd of cattle from that experimental farm a couple of years ago.'

'You mean they *tried* to – the cows walked straight home again. Everyone laughed so much that they called off any further demonstrations. I simply can't imagine that they'd go to all this trouble.' She gestured towards the broken grid.

'It wouldn't be difficult – a small boat at night, a couple of divers – the water's only twenty metres deep.'

'Well, I'll make some inquiries. Meanwhile, I want you to do two things.'

'What?' Brant said, trying not to sound suspicious and failing completely.

'Repair the grid – Tech Stores will give you anything you need. And stop making any more accusations until you're one hundred per cent certain. If you're wrong, you'll look foolish and may have to apologize. If you're right, you may scare the perpetrators away before we can catch them. Understand?'

Brant's jaw dropped slightly: he had never seen the mayor in so incisive a mood. He gathered up Exhibit A and made a somewhat chastened departure.

He might have been even more chastened – or perhaps merely amused – to know that Mayor Waldron was no longer quite so enamoured of him.

Assistant Chief Engineer Loren Lorenson had impressed more than one of Tarna's citizens that morning.

15

Terra Nova

Such a reminder of Earth was an unfortunate name for the settlement, and no one admitted responsibility. But it was slightly more glamorous than 'base camp', and was quickly accepted.

The complex of prefabricated huts had shot up with astonishing speed – literally overnight. It was Tarna's first demonstration of Earthpersons – or rather Earth robots – in action, and the villagers were hugely impressed. Even Brant, who had always considered that robots were more trouble than they were worth, except for hazardous or monotonous work, began to have second thoughts. There was one elegant general-purpose mobile constructor that operated with such blinding speed that it was often impossible to follow its movements. Wherever it went, it was followed by an admiring crowd of small Lassans. When they got in its way, it politely stopped whatever it was doing until the coast was clear. Brant decided that this was exactly the kind of assistant he needed; perhaps there was some way he could persuade the visitors...

By the end of a week, Terra Nova was a fully functioning microcosm of the great ship orbiting beyond the atmosphere. There was plain but comfortable accommodation for a hundred crewmembers, with all the life-support systems they needed – as well as library, gymnasium, swimming pool, and theatre. The Lassans approved of these facilities, and hastened to make full use of them. As a result, the population of Terra Nova was usually at least double the nominal one hundred.

Most of the guests – whether invited or not – were anxious to help and determined to make their visitors' stay as comfortable as possible. Such friendliness, though very welcome and much appreciated, was often embarrassing. The Lassans were insatiably inquisitive, and the concept of privacy was almost unknown to them. A 'Please Do Not Disturb' sign was often regarded as a personal challenge, which led to interesting complications...

'You're all senior officers and highly intelligent adults,' Captain Bey had said at the last staff conference aboard ship. 'So it shouldn't be necessary to tell you this. Try not to get involved in any – ah – entanglements until we know *exactly* how the Lassans think about such matters. They appear very easygoing, but that could be deceptive. Don't you agree, Dr Kaldor?'

'I can't pretend, Captain, to be an authority on Lassan *mores* after so short a period of study. But there are some interesting historical parallels, when the old sailing-ships on Earth put to port after long sea voyages – I expect many of you have seen that classic video antique, *Mutiny on the Bounty*.'

'I trust, Dr Kaldor, that you're not comparing me to Captain Cook – I mean Bligh.'

'It wouldn't be an insult; the real Bligh was a brilliant seaman, and most unfairly maligned. At this stage, all we need are common sense, good manners – and, as you indicated, caution.'

Had Kaldor looked in *his* direction, Loren wondered, when he made that remark? Surely it was not already so obvious...

After all, his official duties put him in contact with Brant Falconer a dozen times a day. There was no way he could avoid meeting Mirissa – even if he wished to.

They had never yet been alone together, and had still exchanged no more than a few words of polite conversation. But already, there was no need to say anything more.

Party Games

'It's called a baby,' Mirissa said, 'and despite appearances, one day it will grow up into a perfectly normal human being.'

She was smiling, yet there was moisture in her eyes. It had never occurred to her, until she noticed Loren's fascination, that there were probably more children in the little village of Tarna than there had been on the entire planet Earth during the final decades of virtually zero birthrate.

'Is it ... yours?' he asked quietly.

'Well, first of all it's not an *it*; it's a he. Brant's nephew Lester – we're looking after him while his parents are on North Island.'

'He's beautiful. Can I hold him?'

As if on cue, Lester started to wail.

'That wouldn't be a good idea,' laughed Mirissa, scooping him up hastily and heading towards the nearest bathroom. 'I recognize the signals. Let Brant or Kumar show you round while we're waiting for the other guests.'

The Lassans loved parties and missed no opportunity for arranging them. The arrival of *Magellan* was, quite literally, the chance of a lifetime – indeed, of many lifetimes. If they had been rash enough to accept all the invitations they received, the visitors would have spent every waking moment staggering from one official or unofficial reception to another. None too soon, the captain had issued one of his infrequent but implacable directives – 'Bey thunderbolts', or simply 'Beybolts', as they were wryly called – rationing his officers to a maximum of one party per five days. There were some who considered that, in view of the time it often took to recover from Lassan hospitality, this was much too generous.

The Leonidas residence, currently occupied by Mirissa, Kumar, and Brant, was a large ring-shaped building that had been the family's home for six generations. One storey high – there were few upper floors in Tarna – it enclosed a grass-covered patio about thirty metres across. At the very centre was a small pond, complete with a tiny island accessible by a picturesque wooden bridge. And on the island was a solitary palm-tree, which did not seem to be in the best of health.

'They have to keep replacing it,' Brant said apologetically. 'Some Terran plants do very well here – others just fade away despite all the chemical boosters we give them. It's the same problem with the fish we've tried to introduce. Freshwater farms work fine, of course, but we don't have space for them. It's frustrating to think that there's a million times as much ocean, if only we could use it properly.'

In Loren's private opinion, Brant Falconer was something of a bore when he started talking about the sea. He had to admit, however, that it was a safer subject of conversation than Mirissa, who had now managed to get rid of Lester and was greeting the new guests as they arrived.

Could he ever have dreamed, Loren asked himself, that he would find himself in a situation like this? He had been in love before, but the memories – even the names – were mercifully blurred by the erasing programs they had all undergone before leaving the solar system. He would not even attempt to recapture them: why torment himself with images from a past that had been utterly destroyed?

Even Kitani's face was blurring, though he had seen her in the hibernaculum only a week ago. She was part of a future they had planned but might never share: Mirissa was here and now – full of life and laughter, not frozen in half a millennium of sleep. She had made him feel whole once more, joyful in the knowledge that the strain and exhaustion of the Last Days had not, after all, robbed him of his youth.

Every time they were together, he felt the pressure that told him he was a man again; until it had been relieved, he would know little peace and would not even be able to perform his work efficiently. There had been times when he had seen Mirissa's face superimposed on the Mangrove Bay plans and flow diagrams, and had been forced to give the computer a PAUSE command, before they could continue their joint mental conversation. It was a peculiarly exquisite torture to spend a couple of hours within metres of her, able to exchange no more than polite trivialities.

To Loren's relief, Brant suddenly excused himself and hurried away. Loren quickly discovered the reason.

'Commander Lorenson!' Mayor Waldron said. 'I hope Tarna's been treating you well.'

Loren groaned inwardly. He knew that he was supposed to be polite to the mayor, but the social graces had never been his strong point.

'Very well, thank you. I don't believe you've met these gentlemen –'

He called, much more loudly than was really necessary, across the patio to a group of colleagues who had just arrived. By good luck, they were all lieutenants; even off duty, rank had its privileges, and he never hesitated to use it.

'Mayor Waldron, this is Lieutenant Fletcher – your first time down, isn't it Owen? Lieutenant Werner Ng, Lieutenant Ranjit Winson, Lieutenant Karl Bosley ...'

Just like the clannish Martians, he thought, always sticking together. Well, that made them a splendid target, and they were a personable group of young men. He did not believe that the mayor even noticed when he made his strategic withdrawal.

Doreen Chang would have much preferred to talk to the captain, but he had made a high-velocity token appearance, downed one drink, apologized to his hosts, and departed.

'Why won't he let me interview him?' she asked Kaldor, who had no such inhibitions and had already logged several days' worth of audio and video time.

'Captain Sirdar Bey,' he answered, 'is in a privileged position. Unlike the rest of us, he doesn't have to explain – or to apologize.'

'I detect a note of mild sarcasm in your voice,' the Thalassa Broadcasting Corporation's star newsperson said.

'It wasn't intended. I admire the captain enormously, and even accept his opinion of me – with reservations, of course. Er – are you recording?'

'Not *now*. Too much background noise.'

'Lucky for you I'm such a trusting person since there's no way I could tell if you were.'

'Definitely off the record, Moses. What *does* he think of you?'

'He's glad to have my views, and my experience, but he doesn't take me very seriously. I know exactly why. He once said, "Moses – you like power but not responsibility. I enjoy both." It was a very shrewd statement; it sums up the difference between us.'

'How did you answer?'

'What could I say? It was perfectly true. The only time I got involved in practical politics was – well, not a disaster, but I never really enjoyed it.'

'The Kaldor Crusade?'

'Oh – you know about that. Silly name – it annoyed me. And that was another point of disagreement between the captain and myself. He thought – still thinks, I'm sure – the Directive ordering us to avoid *all* planets with life-potential is a lot of sentimental nonsense. Another quote from the good captain: "Law I understand. Metalaw is bal – er, balderdash ."

'This is fascinating – one day you must let me record it.'

'Definitely not. What's happening over there?'

Doreen Chang was a persistent lady, but she knew when to give up.

'Oh, that's Mirissa's favourite gas-sculpture. Surely you had them on Earth.'

'Of course. And since we're still off the record, I don't think it's art. But it's amusing.'

The main lights had been switched off in one section of the patio, and about a dozen guests had gathered around what appeared to be a very large soap bubble, almost a metre in diameter. As Chang and Kaldor walked towards it, they could see the first swirls of colour forming inside, like the birth of a spiral nebula.

'It's called "Life",' Doreen said, 'and it's been in Mirissa's family for two hundred years. But the gas is beginning to leak; I can remember when it was much brighter.'

Even so, it was impressive. The battery of electron guns and lasers in the base had been programmed by some patient, long-dead artist to generate a series of geometrical shapes that slowly evolved into organic structures. From the centre of the sphere, ever more complex forms appeared, expanded out of sight, and were replaced by others. In one witty sequence, single-celled creatures were shown climbing a spiral staircase, recognizable at once as a representation of the DNA molecule. With each step, something new was added; within a few minutes, the display had encompassed the four-billion-year odyssey from amoeba to Man.

Then the artist tried to go beyond, and Kaldor lost him. The contortions of the fluorescent gas became too complex and too abstract. Perhaps if one saw the display a few more times, a pattern would emerge –

'What happened to the sound?' Doreen asked when the bubble's maelstrom of seething colours abruptly winked out. 'There used to be some very good music, especially at the end.'

'I was afraid someone would ask that question,' Mirissa said with an apologetic smile. 'We're not certain whether the trouble is in the playback mechanism or the program itself.'

'Surely you have a backup!'

'Oh, yes, of course. But the spare module is somewhere in Kumar's room, probably buried under bits of his canoe. Until you've seen his den, you won't understand what entropy really means.'

'It's not a canoe – it's a kayak,' protested Kumar, who had just arrived with a pretty local girl clinging to each arm. 'And what's entropy?'

One of the young Martians was foolish enough to attempt an explanation by pouring two drinks of different colours into the same glass. Before he could get very far, his voice was drowned by a blast of music from the gas-sculpture.

'You see!' Kumar shouted above the din, with obvious pride, 'Brant can fix *anything*!'

Anything? thought Loren. I wonder … I wonder …

17

Chain of Command

From: Captain
To: All Crew Members

CHRONOLOGY

As there has already been a great deal of unnecessary confusion in this matter, I wish to make the following points:

1. All ship's records and schedules will remain on Earth Time — corrected for relativistic effects — until the end of the voyage. All clocks and timing systems aboard ship will continue to run on ET.
2. For convenience, ground crews will use Thalassan time (TT) when necessary, but will keep all records in ET with TT in parentheses.
3. *To remind you*:

     The duration of the Thalassan Mean Solar Day is 29.4325 hours ET.
     There are 313.1561 Thalassan days in the Thalassan

Sidereal Year, which is divided into 11 months of 28 days. January is omitted from the calendar, but the five extra days to make up the total of 313 follow immediately after the last day (28th) of December. Leap days are intercalated every six years, but there will be none during our stay.

4. Since the Thalassan day is 22% longer than Earth's, and the number of those days in its year is 14% shorter, the actual length of the Thalassan year is only about 5% longer than Earth's. As you are all aware, this has one practical convenience, in the matter of birthdays. Chronological age means almost the same on Thalassa as on Earth. A 21-year-old Thalassan has lived as long as a 20-year old Earthperson. The Lassan calendar starts at First Landing, which was 3109 ET. The current year is 718 TT or 754 Earth years later.

5. Finally — and we can also be thankful for this — there is only one Time Zone to worry about on Thalassa.

Sirdar Bey (Capt.)

3864.05.26.20.30 ET
718.00.02.15.00 TT

'Who would have thought anything so simple could be so complicated!' laughed Mirissa when she had scanned the printout pinned up on the Terra Nova Bulletin Board. 'I suppose this is one of the famous Beybolts. What sort of man is the captain? I've never had a real chance of talking to him.'

'He's not an easy person to know,' Moses Kaldor answered. 'I don't think I've spoken to him in private more than a dozen times. And he's the only man on the ship who everyone calls 'Sir' – *always*. Except maybe Deputy Captain Malina, when they're alone together ... Incidentally, that notice was certainly not a genuine Beybolt – it's too technical. Science Officer Varley and Secretary LeRoy must have drafted it. Captain Bey has a remarkable grasp of engineering principles – much better than I do – but he's primarily an administrator. And occasionally, when he has to be, commander-in-chief.'

'I'd hate his responsibility.'

'It's a job someone has to do. Routine problems can usually be solved by consulting the senior officers and the computer banks. But sometimes a decision has to be made by a single individual, who has the authority to enforce it. That's why you need a captain. You can't run a ship by a committee – at least not all the time.'

'I think that's the way we run Thalassa. Can you imagine President Farradine as captain of *anything?*'

'These peaches are delicious,' Kaldor said tactfully, helping himself to another, though he knew perfectly well that they had been intended for Loren. 'But you've been lucky; you've had no real crisis for seven hundred years! Didn't one of your own people once say: "Thalassa has no history – only statistics"?'

'Oh, that's not true! What about Mount Krakan?'

'That was a natural disaster – and hardly a major one. I'm referring to, ah, political crises: civil unrest, *that* sort of thing.'

'We can thank Earth for that. You gave us a Jefferson Mark 3 Constitution – someone once called it utopia in two megabytes – and it's worked amazingly well. The program hasn't been modified for three hundred years. We're still only on the Sixth Amendment.'

'And long may you stay there,' Kaldor said fervently. 'I should hate to think that we were responsible for a Seventh.'

'If that happens, it will be processed first in the Archives' memory banks. When are you coming to visit us again? There are so many things I want to show you.

'Not as many as I want to see. You must have so much that will be useful for us on Sagan 2, even though it's a very different kind of world.' ('And a far less attractive one,' he added to himself.)

While they were talking, Loren had come quietly into the reception area, obviously on his way from the games room to the showers. He was wearing the briefest of shorts and had a towel draped over his bare shoulders. The sight left Mirissa distinctly weak at the knees.

'I suppose you've beaten everyone, as usual,' Kaldor said. 'Doesn't it get boring?'

Loren gave a wry grin.

'Some of the young Lassans show promise. One's just taken three points off me. Of course, I was playing with my left hand.'

'In the very unlikely event he hasn't already told you,' Kaldor remarked to Mirissa, 'Loren was once table-tennis champion on Earth.'

'Don't exaggerate, Moses. I was only about number five – and standards were miserably low towards the end. Any Third Millennium Chinese player would have pulverized me.'

'I don't suppose you've thought of teaching Brant,' Kaldor said mischievously. 'That should be interesting.'

There was a brief silence. Then Loren answered, smugly but accurately: 'It wouldn't be fair.'

'As it happens,' Mirissa said, 'Brant would like to show *you* something.'

'Oh.'

'You said you've never been on a boat.'

'That's true.'

'Then you have an invitation to join Brant and Kumar at Pier Three – eight-thirty tomorrow morning.'

Loren turned to Kaldor.

'Do you think it's safe for me to go?' he asked in mock seriousness. 'I don't know how to swim.'

'I shouldn't worry,' Kaldor answered helpfully. 'If they're planning a one-way trip for you, that won't make the slightest difference.'

18

Kumar

Only one tragedy had darkened Kumar Leonidas's eighteen years of life; he would always be ten centimetres shorter than his heart's desire. It was not surprising that his nickname was 'The Little Lion' – though very few dared use it to his face.

To compensate for his lack of height, he had worked assiduously on width and depth. Many times Mirissa had told him, in amused exasperation, 'Kumar – if you spent as much time building your brain as your body, you'd be the greatest genius on Thalassa.' What she had never told him – and scarcely admitted even to herself – was that the spectacle of his regular morning exercises often aroused most unsisterly feelings in her breast as well as a certain jealousy of all the other admirers who had gathered to watch. At one time or other this had included most of Kumar's age group. Although the envious rumour that he had made love to all the girls and half the boys in Tarna was wild hyperbole, it did contain a considerable element of truth.

But Kumar, despite the intellectual gulf between him and his sister, was no muscle-bound moron. If anything really interested him, he would not be satisfied until he had mastered it, no matter how long that took. He was a superb seaman and for over two years, with occasional help from Brant, had been building an exquisite four-metre kayak. The hull was complete, but he had not yet started on the deck.

One day, he swore, he was going to launch it and everyone would stop laughing. Meanwhile, the phrase 'Kumar's kayak' had come to mean any unfinished job around Tarna – of which, indeed, there were a great many.

Apart from this common Lassan tendency to procrastinate, Kumar's chief defects were an adventurous nature and a fondness for sometimes risky practical jokes. This, it was widely believed, would someday get him into serious trouble.

But it was impossible to be angry with even his most outrageous pranks, for they lacked all malice. He was completely open, even transparent; no one could ever imagine him telling a lie. For this, he could be forgiven much, and frequently was.

The arrival of the visitors had, of course, been the most exciting event in his life. He was fascinated by their equipment, the sound, video, and sensory recordings they had brought, the stories they told – everything about them. And because he saw more of Loren than any of the others, it was not surprising that Kumar attached himself to him.

This was not a development that Loren altogether appreciated. If there was one thing even more unwelcome than an inconvenient mate, it was that traditional spoilsport, an adhesive kid brother.

19

Pretty Polly

'I still can't believe it, Loren,' Brant Falconer said. 'You've *never* been in a boat – or on a ship?'

'I seem to remember paddling a rubber dinghy across a small pond. That would have been when I was about five years old.'

'Then you'll enjoy this. Not even a swell to upset your stomach. Perhaps we can persuade you to dive with us.'

'No, thanks – I'll take one new experience at a time. And I've learned never to get in the way when other men have work to do.'

Brant was right; he *was* beginning to enjoy himself, as the hydrojets drove the little trimaran almost silently out toward the reef. Yet soon after he had climbed aboard and seen the firm safety of the shoreline rapidly receding, he had known a moment of near panic.

Only a sense of the ridiculous had saved him from making a spectacle of himself. He had travelled fifty light-years – the longest journey ever made by human beings – to reach this spot. And now he was worried about the few hundred metres to the nearest land.

Yet there was no way in which he could turn down the challenge. As he lay at ease in the stern, watching Fa'coner at the wheel (how had he acquired that white scar across his shoulders? – oh, yes, he had mentioned something about a crash in a microflyer, years ago ...), he wondered just what was going through the Lassan's mind.

It was hard to believe that any human society, even the most enlightened and easygoing, could be totally free from jealousy or some form of sexual possessiveness. Not that there was – so far, alas! – much for Brant to be jealous about.

Loren doubted if he had spoken as many as a hundred words to Mirissa; most of them had been in the company of her husband. Correction: on Thalassa, the terms husband and wife were not used until the birth of the first child. When a son was chosen, the mother usually – but not invariably – assumed the name of the father. If the first born was a girl, both kept the mother's name – at least until the birth of the second, and final, child.

There were very few things indeed that shocked the Lassans. Cruelty – especially to children – was one of them. And having a third pregnancy, on this world with only twenty thousand square kilometres of land, was another.

Infant mortality was so low that multiple births were sufficient to maintain a steady population. There had been one famous case – the only one in the whole history of Thalassa – when a family had been blessed, or afflicted, with double quintuplets. Although the poor mother could hardly be blamed, her memory was now surrounded with that aura of delicious depravity that had once enveloped Lucrezia Borgia, Messalina, or Faustine.

I'll have to play my cards very, very carefully, Loren told himself. That Mirissa found him attractive, he already knew. He could read it in her expression and in the tone of her voice. And he had even stronger proof in accidental contacts of hand, and soft collisions of body that had lasted longer than were strictly necessary.

They both knew that it was only a matter of time. And so, Loren was quite sure, did Brant. Yet despite the mutual tension between them, they were still friendly enough.

The pulsation of the jets died away, and the boat drifted to a halt, close to a large glass buoy that was gently bobbing up and down in the water.

'That's our power supply,' Brant said. 'We only need a few hundred watts, so we can manage with solar cells. One advantage of freshwater seas – it wouldn't work on Earth. Your oceans were much too salty – they'd have gobbled up kilowatts and kilowatts.'

'Sure you won't change your mind, uncle?' Kumar grinned.

Loren shook his head. Though it had startled him at first, he had now grown quite accustomed to the universal salutation employed by younger Lassans. It was really rather pleasant, suddenly acquiring scores of nieces and nephews.

'No, thanks. I'll stay and watch through the underwater window, just in case you get eaten by sharks.'

'Sharks!' Kumar said wistfully. 'Wonderful, wonderful animals – I wish we had some here. It would make diving much more exciting.'

Loren watched with a technician's interest as Brant and Kumar adjusted their gear. Compared with the equipment one needed to wear in space, it was remarkably simple – and the pressure tank was a tiny thing that could easily fit in the palm of one hand.

'That oxygen tank,' he said, 'I wouldn't have thought it could last more than a couple of minutes.'

Brant and Kumar looked at him reproachfully.

'Oxygen!' snorted Brant. 'That's a deadly poison, at below twenty metres. This bottle holds air – and it's only the emergency supply, good for fifteen minutes.'

He pointed to the gill-like structure on the backpack that Kumar was already wearing.

'There's all the oxygen you need dissolved in seawater, if you can extract it. But that takes energy, so you have to have a powercell to run the pumps and filters. I could stay down for a week with this unit if I wanted to.'

He tapped the greenly fluorescent computer display on his left wrist.

'This gives all the information I need – depth, powercell status, time to come up, decompression stops – '

Loren risked another foolish question.

'Why are you wearing a facemask, while Kumar isn't?'

'But I am.' Kumar grinned. 'Look carefully.'

'Oh ... I see. Very neat.'

'But a nuisance,' Brant said, 'unless you practically live in the water, like Kumar. I tried contacts once, and found they hurt my eyes. So I stick to the good old facemask – much less trouble. Ready?'

'Ready, skipper.'

They rolled simultaneously over port and starboard sides, their movements so well synchronized that the boat scarcely rocked. Through the thick glass panel set in the keel, Loren watched them glide effortlessly down to the reef. It was, he knew, more than twenty metres down but looked much closer.

Tools and cabling had already been dumped there, and the two divers went swiftly to work repairing the broken grids. Occasionally, they exchanged cryptic monosyllables, but most of the time they worked in complete silence. Each knew his job – and his partner – so well that there was no need for speech.

Time went very swiftly for Loren; he felt he was looking into a new world, as indeed he was. Though he had seen innumerable video records made in the terrestrial oceans, almost all the life that moved below him now was completely unfamiliar. There were whirling discs and pulsating jellies, undulating carpets and corkscrewing spirals – but very few creatures that, by any stretch of the imagination, could be called genuine fish. Just once, near the edge of vision, he caught a glimpse of a swiftly-moving torpedo which he was almost sure he recognized. If he was correct, it, too, was an exile from Earth.

He thought that Brant and Kumar had forgotten all about him when he was startled by a message over the underwater intercom.

'Coming up. We'll be with you in twenty minutes. Everything O.K.?'

'Fine,' Loren answered. 'Was that a fish from Earth I spotted just now?'

'I never noticed.'

'Uncle's right, Brant – a twenty-kilo mutant trout went by five minutes ago. Your welding arc scared it away.'

They had now left the sea bed and were slowly ascending along the graceful catenary of the anchor line. About five metres below the surface they came to a halt.

'This is the dullest part of every dive,' Brant said. 'We have to wait here for fifteen minutes. Channel 2, please – thanks – but not *quite* so loud ...'

The music-to-decompress-by had probably been chosen by Kumar; its jittery rhythm hardly seemed appropriate to the peaceful underwater scene. Loren was heartily glad he was not immersed in it and was happy to switch off the player as soon as the two divers started to move upward again.

'That's a good morning's work,' Brant said, as he scrambled on to the deck. 'Voltage and current normal. Now we can go home.'

Loren's inexpert aid in helping them out of their equipment was gratefully received. Both men were tired and cold but quickly revived after several cups of the hot, sweet liquid the Lassans called tea, though it bore little resemblance to any terrestrial drink of that name.

Kumar started the motor and got under way, while Brant

scrabbled through the jumble of gear at the bottom of the boat and located a small, brightly coloured box.

'No, thanks,' Loren said, as he handed him one of the mildly narcotic tablets. 'I don't want to acquire any local habits that won't be easy to break.'

He regretted the remark as soon as it was made; it must have been prompted by some perverse impulse of the subconscious – or perhaps by his sense of guilt. But Brant had obviously seen no deeper meaning as he lay back, with his hands clasped under his head, staring up into the cloudless sky.

'You can see *Magellan* in the daytime,' Loren said, anxious to change the subject, 'if you know exactly where to look. But I've never done it myself.'

'Mirissa has – often,' Kumar interjected. 'And she showed me how. You only have to call Astronet for the transit time and then go out and lie on your back. It's like a bright star, straight overhead, and it doesn't seem to be moving at all. But if you look away for even a second, you've lost it.'

Unexpectedly, Kumar throttled back the engine, cruised at low power for a few minutes, then brought the boat to a complete halt. Loren glanced around to get his bearings, and was surprised to see that they were now at least a kilometre from Tarna. There was another buoy rocking in the water beside them, bearing a large letter P and carrying a red flag.

'Why have we stopped?' asked Loren.

Kumar chuckled and started emptying a small bucket over the side. Luckily, it had been sealed until now; the contents looked suspiciously like blood but smelled far worse. Loren moved as far away as possible in the limited confines of the boat.

'Just calling on an old friend,' Brant said very softly. 'Sit still – don't make any noise. She's quite nervous.'

She? thought Loren. What's going on?

Nothing whatsoever happened for at least five minutes; Loren would not have believed that Kumar could have remained still for so long. Then he noticed that a dark, curved band had appeared, a few metres from the boat, just below the surface of the water. He traced it with his eyes, and realized that it formed a ring, completely encircling them.

He also realized, at about the same moment, that Brant and Kumar were not watching it; they were watching *him*. So they're trying to give me a surprise, he told himself; well, we'll see about that ...

Even so, it took all of Loren's willpower to stifle a cry of sheer terror when what seemed to be a wall of brilliantly – no, *putrescently* – pink flesh emerged from the sea. It rose, dripping, to about half the height of a man and formed an unbroken barrier around them. And as a final horror, its upper surface was almost completely covered with writhing snakes coloured vivid reds and blues.

An enormous tentacle-fringed mouth had risen from the deep and was about to engulf them ...

Yet clearly they were in no danger; he could tell that from his companions' amused expressions.

'What in God's – Krakan's – name *is* that?' he whispered, trying to keep his voice steady.

'You reacted fine,' Brant said admiringly. 'Some people hide in the bottom of the boat. It's Polly – for polyp. Pretty Polly. Colonial invertebrate – billions of specialized cells, all cooperating. You had very similar animals on Earth though I don't believe they were anything like as large.'

'I'm sure they weren't,' Loren answered fervently. 'And if you don't mind me asking – how do we get out of here?'

Brant nodded to Kumar, who brought the engines up to full-power. With astonishing speed for something so huge, the living wall around them sank back into the sea, leaving nothing but an oily ripple on the surface.

'The vibration's scared it,' Brant explained. 'Look through the viewing glass – now you can see the whole beast.'

Below them, something like a tree-trunk ten metres thick was retracting towards the seabed. Now Loren realized that the 'snakes' he had seen wriggling on the surface were slender tentacles; back in their normal element they were waving weightlessly again, searching the waters for what – or whom – they might devour.

'What a monster!' he breathed, relaxing for the first time in many minutes. A warm feeling of pride – even exhilaration – swept over him. He knew that he had passed another test; he had won Brant's and Kumar's approval and accepted it with gratitude.

'Isn't that thing – *dangerous?*' he asked.

'Of course; that's why we have the warning buoy.'

'Frankly, I'd be tempted to kill it.'

'Why?' Brant asked, genuinely shocked. 'What harm does it do?'

'Well – surely a creature that size must catch an enormous number of fish.'

'Yes, but only Lassan – not fish that *we* can eat. And here's the interesting thing about it. For a long time we wondered how it could persuade fish – even the stupid ones here – to swim into its maw. Eventually we discovered that it secretes some chemical lure, and that's what started us thinking about electric traps. Which reminds me ...'

Brant reached for his comset.

'Tarna Three calling Tarna Autorecord – Brant here. We've fixed the grid. Everything functioning normally. No need to acknowledge. End message.'

But to everyone's surprise, there was an immediate response from a familiar voice.

'Hello, Brant. Dr Lorenson. I'm happy to hear that. And I've got some interesting news for you. Like to hear it!'

'Of course, Mayor,' Brant answered as the two men exchanged glances of mutual amusement. 'Go ahead.'

'Central Archives has dug up something surprising. All this has happened before. Two hundred fifty years ago, they tried to build a reef out from North Island by electroprecipitation – a technique that had worked well on Earth. But after a few weeks, the underwater cables were broken – some of them *stolen*. The matter was never followed up because the experiment was a total failure, anyway. Not enough minerals in the water to make it worth-while. So there you are – you can't blame the Conservers. They weren't around in those days.'

Brant's face was such a study in astonishment that Loren burst out laughing.

'And you tried to surprise *me*!' he said. 'Well, you certainly proved that there were things in the sea that I'd never imagined.'

'But now it looks as if there are some things that *you* never imagined, either.'

20

Idyll

The Tarnans thought it was very funny and pretended not to believe him.

'First you've never been in a boat – now you say you can't ride a bicycle!'

'You should be ashamed of yourself,' Mirissa had chided him, with a twinkle in her eye. 'The most efficient method of transportation ever invented – and you've never tried it!'

'Not much use in spaceships and too dangerous in cities,' Loren had retorted. 'Anyway, what is there to learn?'

He soon discovered that there was a good deal; biking was not quite as easy as it looked. Though it took real talent actually to fall off the low centre-of-gravity, small-wheeled machines (he managed it several times) his initial attempts were frustrating. He would not have persisted without Mirissa's assurance that it was the best way to discover the island – and his own hope that it would also be the best way to discover Mirissa.

The trick, he realized after a few more tumbles, was to ignore the problem completely and leave matters to the body's own reflexes. That was logical enough; if one had to think about every footstep one took, ordinary walking would be impossible. Although Loren accepted this intellectually, it was some time before he could trust his instincts. Once he had overcome that barrier, progress was swift. And at last, as he had hoped, Mirissa offered to show him the remoter byways of the island.

It would have been easy to believe that they were the only two people in the world, yet they could not be more than five kilometres from the village. They had certainly ridden much farther than that, but the narrow cycle track had been designed to take the most picturesque route, which also turned out to be the longest. Although Loren could locate himself in an instant from the position-finder in his comset, he did not bother. It was amusing to pretend to be lost.

Mirissa would have been happier if he had left the comset behind.

'Why must you carry that thing?' she had said, pointing to the control-studded band on his left forearm. 'It's nice to get away from people sometimes.'

'I agree, but ship's regs are very strict. If Captain Bey wanted me in a hurry and I didn't answer –'

'Well – what would he do? Put you in irons?'

'I'd prefer that to the lecture I'd undoubtedly get. Anyway, I've switched to sleep mode. If Shipcom overrides *that*, it will be a real emergency – and I'd certainly want to be in touch.'

Like almost all Terrans for more than a thousand years, Loren would have been far happier without his clothes than without his comset. Earth's history was replete with horror stories of careless or reckless individuals who had died – often within metres of safety – because they could not reach the red EMERGENCY button.

The cycle lane was clearly designed for economy, not heavy traffic. It was less than a metre wide, and at first the inexperienced

Loren felt that he was riding along a tight-rope. He had to concentrate on Mirissa's back (not an unwelcome task) to avoid falling off. But after the first few kilometres he gained confidence and was able to enjoy the other views, as well. If they met anyone coming in the opposite direction, all parties would have to dismount; the thought of a collision at fifty klicks or more was too horrible to contemplate. It would be a long walk home, carrying their smashed bicycles ...

Most of the time they rode in perfect silence, broken only when Mirissa pointed out some unusual tree or exceptional beauty spot. The silence itself was something that Loren had never before experienced in his whole life; on Earth he had always been surrounded by sounds – and shipboard life was an entire symphony of reassuring mechanical noises, with occasional heart-stopping alarms.

Here the trees surrounded them with an invisible, anechoic blanket, so that every word seemed sucked into silence the moment it was uttered. At first the sheer novelty of the sensation made it enjoyable, but now Loren was beginning to yearn for something to fill the acoustic vacuum. He was even tempted to summon up a little background music from his comset but felt certain that Mirissa would not approve.

It was a great surprise, therefore, when he heard the beat of some now-familiar Thalassan dance music from the trees ahead. As the narrow road seldom proceeded in a straight line for more than two or three hundred metres, he could not see the source until they rounded a sharp curve and found themselves confronted by a melodious mechanical monster straddling the entire road surface and advancing towards them at a slow walking pace. It looked rather like a robot caterpillar. As they dismounted and let it trundle past, Loren realized that it was an automatic road repairer. He had noticed quite a few rough patches, and even pot-holes, and had been wondering when the South Island Department of Works would bestir itself to deal with them.

'Why the music?' he asked. 'This hardly seems the kind of machine that would appreciate it.'

He had barely made his little joke when the robot addressed him severely: 'Please do not ride on the road surface within one hundred metres of me, as it is still hardening. Please do not ride on the road surface within one hundred metres of me, as it is still hardening. Thank you.'

Mirissa laughed at his surprised expression.

'You're right, of course – it isn't very intelligent. The music is a warning to oncoming traffic.'

'Wouldn't some kind of hooter be more effective?'

'Yes, but how – *unfriendly*!'

They pushed their bicycles off the road and waited for the line of articulated tanks, control units, and road-laying mechanisms to move slowly past. Loren could not resist touching the freshly extruded surface; it was warm and slightly yielding, and looked moist even though it felt perfectly dry. Within seconds, however, it had become as hard as rock; Loren noted the faint impression of his fingerprint and thought wryly. I've made my mark on Thalassa – until the robot comes this way again.

Now the road was rising up into the hills, and Loren found that unfamiliar muscles in thigh and calf were beginning to call attention to themselves. A little auxiliary power would have been welcomed, but Mirissa had spurned the electric models as too effete. She had not slackened her speed in the least, so Loren had no alternative but to breathe deeply and keep up with her.

What was that faint roar from ahead? Surely no one could be testing rocket engines in the interior of South Island! The sound grew steadily louder as they pedalled onward; Loren identified it only seconds before the source came into view.

By Terran standards, the waterfall was not very impressive – perhaps one hundred metres high and twenty across. A small metal bridge glistening with spray spanned the pool of boiling foam in which it ended.

To Loren's relief, Mirissa dismounted and looked at him rather mischievously.

'Do you notice anything ... *peculiar*?' she asked, waving towards the scene ahead.

'In what way?' Loren answered, fishing for clues. All he saw was an unbroken vista of trees and vegetation, with the road winding away through it on the other side of the fall.

'The trees – the trees!'

'What about them? I'm not a – botanist.'

'Nor am I, but it should be obvious. Just look at them.'

He looked, still puzzled. And presently he understood, because a tree is a piece of natural engineering – and he was an engineer.

A different designer had been at work on the other side of the waterfall. Although he could not name any of the trees among which he was standing, they were vaguely familiar, and he was sure that they came from Earth ... yes, that was certainly an oak, and somewhere, long ago, he had seen the beautiful yellow flowers on that low bush.

Beyond the bridge, it was a different world. The trees – were they really trees? – seemed crude and unfinished. Some had short, barrel-shaped trunks from which a few prickly branches extended; others resembled huge ferns; others looked like giant, skeletal fingers, with bristly haloes at the joints. And there were no flowers ...

'*Now* I understand. Thalassa's own vegetation.'

'Yes – only a few million years out of the sea. We call this the Great Divide. But it's more like a battlefront between two armies, and no one knows which side will win. Neither, if we can help it! The vegetation from Earth is more advanced; but the natives are better adapted to the chemistry. From time to time one side invades the other – and we move in with shovels before it can get a foothold.'

How strange, Loren thought as they pushed their bicycles across the slender bridge. For the first time since landing on Thalassa, I feel that I am indeed on an alien world ...

These clumsy trees and crude ferns could have been the raw material of the coal beds that had powered the Industrial Revolution – barely in time to save the human race. He could easily believe that a dinosaur might come charging out of the undergrowth at any moment; then he recalled that the terrible lizards had still been a hundred million years in the future when such plants had flourished on Earth ...

They were just remounting when Loren exclaimed, 'Krakan and damnation!'

'What's the matter?'

Loren collapsed on what, providentially, appeared to be a thick layer of wiry moss.

'Cramp,' he muttered through clenched teeth, grabbing at his knotted calf muscles.

'Let me,' Mirissa said in a concerned but confident voice.

Under her pleasant, though somewhat amateur, ministrations, the spasms slowly ebbed.

'Thanks,' Loren said after a while. 'That's much better. But please don't stop.'

'Did you really think I would?' she whispered.

And presently, between two worlds, they became one.

IV
Krakan

21

Academy

The membership of the Thalassan Academy of Science was strictly limited to the nice round binary number 100000000 – or, for those who preferred to count on their fingers, 256. *Magellan*'s Science Officer approved of such exclusivity; it maintained standards. And the academy took its responsibilities very seriously; the president had confessed to her that at the moment there were only 241 members, as it had proved impossible to fill all the vacancies with qualified personnel.

Of those 241, no less than 105 were physically present in the academy's auditorium, and 116 had logged in on their comsets. It was a record turnout, and Dr Anne Varley felt extremely flattered – though she could not suppress a fleeting curiosity about the missing 20.

She also felt a mild discomfort at being introduced as one of Earth's leading astronomers – even though, alas, by the date of *Magellan*'s departure, that had been all too true. Time and Chance had given the late director of the – late – Shklovskii Lunar Observatory this unique opportunity of survival. She knew perfectly well that she was no more than competent when judged by the standards of such giants as Ackerley or Chandrasekhar or Herschel – still less by those of Galileo or Copernicus or Ptolemy.

'Here it is,' she began. 'I'm sure you've all seen this map of Sagan – the best reconstruction possible from fly-bys and radioholograms. The detail's very poor, of course – ten kilometres at the best – but it's enough to give us the basic facts.

'Diameter – fifteen thousand kilometres, a little larger than

Earth. A dense atmosphere – almost entirely nitrogen. And no oxygen – *fortunately*.'

That 'fortunately' was always an attention-getter; it made the audience sit up with a jolt.

'I understand your surprise; most human beings have a prejudice in favour of breathing. But in the decades before the Exodus, many things happened to change our outlook on the Universe.

'The absence of other living creatures – past or present – in the solar system and the failure of the SETI programs despite sixteen centuries of effort convinced virtually everyone that life must be very rare elsewhere in the universe, and therefore very precious.

'Hence it followed that all life forms were worthy of respect and should be cherished. Some argued that even virulent pathogens and disease vectors should not be exterminated, but should be preserved under strict safeguards. "Reverence for life" became a very popular phrase during the Last Days and few applied it exclusively to human life.

'Once the principle of biological noninterference was accepted, certain practical consequences followed. It had long been agreed that we should not attempt any settlement on a planet with intelligent life-forms; the human race had a bad enough record on its home world. Fortunately – or unfortunately! – this situation has never arisen.

'But the argument was taken further. Suppose we found a planet on which animal life had just begun. Should we stand aside and let evolution take its course on the chance that megayears hence intelligence might arise?

'Going still further back – suppose there was only plant life? Only single-cell microbes?

'You may find it surprising that, when the very existence of the human race was at stake, men bothered to debate such abstract moral and philosophical questions. But Death focuses the mind on the things that really matter: why are we here, and what should we do?

'The concept of "Metalaw" – I'm sure you've all heard the

term – became very popular. Was it possible to develop legal and moral codes applicable to *all* intelligent creatures, and not merely to the bipedal, air-breathing mammals who had briefly dominated Planet Earth?

'Dr Kaldor, incidentally, was one of the leaders of the debate. It made him quite unpopular with those who argued that since *H. sapiens* was the only intelligent species known, its survival took precedence over all other considerations. Someone coined the effective slogan: "If it's Man or Slime Moulds, I vote for Man!"

'Fortunately, there's never been a direct confrontation – as far as we know. It may be centuries before we get reports from all the seedships that went out. And if some remain silent – well, the slime moulds may have won…

'In 3505, during the final session of the World Parliament, certain guidelines – the famous Geneva Directive – were laid down for future planetary colonization. Many thought that they were too idealistic, and there was certainly no way in which they could ever be enforced. But they were an expression of intent – a final gesture of goodwill towards a Universe which might never be able to appreciate it.

'Only one of the directive's guidelines concern us here – but it was the most celebrated and aroused intense controversy, since it ruled out some of the most promising targets.

'The presence of more than a few per cent oxygen in a planet's atmosphere is definite proof that life exists there. The element is far too reactive to occur in the free state unless it is continually replenished by plants – or their equivalent. Of course, oxygen doesn't necessarily mean *animal* life, but it sets the stage for it. And even if animal life only rarely leads to intelligence, no other plausible route to it has ever been theorized.

'So, according to the principles of Metalaw, oxygen-bearing planets were placed out of bounds. Frankly, I doubt so drastic a decision would have been made if the quantum drive hadn't given us essentially unlimited range – and power.

'Now let me tell you our plan of operation, when we have

reached Sagan 2. As you will see by the map, more than fifty per cent of the surface is ice-covered, to an estimated average depth of three kilometres. All the oxygen we shall ever need!

'When it's established its final orbit, *Magellan* will use the quantum drive, at a small fraction of full-power, to act as a torch. It will burn off the ice and simultaneously crack the steam into oxygen and hydrogen. The hydrogen will quickly leak away into space; we may help it with tuned lasers, if necessary.

'In only twenty years, Sagan 2 will have a ten per cent O_2 atmosphere, though it will be too full of nitrogen oxides and other poisons to be breathable. About that time we'll start dumping specially developed bacteria, and even plants, to accelerate the process. But the planet will still be far too cold; even allowing for the heat we've pumped into it, the temperature will be below freezing everywhere except for a few hours near noon at the Equator.

'So that's where we use the quantum drive, probably for the last time. *Magellan*, which has spent its entire existence in space, will finally descend to the surface of a planet.

'And then, for about fifteen minutes every day at the appropriate time, the drive will be switched on at the maximum power the structure of the ship – and the bedrock on which it is resting – can withstand. We won't know how long the operation will take until we have made the first tests; it may be necessary to move the ship again if the initial site is geologically unstable.

'At a first approximation, it appears that we'll need to operate the drive for thirty years, to slow the planet until it drops sunward far enough to give it a temperate climate. And we'll have to run the drive for another twenty-five years to circularize the orbit. But for much of that time Sagan 2 will be quite livable – though the winters will be fierce until final orbit is achieved.

'So then we will have a virgin planet, larger than Earth, with about forty per cent ocean and a mean temperature of twenty-five degrees. The atmosphere will have an oxygen content seventy per cent of Earth's – but still rising. It will be time to awaken the nine hundred thousand sleepers still in hibernation, and present them with a new world.

'That is the scenario unless unexpected developments – or discoveries – force us to depart from it. And if the worst comes to the worst …'

Dr Varley hesitated, then smiled grimly.

'No – whatever happens, you won't be seeing us again! If Sagan 2 is impossible, there is another target, thirty light-years farther on. It may be an even better one.

'Perhaps we will eventually colonize both. But that is for the future to decide.'

The discussion took a little time to get under way; most of the Academicians seemed stunned, though their applause was certainly genuine. The president, who through long experience always had a few questions prepared in advance, started the ball rolling.

'A trivial point, Dr Varley – but who or what is Sagan 2 named after?'

'A writer of scientific romances, early Third Millennium.'

That broke the ice, just as the president had intended.

'You mentioned, Doctor, that Sagan 2 has at least one satellite. What will happen to it, when you change the planet's orbit?'

'Nothing, apart from very slight perturbations. It will move along with its primary.'

'If the directive of – what was it, 3500 –'

'3505.'

'– had been ratified earlier, would we be here now? I mean, Thalassa would have been out of bounds!'

'It's a very good question, and we've often debated it. The 2751 seeding mission – your Mother Ship on South Island – would certainly have gone against the directive. Luckily, the problem hasn't arisen. Since you have no land animals here, the principle of noninterference hasn't been violated.'

'This is very speculative,' one of the youngest of the Academicians said – to the obvious amusement of many of her elders. 'Granted that oxygen means life, how can you be sure that the reverse proposition is true? One can imagine all sorts of creatures – even intelligent ones – on planets with no oxygen, even with no atmosphere. If our evolutionary successors are intelligent *machines*, as many philosophers have suggested, they'd prefer an atmosphere in which they wouldn't rust. Have you any idea how old Sagan 2 is? It might have passed through the oxygen–biological era; there could be a machine civilization waiting for you there.'

There were a few groans from dissenters in the audience, and someone muttered 'science fiction!' in tones of disgust. Dr Varley waited for the disturbance to die away, then answered briefly, 'We've not lost much sleep over that. And if we did run into a machine civilization, the principle of noninterference would hardly matter. I'd be much more worried about what it would do to *us* than the other way round!'

A very old man – the oldest person Dr Varley had seen in Thalassa – was slowly rising to his feet at the back of the room. The chairman scribbled a quick note and passed it over: 'Prof. Derek Winslade – 115 – GOM of T. science – historian.' Dr Varley puzzled over GOM for a few seconds, before some mysterious flash of insight told her that it stood for 'Grand Old Man'.

And it would be typical, she thought, if the dean of Lassan science was a historian. In all their seven hundred years of history, the Three Islands had produced only a handful of original thinkers.

Yet this did not necessarily merit criticism. The Lassans had been forced to build up the infrastructure of civilization from zero; there had been little opportunity, or incentive, for any research that was not of direct practical application. And there was a more serious and subtle problem – that of population. At any one time, in any one scientific discipline, there would never be enough workers on Thalassa to reach 'critical mass' – the minimum number of reacting minds needed to ignite fundamental research into some new field of knowledge.

Only in mathematics – as in music – were there rare exceptions to this rule. A solitary genius – a Ramanujan or a Mozart – could arise from nowhere, and sail strange seas of thought alone. The famous example from Lassan science was Francis Zoltan (214–242); his name was still revered five hundred years later, but Dr Varley had certain reservations even about his undoubted skills. No one, it seemed to her, had really understood his discoveries in the field of hypertransfinite numbers; still less extended them further – the true test of all genuine break-throughs. Even now, his famous 'Last Hypothesis' defied either proof or disproof.

She suspected – though she was far too tactful to mention this to her Lassan friends – that Zoltan's tragically early death had exaggerated his reputation, investing his memory with wistful hopes of what might have been. The fact that he had disappeared while swimming off North Island had inspired legions of romantic myths and theories – disappointments in love, jealous rivals, inability to discover critical proofs, terror of the hyperinfinite itself – none of which had the slightest factual foundation. But they had all added to the popular image of Thalassa's greatest genius, cut down in the prime of his achievement.

What was the old professor saying? Oh, dear – there was always someone during the question period who brought up a totally irrelevant subject or seized the opportunity to expound a pet theory. Through long practice, Dr Varley was quite good at dealing with such interpolators and could usually get a laugh at their expense. But she would have to be polite to a GOM, surrounded by respectful colleagues, on his own territory.

'Professor – ah – Winsdale' 'Winslade' the chairman whispered urgently, but she decided that any correction would only make matters worse, 'the question you have asked is a very good one but should really be the subject of another lecture. Or series of lectures; even then, it would barely scratch the subject.

'But to deal with your first point. We have heard that criticism several times – it is simply not true. We have made no attempt to keep the secret, as you call it, of the quantum drive. The complete theory is in the ship's Archives, and is among the material being transferred to your own.

'Having said that, I don't want to raise any false hopes. Frankly, there is *no one* in the ship's active crew who really understands the drive. We know how to use it – that's all.

'There are three scientists in hibernation who are supposed to be experts on the drive. If we have to wake them up before we reach Sagan 2, we'll be in really serious trouble.

'Men went insane trying to visualize the geometrodynamic structure of superspace, and asking why the universe originally had eleven dimensions instead of a nice number like ten or twelve. When I took the Propulsion Basics Course, my instructor said, "If you could understand the quantum drive, you wouldn't be here – you'd be up on Lagrange 1 at the Institute for Advanced Studies." And he gave me a useful comparison that helped me get to sleep again when I had nightmares trying to imagine what ten to the minus thirty three centimetres really means.

'"*Magellan's* crew only has to know what the drive *does,*" my instructor told me. "They're like engineers in charge of an electric distribution network. As long as they know how to switch the power around, they don't have to know how it's generated. It may come from something simple, like an oil-fuelled dynamo or a solar panel or a water turbine. They would certainly understand the principles behind these – but they wouldn't need to in order to do their jobs perfectly well.

'"Or the electricity might come from something more complex, like a fission reactor or a thermonuclear fusor or a muon catalyzer or a Penrose Node or a Hawking-Schwarzschild kernel – you see what I mean? *Somewhere* along the line they'd have to give up any hope of comprehension; but they'd still be perfectly competent engineers, capable of switching electric power where and when it was needed."

'In the same way, we can switch *Magellan* from Earth to Thalassa – and, I hope, on to Sagan 2 – without really knowing what we're doing. But one day, perhaps centuries hence, we will again be able to match the genius that produced the quantum drive.

'And – who knows? – you may do it first. Some latter-day Francis Zoltan may be born on Thalassa. And then perhaps *you* will come to visit us.'

She didn't really believe it. But it was a nice way to end, and it drew a tremendous round of applause.

22

Krakan

'We can do it with no trouble, of course,' said Captain Bey thoughtfully. 'Planning's essentially complete – that vibration problem with the compressors seems to be solved – site preparation is ahead of schedule. There's no doubt that we can spare the men and equipment – but is it really a good idea?' He looked at his five senior officers gathered around the oval table in the Terra Nova staff conference room; with one accord they all looked at Dr Kaldor, who sighed and spread his hands in resignation.

'So it's not a purely technical problem. Tell me all I have to know.'

'This is the situation,' Deputy Captain Malina said. The lights dimmed, and the Three Islands covered the table, floating a fraction of a centimetre above it like some beautifully detailed model. But this was no model, for if the scale was expanded enough, one could watch the Lassans going about their business.

'I think the Lassans are still scared of Mount Krakan, though really it's a very well behaved volcano – after all, it's never actually *killed* anyone! And it's the key to the interisland communications system. The summit is six kilometres above sea level – the highest point on the planet, of course. So it's the ideal site for an antenna park; all long-distance services are routed through here and beamed back to the two other islands.'

'It's always seemed a little odd to me,' Kaldor said mildly, 'that after two thousand years we've not found anything better than radio waves.'

'The Universe came equipped with only one electromagnetic spectrum, Dr Kaldor – we have to make the best use of it we can. And the Lassans are fortunate; because even the extreme ends of the North and South Islands are only three hundred kilometres apart, Mount Krakan can blanket them both. They can manage very nicely without comsats.

'The only problem is accessibility – and weather. The local joke is that Krakan's the only place on the planet that has any. Every few years someone has to climb the mountain, repair a few antennas, replace some solar cells and batteries – and shovel away a lot of snow. No real problem but a lot of hard work.'

'Which,' interjected Surgeon-Commander Newton, 'Lassans avoid whenever possible. Not that I blame them for saving their energies for more important things – like sports and athletics.'

She could have added 'making love', but that was already a sensitive subject with many of her colleagues, and the remark might not be appreciated.

'Why do they have to *climb* the mountain?' Kaldor asked. 'Why don't they just fly to the top? They've got vertical-lift aircraft.'

'Yes, but the air's thin up there – and what there is tends to be boisterous. After several bad accidents, the Lassans decided to do it the hard way.'

'I see,' Kaldor said thoughtfully. 'It's the old noninterference problem. Will we weaken their self-reliance? Only to a trivial extent, I'd say. And if we *don't* accede to such a modest request, we'd provoke resentment. Justified, too, considering the help they're giving us with the ice plant.'

'I feel exactly the same way. Any objections? Very good. Mister Lorenson – please make the arrangements. Use whichever spaceplane you think fit, as long as it's not needed for Operation Snowflake.'

Moses Kaldor had always loved mountains; they made him feel nearer to the God whose nonexistence he still sometimes resented.

From the rim of the great caldera, he could look down into a sea of lava, long since congealed but still emitting wisps of smoke from a dozen crevasses. Beyond that, far to the west, both the big islands were clearly visible, lying like dark clouds on the horizon.

The stinging cold and the need to make each breath count, added a zest to every moment. Long ago he had come across a phrase in some ancient travel or adventure book: 'Air like wine.' At the time he had wished he could ask the author just how much wine he'd breathed lately; but now the expression no longer seemed so ridiculous.

'Everything's unloaded, Moses. We're ready to fly back.'

'Thank you, Loren. I felt like waiting here until you collect everyone in the evening, but it might be risky to stay too long at this altitude.'

'The engineers have brought oxygen bottles, of course,'

'I wasn't thinking only of that. My namesake once got into a lot of trouble on a mountain.'

'Sorry – I don't understand.'

'Never mind; it was a long, long time ago.'

As the spaceplane lifted off the rim of the crater, the work party waved cheerfully up at them. Now that all the tools and equipment had been unloaded, they were engaged in the essential preliminary to any Lassan project. Someone was making tea.

Loren was careful to avoid the complex mass of antennas, of practically every known design, as he climbed slowly up into the sky. They were all aimed towards the two islands dimly visible in the west; if he interrupted their multiple beams countless gigabytes of information would be irretrievably lost, and the Lassans would be sorry that they ever asked him to help.

'You're not heading towards Tarna?'

'In a minute. I want to look at the mountain first. Ah – there it is!'

'What?' Oh, I see. Krakan!'

The borrowed expletive was doubly appropriate. Beneath them, the ground had been split into a deep ravine about a hundred metres wide. And at the bottom of that ravine lay Hell.

The fires from the heart of this young world were still burning here, just below the surface. A glowing river of yellow, flecked with crimson, was moving sluggishly towards the sea. How could they be sure, Kaldor wondered, that the volcano had really settled down and was not merely biding its time?

But the river of lava was not their objective. Beyond it lay a small crater about a kilometre across, on the rim of which stood the stump of a single ruined tower. As they came closer, they could see that there had once been three such towers, equally spaced around the rim of the caldera, but of the other two only the foundations were left.

The floor of the crater was covered with a mass of tangled cables and metal sheets, obviously the remains of the great radio reflector that had once been suspended here. At its centre lay the wreckage of the receiving and transmitting equipment, partly submerged in a small lake formed by the frequent rainstorms over the mountain.

They circled the ruins of the last link with Earth, neither caring to intrude on the thoughts of the other. At last Loren broke the silence.

'It's a mess – but it wouldn't be hard to repair. Sagan 2 is only twelve degrees north – closer to the Equator than Earth was. Even easier to point the beam there with an offset antenna.'

'Excellent idea. When we've finished building our shield, we could help them get started. Not that they should need much help, for there's certainly no hurry. After all, it will be almost four centuries before they can hear from us again – even if we start transmitting just as soon as we arrive.'

Loren finished recording the scene, and prepared to fly down the slope of the mountain before turning towards South Island. He had descended scarcely a thousand metres when Kaldor said in a puzzled voice, 'What's that smoke over to the northeast? It looks like a signal.'

Halfway to the horizon, a thin white column was rising against the cloudless blue of the Thalassan sky. It had certainly not been there a few minutes before.

'Let's have a look. Perhaps there's a boat in trouble.'

'You know what it reminds me of?' said Kaldor.

Loren answered with a silent shrug.

'A spouting whale. When they came up to breathe, the big cetaceans used to blow out a column of water vapour. It looked very much like that.'

'There are two things wrong with your interesting theory,' Loren said. 'That column is now at least a kilometre high. Some whale!'

'Agreed. And whale spouts only lasted a few seconds – this is continuous. What's your second objection?'

'According to the chart, that's not open water. So much for the boat theory.'

'But that's ridiculous – Thalassa is *all* ocean – oh, I see. The Great Eastern Prairie. Yes – there's its edge. You'd almost imagine that was land down there.'

Coming swiftly towards them was the floating continent of seaborne vegetation which covered much of the Thalassan ocean and generated virtually all the oxygen in the planet's atmosphere. It was one continuous sheet of vivid – almost virulent – green and looked solid enough to walk upon. Only the complete absence of hills or any other change of elevation, revealed its true nature.

But in one region, about a kilometre across, the floating prairie was neither flat nor unbroken. Something was boiling beneath the surface, throwing up great clouds of steam and occasional masses of tangled weed.

'I should have remembered,' Kaldor said. 'Child of Krakan.'

'Of course,' Loren answered. 'That's the first time it's been active since we arrived. So this is how the islands were born.'

'Yes – the volcanic plume is moving steadily eastward. Perhaps in a few hundred years the Lassans will have a whole archipelago.'

They circled for another few minutes, then turned back towards East Island. To most spectators, this submarine volcano, still struggling to be born, would have been an awesome sight.

But not to men who had seen the destruction of a solar system.

23

Ice Day

The presidential yacht, *alias* Inter-Island Ferry Number 1, had certainly never looked so handsome at any previous stage of its three-centuries-long career. Not only was it festooned with bunting, but it had been given a new coat of white paint. Unfortunately, either paint or labour had become exhausted before the job was quite finished, so the captain had to be careful to anchor with only the starboard side visible from land.

President Farradine was also ceremonially attired in a striking outfit (designed by Mrs President) that made him look like a cross between a Roman emperor and a pioneer astronaut. He did not appear altogether at ease in it; Captain Sirdar Bey was glad that *his* uniform consisted of the plain white shorts, open-neck shirt, shoulder badges, and gold-braided cap in which he felt completely at home – though it was hard to remember when he had last worn it.

Despite the president's tendency to trip over his toga, the official tour had gone very well, and the beautiful onboard model of the freezing plant had worked perfectly. It had produced an unlimited supply of hexagonal ice wafers just the right size to fit into a tumbler of cool drink. But the visitors could hardly be blamed for failing to understand the appropriateness of the name Snowflake; after all, few on Thalassa had ever seen snow.

And now they had left the model behind to inspect the real thing, which covered several hectares of the Tarna coastline. It had taken some time to shuttle the president and his entourage, Captain Bey and his officers, and all the other guests from yacht to shore. Now, in the last light of day, they were standing respectfully around the rim of a hexagonal block of ice twenty metres across and two metres thick. Not only was it the largest mass of frozen water that anyone had ever seen – it was probably the largest on the planet. Even at the Poles, ice seldom had a chance to form. With no major continents to block circulation, the rapidly moving currents from the equatorial regions quickly melted any incipient floes.

'But why is it *that* shape?' the president asked.

Deputy Captain Malina sighed; he was quite sure that this had already been explained several times.

'It's the old problem of covering any surface with identical tiles,' he said patiently. 'You have only three choices – squares, triangles, or hexagons. In our case, the hex is slightly more efficient and easier to handle. The blocks – over two hundred of them, each weighing six hundred tons – will be keyed into each other to build up the shield. It will be a kind of ice-sandwich three layers thick. When we accelerate, all the blocks will fuse together to make a single huge disk. Or a blunt cone, to be precise.'

'You've given me an idea.' The president was showing more animation than he had done all afternoon. 'We've never had ice-skating on Thalassa. It was a beautiful sport – and there was a game called ice-hockey, though I'm not sure I'd like to revive *that*, from the vids I've seen of it. But it would be wonderful if you could make us an ice-rink in time for the Olympics. Would that be possible?'

'I'll have to think about it,' Deputy Captain Malina replied, rather faintly. 'It's a very interesting idea. Perhaps you'll let me know how much ice you'd need.'

'I'll be delighted. And it will be an excellent way of using all this freezing plant when it's done its job.'

A sudden explosion saved Malina the necessity of a reply. The fireworks had started, and for the next twenty minutes the sky above the island erupted with polychromatic incandescence.

The Lassans loved fireworks and indulged in them at every opportunity. The display was intermingled with laser imagery – even more spectacular, and considerably safer, but lacking the smell of gunpowder that added that final touch of magic.

When all the festivities were over and the VIPs had departed to the ship, Deputy Captain Malina said thoughtfully, 'The president's full of surprises, even though he does have a one-track mind. I'm tired of hearing about his damned Olympics – but that ice-rink is an excellent idea and should generate a lot of goodwill for us.'

'I've won my bet, though,' Lieutenant Commander Lorenson said.

'What bet was that?' Captain Bey asked.

Malina gave a laugh.

'I would never have believed it. Sometimes the Lassans don't seem to have any *curiosity* – they take everything for granted. Though I suppose we should be flattered that they have such faith in our technological know-how. Perhaps they think we have antigravity!

'It was Loren's idea that I should leave it out of the briefing – and he was right. President Farradine never bothered to ask what would have been *my* very first question – just how we're going to lift a hundred and fifty thousand tons of ice up to *Magellan*.'

24

Archive

Moses Kaldor was happy to be left alone, for as many hours or days as he could be spared, in the cathedral calm of First Landing. He felt like a young student again, confronted with all the art and knowledge of mankind. The experience was both exhilarating and depressing; a whole universe lay at his fingertips, but the fraction of it he could explore in an entire lifetime was so negligible that he was sometimes almost overwhelmed with despair. He was like a hungry man presented with a banquet that stretched as far as the eye could see – a feast so staggering that it completely destroyed his appetite.

And yet all this wealth of wisdom and culture was only a tiny fraction of mankind's heritage; much that Moses Kaldor knew and loved was missing – not, he was well aware, by accident but by deliberate design.

A thousand years ago, men of genius and goodwill had rewritten history and gone through the libraries of Earth deciding what should be saved and what should be abandoned to the flames. The criterion of choice was simple though often very hard to apply. Only if it would contribute to survival and social stability on the new worlds would any work of literature, any record of the past, be loaded into the memory of the seedships.

The task was, of course, impossible as well as heartbreaking. With tears in their eyes, the selection panels had thrown away the Veda, the Bible, the Tripitaka, the Qur'an, and all the immense body of literature – fiction and nonfiction – that was based upon them. Despite all the wealth of beauty and wisdom these works contained, they could not be allowed to reinfect virgin planets with the ancient poisons of religious hatred, belief in the supernatural, and the pious gibberish with which countless billions of men and women had once comforted themselves at the cost of addling their minds.

Lost also in the great purge were virtually all the works of the supreme novelists, poets, and playwrights, which would in any case have been meaningless without their philosophical and cultural background. Homer, Shakespeare, Milton, Tolstoy, Melville, Proust – the last great fiction writer before the electronic revolution overwhelmed the printed page – all that was left were a few hundred thousand carefully selected passages. Excluded was everything that concerned war, crime, violence, and the destructive passions. If the newly designed – and it was hoped improved – successors to *H. sapiens* rediscovered these, they would doubtless create their own literature in response. There was no need to give them premature encouragement.

Music – except for opera – had fared better, as had the visual arts. Nevertheless, the sheer volume of material was so over-whelming that selection had been imperative, though sometimes arbitrary. Future generations on many worlds would wonder about Mozart's first thirty-eight symphonies, Beethoven's Second and Fourth, and Sibelius's Third to Sixth.

Moses Kaldor was deeply aware of his responsibility, and also conscious of his inadequacy – of *any* one man's inadequacy, however talented he might be – to handle the task that confronted him. Up there aboard *Magellan*, safely stored in its gigantic memory banks, was much that the people of Thalassa had never known and certainly much that they would greedily accept and enjoy, even if they did not wholly understand. The superb twenty-fifth century recreation of the *Odyssey*, the war classics that looked back in anguish across half a millennium of peace, the great Shakespearean tragedies in Feinberg's miraculous Lingua transla-tion, Lee Chow's *War and Peace* – it would take hours and days even to name all the possibilities.

Sometimes, as he sat in the library of the First Landing Complex, Kaldor was tempted to play god with these reasonably happy and far-from-innocent people. He would compare the listings from the memory banks here with those aboard the ship, noting what had been expunged or condensed. Even though he disagreed in principle with any form of censorship, often he had to admit the wisdom of the deletions – at least in the days when the colony was founded. But now that it was successfully established, perhaps a little disturbance, or injection of creativity, might be in order ...

Occasionally, he was disturbed himself either by calls from the ship or by parties of young Lassans being given guided tours back to the beginning of their history. He did not mind the interruptions, and there was one that he positively welcomed.

Most afternoons, except when what passed for urgent business in Tarna prevented her, Mirissa would come riding up the hill on her beautiful palomino gelding, Bobby. The visitors had been much surprised to find horses on Thalassa, since they had never seen any alive on Earth. But the Lassans loved animals, and had recreated many from the vast files of genetic material they had inherited. Sometimes they were quite useless – or even a nuisance, like the engaging little squirrel monkeys that were always stealing small objects from Tarnan households.

Mirissa would invariably bring some delicacy – usually fruit or one of the many local cheeses – which Kaldor would accept with gratitude. But he was even more grateful for her company; who would believe that often he had addressed five million people – more than half the last generation! – yet was now content with an audience of one ...

'Because you've descended from a long line of librarians,' Moses Kaldor said, 'you only think in megabytes. But may I remind you that the name "library" comes from a word meaning *book*. Do you have books on Thalassa?'

'Of course we do,' Mirissa said indignantly; she had not yet learned to tell when Kaldor was joking. 'Millions ... well, thousands. There's a man on North Island who prints about ten a year, in editions of a few hundred. They're beautiful – and very expensive. They all go as gifts for special occasions. I had one on my twenty-first birthday – *Alice in Wonderland*.'

'I'd like to see it someday. I've always loved books, and have almost a hundred on the ship. Perhaps that's why whenever I hear someone talking bytes, I divide mentally by a million and think of one book ... one gigabyte equals a thousand books, and so on. That's the only way I can grasp what's really involved when people talk about data banks and information transfer. Now, how big is your library?'

Without taking her eyes off Kaldor, Mirissa let her fingers wander over the keyboard of her console.

'That's another thing I've never been able to do,' he said admiringly. 'Someone once said that after the twenty-first century, the human race divided into two species – Verbals and Digitals. I *can* use a keyboard when I have to, of course – but I prefer to talk to my electronic colleagues.'

'As of the last hourly check,' Mirissa said, 'six hundred and forty-five terabytes.'

'Um – almost a billion books. And what was the initial size of the library?'

'I can tell you that without looking it up. Six hundred and forty.'

'So in seven hundred years –

'Yes, yes – we've managed to produce only a few million books.'

'I'm not criticizing; after all, quality is far more important than quantity. I'd like you to show me what you consider the best works of Lassan literature – music, too. The problem *we* have to decide is what to give you. *Magellan* has over a thousand megabooks aboard, in the General Access bank. Do you realize just what that implies?'

'If I said "Yes", it would stop you from telling me. I'm not that cruel.'

'Thank you, my dear. Seriously, it's a terrifying problem that's haunted me for years. Sometimes I think that the Earth was destroyed none too soon; the human race was being crushed by the information it was generating.

'At the end of the Second Millennium, it was producing only – only! – the equivalent of a million books a year. And I'm referring merely to information that was presumed to be of some permanent value, so it was stored indefinitely.

'By the Third Millennium, the figure had multiplied by at least a hundred. Since writing was invented, until the end of Earth, it's been estimated that ten thousand million books were produced. And as I told you, we have about ten per cent of that on board.

'If we dumped it all on you, even assuming you have the storage capacity, you'd be overwhelmed. It would be no kindness – it would totally inhibit your cultural and scientific growth. And most of the material would mean nothing at all to you; you'd take centuries to sort the wheat from the chaff ...'

Strange, Kaldor said to himself, that I've not thought of the analogy before. This is precisely the danger that the opponents of SETI kept raising. Well, we never communicated with extraterrestrial intelligence, or even detected it. But the Lassans have done just that – and the ETs are *us* ...

Yet despite their totally different backgrounds, he and Mirissa had so much in common. Her curiosity and intelligence were traits to be encouraged; not even among his fellow crew members was there anyone with whom he could have such stimulating conversations. Sometimes Kaldor was so hard put to answer her questions that the only defence was a counterattack.

'I'm surprised,' he told her after a particularly thorough cross-examination on Solar politics, 'that you never took over from your father and worked here full-time. This would be the perfect job for you.'

'I was tempted. But he spent all his life answering other people's questions and assembling files for the bureaucrats on North Island. He never had time to do anything himself.'

'And you?'

'I like collecting facts, but I also like to see them used. That's why they made me deputy director of the Tarna Development Project.'

'Which I fear may have been slightly sabotaged by our operations. Or so the director told me when I met him coming out of the mayor's office.'

'You know Brant wasn't serious. It's a long-range plan, with only approximate completion dates. If the Olympic Ice Stadium *is* built here, then the project may have to be modified – for the better, most of us believe. Of course, the Northers want to have it on their side – they think that First Landing is quite enough for us.'

Kaldor chuckled; he knew all about the generations-old rivalry between the two islands.

'Well – isn't it? Especially now that you have us as an additional attraction. You mustn't be too greedy.'

They had grown to know – and like – each other so well that they could joke about Thalassa or *Magellan* with equal impartiality. And there were no longer any secrets between them; they could talk frankly about Loren and Brant, and at last Moses Kaldor found he could speak of Earth.

'. . . Oh, I've lost count of my various jobs, Mirissa – most of them weren't very important, anyway. The one I held longest was Professor of Political Science in Cambridge, Mars. And you can't imagine the confusion *that* caused, because there was an older university at a place called Cambridge, *Mass* – and a still older one in Cambridge, England.

'But towards the end, Evelyn and I got more and more involved in the immediate social problems, and the planning for the Final Exodus. It seemed that I had some – well, oratorical talent – and could help people face what future was left to them.

'Yet we never *really* believed that the End would be in our time – who could! And if anyone had ever told me that I should leave Earth and everything I loved...'

A spasm of emotion crossed his face, and Mirissa waited in sympathetic silence until he had regained his composure. There were so many questions she wanted to ask that it might take a lifetime to answer them all; and she had only a year before *Magellan* set forth once more for the stars.

'When they told me I was needed, I used all my philosophical and debating skills to prove them wrong. I was too old; all the knowledge I had was stored in the memory banks; other men could do a better job ... everything except the *real* reason.

'In the end, Evelyn made up my mind for me; it's true, Mirissa, that in some ways women are much stronger than men – but why am I telling *you* that?

' "They need you," said her last message. "We have spent forty years together – now there is only a month left. Go with my love. Do not try to find me."

'I shall never know if she saw the end of the Earth as I did – when we were leaving the solar system.'

25

Scorp

He had seen Brant stripped before, when they had gone on that memorable boat-ride, but had never realized how formidably muscled the younger man was. Though Loren had always taken good care of his body, there had been little opportunity for sport or exercise since leaving Earth. Brant, however, was probably involved in some heavy physical exertion every day of his life – and it showed. Loren would have absolutely no chance against him unless he could conjure up one of the reputed martial arts of old Earth – none of which he had ever known.

The whole thing was perfectly ridiculous. There were his fellow officers grinning their stupid heads off. There was Captain Bey holding a stopwatch. And there was Mirissa with an expression that could only be described as smug.

'... two ... one ... zero ... GO!' said the captain. Brant moved like a striking cobra. Loren tried to avoid the onslaught but discovered to his horror that he had no control over his body. Time seemed to have slowed down ... his legs were made of lead and refused to obey him ... he was about to lose not only Mirissa but his very manhood ...

At that point, luckily, he had woken up, but the dream still bothered him. Its sources were obvious, but that did not make it any the less disturbing. He wondered if he should tell it to Mirissa.

Certainly he could never tell it to Brant, who was still perfectly friendly but whose company he now found embarrassing. Today, however, he positively welcomed it; if he was right, they were now confronted with something very much greater than their own private affairs.

He could hardly wait to see the reaction when Brant met the unexpected visitor who had arrived during the night.

The concrete-lined channel that brought seawater into the freezing plant was a hundred metres long and ended in a circular pool holding just enough water for one snowflake. Since pure ice was an indifferent building material, it was necessary to strengthen it, and the long strands of kelp from the Great Eastern Prairie made a cheap and convenient reinforcement. The frozen composite had been nicknamed icecrete and was guaranteed not to flow, glacierlike, during the weeks and months of *Magellan*'s acceleration.

'There it is.' Loren stood with Brant Falconer at the edge of the pool, looking down through a break in the matted raft of marine vegetation. The creature eating the kelp was built on the same general plan as a terrestrial lobster – but was more than twice the size of a man.

'Have you ever seen anything like *that* before?'

'No,' Brant answered fervently, 'and I'm not at all sorry. What a monster! How did you catch it?'

'We didn't. It swam – or crawled – in from the sea, along the channel. Then it found the kelp and decided to have a free lunch.'

'No wonder it has pinchers like that; those stems are really tough.'

'Well, at least it's a vegetarian.'

'I'm not sure I'd care to put that to the test.'

'I was hoping you could tell us something about it.'

'We don't know a hundredth of the creatures in the Lassan sea. One day we'll build some research subs and go into deep water. But there are so many other priorities, and not enough people are interested.'

They soon will be, Lorenson thought grimly. Let's see how long Brant takes to notice for himself ...

'Science Officer Varley has been checking the records. She tells me that there was something very much like this on Earth millions of years ago. The paleontologists gave it a good name – sea scorpion. Those ancient oceans must have been exciting places.'

'Just the sort of thing Kumar would like to chase,' Brant said. 'What are you going to do with it?'

'Study it and then let it go.'

'I see you've already tagged it.'

So Brant's noticed, thought Loren. Good for him.

'No – we haven't. Look more carefully.'

There was a puzzled expression on Brant's face as he knelt at the side of the tank. The giant scorpion ignored him completely as it continued to snip away at the seaweed with its formidable pinchers.

One of those pinchers was not altogether as nature had designed it. At the hinge of the right-hand claw there was a loop of wire twisted round several times like a crude bracelet.

Brant recognized that wire. His jaw dropped, and for a moment he was at a loss for words.

'So I guessed right,' Lorenson said. 'Now you know what happened to your fish trap. I think we'd better talk to Dr Varley again – not to mention your own scientists.'

'I'm an astronomer,' Anne Varley had protested from her office aboard *Magellan*. 'What you need is a combination of zoologist, paleontologist, ethologist – not to mention a few other disciplines. But I've done my best to set up a search program, and you'll find the result dumped in your Bank 2 under file heading SCORP. Now all you need to do is to search *that* – and good luck to you.'

Despite her disclaimer, Dr Varley had done her usual efficient job of winnowing through the almost-infinite store of knowledge in the ship's main memory banks. A pattern was beginning to emerge; meanwhile, the source of all the attention still browsed peacefully in its tank, taking no notice of the continual flow of visitors who came to study or merely to gape.

Despite its terrifying appearance – those pinchers were almost half a metre long and looked capable of taking off a man's head with one neat snip – the creature seemed completely nonaggressive. It made no effort to escape, perhaps because it had found such an abundant source of food. Indeed, it was generally believed that some trace chemical from the kelp had been responsible for luring it here.

If it was able to swim, it showed no inclination to do so, but was content to crawl around on its six stubby legs. Its four-metre long body was encased in a vividly coloured exoskeleton, articulated to give it surprising flexibility.

Another remarkable feature was the fringe of palps, or small tentacles, surrounding the beaklike mouth. They bore a striking – indeed, uncomfortable – resemblance to stubby human fingers and seemed equally dexterous. Although handling food appeared to be their main function, they were clearly capable of much more, and it was fascinating to watch the way that the scorp used them in conjunction with its claws.

Its two sets of eyes – one pair large, and apparently intended for low light, since during the daytime they were kept closed – must also provide it with excellent vision. Altogether, it was superbly equipped to survey and to manipulate its environment – the prime requirements for intelligence.

Yet no one would have suspected intelligence in such a bizarre creature if not for the wire twisted purposefully around its right claw. That, however, proved nothing. As the records showed, there had been animals on Earth who collected foreign objects – often man-made – and used them in extraordinary ways.

If it had not been fully documented, no one would have believed the Australian bowerbird's, or the North American pack rat's, mania for collecting shiny or coloured objects, and even arranging them in artistic displays. Earth had been full of such mysteries, which now would never be solved. Perhaps the Thalassan scorp was merely following the same mindless tradition, and for equally inscrutable reasons.

There were several theories. The most popular – because it put the least demands on the scorp's mentality – was that the wire bracelet was merely an ornament. Fixing it in place must have required some dexterity, and there was a good deal of debate as to whether the creature could have done it without assistance.

That assistance, of course, could have been human. Perhaps the scorp was some eccentric scientist's escaped pet, but this seemed very improbable. Since everyone on Thalassa knew everyone else, such a secret could not have been kept for long.

There was one other theory, the most farfetched of all – yet the most thought provoking.

Perhaps the bracelet was a badge of rank.

Snowflake Rising

It was highly skilled work with long periods of boredom, which gave Lieutenant Owen Fletcher plenty of time to think. Far too much time, in fact.

He was an angler, reeling in a six-hundred-ton catch on a line of almost unimaginable strength. Once a day the self-guided, captive probe would dive down towards Thalassa, spinning out the cable behind it along a complex, thirty-thousand-kilometre curve. It would home automatically on to the waiting payload, and when all the checks had been completed, the hoisting would begin.

The critical moments were at lift-off, when the snowflake was snatched out of the freezing plant, and the final approach to *Magellan*, when the huge hexagon of ice had to be brought to rest only a kilometre from the ship. Lifting began at midnight, and from Tarna to the stationary orbit in which *Magellan* was hovering, took just under six hours.

If *Magellan* was in daylight during the rendezvous and assembly, the first priority was keeping the snowflake in shadow, lest the fierce rays of Thalassa's sun boil off the precious cargo into space. Once it was safely behind the big radiation shield, the claws of the robot teleoperators could rip away the insulating foil that had protected the ice during its ascent to orbit.

Next the lifting cradle had to be removed, to be sent back for another load. Sometimes the huge metal plate, shaped like a hexagonal saucepan lid designed by some eccentric cook, stuck to the ice, and a little carefully regulated heating was required to detach it.

At last, the geometrically perfect ice floe would be poised motionless a hundred metres away from *Magellan*, and the really tricky part would begin. The combination of six hundred tons of mass with zero weight was utterly outside the range of human instinctive reactions; only computers could tell what thrusts were needed, in what direction, at what moments of time, to key the artificial iceberg into position. But there was always the possibility of some emergency or unexpected problem beyond the capabilities of even the most intelligent robot; although Fletcher had not yet had to intervene, he would be ready if the time came.

I'm helping to build, he told himself, a giant honeycomb of ice. The first layer of the comb was now almost completed, and there were two more to go. Barring accidents, the shield would be finished in another hundred and fifty days. It would be tested under low acceleration, to make sure that all the blocks had fused together properly; and then *Magellan* would set forth upon the final leg of its journey to the stars.

Fletcher was still doing his job conscientiously – but with his mind, not with his heart. That was already lost to Thalassa.

He had been born on Mars, and this world had everything his own barren planet had lacked. He had seen the labour of generations of his ancestors dissolve in flame; why start again centuries from now on yet another world – when Paradise was here?

And, of course, a girl was waiting for him, down there on South Island ...

He had almost decided that when the time came, he would jump ship. The Terrans could go on without him, to deploy their strength and skills – and perhaps break their hearts and bodies – against the stubborn rocks of Sagan 2. He wished them luck; when he had done his duty, his home was here.

Thirty thousand kilometres below, Brant Falconer had also made a crucial decision.

'I'm going to North Island.'

Mirissa lay silent; then, after what seemed to Brant a very long time, she said, 'Why?' There was no surprise, no regret in her voice; so much, he thought, has changed.

But before he could answer, she added, 'You don't like it there.'

'Perhaps it is better than here – as things are now. This is no longer my home.'

'It will always be your home.'

'Not while *Magellan* is still in orbit.'

Mirissa reached out her hand in the darkness to the stranger beside her. At least he did not move away.

'Brant,' she said, 'I never intended this. And nor, I'm quite certain, did Loren.'

'That doesn't help much, does it? Frankly, I can't understand what you see in him.'

Mirissa almost smiled. How many men, she wondered, had said that to how many women in the course of human history? And how many women had said, 'What can you see in *her*?'

There was no way of answering, of course; even the attempt would only make matters worse. But sometimes she had tried, for her own satisfaction, to pinpoint what had drawn her and Loren together since the very moment they had first set eyes upon each other.

The major part was the mysterious chemistry of love, beyond rational analysis, inexplicable to anyone who did not share the same illusion. But there were other elements that could be clearly identified and explained in logical terms. It was useful to know what they were; one day (all too soon!) that wisdom might help her face the moment of parting.

First there was the tragic glamour that surrounded all the Terrans; she did not discount the importance of that, but Loren shared it with all his comrades. What did he have that was so special and that she could not find in Brant?

As lovers, there was little to choose between them; perhaps Loren was more imaginative, Brant more passionate – though had he not become a little perfunctory in the last few weeks? She would be perfectly happy with either. No, it was not *that* ...

Perhaps she was searching for an ingredient that did not even exist. There was no single element but an entire constellation of qualities. Her instincts, below the level of conscious thought, had added up the score; and Loren had come out a few points ahead of Brant. It could be as simple as that.

There was certainly one respect in which Loren far eclipsed Brant. He had drive, ambition – the very things that were so rare on Thalassa. Doubtless he had been chosen for these qualities; he would need them in the centuries to come.

Brant had no ambition whatsoever, though he was not lacking in enterprise; his still-uncompleted fish-trapping project was proof of that. All he asked from the Universe was that it provided him with interesting machines to play with; Mirissa sometimes thought that he included her in that category.

Loren, by contrast, was in the tradition of the great explorers and adventurers. He would help to make history, not merely submit to its imperatives. And yet he could – not often enough but more and more frequently – be warm and human. Even as he froze the seas of Thalassa, his own heart was beginning to thaw.

'What are you going to do on North Island?' Mirissa whispered. Already, they had taken his decision for granted.

'They want me there to help fit out *Calypso*. The Northers don't really understand the sea.'

Mirissa felt relieved; Brant was not simply running away – he had work to do.

Work that would help him to forget – until, perhaps, the time came to remember once again.

27

Mirror of the Past

Moses Kaldor held the module up to the light, peering into it as if he could read its contents.

'It will always seem a miracle to me,' he said, 'that I can hold a million books between my thumb and forefinger. I wonder what Caxton and Gutenberg would have thought.'

'Who?' Mirissa asked.

'The men who started the human race reading. But there's a price we have to pay now for our ingenuity. Sometimes I have a little nightmare and imagine that one of these modules contains some piece of absolutely vital information – say the cure for a raging epidemic – but the address has been lost. It's on *one* of those billion pages, but we don't know which. How frustrating to hold the answer in the palm of your hand and not be able to find it!'

'I don't see the problem,' the captain's secretary said. As an expert on information storage and retrieval, Joan LeRoy had been helping with the transfers between Thalassa Archives and the ship. 'You'll know the key words; all you have to do is set up a search program. Even a billion pages could be checked in a few seconds.'

'You've spoiled my nightmare.' Kaldor sighed. Then he brightened. 'But often you even don't know the key words. How many times have you come across something that you didn't know you needed – until you found it?'

'Then you're badly organized,' said Lieutenant LeRoy.

They enjoyed these little tongue-in-cheek exchanges, and Mirissa was not always sure when to take them seriously. Joan and Moses did not deliberately try to exclude her from their conversations, but their worlds of experience were so utterly different from hers that she sometimes felt that she was listening to a dialogue in an unknown language.

'Anyway, that completes the Master Index. We each know what the other has; now we merely – *merely*! have to decide what we'd like to transfer. It may be inconvenient, not to say expensive, when we're seventy-five lights apart.'

'Which reminds me,' Mirissa said. 'I don't suppose I should tell you – but there was a delegation from North Island here last week. The president of the science academy, and a couple of physicists.'

'Let me guess. The quantum drive.'

'Right.'

'How did they react?'

'They seemed pleased – and surprised – that it really *was* there. They made a copy, of course.'

'Good luck to them; they'll need it. And you might tell them this. Someone once said that the QD's real purpose is nothing as trivial as the exploration of the Universe. We'll need its energies one day to stop the cosmos' collapsing back into the primordial Black Hole – and to start the next cycle of existence.'

There was an awed silence, then Joan LeRoy broke the spell.

'Not in the lifetime of *this* administration. Let's get back to work. We still have megabytes to go, before we sleep.'

It was not all work, and there were times when Kaldor simply had to get away from the Library Section of First Landing in order to relax. Then he would stroll across to the art gallery, take the computer-guided tour through the Mother Ship (never the same route twice – he tried to cover as much ground as possible) or let the Museum carry him back in time.

There was always a long line of visitors – mostly students, or children with their parents – for the Terrama displays. Sometimes Moses Kaldor felt a little guilty at using his privileged status to jump to the head of the queue. He consoled himself with the thought that the Lassans had a whole lifetime in which they could enjoy these panoramas of the world they had never known; he had only months in which to revisit his lost home.

He found it very difficult to convince his new friends that Moses Kaldor had never been in the scenes they sometimes watched together. Everything they saw was at least eight hundred years in his own past, for the Mother Ship had left Earth in 2751 – and he had been born in 3541. Yet occasionally there would be a shock of recognition, and some memory would come flooding back with almost unbearable power.

The 'Sidewalk Cafe' presentation was the most uncanny, and the most evocative. He would be sitting at a small table, under an awning, drinking wine or coffee, while the life of a city flowed past him. As long as he did not get up from the table, there was absolutely no way in which his senses could distinguish the display from reality.

In microcosm, the great cities of Earth were brought back to life. Rome, Paris, London, New York – in summer and winter, by night and day, he watched the tourists and businessmen and students and lovers go about their ways. Often, realizing that they were being recorded, they would smile at him across the centuries, and it was impossible not to respond.

Other panoramas showed no human beings at all, or even any of the productions of Man. Moses Kaldor looked again, as he had done in that other life, upon the descending smoke of Victoria Falls, the Moon rising above the Grand Canyon, the Himalayan snows, the ice cliffs of Antarctica. Unlike the glimpses of the cities, these things had not changed in the thousand years since they were recorded. And though they had existed long before Man, they had not outlasted him.

28

The Sunken Forest

The scorp did not seem to be in a hurry; it took a leisurely ten days to travel fifty kilometres. One curious fact was quickly revealed by the sonar beacon that had been attached, not without difficulty, to the angry subject's carapace. The path it traced along the seabed was perfectly straight, as if it knew precisely where it was going.

Whatever its destination might be, it seemed to have found it, at a depth of two hundred and fifty metres. Thereafter, it still kept moving around, but inside a very limited area. This continued for two more days; then the signals from the ultrasonic pinger suddenly stopped in mid-pulse.

That the scorp had been eaten by something even bigger and nastier than itself was far too naive an explanation. The pinger was enclosed in a tough metal cylinder; any conceivable arrangement of teeth, claws, or tentacles would take minutes – at the very least – to demolish it, and it would continue to function quite happily inside any creature that swallowed it whole.

This left only two possibilities, and the first was indignantly denied by the staff of the North Island Underwater Lab.

'*Every* single component had a back-up,' the director said. 'What's more, there was a diagnostic pulse only two seconds earlier; everything was normal. So it could not have been an equipment failure.'

That left only the impossible explanation. The pinger had been switched off. And to do that, a locking-bar had to be removed.

It could not happen by accident; only by curious meddling – or deliberate intent.

*   *   *

The twenty metre twin-hull *Calypso* was not merely the largest, but the only, oceanographic research vessel on Thalassa. It was normally based on North Island, and Loren was amused to note the good-natured banter between its scientific crew and their Tarnan passengers, whom they pretended to treat as ignorant fishermen. For their part, the South Islanders lost no opportunity of boasting to the Northers that *they* were the ones who had discovered the scorps. Loren did not remind them that this was not strictly in accord with the facts.

It was a slight shock to meet Brant again, though Loren should have expected it, since the other had been partly responsible for *Calypso*'s new equipment. They greeted each other with cool politeness, ignoring the curious or amused glances of the other passengers. There were few secrets on Thalassa; by this time everyone would know who was occupying the main guest-room of the Leonidas home.

The small underwater sledge sitting on the afterdeck would have been familiar to any oceanographer of the last two thousand years. Its metal framework carried three television cameras, a wire basket to hold samples collected by the remote-controlled arm, and an arrangement of water-jets that permitted movement in any direction. Once it had been lowered over the side, the robot explorer could send its images and information back through a fibre-optic cable not much thicker than the lead of a pencil. The technology was centuries old – and still perfectly adequate.

Now the shoreline had finally disappeared, and for the first time Loren found himself completely surrounded by water. He recalled his anxiety on that earlier trip with Brant and Kumar when they had travelled hardly a kilometre from the beach. This time, he was pleased to discover, he felt slightly more at ease, despite the presence of his rival. Perhaps it was because he was on a much larger boat ...

'That's odd,' Brant said, 'I've never seen kelp this far to the west.'

At first Loren could see nothing; then he noticed the dark stain low in the water ahead. A few minutes later, the boat was nosing its way through a loose mass of floating vegetation, and the captain slowed speed to a crawl.

'We're almost there, anyway,' he said. 'No point in clogging our intakes with this stuff. Agreed, Brant?'

Brant adjusted the cursor on the display screen and took a reading.

'Yes – we're only fifty metres from where we lost the pinger. Depth two hundred and ten. Let's get the fish overboard.'

'Just a minute,' one of the Norther scientists said. 'We spent a lot of time and money on that machine, and it's the only one in the world. Suppose it gets tangled up in that damned kelp?'

There was a thoughtful silence; then Kumar, who had been uncharacteristically quiet – perhaps overawed by the high-powered talent from North Island – put in a diffident word.

'It looks much worse from here. Ten metres down, there are almost no leaves – only the big stems, with plenty of room between them. It's like a forest.'

Yes, thought Loren, a submarine forest, with fish swimming between the slender, sinuous trunks. While the other scientists were watching the main video screen and the multiple displays of instrumentation, he had put on a set of full-vision goggles, excluding everything from his field of view except the scene ahead of the slowly descending robot. Psychologically, he was no longer on the deck of *Calypso*; the voices of his companions seemed to come from another world that had nothing to do with him.

He was an explorer entering an alien universe, not knowing what he might encounter. It was a restricted, almost monochrome universe; the only colours were soft blues and greens, and the limit of vision was less than thirty metres away. At any one time he could see a dozen slender trunks, supported at regular intervals by the gas-filled bladders that gave them buoyancy, reaching up from the gloomy depths and disappearing into the luminous 'sky' overhead. Sometimes he felt that he was walking through a grove of trees on a dull, foggy day: then a school of darting fish destroyed the illusion.

'Two hundred fifty metres,' he heard someone call. 'We should see the bottom soon. Shall we use the lights? The image quality is deteriorating.'

Loren had scarcely noticed any change, because the automatic controls had maintained the picture brilliance. But he realized that it must be almost completely dark at this depth; a human eye would have been virtually useless.

'No – we don't want to disturb anything until we have to. As long as the camera's operating, let's stick to available light.'

'There's the bottom! Mostly rock – not much sand.'

'Naturally. _Macrocystis thalassi_ needs rocks to cling to – it's not like the free-floating _Sargassum_.'

Loren could see what the speaker meant. The slender trunks ended in a network of roots, grasping rock-outcroppings so firmly that no storms or surface currents could dislodge them. The analogy with a forest on land was even closer than he had thought.

Very cautiously, the robot surveyor was working its way into the submarine forest, playing out its cable behind it. There seemed no risk of becoming entangled in the serpentine trunks that reared up to the invisible surface, for there was plenty of space between the giant plants. Indeed, they might have been deliberately –

The scientists looking at the monitor screen realized the incredible truth just a few seconds after Loren.

'Krakan!' one of them whispered. 'This isn't a natural forest – it's a – _plantation_!'

29

Sabra

They called themselves Sabras, after· the pioneers who, a millennium and a half before, had tamed an almost equally hostile wilderness on Earth.

The Martian Sabras had been lucky in one respect; they had no human enemies to oppose them – only the fierce climate, the barely perceptible atmosphere, the planet-wide sandstorms. All these handicaps they had conquered; they were fond of saying that they had not merely survived, they had prevailed. That quotation was only one of countless borrowings from Earth, which their fierce independence would seldom allow them to acknowledge.

For more than a thousand years, they had lived in the shadow of an illusion – almost a religion. And, like any religion, it had performed an essential role in their society; it had given them goals beyond themselves, and a purpose to their lives.

Until the calculations proved otherwise, they had believed – or at least hoped – that Mars might escape the doom of Earth. It would be a close thing, of course; the extra distance would merely reduce the radiation by fifty per cent – but that might be sufficient. Protected by the kilometres of ancient ice at the Poles, perhaps Martians could survive when Men could not. There had even been a fantasy – though only a few romantics had really believed it – that the melting of the polar caps would restore the planet's lost oceans. And then, perhaps, the atmosphere might become dense enough for men to move freely in the open with simple breathing equipment and thermal insulation ...

These hopes died hard, killed at last by implacable equations. No amount of skill or effort would allow the Sabras to save themselves. They, too, would perish with the mother world whose softness they often affected to despise.

Yet now, spread beneath *Magellan*, was a planet that epitomized all the hopes and dreams of the last generations of Martian colonists. As Owen Fletcher looked down at the endless oceans of Thalassa, one thought kept hammering in his brain.

According to the star-probes, Sagan Two was much like Mars – which was the very reason he and his compatriots had been selected for this voyage. But why resume a battle, three hundred years hence and seventy-five light-years away, when Victory was already here and now?

Fletcher was no longer thinking merely of desertion; that would mean leaving far too much behind. It would be easy enough to hide on Thalassa; but how would he feel, when *Magellan* left, with the last friends and colleagues of his youth?

Twelve Sabras were still in hibernation. Of the five awake, he had already cautiously sounded out two and had received a favourable response. And if the other two also agreed with him, he knew that they could speak for the sleeping dozen.

Magellan must end its starfaring, here at Thalassa.

30

Child of Krakan

There was little conversation aboard as *Calypso* headed back towards Tarna at a modest twenty klicks; her passengers were lost in their thoughts, brooding over the implications of those images from the seabed. And Loren was still cut off from the outside world; he had kept on the full-view goggles and was playing back yet again the underwater sledge's exploration of the submarine forest.

Spinning out its cable like a mechanical spider, the robot had moved slowly through the great trunks, which looked slender because of their enormous length but were actually thicker than a man's body. It was now obvious that they were ranged in regular columns and rows, so no one was really surprised when they came to a clearly defined end. And there, going about their business in their jungle encampment, were the scorps.

It had been wise not to switch on the floodlights; the creatures were completely unaware of the silent observer floating in the near-darkness only metres overhead. Loren had seen videos of ants, bees, and termites, and the way in which the scorps were functioning reminded him of these. At first sight, it was impossible to believe that such intricate organization could exist without a controlling intelligence – yet their behaviour might be entirely automatic, as in the case of Earth's social insects.

Some scorps were tending the great trunks that soared up towards the surface to harvest the rays of the invisible sun; others were scuttling along the seabed carrying rocks, leaves – and yes, crude but unmistakable nets and baskets. So the scorps were tool-makers; but even that did not prove intelligence. Some bird's nests were much more carefully fashioned than these rather clumsy artifacts, apparently constructed from stems and fronds of the omnipresent kelp.

I felt like a visitor from space, Loren thought, poised above a Stone Age village on Earth, just when Man was discovering agriculture. Could he – or it – have correctly assessed human intelligence from such a survey? Or would the verdict have been: pure instinctive behaviour?

The probe had now gone so far into the clearing that the surrounding forest was no longer visible, though the nearest trunks could not have been more than fifty metres away. It was then that some wit among the Northers uttered the name that was thereafter unavoidable, even in the scientific reports: 'Downtown Scorpville'.

It seemed to be, for want of better terms, both a residential and a business area. An outcropping of rock, about five metres high, meandered across the opening, and its face was pierced by numerous dark holes just wide enough to admit a scorp. Although these little caves were irregularly spaced, they were of such uniform size that they could hardly be natural, and the whole effect was that of an apartment building designed by an eccentric architect.

Scorps were coming and going through the entrances – like office workers in one of the old cities before the age of telecommunications, Loren thought. Their activities seemed as meaningless to him as, probably, the commerce of humans would have been to them.

'Hello,' one of *Calypso*'s other watchers called, 'What's *that*? Extreme right – can you move closer?'

The interruption from outside his sphere of consciousness was jolting; it dragged Loren momentarily from the seabed back to the world of the surface.

His panoramic view tilted abruptly with the probe's change of attitude. Now it was level again and drifting slowly towards an isolated pyramid of rock, which was about ten metres high – judging by the two scorps at its base – and pierced by a single cave entrance. Loren could see nothing unusual about it; then, slowly, he became aware of certain anomalies – jarring elements that did not quite fit into the now-familiar Scorpville scene.

All the other scorps had been busily scurrying about. These two were motionless except for the continual swinging of their heads, back and forth. And there was something else –

These scorps were big. It was hard to judge scale here, and not until several more of the animals had scurried past was Loren quite sure that this pair was almost fifty per cent larger than average.

'What are they doing?' somebody whispered.

'I'll tell you,' another voice answered. 'They're guards – sentries.'

Once stated, the conclusion was so obvious that no one doubted it.

'But what are they guarding?'

'The queen, if they have one? The First Bank of Scorpville?'

'How can we find out? The sled's much too big to go inside – even if they'd let us try.'

It was at this point that the discussion became academic. The robot probe had now drifted down to within less than ten metres of the pyramid's summit, and the operator gave a brief burst from one of the control jets to stop it descending farther.

The sound, or the vibration, must have alerted the sentries. Both of them reared up simultaneously, and Loren had a sudden nightmare vision of clustered eyes, waving palps, and giant claws. I'm glad I'm not *really* here, even though it seems like it, he told himself. And it's lucky they can't swim.

But if they could not swim, they could climb. With astonishing speed, the scorps scrambled up the side of the pyramid and within seconds were on its summit, only a few metres below the sled.

'Gotta get out of here before they jump,' the operator said. 'Those pinchers could snap our cable like a piece of cotton.'

He was too late. A scorp launched itself off the rock, and seconds later its claws grabbed one of the skis of the sled's undercarriage.

The operator's human reflexes were equally swift and in control of a superior technology. At the same instant, he went into full reverse and swung the robot arm downward to the attack. And what was perhaps more decisive, he switched on the floodlights.

The scorp must have been completely blinded. Its claws opened in an almost human gesture of astonishment, and it dropped back to the seabed before the robot's mechanical hand could engage it in combat.

For a fraction of a second, Loren was also blind, as his goggles blacked out. Then the camera's automatic circuits corrected for the increased light level, and he had one startlingly clear close-up of the baffled scorp just before it dropped out of the field of view.

Somehow he was not in the least surprised to see that it was wearing two bands of metal below its right claw.

He was reviewing this final scene as *Calypso* headed back for Tarna, and his senses were still so concentrated on the underwater world that he never felt the mild shockwave as it raced past the boat. But then he became aware of the shouts and confusion around him and felt the deck heel as *Calypso* suddenly changed course. He tore off the goggles and stood blinking in the brilliant sunlight.

For a moment he was totally blind; then, as his eyes adjusted to the glare, he saw that they were only a few hundred metres from South Island's palm-fringed coast. We've hit a reef, he thought. Brant will never hear the last of this...

And then he saw, climbing up over the eastern horizon, something he had never dreamed of witnessing on peaceful Thalassa. It was the mushroom cloud that had haunted men's nightmares for two thousand years.

What was Brant *doing*? Surely he should be heading for land; instead, he was swinging *Calypso* around in the tightest possible turning circle, heading out to sea. But he seemed to have taken charge, while everyone else on deck was staring slack-mouthed towards the east.

'Krakan!' one of the Norther scientists whispered, and for a moment Loren thought he was merely using the overworked Lassan expletive. Then he understood, and a vast feeling of relief swept over him. It was very short-lived.

'No,' Kumar said, looking more alarmed than Loren would have thought possible. 'Not Krakan – much closer. *Child* of Krakan.'

The boat radio was now emitting continuous beeps of alarm, interspersed with solemn warning messages. Loren had no time to absorb any of them when he saw that something very strange was happening to the horizon. *It was not where it should have been.*

This was all very confusing; half of his mind was still down

there with the scorps, and even now he had to keep blinking
against the glare from sea and sky. Perhaps there was something
wrong with his vision. Although he was quite certain that *Calypso*
was now on an even keel, his eyes told him that it was plunging
steeply downward.

No; it was the sea that was rising, with a roar that now
obliterated all other sounds. He dared not judge the height of the
wave that was bearing down upon them; now he understood why
Brant was heading out into deep water, away from the deadly
shallows against which the tsunami was about to expend its fury.

A giant hand gripped *Calypso* and lifted her bow up, up towards
the zenith. Loren started to slide helplessly along the deck; he tried
to grasp a stanchion, missed it, then found himself in the water.

Remember your emergency training, he told himself fiercely.
In sea or in space, the principle is always the same. The greatest
danger is panic, so keep your head...

There was no risk of drowning; his life-jacket would see to that.
But where was the inflation lever? His fingers scrabbled wildly
around the webbing at his waist, and despite all his resolve, he felt
a brief, icy chill before he found the metal bar. It moved easily, and
to his great relief he felt the jacket expand around him, gripping
him in a welcome embrace.

Now the only real danger would be from *Calypso* herself if she
crashed back upon his head. Where was she?

Much too close for comfort, in this raging water, and with part
of her deck-housing hanging into the sea. Incredibly, most of the
crew still seemed on board. Now they were pointing at him, and
someone was preparing to throw a life-belt.

The water was full of floating debris – chairs, boxes, pieces of
equipment – and there went the sled, slowly sinking as it blew
bubbles from a damaged buoyancy tank. I hope they can salvage
it, Loren thought. If not, this will be a very expensive trip, and it
may be a long time before we can study the scorps again. He felt
rather proud of himself for so calm an appraisal of the situation,
considering the circumstances.

Something brushed against his right leg; with an automatic reflex, he tried to kick it away. Though it bit uncomfortably into the flesh, he was more annoyed than alarmed. He was safely afloat, the giant wave had passed, and nothing could harm him now.

He kicked again, more cautiously. Even as he did so, he felt the same entanglement on the other leg. And now this was no longer a neutral caress; despite the buoyancy of his life-jacket, something was pulling him underwater.

That was when Loren Lorenson felt the first moment of real panic, for he suddenly remembered the questing tentacles of the great polyp. Yet those must be soft and fleshy – this was obviously some wire or cable. Of course – it was the umbilical cord from the sinking sled.

He might still have been able to disentangle himself had he not swallowed a mouthful of water from an unexpected wave. Choking and coughing, he tried to clear his lungs, kicking at the cable at the same time.

And then the vital boundary between air and water – between life and death – was less than a metre overhead; but there was no way that he could reach it.

At such a moment, a man thinks of nothing but his own survival. There were no flashbacks, no regrets for his past life – not even a fleeting glimpse of Mirissa.

When he realized it was all over, he felt no fear. His last conscious thought was pure anger that he had travelled fifty light-years, only to meet so trivial and unheroic an end.

So Loren Lorenson died for the second time, in the warm shallows of the Thalassan sea. He had not learned from experience; the first death had been much easier, two hundred years ago.

V

The Bounty Syndrome

31

Petition

Though Captain Sirdar Bey would have denied that he had a milligram of superstition in his body, he always started to worry when things went well. So far, Thalassa had been almost too good to be true; everything had gone according to the most optimistic plan. The shield was being constructed right on schedule, and there had been absolutely no problems worth talking about.

But now, all within the space of twenty-four hours ...

Of course, it could have been much worse. Lieutenant Commander Lorenson had been very, very lucky – thanks to that kid (they'd have to do something for him ...) According to the medics, it had been extremely close. Another few minutes and brain damage would have been irreversible.

Annoyed at letting his attention stray from the immediate problem, the captain reread the message he now knew by heart:

SHIPNET: NO DATE NO TIME
TO: CAPTAIN
FROM: ANON

Sir: A number of us wish to make the following proposal, which we put forward for your most serious consideration. We suggest that our mission be terminated here at Thalassa.
All its objectives will be realized, without the additional risks involved in proceeding to Sagan 2.
We fully recognize that this will involve problems with the existing population, but we believe they can be solved with the technology we possess – specifically, the use of tectonic engineering to increase the available land area.
As per Regulàtions, Section 14, Para 24 (a), we respectfully

request that a Ship's Council be held to discuss this matter as soon as possible.

'Well, Captain Malina? Ambassador Kaldor? Any comments?'

The two guests in the spacious but simply furnished captain's quarters looked at each other simultaneously. Then Kaldor gave an almost imperceptible nod to the deputy captain, and confirmed his relinquishment of priority by taking another slow, deliberate sip of the excellent Thalassan wine their hosts had provided.

Deputy Captain Malina, who was rather more at ease with machines than with people, looked at the printout unhappily.

'At least it's very polite.'

'So I should hope,' Captain Bey said impatiently. 'Have you any idea who could have sent it?'

'None whatsoever. Excluding the three of us, I'm afraid we have 158 suspects.'

'157,' Kaldor interjected. 'Lieutenant Commander Lorenson has an excellent alibi. He was dead at the time.'

'That doesn't narrow the field much,' the Captain said, managing a bleak smile. 'Have *you* any theories, Doctor?'

Indeed I have, Kaldor thought. I lived on Mars for two of its long years; my money would be on the Sabras. But that's only a hunch, and I may be wrong...

'Not yet, Captain. But I'll keep my eyes open. If I find anything, I'll inform you – as far as possible.'

The two officers understood him perfectly. In his role as counsellor, Moses Kaldor was not even responsible to the captain. He was the nearest thing aboard *Magellan* to a father confessor.

'I assume, Dr Kaldor, that you'll certainly let me know – if you uncover information that could endanger this mission.'

Kaldor hesitated, then nodded briefly. He hoped he would not find himself in the traditional dilemma of the priest who received the confession of a murderer – who was still planning his crime.

I'm not getting much help, the captain thought sourly. But I have absolute trust in these two men, and need someone to confide in. Even though the final decision must be mine.

'The first question is should I answer this message or ignore it? Either move could be risky. If it's only a casual suggestion – perhaps from a single individual in a moment of psychological disturbance – I might be unwise to take it too seriously. But if it's from a determined group, then perhaps a dialogue may help. It could defuse the situation. It could also identify those concerned.' And what would you do then? the captain asked himself. Clap them in irons?

'I think you should talk to them,' Kaldor said. 'Problems seldom go away if they're ignored.'

'I agree,' said Deputy Captain Malina. 'But I'm sure it's not any of the Drive or Power crews. I've known all of them since they graduated – or before.'

You could be surprised, Kaldor thought. Who ever *really* knows anyone?

'Very well,' the captain said, rising to his feet. 'That's what I'd already decided. And, just in case, I think I'd better reread some history. I recall that Magellan had a little trouble with his crew.'

'Indeed he did,' Kaldor answered. 'But I trust *you* won't have to maroon anyone.'

Or hang one of your commanders, he added to himself; it would have been very tactless to mention that particular piece of history.

And it would be even worse to remind Captain Bey – though surely he could not have forgotten! – that the great navigator had been killed before he could complete his mission.

32

Clinic

This time, the way back to life had not been prepared so carefully in advance. Loren Lorenson's second awakening was not as comfortable as his first; indeed, it was so unpleasant that he sometimes wished he had been left to sink into oblivion.

When he regained semiconsciousness, he quickly regretted it. There were tubes down his throat, and wires attached to his arms and legs. *Wires!* He felt a sudden panic at the memory of that deadly, downward tugging, then brought his emotions under control.

Now there was something else to worry about. He did not seem to be breathing; he could detect no movement of his diaphragm. How very odd – oh, I suppose they've by-passed my lungs –

A nurse must have been alerted by his monitors, for suddenly there was a soft voice in his ear, and he sensed a shadow falling across eyelids that he was still too tired to open.

'You're doing very well, Mister Lorenson. There's nothing to worry about. You'll be up in a few days – No, don't try to talk.'

I'd no intention of it, Loren thought. I know exactly what's happened –

Then there was the faint hiss of a hypodermic jet, a brief freezing coldness on his arm, and, once more, blessed oblivion.

The next time, to his great relief, everything was quite different. The tubes and wires were gone. Though he felt very weak, he was in no discomfort. And he was breathing again in a steady, normal rhythm.

'Hello,' said a deep male voice from a few metres away. 'Welcome back.'

Loren rolled his head towards the sound, and had a blurred glimpse of a bandaged figure in an adjacent bed.

'I guess you won't recognize me, Mister Lorenson. Lieutenant Bill Horton, communications engineer – and ex-surfboard rider.'

'Oh, hello, Bill – what have *you* been doing –' whispered Loren. But then the nurse arrived and ended that conversation with another well-placed hypodermic.

Now he was perfectly fit and only wanted to be allowed to get up. Surgeon-Commander Newton believed that, on the whole, it was best to let her patients know what was happening to them, and why. Even if they didn't understand, it helped to keep them quiet so that their annoying presence did not interfere too much with the smooth running of the medical establishment.

'You may *feel* all right, Loren,' she said, 'but your lungs are still repairing themselves, and you must avoid exertion until they're back to full capacity. If Thalassa's ocean was like Earth's, there would have been no problem. But it's much less saline – it's drinkable, remember, and you drank about a litre of it. And as your body fluids are saltier than the sea, the isotonic balance was all wrong. So there was a good deal of membrane damage through osmotic pressure. We had to do a lot of high-speed research in Ship's Archives before we could handle you. After all, drowning is not a normal space hazard.'

'I'll be a good patient,' Loren said. 'And I certainly appreciate all you've done. But when can I have visitors?'

'There's one waiting outside right now. You can have fifteen minutes. Then nurse will throw her out.'

'And don't mind me,' Lieutenant Bill Horton said. 'I'm fast asleep.'

33

Tides

Mirissa felt distinctly unwell, and of course it was all the fault of the Pill. But at least she had the consolation of knowing that this could only happen one more time – when (and if!) she had the second child permitted to her.

It was incredible to think that virtually all the generations of women who had ever existed had been forced to endure these monthly inconveniences for half their lives. Was it pure coincidence, she wondered, that the cycle of fertility approximated to that of the Earth's single giant Moon? Just suppose it had worked the same way on Thalassa, with its two close satellites! Perhaps it was just as well that their tides were barely perceptible; the thought of five- and seven-day cycles clashing discordantly together was so comically horrible that she could not help smiling and immediately felt much better.

It had taken her weeks to make the decision, and she had not yet told Loren – still less Brant, busily repairing *Calypso* back on North Island. Would she have done this if he had not left her – for all his bluster and bravado, running away without a fight?

No – that was unfair, a primitive, even prehuman reaction. Yet such instincts died hard; Loren had told her, apologetically, that sometimes he and Brant stalked each other down the corridors of his dreams.

She could not blame Brant; on the contrary, she should be proud of him. It was not cowardice, but consideration, that had sent him north until they could work out both their destinies.

Her decision had not been made in haste; she realized now that it must have been hovering below the verge of consciousness for weeks. Loren's temporary death had reminded her – as if she needed reminding! – that soon they must part forever. She knew what must be done before he set forth for the stars. Every instinct told her that it was right.

And what would Brant say? How would he react? That was another of the many problems yet to be faced.

I love you, Brant, she whispered. I want you to come back; my second child will be yours.

But not my first.

34

Shipnet

How odd, thought Owen Fletcher, that I share my name with one of the most famous mutineers of all time! Could I be a descendant? Let's see – it's more than two thousand years since they landed on Pitcairn Island ... say, a hundred generations, to make it easy ...

Fletcher took a naive pride in his ability to make mental calculations which, though elementary, surprised and impressed the vast majority; for centuries Man had pushed buttons when faced with the problem of adding two and two. Remembering a few logarithms and mathematical constants helped enormously and made his performance even more mysterious to those who did not know how it was done. Of course, he only chose examples that he knew how to handle, and it was very seldom that anyone bothered to check his answers ...

A hundred generations back – so two to the hundred ancestors then. Log two is point three zero one zero – that's thirty point one ... Olympus! – a million, million, million, million, *million* people! Something wrong – nothing like that number ever lived on Earth since the beginning of time – of course, that assumes there was never any overlapping – the human family tree must be hopelessly intertwined – anyway, after a hundred generations everyone must be related to everyone else – I'll never be able to prove it, but Fletcher Christian must be my ancestor – many times over.

All very interesting, he thought, as he switched off the display and the ancient records vanished from the screen. But I'm not a mutineer. I'm a – a *petitioner*, with a perfectly reasonable request. Karl, Ranjit, Bob all agree ... Werner is uncertain but won't give us away. How I wish we could talk to the rest of the Sabras and let them know about the lovely world we've found while they're asleep.

Meanwhile, I have to answer the captain ...

Captain Bey found it distinctly unsettling, having to go about the ship's business not knowing who – or how many – of his officers or crew were addressing him through the anonymity of SHIPNET. There was no way that these unlogged inputs could be traced – confidentiality was their very purpose, built in as a stabilizing social mechanism by the long-dead geniuses who had designed *Magellan*. He had tentatively raised the subject of a tracer with his chief communications engineer, but Commander Rocklyn had been so shocked that he had promptly dropped the matter.

So now he was continually searching faces, noting expressions, listening to voice inflections – and trying to behave as if nothing had happened. Perhaps he was overreacting and nothing important *had* happened. But he feared that a seed had been planted, and it would grow and grow with every day the ship remained in orbit above Thalassa.

His first acknowledgement, drafted after consultation with Malina and Kaldor, had been bland enough:

From: CAPTAIN
To: ANON

In reply to your undated communication, I have no objection to discussions along the lines you propose, either through SHIPNET or formally in Ship's Council.

In fact, he had very strong objections; he had spent almost half his adult life training for the awesome responsibility of transplanting a million human beings across a hundred and twenty-five light-years of space. That was his mission; if the word 'sacred' had meant anything to him, he would have used it. Nothing short of catastrophic damage to the ship or the unlikely discovery that Sagan 2's sun was about to go nova could possibly deflect him from that goal.

Meanwhile, there was one obvious line of action. Perhaps – like Bligh's men! – the crew was becoming demoralized, or at least slack. The repairs to the ice plant after the minor damage caused by the tsunami had taken twice as long as expected, and that was typical. The whole tempo of the ship was slowing down; yes it was time to start cracking the whip again.

'Joan,' he said to his secretary, thirty thousand kilometres below. 'Let me have the latest shield assembly report. And tell Captain Malina I want to discuss the hoisting schedule with him.'

He did not know if they could lift more than one snowflake a day. But they could try.

35

Convalescence

Lieutenant Horton was an amusing companion, but Loren was glad to get rid of him as soon as the electrofusion currents had welded his broken bones. As Loren discovered in somewhat wearisome detail, the young engineer had fallen in with a gang of hairy hunks on North Island, whose second main interest in life appeared to be riding microjet surfboards up vertical waves. Horton had found, the hard way, that it was even more dangerous than it looked.

'I'm quite surprised,' Loren had interjected at one point in a rather steamy narrative. 'I'd have sworn you were ninety per cent hetero.'

'Ninety-two, according to my profile,' Horton said cheerfully. 'But I like to check my calibration from time to time.'

The lieutenant was only half joking. Somewhere he had heard that hundred percenters were so rare that they were classed as pathological. Not that he *really* believed it; but it worried him slightly on those very few occasions when he gave the matter any thought.

Now Loren was the sole patient and had convinced the Lassan nurse that her continuous presence was quite unnecessary – at least when Mirissa was paying her daily visit. Surgeon-Commander Newton, who like most physicians could be embarrassingly frank, had told him bluntly, 'You still need another week to recuperate. If you *must* make love, let her do all the work.'

He had many other visitors, of course. With two exceptions, most were welcome.

Mayor Waldron could bully his little nurse to let her in at any time; fortunately, her visitations never coincided with Mirissa's. The first time the mayor arrived, Loren contrived to be in an almost moribund state, but this tactic proved disastrous, as it made it impossible for him to fend off some moist caresses. On the second visit – luckily there had been a ten-minute warning – he was propped up by pillows and fully conscious. However, by a strange coincidence, an elaborate respiratory function test was in progress, and the breathing-tube inserted in Loren's mouth made conversation impossible. The test was completed about thirty seconds after the mayor's departure.

Brant Falconer's one courtesy visit was something of a strain for them both. They talked politely about the scorps, progress at the

Mangrove Bay freezing plant, North Island politics – anything, in fact, except Mirissa. Loren could see that Brant was worried, even embarrassed, but the very last thing he expected was an apology. His visitor managed to get it off his chest just before he left.

'You know, Loren,' he said reluctantly, 'there was nothing else I could have done about that wave. If I'd kept on course, we'd have smashed into the reef. It was just too bad *Calypso* couldn't reach deep water in time.'

'I'm quite sure,' Loren said with complete sincerity, 'that no one could have done a better job.'

'Er – I'm glad you understand that.'

Brant was obviously relieved, and Loren felt a surge of sympathy – even of pity – for him. Perhaps there had been some criticism of his seamanship; to anyone as proud of his skills as Brant, that would have been intolerable.

'I understand that they've salvaged the sledge.'

'Yes – it will soon be repaired, and as good as new.'

'Like me.'

In the brief comradeship of their joint laughter, Loren was struck by a sudden, ironic thought.

Brant must often have wished that Kumar had been a little less courageous.

36

Kilimanjaro

Why had he dreamed of Kilimanjaro?

It was a strange word; a name, he felt sure – but of what?

Moses Kaldor lay in the grey light of the Thalassan dawn, slowly wakening to the sounds of Tarna. Not that there were many at this hour; a sand-sledge was whirring somewhere on its way to the beach, probably to meet a returning fisherman.

Kilimanjaro.

Kaldor was not a boastful man, but he doubted if any other human being had read quite so many ancient books on such a wide range of subjects. He had also received several terabytes of memory implant, and though information stored that way was not really *knowledge*, it was available if you could recall the access codes.

It was a little early to make the effort, and he doubted if the matter was particularly important. Yet he had learned not to neglect dreams; old Sigmund Freud had made some valid points, two thousand years ago. And anyway, he would not be able to get to sleep again ...

He closed his eyes, triggered the SEARCH command, and waited. Though that was pure imagination – the process took place at a wholly subconscious level – he could picture myriads of Ks flickering past somewhere in the depths of his brain.

Now something was happening to the phosphenes that forever dance in random patterns on the retina of the tightly closed eye. A dark window had appeared magically in the faintly luminescent chaos; letters were forming and there it was:

KILIMANJARO: Volcanic mountain, Africa. Ht. 5.9 km.
              Site of first Space Elevator Earth Terminus.

Well! What did *that* mean? He let his mind play with this scanty information.

Something to do with that other volcano, Krakan – which had certainly been in his thoughts a good deal recently? That seemed rather far fetched. And he needed no warning that Krakan – or its boisterous offspring – might erupt again.

The first space elevator? That was indeed ancient history; it marked the very beginning of planetary colonization by giving mankind virtually free access to the Solar System. And they were employing the same technology here, using cables of super-strength material to lift the great blocks of ice up to *Magellan* as the ship hovered in stationary orbit above the Equator.

Yet this, too, was a very far cry from that African mountain. The connection was too remote; the answer, Kaldor felt certain, must be somewhere else.

The direct approach had failed. The only way to find the link – if he ever would – was to leave it to chance and time, and the mysterious workings of the unconscious mind.

He would do his best to forget about Kilimanjaro, until it chose the auspicious time to erupt in his brain.

37

In Vino Veritas

Next to Mirissa, Kumar was Loren's most welcome – and most frequent – visitor. Despite his nickname, it seemed to Loren that Kumar was more like a faithful dog – or, rather, a friendly puppy – than a lion. There were a dozen much-pampered dogs in Tarna, and someday they might also live again on Sagan 2, resuming their long acquaintanceship with man.

Loren had now learned what a risk the boy had taken in that tumultuous sea. It was well for them both that Kumar never left shore without a diver's knife strapped to his leg; even so, he had been underwater for more than three minutes, sawing through the cable entangling Loren. *Calypso*'s crew had been certain that they had both drowned.

Despite the bond that now united them, Loren found it difficult to make much conversation with Kumar. After all, there were only a limited number of ways in which one could say, 'Thank you for saving my life', and their backgrounds were so utterly dissimilar that they had very few common grounds of reference. If he talked to Kumar about Earth, or the ship, everything had to be explained in agonizing detail; and after a while Loren realized that he was wasting his time. Unlike his sister, Kumar lived in the world of immediate experience; only the here and now of Thalassa were important to him. 'How I envy him!' Kaldor had once remarked. 'He's a creature of today – not haunted by the past or fearful of the future!'

Loren was about to go to sleep on what he hoped would be his last night in the clinic when Kumar arrived carrying a very large bottle, which he held up in triumph.

'Guess!'

'I've no idea,' Loren said, quite untruthfully.

'The first wine of the season, from Krakan. They say it will be a very good year.'

'How do *you* know anything about it?'

'Our family's had a vineyard there for more than a hundred years. The Lion Brands are the most famous in the world.'

Kumar hunted around until he had produced two glasses and poured generous helpings into each. Loren took a cautious sip; it was a little sweet for his taste, but very, *very* smooth.

'What do you call it?' he asked.

'Krakan Special.'

'Since Krakan's nearly killed me once, should I risk it?'

'It won't even give you a hangover.'

Loren took another, longer draught, and in a surprisingly short time the glass was empty. In an even shorter time it was full again.

This seemed an excellent way of spending his last night in hospital, and Loren felt his normal gratitude towards Kumar extending to the entire world. Even one of Mayor Waldron's visits would no longer be unwelcome.

'By the way, how is Brant? I haven't seen him for a week.'

'Still on North Island, arranging repairs to the boat and talking to the marine biologists. Everyone's very excited about the scorps. But no one can decide what to do about them. If anything.'

'You know, I feel rather the same way about Brant.'

Kumar laughed.

'Don't worry. He's got a girl on North Island.'

'Oh. Does Mirissa know?'

'Of course.'

'And she doesn't mind?'

'Why should she? Brant loves her – and he always comes back.'

Loren processed this information, though rather slowly. It occurred to him that he was a new variable in an already complex equation. Did Mirissa have any other lovers? Did he really want to know? Should he ask?

'Anyway,' Kumar continued as he refilled both their glasses, 'all that really matters is that their gene maps have been approved, and they've been registered for a son. When he's born, it will be different. Then they'll only need each other. Wasn't it the same on Earth?'

'Sometimes,' Loren said. So Kumar doesn't know; the secret was still between the two of them.

At least I will see my son, Loren thought, if only for a few months. And then ...

To his horror, he felt tears trickling down his cheeks. When had he last cried? Two hundred years ago, looking back on the burning Earth ...

'What's the matter?' Kumar asked. 'Are you thinking about your wife?' His concern was so genuine that Loren found it impossible to take offence at his bluntness – or at his reference to a subject that by mutual consent, was seldom mentioned, because it had nothing to do with the here and now. Two hundred years ago on Earth and three hundred years hence on Sagan 2 were too far from Thalassa for his emotions to grasp, especially in his present somewhat bemused condition.

'No, Kumar, I was *not* thinking of – my wife –'

'Will you ... ever ... tell her ... about Mirissa?'

'Perhaps. Perhaps not. I really don't know. I feel very sleepy. Did we drink the whole bottle? Kumar? Kumar!'

The nurse came in during the night, and suppressing her giggles, tucked in the sheets so that they would not fall out.

Loren woke first. After the initial shock of recognition, he started to laugh.

'What's so funny?' Kumar said, heaving himself rather blearily out of bed.

'If you really want to know – I was wondering if Mirissa would be jealous.'

Kumar grinned wryly.

'I may have been a little drunk,' he said, 'but I'm quite sure that nothing happened.'

'So am I.'

Yet he realized that he loved Kumar – not because he had saved his life or even because he was Mirissa's brother – but simply because he was Kumar. Sex had absolutely nothing to do with it; the very idea would have filled them not with embarrassment but hilarity. That was just as well. Life on Tarna was already sufficiently complicated.

'And you were right,' Loren added, 'about the Krakan Special. I don't have a hangover. In fact, I feel wonderful. Can you send a few bottles up to the ship? Better still – a few hundred litres.'

38

Debate

It was a simple question, but it did not have a simple answer: What would happen to discipline aboard *Magellan* if the very purpose of the ship's mission was put to the vote?

Of course, any result would not be binding, and he could override it if necessary. He would *have* to, if a majority decided to stay (not that for a moment he imagined ...) But such an outcome would be psychologically devastating. The crew would be divided into two factions, and that could lead to situations he preferred not to contemplate.

And yet – a commander had to be firm but not pig-headed. There was a good deal of sense in the proposal and it had many attractions. After all, he had enjoyed the benefits of presidential hospitality himself and had every intention of meeting that lady decathalon champion again. This was a beautiful world; perhaps they could speed up the slow process of continent building so that there was room for the extra millions. It would be infinitely easier than colonizing Sagan 2 ...

For that matter, they might never reach Sagan 2. Although the ship's operational reliability was still estimated to be ninety-eight per cent, there were external hazards which no one could predict. Only a few of his most trusted officers knew about the section of the ice-shield that had been lost somewhere around light-year 48. If that interstellar meteoroid, or whatever it was, had been just a few metres closer ...

Someone had suggested that the thing could have been an ancient space-probe from Earth. The odds against this were literally astronomical, and of course such an ironic hypothesis could never be proved.

And now his unknown petitioners were calling themselves the New Thalassans. Did that mean, Captain Bey wondered, that there were many of them and they were getting organized into a political movement? If so, perhaps the best thing would be to get them out into the open as soon as possible.

Yes, it was time to call Ship's Council.

Moses Kaldor's rejection had been swift and courteous.

'No, Captain; I can't get involved in the debate – pro or con. If I did, the crew would no longer trust my impartiality. But I'm willing to act as chairman, or moderator – whatever you like to call it.'

'Agreed,' Captain Bey said promptly; this was as much as he had really hoped for. 'And who will present the motions? We can't expect the New Thalassans to come out into the open and plead their case.'

'I wish we could have a straight vote without any arguments and discussions,' Deputy Captain Malina had lamented.

Privately, Captain Bey agreed. But this was a democratic society of responsible, highly educated men, and Ship's Orders recognized that fact. The New Thalassans had asked for a Council to air their views; if he refused, he would be disobeying his own letters of appointment and violating the trust given him on Earth two hundred years ago.

It had not been easy to arrange the Council. Since everyone, without exception, had to be given a chance of voting, schedules and duty rosters had to be reorganized and sleep periods disrupted. The fact that half the crew was down on Thalassa presented another problem that had never arisen before – that of security. Whatever its outcome might be, it was highly undesirable that the Lassans overhear the debate ...

And so Loren Lorenson was alone, with the door of his Tarna office locked for the first time he could recall, when the Council began. Once again he was wearing full-view goggles; but this time he was not drifting through a submarine forest. He was aboard *Magellan*, in the familiar assembly room, looking at the faces of colleagues, and whenever he switched his viewpoint, at the screen on which their comments and their verdict would be displayed. At the moment it bore one brief message:

RESOLVED: That the Starship *Magellan* terminate its mission at Thalassa as all its prime objectives can be achieved here.

So Moses is up on the ship, Loren thought, as he scanned the audience; I wondered why I'd not seen him lately. He looks tired – and so does the captain. Maybe this is more serious than I'd imagined ...

Kaldor rapped briskly for attention.

'Captain, officers, fellow crewmembers – although this is our first Council, you all know the rules of procedure. If you wish to speak, hold up your hand to be recognized. If you wish to make a written statement, use your keypad; the addresses have been scrambled to ensure anonymity. In either case, please be as brief as possible.

'If there are no questions, we will open with Item 001.'

The New Thalassans had added a few arguments, but essentially 001 was still the memorandum that had jolted Captain Bey two weeks ago – a period in which he had made no progress at all in discovering its authorship.

Perhaps the most telling additional point was the suggestion that it was their *duty* to stay here; Lassa *needed* them, technically, culturally, genetically. I wonder, Loren thought, tempted though he was to agree. In any event, we should ask their opinion first. We're not old-style imperialists – or are we?

Everyone had had time to reread the memorandum; Kaldor rapped for attention again.

'No one has, ah, requested permission to speak in favour of the resolution; of course, there will be opportunities later. So I will ask Lieutenant Elgar to put the case against.'

Raymond Elgar was a thoughtful young Power and Communications engineer whom Loren knew only slightly; he had musical talents and claimed to be writing an epic poem about the voyage. When challenged to produce even a single verse, he invariably replied, 'Wait until Sagan 2 plus one year.'

It was obvious why Lieutenant Elgar had volunteered (if indeed he had volunteered) for this role. His poetic pretensions would hardly allow him to do otherwise; and perhaps he really was working on that epic.

'Captain – shipmates – lend me your ears –'

That's a striking phrase, Loren thought. I wonder if it's original?

'I think we will all agree, in our hearts as well as our minds, that the idea of remaining on Thalassa has a great many attractions. But consider these points:

'There are only 161 of us. Have we the right to make an irrevocable decision for the million who are still sleeping?

'And what of the Lassans? It's been suggested that we'll help them by staying on. But will we? They have a way of life that seems to suit them perfectly. Consider *our* background, our training – the goal to which we dedicated ourselves years ago. Do you really imagine that a million of us could become part of Thalassan society without disrupting it completely?

'And there is the question of duty. Generations of men and women sacrificed themselves to make this mission possible – to give the human race a better chance of survival. The more suns we reach, the greater our insurance against disaster. We have seen what the Thalassan volcanoes can do; who knows what may happen here in the centuries to come?

'There has been glib talk of tectonic engineering to make new land, to provide room for the increased population. May I remind you that even on Earth, after thousands of years of research and development, that was still not an exact science. Remember the Nazca Plate Catastrophe of 3175! I can imagine nothing more reckless than to meddle with the forces pent up inside Thalassa.

'There's no need to say any more. There can be only one decision in this matter. We must leave the Lassans to their own destiny; *we* have to go on to Sagan 2.'

Loren was not surprised at the slowly mounting applause. The interesting question was: who had *not* joined it? As far as he could judge, the audience was almost equally divided. Of course, some people might be applauding because they admired the very effective presentation – not necessarily because they agreed with the speaker.

'Thank you, Lieutenant Elgar,' Chairman Kaldor said. 'We particularly appreciate your brevity. Now would anyone like to express the contrary opinion?'

There was an uneasy stirring, followed by a profound silence.

For at least a minute, nothing happened. Then letters began to appear on the screen.

002: WOULD THE CAPTAIN PLEASE GIVE THE LATEST
     ESTIMATE OF PROBABLE MISSION SUCCESS

003. WHY NOT REVIVE A REPRESENTATIVE SAMPLE OF
     THE SLEEPERS TO POLL THEIR OPINION

004. WHY NOT ASK THE LASSANS WHAT THEY THINK.
     IT'S THEIR WORLD

With total secrecy and neutrality, the computer stored and numbered the inputs from the Council members. In two millennia, no one had been able to invent a better way of sampling group opinion and obtaining a consensus. All over the ship – and down on Thalassa – men and women were tapping out messages on the seven buttons of their little one-hand keypads. Perhaps the earliest skill acquired by any child was the ability to touch-type all the necessary combinations without even thinking about them.

Loren swept his eye across the audience and was amused to note that almost everyone had both hands in full view. He could see nobody with the typical far-off look, indicating that a private message was being transmitted via a concealed keypad. But somehow, a lot of people were talking.

015. WHAT ABOUT A COMPROMISE? SOME OF US
     MIGHT PREFER TO STAY. THE SHIP COULD GO ON

Kaldor rapped for attention.

'That's not the resolution we're discussing,' he said, 'but it's been noted.'

'To answer Zero Zero Two,' Captain Bey said – barely remembering in time to get a go-ahead nod from the chairman, 'the figure is ninety-eight per cent. I wouldn't be surprised if our chance of reaching Sagan 2 is better than that of North or South Island staying above water.'

> 021. APART FROM KRAKAN, WHICH THEY CAN'T DO
>   MUCH ABOUT, THE LASSANS DON'T HAVE ANY
>   SERIOUS CHALLENGES. MAYBE WE SHOULD LEAVE
>   THEM SOME. KNR

That would be, let's see ... Of course – Kingsley Rasmussen. Obviously he had no wish to remain incognito. He was expressing a thought that at one time or other had occurred to almost everyone.

> 022 WE'VE ALREADY SUGGESTED THEY REBUILD THE
>   DEEP SPACE ANTENNA ON KRAKAN TO KEEP IN
>   TOUCH WITH US. RMM

> 023. A TEN YEAR JOB AT THE MOST KNR

'Gentlemen,' Kaldor said a little impatiently, 'we're getting away from the point.'

Have I anything to contribute? Loren asked himself. No, I will sit out this debate; I can see too many sides. Sooner or later I will have to choose between duty and happiness. But not yet. Not yet ...

'I'm quite surprised,' Kaldor said after nothing more had appeared on the screen for a full two minutes, 'that no one has anything more to say on such an important matter.'

He waited hopefully for another minute.

'Very well. Perhaps you'd like to continue the discussion informally. We will not take a vote now, but during the next forty-eight hours you can record your opinion in the usual way. Thank you.'

He glanced at Captain Bey, who rose to his feet with a swiftness that showed his obvious relief.

'Thank you, Dr Kaldor. Ship's Council terminated.'

Then he looked anxiously at Kaldor, who was staring at the display screen as if he had just noticed it for the first time.

'Are you all right, Doctor?'

'Sorry, Captain – I'm fine. I've just remembered something important, that's all.'

Indeed he had. For the thousandth time, at least, he marvelled at the labyrinthine workings of the subconscious mind.

Entry 021 had done it. *'The Lassans don't have any serious challenges.'* Now he knew why he had dreamed of Kilimanjaro.

39

The Leopard in the Snows

I'm sorry, Evelyn – it's been many days since I last talked to you. Does this mean that your image is fading in my mind as the future absorbs more and more of my energies and attention?

I suppose so, and logically I should welcome it. Clinging too long to the past is a sickness – as you often reminded me. But in my heart I still can't accept that bitter truth.

Much has happened in the last few weeks. The ship has been infected with what I call the *Bounty* Syndrome. We should have anticipated it – indeed, we did, but only as a joke. Now it's serious, though as far not too serious. I hope.

Some of the crew would like to remain on Thalassa – who can blame them? – and have frankly admitted it. Others want to terminate the whole mission here and forget about Sagan 2. We don't know the strength of this faction, because it hasn't come out into the open.

Forty-eight hours after the Council, we had the vote. Although of course the balloting was secret, I don't know how far the results can be trusted: 151 were for going on; only 6 wanted to terminate the mission here; and there were 4 undecideds.

Captain Bey was pleased. He feels the situation's under control but is going to take some precautions. He realizes that the longer we stay here, the greater the pressure will be not to leave at all. He won't mind a few deserters – 'If they want to go, I certainly don't want to keep them,' was the way he put it. But he's worried about disaffection spreading to the rest of the crew.

So he's accelerating shield construction. Now that the system is completely automatic and running smoothly, we plan to make two lifts a day instead of one. If this works out, we can leave in four months. This hasn't been announced yet. I hope there are no protests when it is, from the New Lassans or anyone else.

And now another matter that may be completely unimportant but which I find fascinating. Do you remember how we used to read stories to each other when we first met? It was a wonderful way of getting to know how people really lived and thought thousands of years ago – long before sensory or even video recordings existed ...

Once you read to me – I had not the slightest *conscious* memory of it – a story about a great mountain in Africa, with a strange name, Kilimanjaro. I've looked it up in Ship's Archives, and now I understand why it's been haunting me.

It seems that there was a cave high up on the mountain, above the snow line. And in that cave was the frozen body of a great hunting cat – a leopard. That's the mystery: no one ever knew what the leopard was doing at such an altitude, so far from its normal territory.

You know, Evelyn, that I was always proud – many people said vain! – about my powers of intuition. Well, it seems to me that something like this is happening here.

Not once but several times, a large and powerful marine animal has been detected a long way from its natural habitat. Recently, the first one was captured; it's a kind of huge crustacean, like the sea scorpions that once lived on Earth.

We're not sure if they're intelligent, and that may even be a meaningless question. But certainly they are highly organized social animals, with primitive technologies – though perhaps that's too strong a word. As far as we've discovered, they don't show any greater abilities than bees or ants or termites, but their scale of operations is different and quite impressive.

Most important of all, they've discovered metal, though as yet they seem to use it only for ornament, and their sole source of supply is what they can steal from the Lassans. They've done this several times.

And recently a scorp crawled up the channel right into the heart of our freezing plant. The naive assumption was that it was hunting for food. But there was plenty where it came from – at least fifty kilometres away.

I want to know what the scorp was doing so far from home; I feel that the answer may be very important to the Lassans.

I wonder if we'll find it before I begin the long sleep to Sagan 2?

40

Confrontation

The instant that Captain Bey walked into President Farradine's office, he knew that something was wrong.

Normally, Edgar Farradine greeted him by his first name and immediately produced the wine decanter. This time there was no 'Sirdar', and no wine, but at least he was offered a chair.

'I've just received some disturbing news, Captain Bey. If you don't mind, I'd like the prime minister to join us.'

This was the first time the Captain had ever heard the president come straight to the point – *whatever* it was – and also the first time he had met the PM in Farradine's office.

'In that case, Mr President, may I ask Ambassador Kaldor to join me?'

The president hesitated only a moment then he replied, 'Certainly.' The captain was relieved to see a ghost of a smile, as if in recognition of this diplomatic nicety. The visitors might be outranked – but not outnumbered.

Prime Minister Bergman, as Captain Bey knew perfectly well, was really the power behind the throne. Behind the PM was the cabinet, and behind the cabinet was the Jefferson Mark 3 Constitution. The arrangement had worked well for the last few centuries; Captain Bey had a foreboding that it was now about to undergo some major perturbation.

Kaldor was quickly rescued from Mrs Farradine, who was using him as a guinea pig to try out her ideas for redecorating the President's House. The prime minister arrived a few seconds later, wearing his usual inscrutable expression.

When they were all seated, the president folded his arms, leaned back in his ornate swivel chair, and looked accusingly at his visitors.

'Captain Bey – Dr Kaldor – we have received some most disturbing information. We would like to know if there is any truth in the report that you now intend to end your mission here – and *not* at Sagan 2.'

Captain Bey felt a great sensation of relief – followed instantly by annoyance. There must have been a bad breach of security; he had hoped that the Lassans would never hear of the petition and Ship's Council – though perhaps that was too much to expect.

'Mr President – Mr Prime Minister – if you have heard such a rumour, I can assure you that there is absolutely no truth in it. Why do you think we are hoisting six hundred tons of ice a day to rebuild our shield? Would we bother to do that if we planned to stay here?'

'Perhaps. If for some reason you've changed your mind, you would hardly alert us by suspending operations.'

The quick rejoiner gave the captain a momentary shock; he had underrated these amiable people. Then he realized that they – and their computers – must have already analysed all the obvious possibilities.

'True enough. But I'd like to tell you – it's still confidential and not yet announced – that we plan to double the rate of hoisting to finish the shield more quickly. Far from staying on, we plan to leave early. I had hoped to inform you of this in more pleasant circumstances.'

Even the prime minister could not completely conceal his surprise; the president did not even try. Before they could recover, Captain Bey resumed his attack:

'And it's only fair, Mr President, that you give us the evidence for your – accusation. Otherwise, how can we refute it?'

The president looked at the prime minister. The prime minister looked at the visitors.

'I'm afraid that's impossible. It would reveal our sources of information.'

'Then it's a stalemate. We won't be able to convince you until we really do leave – one hundred and thirty days from now according to the revised schedule.'

There was a thoughtful and rather gloomy silence; then Kaldor said quietly: 'Could I have a brief private talk with the captain?'

'Of course.'

While they were gone, the president asked the prime minister: 'Are they telling the truth?'

'Kaldor wouldn't lie; I'm certain of that. But perhaps he doesn't know all the facts.'

There was no time to continue the discussion before the parties of the second part returned to face their accusers.

'Mr President,' the captain said, 'Dr Kaldor and I both agree that there is something we should tell you. We'd hoped to keep it quiet – it was embarrassing and we thought the matter had been settled. Possibly we're wrong; in that case, we may need your help.'

He gave a brief summary of the Council proceedings and the events that had led up to them and concluded, 'If you wish, I'm prepared to show you the recordings. We have nothing to hide.'

'That won't be necessary, Sirdar,' the president said, obviously vastly relieved. The prime minister, however, still looked worried.

'Er – just a minute, Mr President. That doesn't dispose of the reports we've received. They were very convincing, you'll recall.'

'I'm sure the captain will be able to explain them.'

'Only if you tell me what they are.'

There was another pause. Then the president moved towards the wine decanter.

'Let's have a drink first,' he said cheerfully. 'Then I'll tell you how we found out.'

41

Pillow Talk

It had gone very smoothly, Owen Fletcher told himself. Of course, he was somewhat disappointed by the vote, though he wondered how accurately it reflected opinion aboard the ship. After all, he had instructed two of his fellow conspirators to register Noes, lest the – still-pitiful – strength of the New Thalassan movement be revealed.

What to do next was, as always, the problem. He was an engineer, not a politician – though he was rapidly moving in that direction – and could see no way of recruiting further support without coming out into the open.

This left only two alternatives. The first, and easier, was to jump ship, as close to launch-time as possible, by simply failing to report back. Captain Bey would be too busy to hunt for them – even if he felt inclined – and their Lassan friends would hide them until *Magellan*'s departure.

But that would be a double desertion – one unheard of in the closely-knit Sabra community. He would have abandoned his sleeping colleagues – including his own brother and sister. What would they think of him, three centuries hence on hostile Sagan 2, when they learned that he could have opened the gates of Paradise for them but had failed to do so?

And now the time was running out; those computer simulations of up-rated lifting schedules could have only one meaning. Though he had not even discussed this with his friends, he saw no alternative to action.

But his mind still shied away from the word sabotage.

Rose Killian had never heard of Delilah and would have been horrified to be compared to her. She was a simple, rather naive Norther who – like so many young Lassans – had been overwhelmed by the glamorous visitors from Earth. Her affair with Karl Bosley was not only her first really profound emotional experience; it was also his.

They were both heartsick at the thought of parting. Rose was weeping on Karl's shoulder late one night when he could bear her misery no longer.

'Promise not to tell *anyone*,' he said, fondling the strands of hair lying along his chest, 'I've some good news for you. It's a big secret – nobody knows it yet. The ship isn't going to leave. We're all staying here on Thalassa.'

Rose almost fell off the bed in her surprise.

'You're not saying this just to make me happy?'

'No – it's true. But don't say a word to anyone. It must be kept *completely* secret.'

'Of course, darling.'

But Rose's closest friend Marion was also weeping for *her* Earth lover, so she had to be told ...

... and Marion passed the good news on to Pauline ... who couldn't resist telling Svetlana ... who mentioned it in confidence to Crystal.

And Crystal was the president's daughter.

42

Survivor

This is a very unhappy business, Captain Bey thought. Owen Fletcher is a good man; I approved his selection myself. How could he have done such a thing?

There was probably no single explanation. If he had not been a Sabra *and* in love with that girl, it might never have happened. What was the word for one plus one adding up to more than two? Sin-something – ah, yes, synergy. Yet he could not help feeling that there was something more, something that he would probably never know.

He remembered a remark that Kaldor, who always had a phrase for every occasion, had made to him once when they were talking about crew psychology.

'We're all *maimed*, Captain, whether we admit it or not. No one who's been through our experiences during those last years on Earth could possibly be unaffected. And we all share the same feeling of guilt.'

'Guilt?' he had asked in surprise and indignation.

'Yes, even though it's not our fault. We're survivors – the *only* survivors. And survivors always feel guilty at being alive.'

It was a disturbing remark, and it might help to explain Fletcher – and many other things.

We're all maimed men.

I wonder what your injury is, Moses Kaldor – and how you handle it. I know mine, and have been able to use it for the benefit of my fellow humans. It brought me to where I am today, and I can be proud of that.

Perhaps in an earlier age I might have been a dictator, or a warlord. Instead, I have been usefully employed as Chief of Continental Police, as General-in-Charge of Space Construction Facilities – and finally as commander of a starship. My fantasies of power have been successfully sublimated.

He walked to the captain's safe, to which he alone held the key, and slipped the coded metal bar into its slot. The door swung smoothly open to reveal assorted bundles of papers, some medals and trophies, and a small, flat wooden box bearing the letters S.B. inlaid in silver.

As the captain placed it on the table, he was happy to feel the familiar stirring in his loins. He opened the lid and stared down at the gleaming instrument of power, snug in its velvet bed.

Once his perversion had been shared by millions. Usually it was quite harmless – in primitive societies, even valuable. And many times it had changed the course of history, for better or for worse.

'I know you're a phallic symbol,' the captain whispered. 'But you're also a gun. I've used you before; I can use you again ...'

The flashback could not have lasted for more than a fraction of a second, yet it seemed to cover years of time. He was still standing by his desk when it was over; just for a moment, all the careful work of the psychotherapists was undone, and the gates of memory opened wide.

He looked back in horror – yet with fascination – on those last turbulent decades which had brought out the best and the worst in humanity. He remembered how, as a young Inspector of Police in Cairo, he had given his first order to fire on a rioting crowd. The bullets were supposed to be merely incapacitating. But two people had died.

What had they been rioting about? He had never even known

– there were so many political and religious movements in the final days. And it was also the great era of the supercriminals; they had nothing to lose and no future to look forward to, so they were prepared to take any risks. Most of them had been psychopaths, but some had been near geniuses. He thought of Joseph Kidder, who had almost stolen a starship. No one knew what had happened to him, and sometimes Captain Bey had been struck by a nightmare fantasy: 'Just suppose that one of my sleepers is really ...'

The forcible running down of the population, the total prohibition of any new births after the year 3600, the absolute priority given to the development of the quantum drive and the building of the *Magellan*-class ships – all these, together with the knowledge of impending doom, had imposed such strains on terrestrial society that it still seemed a miracle that anyone had been able to escape from the solar system. Captain Bey remembered, with admiration and gratitude, those who had burned up their last years for a cause whose success or failure they would never know.

He could see again the last world president, Elizabeth Windsor, exhausted but proud as she left the ship after her tour of inspection, returning to a planet that had only days to live. She had even less time; the bomb in her spaceplane had exploded just before it was due to land at Port Canaveral.

The captain's blood still ran cold at the memory; that bomb had been intended for *Magellan*, and only a mistake in timing had saved the ship. It was ironic that each of the rival cults had claimed responsibility ...

Jonathan Cauldwell and his dwindling but still vocal band of followers proclaimed ever more desperately that all would be well, that God was merely testing Mankind as He had once tested Job. Despite everything that was happening to the Sun, it would soon return to normal, and humanity would be saved – unless those who disbelieved in His mercy provoked His wrath. And *then* He might change His mind ...

The Will of God cult believed the exact opposite. Doomsday had come at last, and no attempt should be made to avoid it. Indeed, it should be welcomed, since after Judgement those who were worthy of salvation would live in eternal bliss.

And so, from totally opposing premises, the Cauldwellites and the WOGs arrived at the same conclusion: The human race should not attempt to escape its destiny. All starships should be destroyed.

Perhaps it was fortunate that the two rival cults were so bitterly opposed that they could not cooperate even towards a goal that they both shared. In fact, after the death of President Windsor their hostility turned to internecine violence. The rumour was started – almost certainly by the World Security Bureau, though Bey's colleagues had never admitted it to him – that the bomb had been planted by the WOGs and its timer sabotaged by the Cauldwellites. The exactly opposite version was also popular; one of them might even have been true.

All this was history, now known only to a handful of men besides himself and soon to be forgotten. Yet how strange that *Magellan* was once again threatened by sabotage.

Unlike the WOGs and the Cauldwellites, the Sabras were highly competent and not unhinged by fanaticism. They could therefore be a more serious problem, but Captain Bey believed he knew how to handle it.

'You're a good man, Owen Fletcher,' he thought grimly. 'But I've killed better ones in my time. And when there was no alternative, I've used torture.'

He was more than a little proud of the fact that he had never enjoyed it, and this time, there was a better way.

43

Interrogation

And now *Magellan* had a new crewmember, untimely awakened from his slumber and still adjusting to the realities of the situation – as Kaldor had done a year ago. Nothing but an emergency justified such action. But according to the computer records only Dr Marcus Steiner, once-Chief Scientist of the Terran Bureau of Investigation, possessed the knowledge and skills that, unfortunately, were needed now.

Back on Earth, his friends had often asked him why he had chosen to become a professor of criminology. And he had always given the same answer: 'The only alternative was to become a criminal.'

It had taken Steiner almost a week to modify the sickbay's standard encephalographic equipment and to check the computer programs. Meanwhile, the four Sabras remained confined to their quarters and stubbornly refused to make any admission of guilt.

Owen Fletcher did not look very happy when he saw the preparations that had been made for him; there were too many similarities to electric chairs and torture devices from the bloodstained history of earth. Dr Steiner quickly put him at ease with the synthetic familiarity of the good interrogator.

'There's nothing to be alarmed at, Owen – I promise you won't feel a thing. You won't even be aware of the answers you're giving me – but there's no way you can hide the truth. Because you're an intelligent man, I'll tell you *exactly* what I'm going to do. Surprisingly enough, it helps me do my job; whether *you* like it or not, your subconscious mind will trust me – and cooperate.'

What nonsense, thought Fletcher; surely he doesn't think he can fool me as easily as that! But he made no reply, as he was seated in the chair and the orderlies fastened leather straps loosely around his forearms and waist. He did not attempt to resist; two of his largest ex-colleagues were standing uncomfortably in the background, carefully avoiding his eye.

'If you need a drink or want to go to the toilet, just say so. This first session will take exactly one hour; we may need some shorter ones later. We want to make you relaxed and comfortable.'

In the circumstances, this was a highly optimistic remark, but no one seemed to think it at all funny.

'Sorry we've had to shave your head, but scalp electrodes don't like hair. And you'll have to be blindfolded, so we don't pick up confusing visual inputs ... Now you'll start getting drowsy, but you'll remain conscious ... We're going to ask you a series of questions which have just three possible answers – Yes, No, Don't Know. But you won't have to reply; your brain will do it for you, and the computer's trinary logic system will know what it's saying.

'And there's absolutely no way you can lie to us; you're very welcome to try! Believe me, some of the best minds of Earth invented this machine – and were never able to fool it. If it gets ambiguous answers, the computer will simply reframe the questions. Are you ready? Very well ... Recorder on high, please ... Check gain on Channel 5 ... Run program.'

YOUR NAME IS OWEN FLETCHER ... ANSWER YES ... OR NO ...

YOUR NAME IS JOHN SMITH ... ANSWER YES ... OR NO ...

YOU WERE BORN IN LOWELL CITY, MARS ... ANSWER YES ... OR NO ....

YOUR NAME IS JOHN SMITH ... ANSWER YES ... OR NO ...

YOU WERE BORN IN AUCKLAND, NEW ZEALAND ... ANSWER YES ... OR NO ...

YOUR NAME IS OWEN FLETCHER ...

YOU WERE BORN ON 3 MARCH 3585 ...

YOU WERE BORN ON 31 DECEMBER 3584 ...

The questions came at such short intervals that even if he had not been in a mildly sedated condition, Fletcher would have been unable to falsify the answers. Nor would it have mattered had he done so; within a few minutes, the computer had established the pattern of his automatic responses to all the questions whose answers were already known.

From time to time the calibration was rechecked (YOUR NAME IS OWEN FLETCHER ... YOU WERE BORN IN CAPETOWN, ZULULAND ...), and questions were occasionally repeated to confirm answers already given. The whole process was completely automatic, once the physiological constellation of YES – NO responses had been identified.

The primitive 'lie detectors' had tried to do this with fair success – but seldom complete certainty. It had taken no more than two hundred years to perfect the technology and thereby to revolutionize the practice of law, both criminal and civil, to the point when few trials ever lasted more than hours.

It was not so much an interrogation as a computerized – and cheat-proof – version of the ancient game Twenty Questions. In principle, *any* piece of information could be quickly pinned down by a series of YES – NO replies, and it was surprising how seldom as many as twenty were needed when an expert human cooperated with an expert machine.

When a rather dazed Owen Fletcher staggered from the chair, exactly one hour later, he had no idea what he had been asked or how he had responded. He was fairly confident, however, that he had given nothing away.

He was mildly surprised when Dr Steiner said cheerfully, 'That's it, Owen. We won't need you again.'

The professor was proud of the fact that he had never hurt anybody, but a good interrogator had to be something of a sadist – if only a psychological one. Besides, it added to his reputation for infallibility, and that was half the battle.

He waited until Fletcher had regained his balance and was being escorted back to the detention cell.

'Oh, by the way, Owen – that trick with the ice would never have worked.'

In fact, it might well have done; but that didn't matter now. The expression on Lieutenant Fletcher's face gave Dr Steiner all the reward he needed for the exercise of his considerable skills.

Now he could go back to sleep until Sagan 2. But first he would relax and enjoy himself, making the most of this unexpected interlude.

Tomorrow he would have a look at Thalassa and perhaps go swimming off one of those beautiful beaches. But for the moment he would enjoy the company of an old and beloved friend.

The book he drew reverently out of its vacuum-sealed package was not merely a first edition; it was now the *only* edition. He opened it at random; after all, he knew practically every page by heart.

He started to read, and fifty light-years from the ruins of Earth, the fog rolled once more down Baker Street.

'The cross-checking has confirmed that only the four Sabras were involved,' Captain Bey said. 'We can be thankful that there's no need to interrogate anyone else.'

'I still don't understand how they hoped to get away with it,' Deputy Captain Malina said unhappily.

'I don't believe they would, but it's lucky it was never put to the test. Anyway, they were still undecided.

'Plan A involved damaging the shield. As you know, Fletcher was on the assembly crew and was working out a scheme to reprogram the last stage of the lifting procedure. If a block of ice could be allowed to impact at just a few metres a second – you see what I mean?

'It could be made to look like an accident, but there was risk that the subsequent inquiry would soon prove it was nothing of the sort. And even if the shield was damaged, it could be repaired.

Fletcher hoped that the delay would give time to acquire more recruits. He might have been right; another year on Thalassa ...

'Plan B involved sabotaging the life-support system, so that the ship had to be evacuated. Again, the same objections.

'Plan C was the most disturbing one because it would have terminated the mission. Luckily, none of the Sabras was in propulsion; it would have been very hard for them to get at the drive ...'

Everyone looked shocked – though none more so than Commander Rocklyn.

'It would not have been at all difficult, Sir, if they were sufficiently determined. The big problem would have been to arrange something that would put the drive out of action – *permanently* – without damaging the ship. I very much doubt if they'd have the technical knowledge necessary.'

'They were working on it,' the captain grimly said. 'We have to review our security proceedings, I'm afraid. There will be a conference on that tomorrow for all senior officers – here, at noon.'

And then Surgeon-Commander Newton put the question that everyone hesitated to ask.

'Will there be a court martial, Captain?'

'It's not necessary; guilt has been established. According to Ship's Orders, the only problem is the sentence.'

Everyone waited. And waited.

'Thank you, ladies and gentlemen,' the captain said, and his officers left in silence.

Alone in his quarters, he felt angry and betrayed. But at least it was over; *Magellan* had ridden out the man-made storm.

The other three Sabras were – perhaps – harmless; but what about Owen Fletcher?

His mind strayed to the deadly plaything in his safe. He was captain: it would be easy to arrange an accident ...

He put the fantasy aside; he could never do it, of course. In any event, he had already made up his mind and was certain that there would be universal agreement.

Someone had once said that for every problem there is a solution that is simple, attractive – and wrong. But this solution, he was certain, was simple, attractive – and absolutely right.

The Sabras wanted to remain on Thalassa; they could do so. He did not doubt that they would become valuable citizens – perhaps exactly the aggressive, forceful type that this society needed.

How strange that History was repeating itself; like Magellan, he would be marooning some of his men.

But whether he had punished them or rewarded them, he would not know for three hundred years.

VI

The Forests of the Sea

44

Spyball

The North Island Marine Lab had been less than enthusiastic.

'We still need a week to repair *Calypso*,' the director said, 'and we were lucky to find the sledge. It's the only one on Thalassa, and we don't want to risk it again.'

I know the symptoms, thought Science Officer Varley; even during the last days on Earth, there were still some lab directors who wanted to keep their beautiful equipment unsullied by actual use.

'Unless Krakan Junior – or Senior – misbehaves again, I don't see that there's any risk. And haven't the geologists promised that they'll be quiet again for at least fifty years?'

'I've a small bet with them on *that*. But frankly – why do you think this is so important?'

What tunnel vision! Varley thought. Even if the man *is* a physical oceanographer, one would have expected him to have some interest in marine life. But perhaps I've misjudged him; he may be sounding me out ...

'We have a certain emotional interest in the subject since Dr Lorenson was killed – luckily not permanently. But quite apart from that, we find the scorps fascinating. *Anything* we can discover about alien intelligence could be of vital importance someday. And to *you* even more than to us since they're on your doorstep.'

'I can appreciate that. Perhaps it's lucky we occupy such different ecological niches.'

For how long? the Science Officer thought. If Moses Kaldor is right ...

'Tell me just what a spyball does. The name's certainly intriguing.'

'They were developed a couple of thousand years ago for security and espionage but had many other applications. Some weren't much bigger than pinheads – the one we'll use is the size of a football.'

Varley spread the drawings on the director's table.

'This one was designed especially for underwater use – I'm surprised you're not familiar with it – the reference date is as early as 2045. We found complete specifications in Tech Memory, and fed them into the replicator. The first copy wouldn't work – we still don't know why – but No. 2 tests out fine.

'Here are the acoustic generators – ten megahertz – so we've got millimetre resolution. Hardly video quality, of course, but good enough.

'The signal-processor is quite intelligent. When the spyball's switched on, it sends out a single pulse which builds up an acoustical hologram of everything within twenty or thirty metres. It transmits this information on a two-hundred-kilohertz narrowband to the buoy floating topside, which radios it back to base. The first image takes ten seconds to build up; then the spyball pulses again.

'If there's no change in the picture, it sends a null signal. But if something happens, it transmits the new information so that an updated image can be generated.

'What we get, then, is a snapshot every ten seconds, which is good enough for most purposes. Of course, if things happen quickly, there will be bad image smearing. But you can't have everything; the system will work anywhere, in total darkness – it isn't easy to spot – and it's economical.'

The director was obviously interested and was doing his best to keep his enthusiasm from showing.

'It's a clever toy – may be useful for our work. Can you give us the specs – and a few more models?'

'The specs – certainly and we'll check that they interface with your replicator so you can make as many copies as you like. The first working model – and maybe the next two or three – we want to dump on Scorpville.

'And then we'll just wait and see what happens.'

45

Bait

The image was grainy, and sometimes hard to interpret despite the false-colour coding which revealed details the eye could not otherwise detect. It was a flattened-out 360-degree panorama of seabed, with a distant view of kelp on the left, a few rock outcroppings at centre, and kelp again on the right. Though it looked like a still photograph, the changing numbers at the lower left-hand corner revealed the passage of time; and occasionally the scene changed with a sudden jerk when some movement altered the information pattern being transmitted.

'As you'll see,' Commander Varley told the invited audience in the Terra Nova auditorium, 'there were no scorps around when we arrived, but they may have heard – or felt – the bump when our, ah, package landed. Here's the first investigator at one minute twenty seconds.'

Now the image was changing abruptly at every ten-second interval, and more scorps were appearing in each frame.

'I'll freeze this one,' said the science officer, 'so that you can study the details. See that scorp on the right? Look at his left claw – no less than five of those metal bands! And he seems to be in a position of authority – in the next frames the other scorps have moved out of his way – now he's examining the mysterious pile of junk that's just fallen out of his sky – this is a particularly good shot – see how he uses claws and mouth palps together – one set for power, the other for precision – now he's pulling at the wire, but our little gift is-too heavy to move – look at his attitude – I'll swear he's giving orders, though we haven't detected any signal – maybe it's subsonic – here comes another of the big fellows –'

The scene shifted abruptly, tilting at a crazy angle.

'Here we go; they're dragging us along – and you were right, Dr Kaldor – they're heading for that cave in the rock pyramid – the package is too big to go inside – just the way we planned it, of course – *this* is the really interesting part –'

A good deal of thought had gone into the present for the scorps. Although it consisted mostly of junk, that junk had been carefully selected. There were bars of steel, copper, aluminium, and lead; wooden planks; tubes and sheets of plastic; pieces of iron chain; a metal mirror – and several coils of copper wire of assorted gauges. The entire mass weighed over a hundred kilograms, and had been carefully fastened together so that it could only be moved as a single unit. The spyball nestled inconspicuously at one corner, attached by four separate short cables.

The two big scorps were now attacking the pile of junk with determination and, it seemed, a definite plan. Their powerful claws quickly disposed of the wires holding it together, and they immediately discarded the pieces of wood and plastic; it was obvious that they were only interested in the metal.

The mirror gave them pause. They held it up and stared at their reflections – invisible, of course, in the spyball's acoustical image.

'We rather expected them to attack – you can start a good fight by putting a mirror in a tank of fish. Perhaps they recognize themselves. That seems to indicate a fair level of intelligence.'

The scorps abandoned the mirror and began to drag the rest of the debris across the seabed. For the next frames, the views were hopelessly confused. When the image stabilized again, it showed a completely different scene.

'We were in luck – things worked out exactly as we'd hoped. They've dragged the spyball into that guarded cave. But it isn't the

Queen Scorp's throne room – if there *is* a Queen Scorp, which I very much doubt ... Theories, anyone?'

There was silence for a long time while the audience studied the strange spectacle. Then someone remarked, 'It's a junk room!'

'But it must have a purpose –'

'Look – that's a ten-kilowatt outboard motor – someone must have dropped it!'

'Now we know who's been stealing our anchor chains!'

'But *why* – it doesn't make sense.'

'Obviously it does – to them.'

Moses Kaldor gave his attention-demanding cough, which seldom failed to work.

'This is still only a theory,' he began, 'but more and more the facts seem to support it. You'll notice that everything here is metal, carefully collected from a wide variety of sources ...

'Now, to an intelligent marine creature, metal would be very mysterious, something quite different from all the other natural products of the ocean. The scorps seem to be still in the Stone Age – and there's no way they can get out of it as we land animals did on Earth. Without fire, they are trapped in a technological *cul-de-sac.*

'I think we may be seeing a replay of something that happened long ago on our own world. Do you know where prehistoric man got his first supplies of iron? From space!

'I don't blame you for looking surprised. But pure iron never occurs in nature – it rusts too easily. Primitive man's only source of supply was meteorites. No wonder they were worshipped; no wonder our ancestors believed in supernatural beings beyond the sky ...

'Is the same story happening here? I urge you to consider it seriously. We still don't know the level of intelligence of the scorps. Perhaps they are collecting metals out of mere curiosity and fascination with their – shall I say magical? – properties. But will they discover how to use them, for anything more than decoration? How far can they progress – while they stay underwater? *Will* they stay there?

'My friends, I think you should learn all you possibly can about the scorps. You may be sharing your planet with another intelligent race. Are you going to cooperate or fight? Even if they are not really intelligent, the scorps could be a deadly menace – or a useful tool. Perhaps you should cultivate them. By the way, look up the reference Cargo Cult in your History Banks ... that's C-A-R-G-O C-U-L-T.

'I would love to know the next chapter in this story. Are there scorp philosophers, even now, gathering in the kelp forests – to consider what to do about us?

'So *please*, repair the deep-space antenna so we can keep in touch! *Magellan*'s computer will be waiting for your report – as it watches over us on the road to Sagan 2.'

46

Whatever Gods May Be...

'What is God?' Mirissa asked.

Kaldor sighed and looked up from the centuries-old display he was scanning.

'Oh, dear. Why do you ask?'

'Because Loren said yesterday, "Moses thinks the scorps may be looking for God."'

'Did he indeed? I'll speak to him later. And you, young lady, are asking me to explain something that has obsessed millions of men for thousands of years and generated more words than any other single subject in history. How much time can you spare this morning?'

Mirissa laughed. 'Oh, at least an hour. Didn't you once tell me that anything really important can be expressed in a single sentence?'

'Umm. Well, I've come across some exceedingly long-winded sentences in my time. Now, where shall I start ...'

He let his eyes wander to the glade outside the library window and the silent – yet so eloquent! – hulk of the Mother Ship looming above it. Here human life began on this planet; no wonder it often reminds me of Eden. And am I the Snake, about to destroy its innocence? But I won't be telling a girl as clever as Mirissa anything that she doesn't already know – or guess.

'The trouble with the word God,' he began slowly, 'is that it never meant the same thing to any two people – especially if they were philosophers. That's why it slowly dropped out of use during the Third Millennium except as an expletive – in some cultures, too obscene for polite use.

'Instead, it was replaced by a whole constellation of specialized words. This at least stopped people arguing at cross-purposes, which caused ninety per cent of the trouble in the past.

'The Personal God, sometimes called God One, became Alpha. It was the hypothetical entity supposed to watch over the affairs of everyday life – every individual, every *animal*! – and to reward good and punish evil, usually in a vaguely described existence after death. You worshipped Alpha, prayed to it, carried out elaborate religious ceremonies, and built huge churches in its honour ...

'Then there was the God who created the universe and might or might not have had anything to do with it since then. That was Omega. By the time they'd finished dissecting God, the philosophers had used up all the other twenty or so letters of the ancient Greek alphabet, but Alpha and Omega will do very nicely for this morning. I'd guess that not more than ten billion man-years were ever spent discussing them.

'Alpha was inextricably entangled with religion – and that was its downfall. It might still have been around right up to the destruction of the Earth if the myriads of competing religions had left each other alone. But they couldn't do that, because each claimed to possess the One and Only Truth. So they had to destroy their rivals – which means, in effect, not only every other religion but dissenters inside their own faith.

'Of course, I'm grossly simplifying; good men and women often transcended their beliefs, and it's quite possible that religion was *essential* to early human societies. Without supernatural sanctions to restrain them, men might never have cooperated in anything larger than tribal units. Not until it became corrupted by power and privilege did religion become an essentially antisocial force, the great good it had done being eclipsed by greater evils.

'You've never heard, I hope, of the Inquisition, of Witch Hunts, of Jihads. Would you believe that even well into the Space Age there were nations in which children could be officially executed because their *parents* adhered to a heretical subset of the state's particular brand of Alpha? You look shocked, but these things – and worse – happened while our ancestors were beginning the exploration of the Solar System.

'Fortunately for mankind, Alpha faded out of the picture, more or less gracefully, in the early 2000s. It was killed by a fascinating development called statistical theology. How much time do I have left? Won't Bobby be getting impatient?'

Mirissa glanced out of the big picture window. The palomino was happily munching at the grass around the base of the Mother Ship, and was clearly perfectly content.

'He won't wander off – as long as there's something to eat here. What was statistical theology?'

'It was the final assault on the problem of Evil. What brought it to a head was the rise of a very eccentric cult – they called themselves Neo-Manichees, don't ask me to explain why – around 2050. Incidentally, it was the first orbital religion; although all the other faiths had used communications satellites to spread their doctrines, the NMs relied on them exclusively. They had no meeting place except the television screen.

'Despite this dependence on technology, their tradition was actually very old. They believed that Alpha existed, but was completely evil – and that mankind's ultimate destiny was to confront and destroy it.

'In support of their faith, they marshalled an immense array of horrible facts from history and zoology. I think they must have been rather sick people, because they seemed to take a morbid delight in collecting such material.

'For example – a favourite proof of Alpha's existence was what's called the Argument from Design. We now know it's utterly fallacious, but the NMs made it sound totally convincing and irrefutable.

'If you find a beautifully designed system – their favourite example was a digital watch – then there must be a planner, a creator, behind it. So just look at the world of Nature –

'And they did, with a vengeance. Their special field was parasitology – you don't know how lucky you are on Thalassa, by the way! I won't revolt you by describing the incredibly ingenious methods and adaptations that various creatures used to invade other organisms – humans especially – and to prey on them, often until they were destroyed. I'll only mention one special pet of the NMs, the ichneumon fly.

'This delightful creature laid its eggs in other insects, after first paralyzing them so that when their larvae hatched out, they would have an ample supply of fresh – *living* – meat.

'The NMs could go on for hours along these lines, expounding the wonders of Nature as proof that Alpha was, if not supremely evil, then utterly indifferent to human standards of morality and goodness. Don't worry – I can't imitate them, and won't.

'But I must mention another of their favourite proofs – the Argument from Catastrophe. A typical example, which could be multiplied countless times: Alpha worshippers gather to appeal for help in the face of disaster – and are all killed by the collapse of their refuge, whereas most of them would have been saved had they stayed at home.

'Again, the NMs collected volumes of such horrors – burning hospitals and old people's homes, infant schools engulfed by earthquakes, volcanoes, or tidal waves destroying cities – the list is endless.

'Of course, rival Alpha worshippers didn't take this lying down. *They* collected equal numbers of counterexamples – the wonderful things that had happened, time and again, to *save* devout believers from catastrophe.

'In various forms, this debate had been going on for several thousand years. But by the twenty-first century, the new information technologies and methods of statistical analysis as well as a wider understanding of probability theory allowed it to be settled.

'It took a few decades for the answers to come in, and a few more before they were accepted by virtually all intelligent men: Bad things happened just as often as good; as had long been suspected, the universe simply obeyed the laws of mathematical probability. Certainly there was no sign of any supernatural intervention, either for good or for ill.

'So the problem of Evil never really existed. To expect the universe to be benevolent was like imagining one could *always* win at a game of pure chance.

'Some cultists tried to save the day by proclaiming the religion of Alpha the Utterly Indifferent and used the bell-shaped curve of normal distribution as the symbol of their faith. Needless to say, so abstract a deity didn't inspire much devotion.

'And while we're on the subject of mathematics, it gave Alpha another devastating blow in the twenty-first (or was it the twenty-second?) century. A brilliant Terran named Kurt Gödel proved that there were certain absolutely fundamental limits to knowledge, and hence the idea of a completely Omniscient Being – one of the definitions of Alpha – was logically absurd. This discovery has come down to us in one of those unforgettable bad puns: 'Gödel Deleted God.' Students used to write graffiti on walls with the letters G, O, and the Greek Delta; and of course there were versions that read: "God Deleted Gödel".

'But back to Alpha. By mid-millennium, it had more or less

faded from human concerns. Virtually all thinking men had finally come to agree with the harsh verdict of the great philosopher Lucretius: *all* religions were fundamentally immoral, because the superstitions they peddled wrought more evil than good.

'Yet a few of the old faiths managed to survive, though in drastically altered forms, right up to the end of the Earth. The Latter Day Mormons and the Daughters of the Prophet even managed to build seedships of their own. I often wonder what happened to them.

'With Alpha discredited, that left Omega, the Creator of everything. It's not so easy to dispose of Omega; the universe takes a certain amount of explaining. Or does it? There's an ancient philosophical joke that's much subtler than it seems. Question: Why is the universe here? Answer: Where else would it be? And I think *that's* quite enough for one morning.'

'Thank you, Moses,' Mirissa answered, looking slightly dazed. 'You've said it all before, haven't you?'.

'Of course I have – many times. And promise me this –'

'What is it?'

'Don't believe *anything* I've told you – merely because I said it. No serious philosophical problem is ever settled. Omega is still around – and sometimes I wonder about Alpha ...'

VII
As the Sparks Fly Upward

47

Ascension

Her name was Carina; she was eighteen years old, and though this was the first time she had ever been out at night in Kumar's boat, it was not by any means the first time she had lain in his arms. She had, indeed, perhaps the best title to the much-disputed claim of being his favourite girl.

Though the sun had set two hours ago, the inner moon – so much brighter and closer than the lost Moon of Earth – was almost full, and the beach, half a kilometre away, was awash with its cold, blue light. A small fire was burning just outside the line of the palm-trees, where the party was still in progress. And the faint sound of music could be heard from time to time above the gentle murmur of the jet drive operating at its very lowest power. Kumar had already arrived at his prime goal and was in no great hurry to go elsewhere. Nevertheless, like the good seaman he was, he occasionally disengaged himself to speak a few words of instruction to the autopilot and made a swift scan of the horizon.

Kumar had spoken the truth, thought Carina blissfully. There was something very erotic about the regular, gentle rhythm of a boat, especially when it was amplified by the airbed on which they were lying. After *this*, would she ever be satisfied by lovemaking on dry land?

And Kumar, unlike quite a few other young Tarnans she could mention, was surprisingly tender and considerate. He was not one of those men who was only concerned with his own satisfaction; his pleasure was not complete unless it was shared. While he's in me, Carina thought, I feel I'm the only girl in his universe – even though I know perfectly well that isn't true.

Carina was vaguely aware that they were still heading away from the village, but she did not mind. She wished that this moment could last forever and would hardly have cared if the boat had been driving at full speed out into the empty ocean, with no land ahead until the circumnavigation of the globe. Kumar knew what he was doing – in more ways than one. Part of her pleasure derived from the utter confidence he inspired; within his arms, she had no worries, no problems. The future did not exist; there was only the timeless present.

Yet time did pass, and now the inner moon was much higher in the sky. In the aftermath of passion, their lips were still languidly exploring the territories of love when the pulsing of the hydrojet ceased and the boat drifted to a stop.

'We're here,' Kumar said, a note of excitement in his voice.

And where may 'here' be? Carina thought lazily as they rolled apart. It seemed hours since she had last bothered to glance at the coastline ... even assuming that it was still within sight.

She climbed slowly to her feet, steadying herself against the gentle rocking of the boat – and stared wide-eyed at the Fairyland that, not long ago, had been the dismal swamp hopefully but inaccurately christened Mangrove Bay.

It was not, of course, the first time she had encountered high technology; the fusion plant and Main Replicator on North Island were much larger and more impressive. But to see this brilliantly illuminated labyrinth of pipes and storage tanks and cranes and handling mechanisms – this bustling combination of shipyard and chemical plant, all functioning silently and efficiently under the stars with not a single human being in sight – was a real visual and psychological shock.

There was a sudden splash, startling in the utter silence of the night, as Kumar threw out the anchor.

'Come on,' he said mischievously 'I want to show you something.'

'Is it safe?'

'Of course – I've been here lots of times.'

And not by yourself, I'm sure, Carina thought. But he was already over the side before she could make any comment.

The water was barely more than waist deep and still retained so much of the day's heat that it was almost uncomfortably warm. When Carina and Kumar walked up on to the beach, hand in hand, it was refreshing to feel the cool night breeze against their bodies. They emerged from the random rippling of tiny wavelets like a new Adam and Eve given the keys to a mechanized Eden.

'Don't worry!' Kumar said. 'I know my way around. Dr Lorenson's explained everything to me. But I've found something I'm sure *he* doesn't know.'

They were walking along a line of heavily insulated pipes, supported a metre from the ground, and now for the first time Carina could hear a distinct sound – the throbbing of pumps forcing cooling fluid through the maze of plumbing and heat exchangers that surrounded them.

Presently they came to the famous tank in which the scorp had been found. Very little water was now visible; the surface was almost completely covered with a tangled mass of kelp. There were no reptiles on Thalassa, but the thick flexible stalks reminded Carina of intertwining snakes.

They walked along a series of culverts and past small sluice gates, all of them closed at the moment, until they reached a wide, open area, well away from the main plant. As they left the central complex, Kumar waved cheerfully at the lens of a pointing camera. No one ever discovered, later, why it had been switched off at the crucial moment.

'The freezing tanks,' Kumar said. 'Six hundred tons in each. Ninety-five per cent water, five per cent kelp. What's so funny?'

'Not funny – but very *strange*,' answered Carina, still smiling. 'Just think of it – carrying some of our ocean forest, all the way to the stars. Who would ever imagine such a thing! But *that's* not why you brought me here.'

'No,' said Kumar softly. 'Look ...'

At first, she could not see what he was pointing at. Then her mind interpreted the image that flickered at the very edge of vision, and she understood.

It was an old miracle, of course. Men had done such things on many worlds, for over a thousand years. But to witness it with her own eyes was more than breathtaking – it was awesome.

Now that they had walked closer to the last of the tanks, she could see it more clearly. The thin thread of light – it could not have been more than a couple of centimetres wide! – climbed upward to the stars, straight and true as a laser beam. Her eyes followed it until it narrowed into invisibility, teasing her to decide the exact place of its disappearance. And still her gaze swept onward, dizzyingly, until she was staring at the zenith itself, and at the single star that was poised motionless there while all its fainter, natural companions marched steadily past it towards the west. Like some cosmic spider, *Magellan* had lowered a thread of gossamer and would soon be hoisting the prize it desired from the world below.

Now that they were standing at the very edge of the waiting ice block, Carina had another surprise. Its surface was completely covered with a glittering layer of golden foil, reminding her of the gifts that were presented to children on their birthdays or at the annual Landing Festival.

'Insulation,' Kumar explained. 'And it really *is* gold – about two atoms thick. Without it, half the ice would melt again before it could get up to the shield.'

Insulation or no, Carina could feel the bite of cold through her bare feet as Kumar led her out on to the frozen slab. They reached its centre in a dozen steps – and there, glittering with a curious nonmetallic sheen, was the taut ribbon that stretched, if not to the stars, at least the thirty thousand kilometres up to the stationary orbit in which *Magellan* was now parked.

It ended in a cylindrical drum, studded with instruments and control jets, which clearly served as a mobile, intelligent crane-hook, homing on to its load after its long descent through the atmosphere. The whole arrangement looked surprisingly simple and even unsophisticated – deceptively so, like most products of mature, advanced technologies.

Carina suddenly shivered, and not from the cold underfoot, which she now scarcely noticed.

'Are you sure it's safe here?' she asked anxiously.

'Of course. They always lift at midnight, on the second – and that's still hours away. It's a wonderful sight, but I don't think we'll stay so late.'

Now Kumar was kneeling, placing his ear against the incredible ribbon that bound ship and planet together. If it snapped, she wondered anxiously, would they fly apart?

'Listen,' he whispered ...

She had not known what to expect. Sometimes in later years, when she could endure it, she tried to recapture the magic of this moment. She could never be sure if she had succeeded.

At first it seemed that she was hearing the deepest note of a giant harp whose strings were stretched between the worlds. It sent shivers down her spine, and she felt the little hairs at the nape of her neck stirring in that immemorial fear response forged in the primeval jungles of Earth.

Then, as she grew accustomed to it, she became aware of a whole spectrum of shifting overtones covering the range of hearing to the very limits of audibility – and doubtless far beyond. They blurred and merged one into the other, as inconstant yet steadily repeating as the sounds of the sea.

The more she listened the more she was reminded of the endless beating of the waves upon a desolate beach. She felt that she was hearing the sea of space wash upon the shores of all its worlds – a sound terrifying in its meaningless futility as it reverberated through the aching emptiness of the universe.

And now she became aware of other elements in this immensely complex symphony. There were sudden, plangent twangings as if giant fingers had plucked at the ribbon somewhere along its thousands of taut kilometres. Meteorites? Surely not. Perhaps some electrical discharge in Thalassa's seething ionosphere? And – was this pure imagination, something created by her own unconscious fears? – it seemed that from time to time she heard the faint wailing of demon voices or the ghostly cries of all the sick and starving children who had died on Earth during the Nightmare Centuries.

Suddenly, she could bear it no longer.

'I'm frightened, Kumar,' she whispered, tugging at his shoulder. 'Let's go.'

But Kumar was still lost in the stars, his mouth half open as he pressed his head against that resonant ribbon, hypnotized by its siren song. He never even noticed when, angry as much as scared, Carina stomped across the foil-covered ice and stood waiting for him on the familiar warmth of dry land.

For now he had noticed something new – a series of rising notes that seemed to be calling for his attention. It was like a Fanfare for Strings, if one could imagine such a thing, and it was ineffably sad and distant.

But it was coming closer, growing louder. It was the most thrilling sound that Kumar had ever heard, and it held him paralysed with astonishment and awe. He could almost imagine that *something* was racing down the ribbon towards him ...

Seconds too late, he realized the truth as the first shock of the precursor wave jolted him flat against the golden foil and the ice block stirred beneath him. Then, for the very last time, Kumar Leonidas looked upon the fragile beauty of his sleeping world, and the terrified, upturned face of the girl who would remember this moment until her own dying day.

Already, it was too late to jump. And so the Little Lion ascended to the silent stars – naked and alone.

48

Decision

Captain Bey had graver problems on his mind and was very glad to delegate this task. In any event, no emissary could have been more appropriate than Loren Lorenson.

He had never met the Leonidas elders before and dreaded the encounter. Though Mirissa had offered to accompany him, he preferred to go alone.

The Lassans revered their old folk and did everything possible for their comfort and happiness. Lal and Nikri Leonidas lived in one of the small, self-contained retirement colonies along the south coast of the island. They had a six-room chalet with every conceivable labour-saving device, including the only general-purpose house robot that Loren had ever seen on South Island. By Earth chronology, he would have judged them to be in their late sixties.

After the initial subdued greetings, they sat on the porch, looking out to sea while the robot fussed around bearing drinks and plates of assorted fruit. Loren forced himself to eat a few morsels, then gathered his courage and tackled the hardest task of his life.

'Kumar –' The name stuck in his throat, and he had to begin again. 'Kumar is still on the ship. I owe my life to him; he risked his to save mine. You can understand how I feel about this – I would do *anything* . . .'

Once more he had to fight for control. Then, trying to be as brisk and scientific as he could – like Surgeon–Commander Newton during her briefing – he made yet another start.

'His body is almost undamaged, because decompression was

slow and freezing took place immediately. But, of course, he is clinically dead – just as I was myself a few weeks ago ...

'However, the two cases are very different. My – body – was recovered before there was time for brain damage, so revival was a fairly straightforward process.

'It was hours before they recovered Kumar. Physically, his brain is undamaged – but there is no trace of any activity.

'Even so, revival *may* be possible with extremely advanced technology. According to our records – which cover the entire history of Earth's medical science – it has been done before in similar cases, with a success rate of sixty per cent.

'And that places us in a dilemma, which Captain Bey has asked me to explain to you frankly. We do not have the skills or the equipment to carry out such an operation. But we may – in three hundred years' time ...

'There are a dozen brain experts among the hundreds of medical specialists sleeping aboard the ship. There are technicians who can assemble and operate every conceivable type of surgical and life-support gear. All that Earth ever possessed will be ours again – soon after we reach Sagan 2 ...'

He paused to let the implications sink in. The robot took this inopportune moment to offer its services; he waved it away.

'We would be willing – no, glad, for it is the very least we can do – to take Kumar with us. Though we cannot guarantee it, one day he may live again. We would like you to think it over; there is plenty of time before you have to make the decision.'

The old couple looked at each other for a long, silent moment while Loren stared out to sea. How quiet and peaceful it was! He would be glad to spend his own declining years here, visited from time to time by children and grandchildren ...

Like so much of Tarna, it might almost be Earth. Perhaps through deliberate planning, there was no Lassan vegetation anywhere in sight; all the trees were hauntingly familiar.

Yet something essential was lacking; he realized that it had been puzzling him for a long time – indeed, ever since he had landed on this planet. And suddenly, as if this moment of grief had triggered the memory, he knew what he had missed.

There were no sea gulls wheeling in the sky, filling the air with the saddest and most evocative of all the sounds of Earth.

Lal Leonidas and his wife had still not exchanged a word, yet somehow Loren knew that they had made their decision.

'We appreciate your offer, Commander Lorenson; please express our thanks to Captain Bey.

'But we do not need any time to consider it. Whatever happens, Kumar will be lost to us forever.

'Even if you succeed – and as you say, there is no guarantee – he will awaken in a strange world, knowing that he will never see his home again and that all those he loved are centuries dead. It does not bear thinking of. You mean well, but that would be no kindness to him.

'We know what he would have wished and what must be done. Give him back to us. We will return him to the sea he loved.'

There was nothing more to be said. Loren felt both an overwhelming sadness and a vast relief.

He had done his duty. It was the decision he had expected.

49

Fire on the Reef

Now the little kayak would never be completed; but it would make its first and its last voyage.

Until sunset, it had lain at the water's edge, lapped by the gentle waves of the tideless sea. Loren was moved, but not surprised, to see how many had come to pay their last respects. All Tarna was here, but many had also come from all over South Island – and even from North. Though some, perhaps, had been drawn by morbid curiosity – for the whole world had been shocked by the uniquely spectacular accident – Loren had never seen such a genuine outpouring of grief. He had not realized that the Lassans were capable of such deep emotion, and in his mind he savoured once again a phrase that Mirissa had found, searching the Archives for consolation: 'Little friend of all the world'. Its origin was lost, and no one could guess what long-dead scholar, in what century, had saved it for the ages to come.

Once he had embraced them both with wordless sympathy, he had left Mirissa and Brant with the Leonidas family, gathered with numerous relatives from both islands. He did not want to meet any strangers, for he knew what many of them must be thinking. 'He saved you – but you could not save him.' That was a burden he would carry for the rest of his life.

He bit his lip to check the tears that were not appropriate for a senior officer of the greatest starship ever built and felt one of the mind's defence mechanisms come to his rescue. At moments of deep grief, sometimes the only way to prevent loss of control is to evoke some wholly incongruous – even comic – image from the depths of memory.

Yes – the universe had a strange sense of humour. Loren was almost forced to suppress a smile; how Kumar would have enjoyed the final joke it had played on him!

'Don't be surprised,' Commander Newton had warned as she opened the door of the ship's morgue and a gust of icy, formalin-tainted air rolled out to meet them. 'It happens more often than you think. Sometimes it's a final spasm – almost like an unconscious attempt to defy death. This time, it was probably caused by the loss of external pressure and the subsequent freezing.'

Had it not been for the crystals of ice defining the muscles of the splendid young body, Loren might have thought that Kumar was not merely sleeping but lost in blissful dreams.

For in death, the Little Lion was even more male than he had been in life.

And now the sun had vanished behind the low hills to the west, and a cool evening breeze was rising from the sea. With scarcely a ripple, the kayak slipped into the water, drawn by Brant and three other of Kumar's closest friends. For the last time Loren glimpsed the calm and peaceful face of the boy to whom he owed his life.

There had been little weeping until now, but as the four swimmers pushed the boat slowly out from the shore, a great wail of lamentation rose from the assembled crowd. Now Loren could no longer contain his tears and did not care who saw them.

Moving strongly and steadily under the powerful drive of its four escorts, the little kayak headed out to the reef. The quick Thalassan night was already descending as the craft passed between the two flashing beacons that marked the channel to the open sea. It vanished beyond them and for a moment was hidden by the white line of breakers foaming lazily against the outer reef.

The lamentation ceased; everyone was waiting. Then there was a sudden flare of light against the darkling sky, and a pillar of fire rose out of the sea. It burned cleanly and fiercely, with scarcely any smoke; how long it lasted, Loren never knew, for time had ceased on Tarna.

Then, abruptly, the flames collapsed; the crown of fire shrank back into the sea. All was darkness; but for a moment only.

As fire and water met, a fountain of sparks erupted into the sky. Most of the embers fell back upon the sea, but others continued to soar upward until they were lost from view.

And so, for the second time, Kumar Leonidas ascended to the stars.

VIII

The Songs of Distant Earth

50

Shield of Ice

The lifting of the last snowflake should have been a joyful occasion; now it was merely one of sombre satisfaction. Thirty thousand kilometres above Thalassa, the final hexagon of ice was jockeyed into position, and the shield was complete.

For the first time in almost two years, the quantum drive was activated, though at minimum power. *Magellan* broke away from its stationary orbit, accelerating to test the balance and the integrity of the artificial iceberg it was to carry out to the stars. There were no problems; the work had been well done. This was a great relief to Captain Bey, who had never been able to forget that Owen Fletcher (now under reasonably strict surveillance on North Island) had been one of the shield's principal architects. And he wondered what Fletcher and the other exiled Sabras had thought when they watched the dedication ceremony.

It had begun with a video retrospective showing the building of the freezing plant and the lifting of the first snowflake. Then there had been a fascinating, speeded-up space ballet showing the great blocks of ice being manoeuvred into place and keyed into the steadily growing shield. It had started in real time, then rapidly accelerated until the last sections were being added at the rate of one every few seconds. Thalassa's leading composer had contrived a witty musical score beginning with a slow pavane and culminating in a breathless polka – slowing down to normal speed again at the very end as the final block of ice was jockeyed into position.

Then the view had switched to a live camera hovering in space a kilometre ahead of *Magellan* as it orbited in the shadow of the planet. The big sun-screen that protected the ice during the day had been moved aside, so the entire shield was now visible for the first time.

The huge greenish-white disc gleamed coldly beneath the floodlights; soon it would be far colder as it moved out into the few-degrees-above-absolute zero of the galactic night. There it would be warmed only by the background light of the stars, the radiation leakage from the ship – and the occasional rare burst of energy from impacting dust.

The camera drifted slowly across the artificial iceberg, to the accompaniment of Moses Kaldor's unmistakable voice.

'People of Thalassa, we thank you for your gift. Behind this shield of ice, we hope to travel safely to the world that is waiting for us, seventy-five light-years away, three hundred years hence.

'If all goes well, we will still be carrying at least twenty thousand tons of ice when we reach Sagan 2. That will be allowed to fall on to the planet, and the heat of reentry will turn it into the first rain that frigid world has ever known. For a little while, before it freezes again, it will be the precursor of oceans yet unborn.

'And one day our descendants will know seas like yours, though not as wide or as deep. Water from our two worlds will mingle together, bringing life to our new home. And we will remember you, with love and gratitude.'

51

Relic

'It's beautiful,' Mirissa said reverently. 'I can understand why gold was so prized on Earth.'

'The gold is the least important part,' Kaldor answered, as he slid the gleaming bell out of its velvet-lined box. 'Can you guess what this is?'

'It's obviously a work of art. But it must be something much more for you to have carried it across fifty light-years.'

'You're right, of course. It's an exact model of a great temple, more than a hundred metres tall. Originally, there were seven of these caskets, all identical in shape, nesting one inside the other – this was the innermost, holding the Relic itself. It was given to me by some old and dear friends on my very last night on Earth. "All things are impermanent," they reminded me. "But we have guarded this for more than four thousand years. Take it with you to the stars, with our blessings."

'Even though I did not share their faith, how could I refuse so priceless an offering? And now I will leave it here, where men first came to this planet – another gift from Earth – perhaps the last.'

'Don't say that,' Mirissa said. 'You have left so many gifts – we will never be able to count them all.'

Kaldor smiled wistfully and did not answer for a moment as he let his eyes linger on the familiar view from the library window. He had been happy here, tracing the history of Thalassa and learning much that might be of priceless value when the new colony was started on Sagan 2.

Farewell, old Mother Ship, he thought. You did your work well. We still have far to go; may *Magellan* serve us as faithfully as you served the people we have grown to love.

'I'm sure my friends would have approved – I've done my duty. The Relic will be safer here, in the Museum of Earth, than aboard the ship. After all, we may never reach Sagan 2.'

'Of course you will. But you haven't told me what's inside this seventh casket.'

'It's all that's left of one of the greatest men who ever lived; he founded the only faith that never became stained with blood. I'm sure he would have been most amused to know that, forty centuries after his death, one of his teeth would be carried to the stars.'

52

The Songs of Distant Earth

Now was the time of transition, of farewells – of partings as deep as death. Yet for all the tears that were shed – on Thalassa as well as the ship – there was also a feeling of relief. Though things would never be quite the same again, life could now return to normal. The visitors were like guests who had slightly overstayed their welcome; it was time to go.

Even President Farradine now accepted this and had abandoned his dream of an interstellar Olympics. He had ample consolation; the freezing units at Mangrove Bay were being transferred to North Island, and the first skating rink on Thalassa would be ready in time for the Games. Whether any competitors would also be ready was another question, but many young Lassans were spending hours staring incredulously at some of the great performers of the past.

Meanwhile, everyone agreed that some farewell ceremony should be arranged to mark *Magellan*'s departure. Unfortunately, few could agree what form it should take. There were innumerable private parties – which put a considerable mental and physical strain on all concerned – but no official, public one.

Mayor Waldron, claiming priority on behalf of Tarna, felt that the ceremony should take place at First Landing. Edgar Farradine argued that the President's Palace, despite its modest size, was more appropriate. Some wit suggested Krakan as a compromise, pointing out that its famous vineyards would be an appropriate place for the farewell toasts. The matter was still unresolved when the Thalassan Broadcasting Corporation – one of the planet's more enterprising bureaucracies – quietly preempted the entire project.

The farewell concert was to be remembered, and replayed, for generations to come. There was no video to distract the senses – only music and the briefest of narration. The heritage of two thousand years was ransacked to recall the past and to give hope for the future. It was not only a Requiem but also a Berceuse.

It still seemed a miracle that after their art had reached technological perfection, composers of music could find anything new to say. For two thousand years, electronics had given them complete command over every sound audible to the human ear, and it might have been thought that all the possibilities of the medium had been long exhausted.

There had, indeed, been about a century of beepings and twitterings and electro-eructations before composers had mastered their now infinite powers and had once again successfully married technology and art. No one had ever surpassed Beethoven or Bach; but some had approached them.

To the legions of listeners, the concert was a reminder of things they had never known – things that belonged to Earth alone. The slow beat of mighty bells, climbing like invisible smoke from old cathedral spires; the chant of patient boatmen, in tongues now lost forever, rowing home against the tide in the last light of day; the songs of armies marching into battles that Time had robbed of all their pain and evil; the merged murmur of ten million voices as man's greatest cities woke to meet the dawn; the cold dance of the aurora over endless seas of ice; the roar of mighty engines climbing upward on the highway to the stars. All these the listeners heard in the music that came out of the night – the songs of distant Earth, carried across the light-years . . .

For the concluding item, the producers had selected the last great work in the symphonic tradition. Written in the years when Thalassa had lost touch with Earth, it was totally new to the audience. Yet its oceanic theme made it peculiarly appropriate to this occasion – and its impact upon the listeners was everything the long-dead composer could have wished.

'... When I wrote "Lamentation for Atlantis", almost thirty years ago, I had no specific images in mind; I was concerned only with emotional reactions, not explicit scenes; I wanted the music to convey a sense of mystery, of sadness – of overwhelming loss. I was not trying to paint a sound-portrait of ruined cities full of fish. But now something strange happens, whenever I hear the *Lento lugubre* – as I am doing in my mind at this very moment ...

'It begins at Bar 136, when the series of chords descending to the organ's lowest register first meets the soprano's wordless aria, rising higher and higher out of the depths ... You know, of course, that I based that theme on the songs of the great whales, those mighty minstrels of the sea with whom we made peace too late, too late ... I wrote it for Olga Kondrashin, and no one else could ever sing those passages without electronic backing ...

'When the vocal line begins, it's as if I'm seeing something that really exists. I'm standing in a great city square almost as large as St Mark's or St Peter's. All around are half-ruined buildings, like Greek temples, and overturned statues draped with seaweeds, green fronds waving slowly back and forth. Everything is partly covered by a thick layer of silt.

'The square seems empty at first; then I notice something – *disturbing*. Don't ask me why it's always a surprise, why I'm always seeing it for the first time ...

'There's a low mound in the centre of the square, with a pattern of lines radiating from it. I wonder if they are ruined walls, partly buried in the silt. But the arrangement makes no sense; and then I see that the mound is – *pulsing*.

'And a moment later I notice two huge, unblinking eyes staring out at me.

'That's all; nothing happens. Nothing *has* happened here for six thousand years, since that night when the land barrier gave way and the sea poured in through the Pillars of Hercules.

'The *Lento* is my favourite movement, but I couldn't end the symphony in such a mood of tragedy and despair. Hence the *Finale*, "Resurgence".

'I know, of course, that Plato's Atlantis never really existed. And for that very reason, it can never die. It will always be an ideal – a dream of perfection – a goal to inspire men for all ages to come. So that's why the symphony ends with a triumphant march into the future.

'I know that the popular interpretation of the *March* is a New Atlantis emerging from the waves. That's rather too literal; to me the *Finale* depicts the conquest of space. Once I'd found it and pinned it down, it took me months to get rid of that closing theme. Those damned fifteen notes were hammering away in my brain night and day …

'Now, the *Lamentation* exists quite apart from me; it has taken on a life of its own. Even when Earth is gone, it will be speeding out towards the Andromeda Galaxy, driven by fifty thousand megawatts from the Deep Space transmitter in Tsiolkovski Crater.

'Someday, centuries of millennia hence, it will be captured – and understood.'

Spoken Memoirs – Sergei Di Pietro (3411–3509).

53

The Golden Mask

'We've always pretended she doesn't exist,' Mirissa said. 'But now I would like to see her – just once.'

Loren was silent for a while. Then he answered, 'You know that Captain Bey has never allowed any visitors.'

Of course she knew that; she also understood the reasons why.

Although it had aroused some resentment at first, everyone on Thalassa now realized that *Magellan*'s small crew was far too busy to act as tour guides – or nursemaids – to the unpredictable fifteen per cent who would become nauseated in the ship's zero-gravity sections. Even President Farradine had been tactfully turned down.

'I've spoken to Moses – and he's spoken to the captain. It's all arranged. But it's to be kept secret until the ship has left.'

Loren stared at her in amazement; then he smiled. Mirissa was always surprising him; that was part of her attraction. And he realized, with a twinge of sadness, that no one on Thalassa had a better right to this privilege; her brother was the only other Lassan to have made the journey. Captain Bey was a fair man, willing to alter the rules when necessary. And once the ship had left, only three days from now, it would not matter.

'Suppose you're spacesick?'

'I've never even been seasick –'

'– that doesn't prove anything –'

'– and I've seen Commander Newton. She's given me a ninety-five per cent rating. And she suggests the midnight shuttle – there won't be any villagers around then.'

'You've thought of everything, haven't you?' Loren said in frank admiration. 'I'll meet you at Number Two Landing, fifteen minutes before midnight.'

He paused, then added with difficulty, 'I won't be coming down again. Please say good-bye to Brant for me.'

That was an ordeal he could not face. Indeed, he had not set foot in the Leonidas residence since Kumar had made his last voyage and Brant had returned to comfort Mirissa. Already, it was almost as if Loren had never entered their lives.

And he was inexorably leaving theirs, for now he could look on Mirissa with love but without desire. A deeper emotion – one of the worst pains he had ever known – now filled his mind.

He had longed, and hoped, to see his child – but *Magellan*'s new schedule made that impossible. Though he had heard his son's heartbeats, mingled with his mother's, he would never hold him in his arms.

The shuttle made its rendezvous on the day side of the planet, so *Magellan* was still almost a hundred kilometres away when Mirissa first saw it. Even though she knew its real size, it looked like a child's toy as it glittered in the sunlight.

From ten kilometres, it seemed no larger. Her brain and eyes insisted that those dark circles round the centre section were only portholes. Not until the endless, curving hull of the ship loomed up beside them did her mind admit that they were cargo and docking hatches, one of which the ferry was about to enter.

Loren looked at Mirissa anxiously as she unbuckled her seatbelt; this was the dangerous moment when, free from restraints for the first time, the overconfident passenger suddenly realized that zero-gravity was not as enjoyable as it looked. But Mirissa seemed completely at ease as she drifted through the airlock, propelled by a few gentle pushes from Loren.

'Luckily there's no need to go into the one-gee section, so you'll avoid the problem of re-adapting twice. You won't have to worry about gravity again until you're back on the ground.'

It would have been interesting, Mirissa thought, to have visited the living quarters in the spinning section of the ship – but that would have involved them in endless polite conversations and personal contacts, which were the last things she needed now. She was rather glad that Captain Bey was still down on Thalassa; there was no need even for a courtesy visit of thanks.

Once they had left the airlock they found themselves in a tubular corridor that seemed to stretch the whole length of the ship. On one side was a ladder, on the other, two lines of flexible loops, convenient for hands or feet, glided slowly in either direction along parallel slots.

'This is not a very good place to be when we're accelerating,' Loren said. 'Then it becomes a vertical shaft – two kilometres deep. That's when you *really* need the ladder and handholds. Just grab that loop, and let it do all the work.'

They were swept effortlessly along for several hundred metres, then switched to a corridor at right angles to the main one. 'Let go of the strap,' Loren said when they had travelled a few dozen metres. 'I want to show you something.'

Mirissa released her hold, and they drifted to a stop beside a long, narrow window set in the side of the tunnel. She peered through the thick glass into a huge, brightly-lit metal cavern. Though she had quite lost her bearings, she guessed that this great cylindrical chamber must span almost the entire width of the ship – and that central bar must therefore lie along its axis.

'The quantum drive,' Loren said proudly.

He did not even attempt to name the shrouded metal and crystal shapes, the curiously-formed flying buttresses springing from the walls of the chamber, the pulsing constellations of lights, the sphere of utter blackness that, even though it was completely featureless, somehow seemed to be spinning ... But after a while he said:

'The greatest achievement of human genius – Earth's last gift to its children. One day it will make us masters of the galaxy.'

There was an arrogance about the words that made Mirissa wince. That was the old Loren speaking again, before he had been mellowed by Thalassa. So be it, she thought; but part of him has been changed forever.

'Do you suppose,' she asked gently, 'that the galaxy will even notice?'

Yet she was impressed, and stared for a long time at the huge and meaningless shapes that had carried Loren to her across the light-years. She did not know whether to bless them for what they had brought her or to curse them for what they would soon take away.

Loren led her on through the maze, deeper into *Magellan*'s heart. Not once did they meet another person; it was a reminder of the ship's size – and the smallness of its crew.

'We're nearly there,' Loren said in a voice that was now hushed and solemn. 'And *this* is the Guardian.'

Taken completely by surprise, Mirissa floated towards the golden face staring at her out of the alcove until she was about to collide with it. She put out her hand, and felt cold metal. So it was real – and not, as she had first imagined, a holodisplay.

'What – who – is it?' she whispered.

'We have many of Earth's greatest art treasures on board,' Loren said with sombre pride. 'This was one of the most famous. He was a king who died very young – when he was still a boy ...'

Loren's voice faded away as they shared the same thought. Mirissa had to blink away her tears before she could read the inscription below the mask.

TUTANKHAMUN
1361–1353 BC
(Valley of the Kings, Egypt, AD 1922)

Yes, he had been almost exactly the same age as Kumar. The golden face stared out at them across the millennia, and across the light-years – the face of a young god struck down in his prime. There was power and confidence here but not yet the arrogance and cruelty that the lost years would have given.

'Why here?' Mirissa said, half guessing the answer.

'It seemed an appropriate symbol. The Egyptians believed that if they carried out the right ceremonies, the dead would exist again in some kind of afterworld. Pure superstition, of course – yet here we have made it come true.'

But not in the way I would have wished, Mirissa thought sadly. As she stared into the jet-black eyes of the boy king, looking out at her from his mask of incorruptible gold, it was hard to believe that this was only a marvellous work of art and not a living person.

She could not tear her eyes away from that calm yet hypnotic gaze across the centuries. Once more she put forth her hand, and stroked a golden cheek. The precious metal suddenly reminded her of a poem she had found in the First Landing Archives, when she set the computer searching the literature of the past for words of solace. Most of the hundreds of lines had been inappropriate, but this one ('Author unknown – ?1800–2100') fitted perfectly:

They carry back bright to the coiner the mintage of man,
The lads that will die in their glory and never be old.

Loren waited patiently until Mirissa's thoughts had run their course. Then he slid a card into an almost invisible slot beside the death-mask, and a circular door opened silently.

It was incongruous to find a cloak-room full of heavy furs inside a spaceship, but Mirissa could appreciate the need for them. Already the temperature had fallen many degrees, and she found herself shivering with the unaccustomed cold.

Loren helped her into the thermosuit – not without difficulty in zero gravity – and they floated towards a circle of frosted glass set in the far wall of the little chamber. The crystal trapdoor swung towards them like an opening watchglass, and out of its swirled a blast of frigid air such as Mirissa had never imagined far less experienced. Thin wisps of moisture condensed in the freezing air, dancing round her like ghosts. She looked at Loren as if to say, 'Surely you don't expect me to go in *there!*'

He took her arm reassuringly and said, 'Don't worry – the suit will protect you, and after a few minutes you won't notice the cold on your face.'

She found this hard to believe; but he was right. As she followed him through the trapdoor, breathing cautiously at first, she was surprised to find the experience not at all unpleasant. Indeed, it was positively stimulating; for the first time she could understand why people had willingly gone into the polar regions of the Earth.

She could easily imagine that she was there herself, for she seemed to be floating in a frigid, snow-white universe. All around her were glittering honeycombs that might have been made of ice, forming thousands of hexagonal cells. It was almost like a smaller version of *Magellan*'s shield – except that here the units were only about a metre across, and laced together with clusters of pipes and bundles of wiring.

So here they were, sleeping all around her – the hundreds of thousands of colonists to whom Earth was still in literal truth, a memory of only yesterday. What were they dreaming, she wondered, less than halfway through their five-hundred-year sleep? Did the brain dream at all in this dim no-man's-land between life and death? Not according to Loren; but who could be really sure?

Mirissa had seen videos of bees scurrying about their mysterious business inside a hive; she felt like a human bee as she followed Loren, hand over hand along the grid-work of rails crisscrossing the face of the great honeycomb. She was now quite at ease in zero gravity and was no longer even aware of the bitter cold. Indeed, she was scarcely aware of her body and sometimes had to persuade herself that this was not all a dream from which she would presently awake.

The cells bore no names but were all identified by an alphanumeric code; Loren went unerringly to H-354. At the touch of a button, the hexagonal metal-and-glass container slid outward on telescopic rails to reveal the sleeping woman inside.

She was not beautiful – though it was unfair to pass judgement on any woman without the crowning glory of her hair. Her skin was of a colour that Mirissa had never seen and which she knew had become very rare on Earth – a black so deep that it held almost a hint of blue. And it was so flawless that Mirissa could not resist a spasm of envy; into her mind came a fleeting image of intertwined bodies, ebon and ivory – an image which, she knew, would haunt her in the years ahead.

She looked again at the face. Even in this centuries-long repose, it showed determination and intelligence. Would we have been friends? Mirissa wondered. I doubt it; we are too much alike.

So you are Kitani, and you are carrying Loren's first child out to the stars. But will she really be the first, since she will be born centuries after mine? First or second, I wish her well ...

She was still numb, though not only with cold, when the crystal door closed behind them. Loren steered her gently back along the corridor and past the Guardian.

Once more her fingers brushed the cheek of the immortal golden boy. For a shocked moment, it felt warm to her touch; then she realized that her body was still adjusting to normal temperature.

That would take only minutes; but how long, she wondered, before the ice would melt around her heart?

54

Valediction

This is the last time I shall talk to you, Evelyn, before I begin my longest sleep. I am still on Thalassa, but the shuttle will be lifting for *Magellan* in a few minutes; there is nothing more for me to do – until planetfall, three hundred years from now ...

I feel a great sadness, for I have just said good-bye to my dearest friend here, Mirissa Leonidas. How you would have enjoyed meeting her! She is perhaps the most intelligent person I have met on Thalassa, and we had many long talks together – though I fear that some were more like the monologues for which you so often criticized me ...

She asked about God, of course; but perhaps her shrewdest question was one I was quite unable to answer.

Soon after her beloved young brother was killed, she asked me, 'What is the purpose of grief? Does it serve any biological function?'

How strange that I had never given any serious thought to that!

One could imagine an intelligent species which functioned perfectly well if the dead were remembered with no emotion – if indeed they were remembered at all. It would be an utterly inhuman society, but it could be at least as successful as the termites and the ants were on Earth.

Could grief be an accidental – even a pathological – by-product of love, which of course *does* have an essential biological function? It's a strange and disturbing thought. Yet it's our emotions that make us human; who would abandon them, even knowing that each new love is yet another hostage to those twin terrorists, Time and Fate?

She often talked to me about you, Evelyn. It puzzled her that a man could love only one woman in all his life and not seek another when she was gone. Once I teased her by saying that fidelity was almost as strange to the Lassans as jealousy; she retorted that they had gained by losing both.

They are calling me; the shuttle is waiting. Now I must say good-bye to Thalassa forever. And your image, too, is beginning to fade. Though I am good at giving advice to others, perhaps I have clung too long to my own grief, and it does no service to your memory.

Thalassa has helped to cure me. Now I can rejoice that I knew you rather than mourn because I lost you.

A strange calmness has come upon me. For the first time, I feel that I really understand my old Buddhist friends' concepts of Detachment – even of Nirvana ...

And if I do not wake on Sagan 2, so be it. My work here is done, and I am well content.

55

Departure

The trimaran reached the edge of the kelp bed just before midnight, and Brant anchored in thirty metres of water. He would start to drop the spyballs at dawn until the fence was laid between Scorpville and South Island. Once that was established, any comings and goings would be observed. If the scorps found one of the spyballs and carried it home as a trophy, so much the better. It would continue to operate, doubtless providing even more useful information than in the open sea.

Now there was nothing to do but to lie in the gently rocking boat and listen to the soft music from Radio Tarna, tonight uncharacteristically subdued. From time to time there would be an announcement or a message of goodwill or a poem in honour of the villagers. There could be few people sleeping on either island tonight; Mirissa wondered fleetingly what thoughts must be passing through the minds of Owen Fletcher and his fellow exiles, marooned on an alien world for the rest of their lives. The last time she had seen them on a Norther Videocast, they had not appeared at all unhappy and had been cheerfully discussing local business opportunities.

Brant was so quiet that she would have thought he was sleeping, except that his grip on her hand was as firm as ever, as they lay side by side, looking up at the stars. He had changed – perhaps even more than she had. He was less impatient, more considerate. Best of all, he had already accepted the child, with words whose gentleness had reduced her to tears: 'He will have two fathers.'

Now Radio Tarna was starting the final and quite unnecessary launch countdown – the first that any Lassan had ever heard except for historic recordings from the past. Will we see anything at all, Mirissa wondered? *Magellan* is on the other side of the world, hovering at high noon above a hemisphere of ocean. We have the whole thickness of the planet between us ...

'... Zero ...' Tarna Radio said – and instantly was obliterated by a roar of white noise. Brant reached for the gain control and had barely cut off the sound when the sky erupted.

The entire horizon was ringed with fire. North, south, east, west – there was no difference. Long streamers of flame reached up out of the ocean, halfway towards the zenith, in such an auroral display, as Thalassa had never witnessed before, and would never see again.

It was beautiful but awe-inspiring. Now Mirissa understood why *Magellan* had been placed on the far side of the world; yet this was not the quantum drive itself but merely the stray energies leaking from it, being absorbed harmlessly in the ionosphere. Loren had told her something incomprehensible about superspace shockwaves, adding that not even the inventors of the drive had ever understood the phenomenon.

She wondered, briefly, what the scorps would make of these celestial fireworks; some trace of this actinic fury must filter down through the forests of kelp to illuminate the byways of their sunken cities.

Perhaps it was imagination, but the radiating, multicoloured beams that formed the encircling crown of light seemed to be creeping slowly across the sky. The source of their energy was gaining speed, accelerating along its orbit as it left Thalassa forever. It was many minutes before she could be quite sure of the movement; in the same time, the intensity of the display had also diminished appreciably.

Then abruptly, it ceased. Radio Tarna came back on the air, rather breathlessly.

'... everything according to plan ... the ship is now being reoriented ... other displays later, but not so spectacular ... all stages of the initial breakaway will be on the other side of the world, but we'll be able to see *Magellan* directly in three days, when it's leaving the system ...'

Mirissa scarcely heard the words as she stared up into the sky to which the stars were now returning – the stars that she could never seen again without remembering Loren. She was drained of emotion now; if she had tears, they would come later.

She felt Brant's arm around her and welcomed their comfort against the loneliness of space. This was where she belonged; her heart would not stray again. For at last she understood; though she had loved Loren for his strength, she loved Brant for his weakness.

Good-bye, Loren, she whispered – may you be happy on that far world which you and your children will conquer for mankind. But think of me sometimes, three hundred years behind you on the road from Earth.

As Brant stroked her hair with clumsy gentleness, he wished he had words to comfort her, yet knew that silence was the best. He felt no sense of victory; though Mirissa was his once more, their old, carefree companionship was gone beyond recall. All the days of his life, Brant knew, the ghost of Loren would come between them – the ghost of a man who would not be one day older when they were dust upon the wind.

When, three days later, *Magellan* rose above the eastern horizon, it was a dazzling star too brilliant to look upon with the naked eye even though the quantum drive had been carefully aligned so that most of its radiation leakage would miss Thalassa.

Week by week, month by month, it slowly faded, though even when it moved back into the daylight sky it was still easy to find if one knew exactly where to look. And at night for years it was often the brightest of the stars.

Mirissa saw it one last time, just before her eyesight failed. For a few days the quantum drive – now harmlessly gentled by distance – must have been aimed directly towards Thalassa.

It was then fifteen light-years away, but her grandchildren had no difficulty in pointing out the blue, third magnitude star, shining above the watchtowers of the electrified scorp-barrier.

56

Below the Interface

They were not yet intelligent, but they possessed curiosity – and that was the first step along the endless road.

Like many of the crustaceans that had once flourished in the seas of Earth, they could survive on land for indefinite periods. Until the last few centuries, however, there had been little incentive to do so; the great kelp forests provided for all their needs. The long, slender leaves supplied food; the tough stalks were the raw material for their primitive artifacts.

They had only two natural enemies. One was a huge but very rare deep-sea fish – little more than a pair of ravening jaws attached to a never-satisfied stomach. The other was a poisonous, pulsing jelly – the motile form of the giant polyps – which sometimes carpeted the seabed with death, leaving a bleached desert in its wake.

Apart from sporadic excursions through the air–water interface, the scorps might well have spent their entire existence in the sea, perfectly adapted to their environment. But – unlike the ants and termites – they had not yet entered any of the blind alleys of evolution. They could still respond to change.

And change, although as yet only on a very small scale, had indeed come to this ocean world. Marvellous things had fallen out of the sky. Where these had come from, there must be more. When they were ready, the scorps would go in search of them.

There was no particular hurry in the timeless world of the Thalassan sea; it would be many years before they made their first assault upon the alien element from which their scouts had brought back such strange reports.

They could never guess that other scouts were reporting on *them*. And when they finally moved, their timing would be most unfortunate.

They would have the bad luck to emerge on land during President Owen Fletcher's quite unconstitutional, but extremely competent, second term of office.

IX
Sagan 2

57

The Voices of Time

The starship *Magellan* was still no more than a few light-hours distant when Kumar Lorenson was born, but his father was already sleeping and did not hear the news until three hundred years later.

He wept to think that his dreamless slumber had spanned the entire lifetime of his first child. When he could face the ordeal, he would summon the records that were waiting for him in the memory banks. He would watch his son grow to manhood and hear his voice calling across the centuries with greetings he could never answer.

And he would see (there was no way he could avoid it) the slow ageing of the long-dead girl he had held in his arms – only weeks ago. Her last farewell would come to him from wrinkled lips long turned to dust.

His grief, though piercing, would slowly pass. The light of a new sun filled the sky ahead; and soon there would be another birth, on the world that was already drawing the starship *Magellan* into its final orbit.

One day the pain would be gone; but never the memory.

CHRONOLOGY

(Terran years)

Terran	Event		Thalassa
1956	Detection of neutrino		
1967	Solar neutrino anomaly discovered		
2000			
	Sun's fate confirmed		
100			
	Interstellar probes		
200			
300	Robot seeders planned		
400			
	Seeding started		
2500	(embryos)		
600	(DNA codes)		
700			
751	SEEDER LEAVES FOR THALASSA		
800			
900			
999	LAST MILLENNIUM		
3000		THALASSA	
100			
		3109 First Landing	0
200	LORDS	Birth of Nation	100
	OF	Contact with Earth	
300	THE		200
	LAST	Mt Krakan Erupts	
400	DAYS	Contact Lost	300
3500			400
	QUANTUM DRIVE		
600	FINAL EXODUS	Stasis	
617	STARSHIP MAGELLAN		
3620	END OF EARTH		
		3864 *Magellan* arrives	718
		3865 *Magellan* leaves	720
		4135 SAGAN 2	1026

Bibliographical Note

The first version of this novel, a 12,500-word short story, was written between February and April 1957 and subsequently published in *IF* Magazine (US) for June 1958 and *Science Fantasy* (UK) in June 1959. It may be more conveniently located in my own Harcourt, Brace, Jovanovich collections *The Other Side of the Sky* (1958) and *From the Ocean, From the Stars* (1962).

In 1979, I developed the theme in a short movie outline that appeared in *OMNI Magazine* (Vol. 3, No. 12, 1980). This has since been published in the illustrated Byron Preiss/Berkley collection of my short stories, *The Sentinel* (1984), together with an introduction explaining its origin and the unexpected manner in which it led to the writing and filming of *2010: Odyssey Two*.

This novel, the third and final version, was begun in May 1983 and completed in June 1985.

COLOMBO, SRI LANKA
1 JULY 1985

Acknowledgements

The first suggestion that vacuum energies might be used for propulsion appears to have been made by Shinichi Seike in 1969. ('Quantum electric space vehicle'; 8th Symposium on Space Technology and Science, Tokyo.)

Ten years later, H. D. Froning of McDonnell Douglas Astronautics introduced the idea at the British Interplanetary Society's Interstellar Studies Conference, London (September 1979) and followed it up with two papers: 'Propulsion Requirements for a Quantum Interstellar Ramjet' (*JBIS*, Vol. 33, 1980) and 'Investigation of a Quantum Ramjet for Interstellar Flight' (*AIAA Preprint* 81–1534, 1981).

Ignoring the countless inventors of unspecified 'space drives,' the first person to use the idea in fiction appears to have been Dr Charles Sheffield, Chief Scientist of Earth Satellite Corporation; he discusses the theoretical basis of the 'quantum drive' (or, as he has named it, 'vacuum energy drive') in his novel *The McAndrew Chronicles* (*Analog* magazine 1981; Tor, 1983).

An admittedly naive calculation by Richard Feynman suggests that every cubic centimetre of vacuum contains enough energy to boil all the oceans of Earth. Another estimate by John Wheeler gives a value a mere seventy-nine orders of magnitude *larger*. When two of the world's greatest physicists disagree by a little matter of seventy-nine zeros, the rest of us may be excused a certain scepticism; but it's at least an interesting thought that the vacuum inside an ordinary light bulb contains enough energy to destroy the galaxy ... and perhaps, with a little extra effort, the cosmos.

In what may hopefully be an historic paper ('Extracting electrical energy from the vacuum by cohesion of charged foliated conductors,' *Physical Review*, Vol. 30B, pp. 1700–1702, 15 August 1984) Dr Robert L. Forward of the Hughes Research Labs has shown that at least a minute fraction of this energy can be tapped. If it can be harnessed for propulsion by anyone besides science-fiction writers, the purely engineering problems of interstellar – or even intergalactic – flight would be solved.

But perhaps not. I am extremely grateful to Dr Alan Bond for his detailed mathematical analysis of the shielding necessary for the mission described in this novel and for pointing out that a blunt cone is the most advantageous shape. It may well turn out that the factor limiting high-velocity interstellar flight will not be energy but ablation of the shield mass by dust grains, and evaporation by protons.

The history and theory of the 'space elevator' will be found in my address to the Thirtieth Congress of the International Astronautical Federation, Munich, 1979: 'The Space Elevator: "Thought Experiment" or key to the Universe?' (Reprinted in *Advances in Earth Orientated Applications of Space Technology*, Vol. I, No. 1, 1981, pp. 39–48 and *Ascent to Orbit*: John Wiley, 1984). I have also developed the idea in the novel *The Fountains of Paradise* (Del Rey, Gollancz, 1978).

My apologies to Jim Ballard and J. T. Frazer for stealing the title of their own two very different volumes for my final chapter.

My special gratitude to the Diyawadane Nilame and his staff at the Temple of the Tooth, Kandy, for kindly inviting me into the Relic Chamber during a time of troubles.